LOVING UNDER DANGER'S CLOUD

Loving him, secure in his love for her, she had to believe the truth of what he said, that nothing and no one could truly touch or diminish what they had created together. Nothing—not the world, the war, not parents, brothers, sisters, in-laws, or dear friends— could reach or destroy their essential oneness. They were Abby and Joseph, an entity apart from all others, so inextricably bound one to the other that not even death could separate them for more than an instant . . .

DREAMS AND SHADOWS

DREAMS
AND
SHADOWS

Rosemary Simpson

BANTAM BOOKS
TORONTO · NEW YORK · LONDON · SYDNEY · AUCKLAND

DREAMS AND SHADOWS

*A Bantam Book / published by arrangement with
St. Martin's Press*

PRINTING HISTORY

*St. Martin's edition published 1986
Bantam edition / June 1987*

*Bantam Books are published by Bantam Books, Inc. Its trademark,
consisting of the words "Bantam Books" and the portrayal of
a rooster, is Registered in U.S. Patent and Trademark Office
and in other countries. Marca Registrada. Bantam Books, Inc.,
666 Fifth Avenue, New York, New York 10103.*

PRINTED IN THE UNITED STATES OF AMERICA

KR   0 9 8 7 6 5 4 3 2 1

Contents

Contents

PART ONE

Abby

1925

1

The notice in *Variety* was small, tucked away between an ad for a singing bear and a call for midget tap dancers. "Redheads only. Follies-Scandals types."

"If I had your looks, I'd be down there right now. You're crazy if you don't try it, Tess. You and Abby both."

"I don't know, Sheila."

"Well, I do." Sheila Cohen folded the newspaper into a tight little rectangle. She pushed it across the desk toward her friend and took another bite out of the sandwich she'd brought from home that morning. "God, I hate cheese," she said. "It's a Sammy Rosen thing. He's had a piece of a lot of shows, Tess."

"I've never acted in my life."

"Who said anything about acting? He's auditioning bodies, not brains. All you have to do is walk across the stage, strike a couple of poses, maybe sing and dance a little. Jesus H. Christ, Tess, do you have any idea what showgirls make? Some of them get up to a hundred bucks a week, and that's just the beginning. You could work for Saul Gruber for the rest of your life and never see that much money."

"I'll have to ask Abby."

"So ask her."

"Ask me what?" The tall young woman who came into the cramped little office carried a sheaf of letters in one hand, a long thin ledger book in the other. "Mr. Gruber won't sign these, Tess. He says he's never seen worse typing in his life and if they're not done over by the time he's ready to leave, you're fired. You didn't even check them."

"See. What've you got to lose?" Sheila Cohen threw the

3

crusts of her stale sandwich into the wastebasket and picked up a cardboard cup of lukewarm deli coffee. As long as she lived, she'd never understand the Irish.

The one ambition of Sheila's life was to act on the Broadway stage, any stage, really, as long as it eventually led to the magic theaters clustered around Forty-second Street. She read every issue of *Variety*, every theater column in the New York papers, worked at night and on weekends with groups of other hopefuls, turned up at any call that sounded even remotely promising, spent hours rehearsing in front of the tiny mirror in her bedroom, and paid out every spare dollar she could save on lessons that seemed to lead nowhere. She was dark, she was short, and no matter how many diets she went on, her clothes were always just a shade too tight. Five years ago, on her first day in Saul Gruber's office, she'd drafted the letter of resignation she expected to hand him within six months. But the breaks hadn't come her way. Cousin of a cousin, good old Saul would never fire her, no matter how often the hour she got for lunch stretched into three or four.

Recently she'd started seeing Arnie Gruber, who worked in the business during the day and was going to CCNY Law School at night. She had nothing against Arnie except that he was short, dark, plump, and unexciting. "He'll be a lawyer someday, Sheila," her mother said. "I know, Mom. I'm impressed. As long as he'll take me to a show, I'll go out with him." Arnie always fell asleep during the second act, always apologized, and always asked her out again. Pearl Gruber and Sarah Cohen spent long hours on the telephone discussing the progress of the match they were making. Their children were perfect for each other, even if Sheila was too stubborn to admit it.

Once, just once, Sheila would have liked to be called into the showroom to model a coat for a customer. But it never happened. Saul Gruber's business ran on a very thin profit margin; the furs his workmen fashioned into jackets and scarves and full-length coats were as good as he could afford, but it took skill, dim lights, and tall Gentile girls to sell them. On Sheila they would have looked worse than on the animals who had been their original owners. The girls who modeled the coats came and went, typing and filing without much expertise and even less interest, twirling and holding their heads high in the showroom on the days when customers came to inspect Saul's merchandise, quitting as soon as something better came along. Quite a few of them had made it into chorus lines, others had picked up their own apartments and bank accounts from men who had watched them twirl and smile and show more silk-clad leg than Saul approved of. After a while Sheila had grown able to predict down to the last minute how long a girl would last. The only ones she'd ever bothered to make friends with were Tess and Abby Sullivan.

They fascinated her because they were so alike and yet so different from each other. Abby did all her own work and much of her sister's, never complained, always arrived on time in the morning, often stayed late without being asked. Saul held his breath every time she put on one of his coats and went into the showroom. But even after four years of looks that no other girl could have misinterpreted, Abby seemed not to realize how extraordinarily beautiful she was.

Her bobbed hair curled sedately around her face, the red and the gold strands so mingled that a word hadn't been invented to describe their combined color. She had the fine features of some of the more fortunate Irish, fragile bones thinly covered with white, unfreckled skin, long, slender hands and feet, eyes that were gray on dark days, green or perhaps blue in the sunshine that occasionally pierced through the dingy window beside her desk. Once you got past the startling fact of her beauty, you were struck by the dignified way in which she held herself, the calm, orderly way in which she carried out every task assigned to her, the absence of laughter when you knew, you had heard so often, that all the Irish laughed all the time. She took life very seriously, did Abby Sullivan, taught to do so by a mother once as beautiful as she, but worn out by twenty-four years of marriage and the bearing of more children, living and dead, than even the parish priest secretly thought God could really intend.

Tess belonged to another type of Irish. She had the same height, the same white skin and delicate bone structure as her sister, but her hair was redder, her eyes a deeper, truer blue, and she never, never could get the hang of working. When Abby offered to bring her sister into Saul Gruber's office to replace the blond Swede who hadn't bothered to give notice, the furrier had drunk a glass of wine at lunch to celebrate his good fortune and hired Tess without the formality of an interview. His files a shambles after only two months, his correspondence suddenly unreadable, he was now determined to fire her. Tess could wear coats and walk like a queen, but that was about all she could do. Before he sent her into the showroom he had to tell Sheila to make sure that there were no runs in her silk stockings, that her wild, flyaway hair was combed, and that she'd wiped the mustard or the crumbs of doughnut off her upper lip. "She's a slob," he raged to his wife Pearl, "beautiful, but a slob." Her typing was disastrous, her filing a mystery even to herself, her conception of time as remote as though she'd never heard of regular business hours. She could wear coats, she could laugh, she could play terribly mischievous jokes on everyone from the shipping clerks to Saul Gruber himself, and her smile could wrap itself around your heart like that of your own child. "What she needs is a rich husband," Pearl concluded, busy with arranging yet another theater date for Arnie and her best friend's daughter. "Is she at least smart enough to know that?"

"She's the dumbest mick in the world," Saul mourned. "Somebody should have made her a nun."

Fortunately, none of Bridget Sullivan's children had a religious vocation. The family couldn't afford to give one of its members to God, especially after Patrick Sullivan had fallen off the scaffolding at the new hotel job he'd been so happy to get. His legs were crushed beneath the bricks that had tumbled down on top of him, and even after four years there were days on which he could barely hobble to the bathroom to relieve himself.

Sean Fitzgerald and the Democratic party had come through with a job for Bridget, and Mrs. Goldbaum across the hall had taken Abby, newly graduated from high school, to see her dead husband's relative, Saul Gruber. But the end of every week was still grim, with milk and potatoes barely enough for the little ones, and all the adults sucking in their stomachs until Bridget, Abby, and now Tess were paid. Bridget Sullivan said novenas and lit candles in front of the statue of Our Lady in Holy Rosary Church, but the maintenance of life was a shaky business at best. Yet her children were handsome and healthy, thank God; she could look at her wedding photograph and remember how red her hair had been before it turned gray and washed out, and even when she changed the soiled linen on the daybed where Pat spent his waking and sleeping hours, she could still recall the ambitious, loving man he had once been. "Education is everything in America," Mrs. Goldbaum said, sucking in tea through teeth too rotten to tolerate sugar, and she was right. The Jews sent their children to night school at the virtually free City College of New York or scrabbled together quarters and half-dollars to pay the tuition at Columbia. Maybe Thomas, who at sixteen was brighter and more hungry for knowledge than his twenty-year-old friend, CCNY student Leon Goldbaum, would make it that far; but for the girls, four years to get a high school diploma was all the time Bridget Sullivan could spare them.

"Come on, Tess. You're going to get fired anyway." Sheila was never jealous. If she'd been just a little bit pretty, she might have learned to envy girls like the Sullivan sisters. As it was, the physical gulf between them was so great that it never occurred to her to resent what she couldn't have even in her dreams. Everyone in the little theater groups to which she belonged swore she had more talent than any of the rest of them. And she was smart. Even if you had a friend who only paraded around on a stage dressed in feathers and spangles, it was still a friend in show business. One thing led to another; showgirls sometimes hung around with real actors, might even know when a part was being vacated and needed to be recast before the notice appeared in *Variety*. Timing was as important as talent.

"What do you think, Abby?" Tess picked up the folded newspaper and sauntered over to where her sister was working through her lunch hour. Even in the narrow aisle between the desks she managed to give the impression of space and a well-lit runway. "Take a look at this."

"What about those letters?"

"Forget the letters. Sheila thinks I'd be crazy to pass this up."

It took Abby only a few seconds to skim the ad, even less time to remind Tess that nobody hired girls who walked in off the street with no experience. Look how long Sheila had been running to every audition she heard or read about. "If you start right away, you can get at least two or three of those letters finished, and I'll do the rest of them for you. Mr.

Gruber is leaving early this afternoon. He won't know the difference." Abby dropped the copy of *Variety* into her wastebasket.

"Abby." Now it was Sheila bending over her desk, one hand covering the pages of the ledger, her deep, expressive brown eyes pleading, persuading. "Face it, kid. The only thing Tess has that's worth anything is her body, and she's not using it. Have you ever been to one of those shows? Half the girls in them would look like hags standing next to her. Somebody like Sammy Rosen would hire her in a minute. I know he would."

"And I'm going to get fired anyway," Tess pointed out.

"Why do you need my approval, Tess? I think Sheila's already made your mind up for you. When was the last time you listened to me?"

Tess was at her best when she wanted something. Her blue eyes seemed to melt with sweetness and innocence, her mouth curved in the most candid of smiles, her voice, normally so loud and high-pitched that Saul Gruber could hear it through the closed door of his private office, dropped to a whisper. "I don't want to go by myself, Abby."

"Take Sheila with you. Neither one of you does enough work around here to be missed."

"Look, Abby, the whole point of one of these cattle calls is to get yourself noticed. I know Sammy Rosen would want her if he got a good look at her, but every redhead in New York will be milling around in that rehearsal hall. Tess needs a gimmick, and you're it. How many sets of gorgeous twins do you think he sees in a day?"

"Nobody is going to mistake us for twins, Sheila."

"Maybe not up close. But by that time he'll already be interested enough to want a better look. You might buy yourselves five extra minutes, and believe me, five minutes is more than most girls get. Just stand together, apart from everybody else, preferably under a light if you can manage it. Don't talk, don't giggle, don't move a muscle. Just stand there. Sometimes they call out just the last name, and if they do, the two of you walk out at the same time. You can do it. You've done it in the showroom often enough."

It was Saul Gruber's favorite customer razzle-dazzle, Tess and Abby Sullivan parading side by side in dark full-length mink. There was always a little gasp, a heartbeat of silence before pencils scratched over pads again and heads bent toward one another to comment on the quality of the furs and the cut of the coats. More often than not, the two redheads made a difference, and a maybe became a sale.

"Please, Abby. You'll never have to get me another job again." Tess could wheedle like a child when she sensed that her sister was weakening.

"I don't know. I have to think about it. And I've got work to do." She was more than half won over, but there were other considerations besides the obvious one of realizing that even Tess was not likely to be fired from a job for which, for a change, she seemed to have all the qualifications.

Mom wouldn't approve, but she'd take the good money Tess brought home, light extra candles to the Blessed Mother to keep her child safe, and say no more about it. Patrick was another problem altogether. Mrs. Goldbaum across the hall always said she could understand every word Mr. Sullivan shouted when he was in one of his rages. So could everyone else in the building. It wasn't Pat's style to hold himself in, nor did he ever bother about the Murphys below them when he pounded his cane on the splintery wood floor that was also the Murphys' ceiling. Murphy didn't complain, being Irish himself and inclined to loud singing whenever he bottled up a new batch of the beer he brewed in his bathtub, but it mortified proud Abby to know how often the neighbors were privy to language that her father permitted no one else to use. Pat had stricter rules for his two girls than he ever attempted to force on the boys, and none of them, she was sure, was flexible enough to allow him to permit one of his daughters to gallivant around half naked on a public stage, staying out until all hours of the night, and coming home by herself at God knew what time.

Only the fact of all that money coming in might make a difference, that and Tess's sworn oath to quit as soon as their father was able to work again. Before she left, the Swede had boasted that she'd be earning three times what Saul Gruber considered tops for his girls. Three times! For easy work, work that was exciting and fun, that didn't leave you so tired at the end of the day that you wondered how you'd ever manage to drag yourself out of bed the next morning. Once, about six months ago, a customer had handed Abby his card, a phone number scrawled in pencil on the back of it. "That's a private line, sweetheart," he'd said. "Call me anytime." She'd given it to the stock boy to slip into the pocket of the coat the customer was having sent to his wife, but the feel of the pasteboard had stayed on her fingers for days.

His own private little Catholic saint was what Saul Gruber called her, so often and with such unmistakable self-satisfaction in his voice at having found so rare a gem that sometimes it was all she could do to smile sweetly at him and accept the compliment. But there were depths to Abby Sullivan that no one suspected, hungers that gnawed so cruelly she wanted to howl with the pain of them. Bridget found peace kneeling in the jeweled light of Holy Rosary's stained-glass windows, but Abby's yearning heart and soul cried out for beauty that did not spill itself mockingly over dark-clothed, despairing women, over broken, beaten men, beauty that did not disappear because clouds hid the sun.

In her last year of high school she had made a pact with a sympathetic nun who taught the commercial courses most girls took. In Sister Anthony's advanced English class Abby gulped down literature and poetry like the starved creature she was; after school, for an hour every day, Sister Mark taught her the skills by which she would have to earn her living.

There was never any real hope. She had known it from the beginning. On the evening of Patrick Sullivan's accident, she returned Sister Anthony's books of poetry to Holy Rosary Convent, managing somehow to speak to the nun without bitterness or anger. There wasn't time now for anything except more and longer hours devoted to learning bookkeeping, stenography, and typing. There wasn't any time left at all for dreaming of a different life, for anything but accepting the truth of a crippled father, hungry little brothers, a mother whose eyes told her there was no escape. At graduation Sister Mark told her that she had tested higher than any other girl in the commercial course. Abby never forgot the catch in the nun's voice, nor Sister Anthony's consoling hug.

She ran Saul Gruber's office almost single-handedly, bringing efficiency and calm control to a business that was often erratic and always hectic, and most days she managed an inner calm also. But there were moments, she thought there would always be moments, when the wanting something better churned her stomach and clenched her fists. The sight of Patrick's useless legs stretched out on the daybed made her want to weep with the hopelessness of it, the helplessness. Bridget's straight back as she went out the door each night to work brought a guilt that was sharper than the wanting. The brothers looked to her for smiles and reassurances that all was well. And every morning she promised herself that she would not fail them, that she would get through this day, and the next. And all the dreary days to come.

Shortly after two o'clock she carried Tess's letters, retyped and proofread, into Saul Gruber's office. She laid them on the desk beside the ledger and waited while he signed them.

"How many of these did you do, Abby?" he asked. He had a cigar clamped in his mouth and his hat was pushed to the back of his head.

"Just a few, Mr. Gruber. I know she's slow, but I think she's getting better."

He sighed and stubbed the cigar out in an ashtray already filled with reeking dead butts and inch-long ashes. "I'm sorry, Abby, I really am. But you've got to look at it from my point of view. I can't afford to pay her just to wear coats. Believe me, it's nothing personal. You want me to tell her or can you do it?"

"I'll tell her."

"You're a good girl, Abby. I don't know what I'd do without you." He had his coat on and was moving around his desk toward the door. "Look, I tell you what. It's Friday, nothing much is going on. Why don't you girls close up the office and go home early? Maybe do a little shopping. Mrs. Gruber always buys herself something new when she's feeling bad."

"Maybe we will. Have a nice weekend, Mr. Gruber."

"I'm really sorry, Abby. Tell her that if I hear of anything else opening up, I'll let you know about it."

"Thanks, Mr. Gruber."

He left the door open when he went out. Tess didn't look up from the invoice she was pretending to complete, and Sheila was already picking the wrinkled copy of *Variety* out of Abby's wastebasket.

"I know. I heard. We've got the rest of the afternoon

off." Sheila held *Variety* over her head like a sword. "What about it?"

"On one condition. You start looking for another job on Monday morning, Tess."

"I will, Abby. I promise."

"Don't worry, kid," Sheila said. "That's one promise you'll never have to keep. I've got a feeling about this. You're going to have it made."

By the time they came up out of the subway in the theater district, Abby was already regretting the impulse that had made her agree to come this far. Sheila's description of what went on at a cattle call for chorus girls hadn't been in the least reassuring.

"It can't be much different from the auditions I've been to," she said. "They're looking for a certain type of girl, and most of the time all you do is walk past a table with three or four men behind it, let them see what you look like, and then leave. Once in a while they ask somebody to read a few lines, but usually it's 'Thank you. We'll let you know,' and you're finished. Believe me, there's nothing to it. Okay now. Stand still, and let me do a little gilding of the lilies."

They were halfway up the flight of dirty stairs leading to the rehearsal hall. Girls were pushing past them, looking narrowly, assessingly at one another on the way up, coming down with tight mouths and that special flatness of yet another rejection in their eyes. "Not bad, not bad at all." Sheila had run a comb lightly through their short hair, smudged a trace of blue over their eyelids, darkened their lips with a shade of red that had enough coral in it to bring out the red gold of their hair. "I'll hold your coats and bags once we get inside," she said. "I think you're going to make it, Tess, I really do." She was as excited as if she were the one auditioning, as fussy and hopeful as any stage mother. Tess's eyes were shining and a nervous flush colored her cheeks. Abby's complexion, too, had heightened, but from embarrassment and the conviction that this was the most foolish thing Tess had ever persuaded her to do.

One side of the high-ceilinged rehearsal room was paneled in mirrors that stretched ten feet from the floor. Opposite the mirrors, a long strip of black tape had been stuck to the wall at a height of five feet, eight inches. A short, mannish-looking woman wearing a baggy gray sweater and holding a clipboard against her flat chest stood in the doorway. Fifteen or twenty girls sat on low benches, nervously combing and recombing their hair, running their hands over their stockings and pulling at their skirts.

"All right, ladies, let's have your names," she said, assessing red hair and height with one quick glance. "Take off your shoes and go stand against the tape. Feet flat on the floor, backs against the wall." She looked at Sheila and shook her head. "Wrong color hair, sweetheart." She was brusque, but there was a trace of kindness, maybe a tinge of pity in her voice.

"I'm just holding coats," Sheila said. "Okay if I come inside to wait? The stairs are as cold as a monkey's rear end."

It wasn't really all right, but it was late in the day and there was something feisty, tough, and endearing about the girl who looked like an ugly duckling amidst all these swans. "Sure, why not? Just don't try to get in to see Mr. Rosen."

"What do you think I am? Crazy?"

"It happens." The woman shrugged her shoulders and smiled. "It happens all the time." She walked over to where Tess and Abby were standing, shoes dangling from their hands. "Five ten. Good enough," she said, writing it down on her clipboard. "What is this, a sister act? You've got a hole in your stocking, kid." Tess curled her big toe into the ripped silk. "But I guess that's what shoes are for, right? Any experience?"

That was the question Abby had been dreading. In and out. They wouldn't even get the five minutes Sheila was hoping for.

"Modeling," Tess said. "You name it, we've worn it."

"Sure you have. Put your shoes back on and find yourselves somewhere to sit. When I call your names, go through that door over there, give this piece of paper to one of the men inside, do a little walking, make a few turns, and get out quick. Got it?" She lit a cigarette, threw the spent match on the floor, and went back to her guard-dog position at the door.

"Forget about sitting down," Sheila hissed. "Remember what I told you."

"I feel like a fool," Abby whispered. They were standing by one of the big windows overlooking the street, motionless as statues, the wintry afternoon light pooling feebly over them. "There's no one to see us, Tess. Sheila was all wrong about this."

The room emptied quickly. At five minutes to four the woman in the gray sweater closed the door. There were three or four frantic bursts of knocking, which she ignored, followed by the sound of defeated feet clopping down the stairs. Sheila gave them a thumbs-up sign, bright smile plastered across her face.

At four o'clock precisely, the door to the inner room opened and a skinny young man in his mid-twenties came out, shrugging on his coat. "Mr. Rosen says to hold it for a while," he said to the woman. "How many more?" He looked around the rehearsal hall and darted through the door again, returning in a few seconds. "Okay, he'll see the rest of them, but that's all for today. I'm going down to the deli for coffee and a sandwich. You want something?"

"Coffee, white. You need any money?"

"It's on the house."

"Who was that?" Sheila asked. "I think I've seen him before." She'd borrowed a match from the woman in the gray sweater and was standing next to her, smoking companionably, somehow giving the impression that she belonged here in this room. She could worm her way in anywhere if there was the chance of picking up useful information.

"Bobby Stein. He's a dancer, but he'll be doing some of the choreography and taking the rehearsals."

"Does he act?"

"Who doesn't?"

"That's where I recognize him from. I think we've been to a few auditions together. He's good." You could see her quick mind working, filing away the name and the face for future reference.

"Forget it, kid. Mr. Rosen does the picking for this show." All these girls wore hungry, eternally hopeful looks. Fifteen years of working backstage, and Bette Blumfeld had never known it to be any different. She'd seen a lot of girls like Sheila Cohen. They could break your heart if you let it get to you. That was one of the reasons she'd made the switch from plays to song-and-dance shows. Chorines were tough-skinned and a lot more stupid than the kids who wasted their years in little theater groups and showed up in droves every time a new play was being cast. She knew about it because she'd been one of them herself, a long, long time ago. This one, like so many of them, didn't have a prayer. If Bette Blumfeld had ever taken the time to get married and retire from this madness, she probably would have produced a daughter very similar in looks and size to Sheila Cohen.

"Has Bobby already gone?" The girls sitting on the benches couldn't see the face of the man hidden by the partially opened door, but they straightened with a nearly audible snap when Bette Blumfeld answered him.

"Yes, Mr. Rosen. You want me to go after him?"

"No, never mind. Give us another five minutes, then we'll finish up." The door moved a fraction of an inch, half a foot. A hand reached out to take Bette Blumfeld's clipboard. "Let's see what you've got."

"Oh my God. Jeez, I'm sorry, Mr. Rosen." All kinds of junk was falling out of Tess's purse, rolling across the floor. Sheila, a tangle of coats tripping her up awkwardly, was down on her hands and knees, scrabbling after the comb, the lipstick, the dirty balled-up handkerchief. He could step backward or forward to avoid them. Nice, Bette Blumfeld thought, very nicely done. She took a couple of steps back out of the way of the scuttling Sheila, clipboard still in her hand. Sammy Rosen, as was inevitable under the circumstances, followed.

"What the hell . . . ?" When he looked up from the debris under his feet and the chubby little kid who seemed to be close to tears, his eyes had nowhere to go but to the benches and the wall of windows. And as Sheila had intended, he saw Tess and Abby Sullivan in exactly the pose she had coached them to assume. Precisely the same height, turned in a half-profile so that their faces were outlined against grayness, one vagrant beam of light skirting over the tops of their heads, they might have been frozen in one of the tableaux vivants that were always a popular part of every show. He was too experienced and had seen too many beautiful girls to allow any expression to show on his face, but as he turned away and bent over the clipboard, he whispered something to Bette Blumfeld.

"I don't think so," she whispered back. "Sisters, anyway."

A moment later he was gone, and Sheila, suddenly efficient, cleared the floor and sank back into her seat with a gleam of immense satisfaction in her eyes. Timing and luck. You never got anywhere if you didn't take chances.

By the time Bobby Stein returned with the coffee, only Sheila and her protégées remained in the rehearsal hall. Except for calling out the names of the other girls, who were in and out of the inner room as though through a revolving door, Bette Blumfeld hadn't said a thing, hadn't given a hint of whatever it was Sammy Rosen had said to her, hadn't dared look at Sheila Cohen. She wouldn't have been able to stop herself from smiling conspiratorily if she had.

"Okay, you two," she said, coffee in one hand, clipboard in the other, a freshly lit cigarette dangling from between her lips. "Mr. Rosen wants to see you together. Get the door for me, will you, kid? I'm sitting in on this one." As she passed through, dwarfed and looking bulkier than ever behind the tall, slender Sullivan sisters, she winked at Sheila Cohen.

It was smoky and hot in the room, which was as long but only a fraction as wide as the rehearsal hall. Sammy Rosen and Bobby Stein sat at a table littered with used paper cups, greasy sheets of butcher's paper, pads covered with notes and doodlings. Bette Blumfeld laid the clipboard in front of them.

"All right, girls. Tess and Abby, is it?" Sammy Rosen smiled encouragingly at them. "Let's see who's who. Tess, why don't you walk a little for us. Over there and back. Nice and slow. Big smile. Good long steps. Stretch them out. That's it. A couple more times." He bent forward, twirling the stub of a pencil between his fingers. Bobby Stein wrote something on a scrap of paper and handed it to him. "Right. Okay, Tess, we need a back view. Can you walk over to the window and stand there for a minute? Nice, very nice. Raise your arms up over your head. No, that's too high. Bobby, go show her what we want."

Watching Tess glide and posture, raise and lower her arms, hold her smile and toss her head in front of these men whose eyes seemed cold and impersonally intrusive, Abby suddenly knew she had to get out of this room before the disgust in the pit of her stomach turned to sickness. She'd gotten her sister her five extra minutes, for what they were worth, but she was finished with the whole thing now, nausea rising in her throat as she thought how different this was from modeling coats, how much closer to offering oneself for sale.

She had her hand on the knob of the door, but her palm was wet and it slipped against the metal when she tried to turn it.

"Hey, wait a minute. Where are you going?" Bobby Stein's lithe dancer's body seemed to drift across the room. "What's the matter?"

"Nothing. I've just changed my mind, that's all."

"Look, sit down for a second. You're not going to be sick, are you?" Abby's face was so white that Stein's arm went out to hold her up. Any minute now and she'd faint. He led her to the table, pulled out a chair, and more or less pushed her into it. Some of these girls starved themselves for days before an audition. The lights put ten pounds on everybody, even the skinny ones.

"Tess, why don't you wait outside for a few minutes," Sammy Rosen said. "Bring us some water, Bette."

The cup was in Abby's hand, water sloshing over the sides, before he spoke again. "Bobby, go put Tess through a few steps of one of the basic routines. I'll call you when I want you." The door clicked softly behind him.

Sammy Rosen got up and came around the table to lean against it. He waited for Abby to take a few sips of the water, waited until some color came back into her cheeks. "All right, Miss Sullivan," he said. "You want to look at me for a minute and tell me what the problem is?"

"Mr. Rosen." She put the cup carefully on the table, straightened her shoulders and lifted her head. It was the first time she'd really seen him. He was about thirty, maybe a few years older, tall because she had to crane her neck back to meet his eyes. His skin was dark, tanned and smooth and very soft-looking, as though he'd spent part of the winter on a beach somewhere. He had a tiny little cleft in his chin and wrinkles at the corners of his eyes, brown eyes that were as warm and harmless-looking as any she'd ever seen. His hair was black and curly, with an almost white streak of gray over his left temple. Sammy Rosen was handsome in a very un-Irish, very eastern-European way. For a minute she just looked at him, forgetting what it was he had asked her.

"You were going to tell me what the problem is." It wasn't the first time a showgirl had lost her voice when he turned on the charm.

It would be easier if she stood up, if she could move

away from him. "I just came with my sister, Mr. Rosen. I never intended to audition."

"You let Bette put your name on the list." She had more presence than her sister, an almost royal way of holding herself.

"I'm sorry about that. I'm sorry I wasted your time. A friend of ours said that Tess would stand a better chance if she had some sort of gimmick."

"Like maybe I thought I was seeing a pair of twins?" He was laughing at her, an amused little rumble that barely reached her ears.

"I already have a job, Mr. Rosen. I'm not looking for another one."

"And what about Tess? Does she have a job too?" He knew she didn't. He had seen hundreds of Tesses, though only a few who could compete with her for that rare combination of red hair and unfreckled skin. The Tesses, after they'd been fired from every office job they got, always made the best showgirls. They liked the adulation and they got smart after a while, a kind of smart that he sensed this girl would despise. "Never mind, it doesn't matter. If Bobby thinks your sister can learn to dance, I'll give her a try at it. Listen, Abby. Can I call you Abby? No harm done. Okay?"

"Thank you, Mr. Rosen. I'm really sorry about this."

God, she was beautiful when she smiled like that. He'd hired a lot of Irish girls in his time, taught them how to walk and dress, how to dance and belt out a tune on key, got them started, so to speak, introduced them to some of the men who put money into his shows. His one rule was that you didn't play favorites, you didn't get involved, but he could feel himself already wondering whether it wasn't time to make an exception in this case. The funny thing about some of these Irish girls was that they didn't seem very aware of how far they could go with that kind of looks. They had to be pushed, toughened up, the cobwebs dusted from their eyes. Sammy Rosen had a great deal of experience brushing away cobwebs.

"Let's get Tess back in here. I want to give her the good news." He leaned over and grazed his lips against Abby's cheek. A theatrical kiss. It meant nothing. He didn't even look back when he opened the door and called out to his choreographer. "Hey, Bobby, you want to get a bite of something to eat with the newest member of the cast and her sister?"

Sheila Cohen slipped down the stairs as though there were wings attached to her feet. Who said there was no such thing as a break in this business?

Two and a half weeks later Abby Sullivan gave her notice in to Saul Gruber.

"You're making a mistake, Abby. Why do you want to get yourself mixed up in a business like that? Is it money? I'll give you more money. You want to come in a little later in the morning? That's okay with me too."

"Mr. Gruber, I'd rather not talk about it. You can get someone to replace me just by picking up the phone. I'll stay long enough to train her."

"How long?"

"Until the middle of next week. I'm not going to change my mind, Mr. Gruber. I'm sorry."

"You're sorry, I'm miserable." She'd changed in the past few weeks, in subtle ways that only a man used to looking at girls who earned half their living by being beautiful would notice. There was a quality of languor about her all the time, as though she were moving slowly under water. She wasn't quite as pale as she'd been; he'd caught her smiling to herself as she totaled up his accounts, and when he interrupted her she'd blushed, some secret thought or desire too fragile to stand up to his scrutiny and good-natured teasing. Sheila hadn't said anything. He'd gotten the story from Pearl, who had gotten it from Sarah Cohen. "Why don't you hire some nice Jewish girls to wear the coats for a change?" his wife had suggested. "You want me to drive away the few customers I've got?" he asked her. "Thanks, but no thanks. I'll stick to the way I've always done things. Saul Gruber, unpaid theatrical agent and placement service. Furs on the side."

There wasn't a show yet, but at least there was a little money. Eighteen girls were learning the rudiments of tap dancing from four to seven o'clock every afternoon, moving their bodies stiffly in time to the rhythm of tunes banged out on a bad piano, sweating and stumbling along behind the amazingly even-tempered Bobby Stein. "Nobody quits her regular job until I get the contract from Paris," Sammy Rosen had told them. "The frogs may change their minds." "Remind him that you haven't got a job," Abby told Tess when she heard about the contract that hadn't even been signed yet. It was driving Bette Blumfeld toward high blood pressure, but Tess was answering the phone in Sammy Rosen's office now, getting callers' names wrong and thoroughly confusing long-distance operators, but at least she was making as much as Saul Gruber had paid her, and at home no one suspected that she wasn't still working for him. "There's no point upsetting everyone if it doesn't work out," Abby had said sensibly.

It was one of the last really practical thoughts she'd had after that first dinner with Sammy Rosen. And Tess and Bobby Stein too, of course. They hadn't gone anywhere famous or fancy, anywhere notorious or flamboyant. The girls hadn't been dressed for that, and it wasn't Sammy Rosen's style to go for the big first impression. He was too smooth and too confident to play kids' games. They went to a small, intimate place where it was possible to talk quietly as well as eat. Candles on the tables. A thin girl in a black dress singing melancholy songs, barely brushing her fingers over the keys of her piano. Couples, mainly couples in the restaurant.

He and Bobby talked shop for a few minutes, just long enough to set Tess's eyes to shining and make Abby begin to forget how horrible the audition had seemed. People she'd only read about in the gossip columns were mentioned as casually as if they weren't famous, weren't envied, as if they really existed in the ordinary workaday world.

"It's a simple idea," Sammy Rosen explained. "That's what makes it so good. American girls are the most beautiful in the world. The Europeans all love them, especially the French. So what I do is provide a ready-made, hand-picked chorus line. They tell me what types they want, what routines they should learn, what songs they're going to sing. I audition them, Bobby does the dance work, we bring in a teacher if they've got to sing in French. Most of the time they'll probably sing in English, it'll be part of their appeal. We rehearse here, they rehearse there, we put it together in a couple of weeks in Paris, and we're ready to open. I'm starting off with redheads because the French are crazy about them. How many Frenchwomen have you ever heard of with red hair?"

"This is the first time you've done this, Mr. Rosen?"

"How can I call you Abby if you call me 'Mr. Rosen'?

After all, you're not working for me. Tess now, she calls me 'Mr. Rosen.' To you it's Sammy." He could charm the birds out of the trees, as Bridget Sullivan was fond of remarking about the young Patrick she'd loved enough to follow to America. "It's the first time, but it's not going to be the last. I set it up in Paris last year, saw Josephine Baker and talked to her after her show. She's a smart girl. She saw the possibilities as soon as I told her what I had in mind. She knew right away that she'd look even more gorgeous and exotic against a background of American redheads. But hers isn't the only show. Music may be a universal language, but so is beauty. That's an American girl's stock-in-trade. It's taken a while to make the contacts, convince a few people, find the seed money, but we're just about through the talking stage. I've got an informal agreement with a man by the name of Louvier, and my lawyer sent him the contract a week ago. As soon as his signature is on the dotted line, I buy the tickets. I'm taking the first group over personally, and maybe I'll bring some French girls back. Anything French sells in New York."

Strange. Even though Sammy Rosen was all business, all fast-paced, factual explanation, Abby felt as if she were being wooed, as if, beneath the patter and the convincing tone of his voice, he was really saying other things, moving closer to her even though the width of the table lay between them. It was something in his eyes, something in the way they glanced at Tess, darted to Bobby Stein, came back, always came back to linger on her, almost, at times, seeming to shut the others out from what was not a private conversation at all. It was hard to read his expression; his face was too mobile, too constantly changing for her to fix any one look in her mind. He told her, just once, that she could join the line if she wanted to, and when she shook her head he laughed and said, "Think about it." She was beginning to find it difficult to remember why she'd refused his offer in the first place.

On Monday Tess rode the subway to Saul Gruber's office as usual. "It's ridiculous," she protested, "I could have stayed in bed." She hid in the stockroom all morning, drinking coffee, eating doughnuts, and enthralling her former co-workers with the story of her soon-to-be-realized success, repeating it all, with lavish embellishments, over a long lunch with Sheila. By three-thirty she was on her way to the first of many sessions with Bobby Stein, and by six o'clock she had what

Abby had told her to ask for, a regular morning job answering Sammy Rosen's phone. "And listen, Abby," she said, "he asked could I wait around for an hour or so tonight so Bette Blumfeld could show me how he likes things done. She's not coming in tomorrow. She's getting the flu or something. Why don't you come over and wait? We can go home together."

Sammy Rosen worked out of a set of messy, cluttered offices in a building that was never quiet. Dancers thumped in the studio that adjoined his three rooms, out-of-work performers trailed up and down the stairs to booking and agents' offices, music blared from a radio in a sweatshop that specialized in hand sewing sequins onto skimpy chorus-line costumes, bill collectors and process servers lounged in the hallways. "Isn't this great?" Tess asked. "Great," Abby agreed, brushing aside the huge white tomcat who leaped into her lap. There were white hairs all over her dark skirt.

"I never hire anyone my cat doesn't approve of," Sammy Rosen said. "Superstition. Everyone in show business is superstitious."

"So are the Irish," Abby said.

"That's why they make the world's best actors."

The phone began to ring, and on the fourth shrill cry, Tess answered it. Sammy Rosen shook his head and pantomimed taking a message. It took Tess longer than it should have to find a pencil and a scrap of paper, but at last she was hunched over the receiver, laboriously writing down the caller's message.

"The best of the Irish is Laurette Taylor. Have you ever seen her?" Sammy Rosen's hand was on the back of Abby's chair. She had to turn halfway around to look at him. They were as effectively alone in the little office as if a curtain had been pulled shut in front of them.

"No, I haven't," she said. "I've never been to a play at all."

"That's a crime. Everybody ought to see Laurette Taylor at least once in his life." He smiled at her, the warm, slow smile that had made her feel so comfortable with him three days before. The cat wound itself around his legs. He scooped it up, rubbed the flat space between its eyes until the sound of its purring filled the office, then leaned over and placed the animal in Abby's lap. "Wait here a minute," he said. "I've got to make a phone call." The cat kneaded itself a nest on her thighs, its heavy body a weight she balanced carefully. "I've never known Banquo to take to anyone so quickly."

"What a funny name for a cat," Tess said. She wasn't sure whether the message she had taken was important enough to interrupt Mr. Rosen, who had gone into his office and closed the door behind him, or whether it could wait until morning. Wait until morning, she decided. She might not have gotten it right anyway. "Sounds Italian."

"It's from *Macbeth*, Tess. Banquo is murdered, but his ghost comes to sit in Macbeth's chair." Abby's hand stroked the animal's head. The fur snapped electrically and clung to her fingers.

"I'm ready to go." Tess propped the message against the phone and covered the typewriter. She didn't bother attempting to clear off the desk. Bette Blumfeld had told her not to touch anything. She knew exactly where everything was and she wanted it to stay that way.

"Sammy asked me to wait."

Somehow Tess had lost the inside track. She was the only one of the two who ought to feel at home in this office, but Abby was sitting there with Mr. Rosen's cat on her lap as if she owned the place. Maybe it hadn't been such a good idea after all to ask her to meet there. Actually, she would never have thought of it if Mr. Rosen hadn't made the suggestion. Mr. Rosen. Sammy. She reached for her hat and coat, a tickling, hilarious suspicion sneaking up on her—the same way Sammy Rosen was sneaking up on Abby. She wondered how long it would be before her sister caught on to what was happening.

"I've got two tickets to see Laurette Taylor tonight in *Pierre the Prodigal*," Sammy Rosen said. "We can pick them up at the box office anytime before the curtain goes up. What about it, Abby?"

Two tickets. With his connections he could just as easily have gotten three. "Go ahead, Abby," Tess said. "I'll tell Mom you'll be late and not to worry."

"Call her if you want to. Tell her I'll bring you home in a cab."

"We don't have a phone, Mr. Rosen." There it was, the gulf between them, a family that was too poor to afford a telephone and a working girl who suddenly felt the need for formality.

Tess was halfway out the door. If Saul Gruber hadn't been old and very, very married, he would never have fired Abby Sullivan's sister. But if he hadn't, Tess wouldn't be where she was now. Sammy Rosen wasn't married, and he was definitely, very definitely showing signs of a more than casual interest in Bridget Sullivan's eldest daughter. I won't say anything about his being a Jew, Tess decided, remembering Patrick's rule about going out only with young men who were both Catholic and Irish. I'll just say I don't know what his name is. "Have a good time," she said. "Don't worry about Mom and Dad. Have you got a key?"

The evening was magic. Laurette Taylor, tiny, exquisitely beautiful, with a voice whose whisper could reach to the farthest corner of the theater, wove an unbreakable spell around Abby Sullivan's Irish heart and soul. She sank into the nighttime world of the theater so completely that for the space of a few hours she forgot that daylight and Saul Gruber's office even existed. Of the hundreds of plays she was to see in later years, *Pierre the Prodigal* was always the one she remembered best, always the one whose opening and closing lines remained engraved on her memory. And Sammy Rosen, sitting beside her in the dark, watching the play of expressions across her face rather than the actors on the stage, knew that if he had cast the line, Laurette Taylor was the hook on which Abby Sullivan would be reeled in.

"Would you like to go backstage to meet her?" he asked. Too stunned even to applaud, Abby had sat as motionless as a child overwhelmed by the lights of its first Christmas tree, staring at the curtain as if by willing it to open she could make the magic begin all over again.

"Backstage?"

"I could arrange it if you like."

"Oh, no. No. What would I say to her?"

" 'You were wonderful, Miss Taylor.' That's what everyone says."

"She *was* wonderful, wasn't she, Mr. Rosen?"

"Sammy."

"Sammy. And it's not just because it's the first play I've ever seen. Is it always like this?"

"Like what?"

"Magic." It was the only word she could think of.

"That's what the theater is, Abby. Real magicians and a lot of people who just think they are, all of them trying to create believable illusions."

"Could we really go backstage?"

"As easy as one, two, three."

"That's good enough then, just knowing it's possible. Please don't laugh at me."

"I wouldn't dare."

"I don't want to destroy the illusion. I don't want to find out that that's all it is."

"You're showing the classic symptoms of having been bitten by the bug," he said. "Do you have any idea what I'm talking about? No? Then ask your little friend who so conveniently dropped her purse last Friday. Bette Blumfeld told me all about it. She'll know."

He held her arm in his as they walked up the aisle, through the lobby, out under the marquee to where a line of taxis was drawn up against the curb. People turned their heads as they passed, wondering who the tall young woman was who seemed to walk in a radiance that began with the brightness of her hair and glowed in her face. She had to be somebody, dressed like that, somebody pretending to be nobody, someone they ought to know who was trying to slip by them unrecognized. Tentative smiles came her way, but she didn't see them, and that was all the more convincing. Sammy Rosen heard it once, the whispered "Who is she?" He tightened his grip on her arm, walked a little faster and knew he looked conspiratorial.

"Would you like to go somewhere?" he asked when they were settled in the close dimness of the cab. He held her ungloved hand in his, warming the cold fingers, no nearer than when the shared arm of their seats had been between them.

"Home, please," she said, and he knew better than to intrude on her dream during the long ride to the crowded apartment house where too many people lived and a man named Murphy brewed beer in his bathtub.

2

The explosion came in the same week that Abby quit Saul Gruber and it came, as she should have known it would, via Mrs. Goldbaum across the hall. Fools may live in paradise, but never for very long.

Mrs. Goldbaum met them at the subway station, so upset by the sounds she'd heard coming from the Sullivan apartment that her black wig had slipped sideways on her head and she'd come out into the cold in her house slippers.

"I never would have said a thing, Abby dear. You know I don't go looking for trouble, Tess. I thought they knew." Miserable and fearful as she was, she could still look accusingly at daughters who hid things from their parents. God forbid Leon should ever have such a secret. "You should have told them. Finding out like this, your father is going to have a stroke. Take my advice. Go get Father Phelan and take him home with you. In front of a priest, what can he say?"

"What happened, Mrs. Goldbaum?" Abby was as calm as she'd been on the day Sean Fitzgerald had come to take her mother to the hospital, the day that Bridget had turned despairing, childlike eyes on her daughter and given a portion of her own mothering endurance over to her. Tess's teeth were chattering and she was stripping the gloves off her hands. She'd been ready for this fight for a long time, much longer than Abby.

"Arnie Gruber told my Leon, and Leon told me. I couldn't believe it. I told him he was crazy. My own son, I told him he didn't know what he was talking about. That was a good job I got you, Abby," she mourned. "I'll never be able to look Saul Gruber in the face again."

"What exactly did Arnie say, Mrs. Goldbaum?"

"What do you think he said? His father has to find a new girl because the one I personally brought to his office is walking out on him to take her clothes off in front of the whole world. That's what he said."

"He fired me," Tess said. "What could I do? I had to find another job."

"You I'm not talking about. I'm not surprised, if you'll pardon my saying so. Let Father Phelan find you a job if you're still alive tomorrow morning."

"This isn't getting us anywhere, Mrs. Goldbaum."

Leon's mother straightened her wig and looked down at her feet, surprised at the damp cold that was numbing her toes. "Look at this," she said. "What I do for you girls out of the goodness of my heart."

"Is Mom home?"

"Is your mother home? Where else would she be, with news like this? Every afternoon we drink a cup of tea together. Today she should have told me to go away. Better for her if she had." She started walking gingerly along the sidewalk, skirting the puddles of melted snow that had already wrecked her slippers. "So. After I yelled at Leon, after I called my only son a liar, I went down to the drugstore and called Saul Gruber. 'Saul,' I said, 'somebody, not mentioning names, is saying terrible things about Abby Sullivan, and for her mother's sake, I want to hear you tell me they're not true.' 'What?' he says. So I tell him what Arnie told Leon. You should have heard the man. It would break your heart. Tears, real tears in his voice. 'All right,' I said, 'maybe it's not that bad. So it's show business, but maybe it isn't *that* kind of show business. Maybe it's a real play, and Mrs. Sullivan already knows about it. She's keeping it a surprise in case something goes wrong. A lot of plays never get anywhere. You read about it in the papers all the time.' 'Ask her,' he says."

"And that's what you did." They were only half a block from the apartment house. Tess stopped and pulled Mrs. Goldbaum under a streetlight. She looked terrible.

"Not right away. In case she didn't want to talk about it. 'Isn't it nice about the girls,' I said. 'All that extra money coming in.' 'What extra money?' your mother asks. So then I realized she didn't know. 'Excuse me,' I said, 'I've got to go put Leon's supper on.' And then Mr. Sullivan comes roaring across the room at me, waving his cane and yelling, 'What extra money?' "

"And that was it?"

"Who am I to keep secrets from your father when he's threatening me with his cane and yelling at the top of his lungs?"

"It was nice of you to come out in this weather to warn us, Mrs. Goldbaum." Instinctively, Abby moved out of the circle of light from the street lamp. Down the block she could see light pouring from the front room of the apartment where her father and mother waited.

Mrs. Goldbaum shrugged her shoulders. "Maybe it's not too late," she said. "You don't even have to ask Saul Gruber if he'll take you back. Just walk into his office Monday and tell him you've changed your mind."

"It's too late for that."

"Much too late," Abby agreed. There had been too many lunches, too many dinners, too many plays in Sammy Rosen's company. "Good night, Mrs. Goldbaum."

"Something bad happens, come knock on my door. You can sleep on the couch. It folds out into a bed. In the morning you make up with him. Your poor mother. It's the least I can do." She touched each of the girls lightly on the cheek, then shuffled off down the sidewalk, muttering to herself and shaking her head.

"Are you ready for 'The Troubles'?" Tess asked.

"Worse," said Abby. "The Battle of the Boyne."

The apartment was on the third floor, at the head of a tunnel of narrow stairs flanked by a sticky, splintery railing and a wall from which the dark-brown paint had peeled off in irregular dirty-white patches. Trash bins stood on every landing, never empty, always overflowing. From under the doors behind which the Irish lived seeped the odors of cooking cabbage and steeped tea leaves, wet diapers and woolen coats hung to dry over the stove. The old building had absorbed so many generations of living that its porous walls could hold no more. Sausages were being fried in olive oil somewhere on the second floor, the sunny smells of garlic and tomatoes grown on faraway hillsides cut through the damp of the wintry night air, and the fragrance of candles and chicken soup lingered outside Mrs. Goldbaum's three rooms. The children who should have been playing jacks and marbles in the hallways were missing, pulled inside by parents who would open their doors just a crack when Mr. Sullivan got good and warmed up again. All the little cubicles piled one atop the other, floors, ceilings, and walls a shared membrane of pulsating sound, made for exciting and very public airing of private joys and griefs.

Someday, Abby thought, she would try to explain to Sammy Rosen what it was like to try to live here. Perhaps he already knew. Scratch a New Yorker and it was more than likely you'd find the son or daughter of an immigrant. He had never come into the building with her, never done more than stand on the sidewalk beside his waiting taxi until she twitched back the curtain of the front room and waved to him that she was in the apartment and safe. That was the way she wanted it, and he didn't argue with her. Working people, men and women who fed their families and paid their rent by the labor of their muscles, went to bed early and slept soundly. The expensive taxi that would have set tongues to wagging in daylight had driven unnoticed down this street at night. She didn't know where Sammy Rosen went after he took her home. He had an apartment somewhere, rooms unshared with anyone else, space in which to do and think and be in privacy, a place to which he had never invited her, knowing she would not, could not have gone. She imagined them in terms of a theater set—fine furniture, white couches, paintings on the walls, lamps with fringed shades sitting on polished tables, books on shelves, lights that dimmed slowly with the turning of a knob. How else could he live?

Patrick Sullivan sat at the head of the table at which the family gathered for its meals, the crook of his cane hooked over the high back of his chair, an untouched cup of tea cooling in front of him. The mother, a pot of fresh tea in her hand, froze beside him at the first sound of the door opening on its uneven hinges. She didn't greet the two girls, didn't cluck over their wet shoes, didn't rush to set cups and milk and sugar and slices of toasted bread before them, made none of the reassuringly normal noises that usually welcomed them home. The rooms were as silent as if not a single soul lived there. The five boys, from Thomas, the oldest, to four-year-old Seamus, were waiting out the storm and the shame of it all in the warm Murphy kitchen.

"I've never hit a one of you yet," Patrick said through clenched teeth. "But maybe it's time I started, by God."

"Can you spare me a minute to take off my coat?" Tess asked. "I wouldn't want to make it too difficult for you." The skin around her lips was as white as frost, but her eyes were dancing like the blue flames over the peat bogs in the old country. She was the only one in the family with a temper to match her father's.

The teapot fell from Bridget's hand and crashed to the floor. A steaming brown pool eddied at her feet, but she didn't reach for mop or rag to wipe it up before it ruined the bit of carpet that was threadbare with brushing and cleaning. She had one strong hand on her husband's shoulder and the other on his cane before the noise of breaking pottery died away. "Have patience, Patrick," she pleaded. "You promised."

"Sit down," he shouted, his shoulder muscles, which had grown stronger since the accident, twitching beneath her fingers. "Sit down, the both of you."

The heels on Tess's shoes clicked over the floor as she walked to the table. She pulled out a chair, grimly satisfied with the scraping noise that was sure to tell the Murphys that the battle was about to begin in earnest. All their snub, rabbity noses were probably pointed up at the cracks in the ceiling right this minute. It didn't bother her in the least to have an audience. Breaking dishes, shouts, and overturned furniture were merely the background noises of any decent fight, like the whinnying of horses and the blowing of horns when an army marched out onto the field. Abby moved so quietly that she might have been a ghost slipping sideways through the air. She still had her coat on, dressed more for flight than for combat. Her face was set in that same queer expression she'd worn the day Tess had auditioned for Sammy Rosen, as if she were naked but hoped no one would notice it.

"I want the whole story," Patrick Sullivan said. He pushed the cup of tea away from him, and when the milky liquid slopped over his fingers, he swept cup, saucer, and spoon to the floor. "And I want the truth."

At this rate we'll have no dishes left in the house at all, Tess thought. She was trying to make up her mind how much to tell, how many small lies she could slip between the facts to soften them. But when she opened her mouth to speak, her father slapped the table with the palm of his hand, silencing her with a finger that stuck out from his clenched fist like a stick from the knobby branch of a tree.

"Not you," he commanded. "You'd lie to Almighty God Himself if you thought you could get away with it. Not one word from you, my girl, not one word." He turned away from her, turned toward Abby, and for just a fraction of a second there was a suggestion of both pain and softness at the corners of his eyes. Abby was his favorite child, his Bridget as she had been in Ireland, before the hard work in America and the children he couldn't stop himself from giving her had worn out the fey beauty, gnarled and roughened the once slender hands, driven her to lay her troubles at the Blessed Mother's altar at six-o'clock Mass every morning, like all the rest of the women who had precious little but their faith to sustain them. "Have patience," Bridget had implored, "promise me you won't lose your temper." He'd promised her that, much good it would do. The only unbroken vow of the many he'd made over the years was the one to remain faithful. He'd never so much as looked at another woman, but everything else he'd done wrong.

"Don't keep your father waiting, Abby," Bridget said. Not me, not us. The father, always the father, as if he were the more fragile of the two, the one more to be loved and obeyed, the one, if a choice had to be made, to protect and cherish.

Abby's face was cold, her lips were stiff. She took a deep breath and folded her hands in her lap, the way she'd done for years and years when waiting to be called on to recite her catechism lessons in the musty classrooms of Holy Rosary School. Only this time she had no words committed to memory, there were no short, easy questions, no answers that she could give without stumbling over them.

"Tess was fired," she began. The sound of her own voice surprised her. Steady and low, not at all frightened, as if she were reading from a story in a newspaper. "Three weeks ago today. There was an ad in *Variety*, and I went with her to answer it. She got the job. That's where the money's been coming from. There'll be more, a lot more. Right now she's answering the phone in Mr. Rosen's office in the morning and learning to dance in the afternoon. In a couple of months he's taking all the girls to Paris."

"No Jew is taking a daughter of mine anywhere," Patrick Sullivan shouted. "Take your hands off me, woman."

"He already has," Abby said in the same deadly, matter-of-fact voice. "He's taken me to dinners and plays. Almost every night." The last in a whisper, as if only now did she realize how many hours she had spent in his company.

"Jesus, Mary, and Joseph," Bridget moaned. Her hand was a blur flinging a cross over the upper part of her body, coming to rest against her heart.

"We've got our own lives to live, Dad, and they won't be ruined by the Church and the smell of cabbage in a place like this." Tess had found her tongue in spite of Patrick's warning. For once in her life she wasn't laughing, wasn't teasing for the pure fun of it. "For God's sake, do you want us to end up like Mother? Look at her. When was the last time she had a new dress? When did she ever eat a meal without stinting herself so that everyone else could have enough? How long does she have to go on kissing Sean Fitzgerald's ass to keep a miserable, stinking job that'll be the death of her before it's over with?"

He could move fast when he wanted to, swift and crablike on the bowed legs in which hundreds of pieces of fractured bone had knitted together in painful knobs and points. There was nothing wrong with his arms, nothing of the cripple in the way they reached out for his daughter, nothing but fine strength in the hand that pulled her from her chair and the open palm that stung against her cheek and snapped her head far back on her neck. "You're not fit to be in the same room with her," he panted. "Not fit to live in the same house."

A trickle of blood oozed from the side of Tess's mouth, drops spattered on the back of the hand that Bridget caught and held in a grip tighter than death. She pushed her body between her husband and the defiant, injured young woman who had challenged him with words no child of hers should ever have spoken. Burned by the hot fire that was Patrick licked to killing rage, paralyzed by the ice that was Tess, she swayed against the edge of the table, losing her footing as the unyielding wood bit into the thin flesh of her hip, holding on desperately, unbalancing her husband, bringing him down on top of her as she fell sideways and crumpled into the sticky mess of spilled tea. He went down, and without his cane or the supporting arm of his wife he couldn't get up again, but he was still the father, still the lawgiver, always and forever the victor. Before Bridget could begin to fear that she'd hurt him for the sake of saving her daughter, he'd disowned the child.

"Pack your things and get out," he shouted, the pain of what had been done to him swirling like blood in his brain, dropping a curtain of red that glowed over Tess's hair and spread scarlet from chin to forehead. "You're no daughter of mine, do you hear? Go to the devil if he'll have you."

"It doesn't have to be like this, Dad." Abby was down on her knees beside him, reaching out to help him to his feet. "Please, Mom, tell him it's not what he thinks."

"What is it then, Abby?" Bridget asked. Caught between her husband and her most loving, most responsible child, she wanted desperately to understand, wanted, more than anything else, to be told that nothing had changed, that the world was not reaching out its fingers to ensnare her daughters and tempt them away from family and Church. The lines were so rigidly drawn, the consequences so terrible when a good Catholic girl allowed herself to enjoy the company of a man not of her faith. Every mother knew it, that was why the rules had been made in the first place, that was the real meaning behind the vague designation of "occasions of sin" applied to so many people and places they were commanded to avoid.

They had Patrick back in his chair again, the heavy, destructive cane well beyond his grasp, both of them soothing and settling him, the clucking of their tongues an odd counterpoint to the rasping noise of his lungs. As long as he didn't catch sight of Tess, there was a chance of calming him down. They could hear the angry sound of drawers being opened and the thump of clothes and shoes being hurled into a suitcase.

"Please, Dad, look at me," Abby pleaded. She held his right hand in both of hers. "Just listen for a minute."

"Give her a chance to explain, Patrick." Bridget held his other hand. The glazed look in his eyes frightened her.

"What we're doing isn't wrong, Dad, it's not a sin. And

Tess didn't mean what she said. She just opened her mouth without thinking."

"Then why didn't you tell us?" Bridget asked softly. "Why did we have to hear it from Mrs. Goldbaum? How can you think there's nothing wrong if you're ashamed to tell your own parents what you're doing?"

"People who aren't in show business don't understand what it's like." That was what Sammy Rosen had told her, what Sheila Cohen had confirmed. But it didn't answer the question and it was begging the point. Abby at least *had* been ashamed. Tess had wanted to bring everything out in the open right away, had been correct, as it turned out, in believing that, then or later, the reaction would be the same. "What Tess is doing is hard work, just as hard as slaving in an office all day. Mr. Rosen isn't an evil man, and the girls he hires aren't tramps."

"Whores is what they are," Patrick Sullivan muttered. "Whores slipping down to hell as fast as their backsides will take them."

"That's not fair, Dad, and it's not true."

"I'll not call any dirty whore a daughter of mine," Patrick shouted. He shook off Abby's cold hands and made the sign of the cross. The vague look was gone from his eyes, as though he'd accepted the worst of what they had seen and would no longer fight to believe that it wasn't true. He was still a man after all. He knew why beautiful young girls dressed themselves up in bits of clothing that wouldn't cover the nakedness of a small child, why they painted their faces and twitched their fannies, why they needed to move out of their parents' homes to live alone or with other girls no better than themselves. The men who sent notes and flowers to their dressing rooms, who waited in the dark alleyways after the show was over, who took them out to restaurants, bought them jewelry, paid their rent, these men didn't waste their time and their money on girls who gave them no reward for their pains. It wasn't a world in which Patrick had ever lived, but it was one about which every newspaper constantly wrote, every priest preached horrifying sermons, and every poor girl dreamed. He'd been wrong to discourage the Irish boys who had come sniffing around when Tess and Abby were still in school, wrong to think they would be safe in the jobs they had gotten. If there had been money enough to keep them at home, if the accident had never happened, if Sean Fitzgerald had been quicker to help than Mrs. Goldbaum, all this might never have happened. They might be married right now, with children on the way, and strong, healthy husbands to love and care for them as God intended.

"It's not too late," Bridget said, reading his thoughts as she always did. "I can see Sean Fitzgerald in the morning. He'll find something for them."

"She'll have to go down on her knees in front of you, Bridget. Nothing less after what she said."

"I'll talk to her, Patrick."

"Any talking that's done will be done here and now. She won't sleep under my roof until she's apologized. And they're not leaving this house again until Fitzgerald himself tells me he's found them decent work."

Tess had two heavy suitcases in her hands. No one had heard her come out of the bedroom; no one knew how long she'd been standing there in the doorway. "I packed your things too, Abby," she said. "You can tell him for me that I'd rather sleep in the street than take back one word. Tell him, too, that a man who won't admit to the truth when he hears it is a fool." Two brilliant spots of red burned on her cheeks and her head was very high, her neck so stiff that it would never bend again. She paused for a second to look into her mother's eyes, then carried the suitcases out into the hall. "Bring my coat when you come, Abby," she said. The suitcases bumped against the stairs, loud and defiant like thunderclaps in a dark sky.

Abby didn't look at Patrick, didn't look at Bridget. Tears pricked behind her eyelids, she would choke on the love and the pain of it all if she attempted to speak. She closed the apartment door very quietly behind her, waiting for a moment to hear her father call out to her or her mother to open it again and take her, weeping, into her arms. Nothing happened. Mrs. Goldbaum's tiny head bobbed from side to side, and she stroked Abby's sleeve once, a tentative little gesture immeasurably sad and contrite. She didn't go back into her own apartment until Abby was halfway down the stairs.

Thomas was waiting for them on the first-floor landing, shivering from the cold and what everyone in the building had heard Patrick Sullivan call his daughters. He'd be bloody for a week with all the fighting he'd have to do every time another boy taunted him with the word.

Abby held him tightly for a moment. He wasn't a man yet, even though he was as tall as she. He hadn't enough muscle on his bones, not enough hair growing on his face to need a razor. "Don't worry about us," she said, letting him go, fussing with the collar of his shirt exactly as Bridget always did. "When you get a chance to talk to Mom alone, tell her that everything will be all right. Tell her we'll get some money to her and we'll find some way to see her before we leave. Give her this." She took her week's pay out of her handbag and closed his fingers over it. "Don't let Dad see you. He wouldn't let her keep it. Understand?" He nodded and squirmed as Abby ruffled his hair and pulled at the tight, bright curls. "Go back to the Murphys now, and if anybody asks, tell them that your sisters are going to be the most famous actresses on two continents. Don't take anything off any of them."

"I won't."

At the last minute, halfway out into the night, Abby turned back. "If something happens, if you really need us," she said, "tell Mrs. Goldbaum. She'll know how to get in touch with us. Promise?" She would never forget the sight of her thin younger brother waving at them from the stoop of the building, seeming to grow smaller, younger, and more burdened by what they had left him to live with than was fair or just.

"We're taking a cab, Abby," Tess said. "I'm not dragging these suitcases through the subway. We'll find one over on the avenue or we'll call from a drugstore. And don't keep looking back like that. Nobody's coming after us."

"I know. I just wanted to make sure Thomas went back inside."

"Thomas will be all right. They all will. The sooner you realize that, the better. I meant it when I said we had our own lives to lead." Tess grinned, and suddenly the girl who had been hard and grim disappeared. A mischievous light came back into her eyes and she actually laughed, there on the street with everything she owned packed into a battered old suitcase and nowhere to go for the night. Adventure was what Tess thrived on; she had never, for as far back as Abby could remember, been any different.

"Do you want to tell me where we're going, once we do find a cab?" Abby asked. Holy Rosary Church was a pile of dirty gray brick on the corner. "We could spend the night in one of the confessionals. The church isn't locked up yet."

"I have a much better idea," Tess said. She dug around in her purse and held up a key. "Bette Blumfeld gave me this last week, just in case I ever remembered to get to the office on time."

"Tess, there won't be anybody there until Monday morning."

"So much the better. You're not afraid of an empty building, are you?"

Even if she was, there was no point in admitting it. Spending the night in a church would be just as frightening and a lot less comfortable. "Who gets the couch?" she asked.

"You do," Tess laughed. "It's two inches deep in cat hair and I can't stand that animal."

There was no heat in the building over the weekend, only the smelly warmth of the cat, who would leave neither of them alone. It was a strange night in an even stranger place, everything that was familiar by day transformed by darkness. The only sound after midnight was the occasional heavy footstep of a patrolman and the tap of his nightstick in the palm of his hand.

"We could turn the lights on," Tess said. "I do work here, after all."

"I'd rather not take a chance," Abby whispered. Somehow you didn't talk in normal tones at a time and in a place like this.

They tried to sleep, both of them did. Banquo purred and stretched and snored, kneading his front paws against them, whipping his tail in his dreams, releasing clouds of fine cat hair every time his muscles twitched.

"You weren't going to stay, were you, Abby?" Tess finally asked. She lit a cigarette from a pack Bette Blumfeld had left on the desk and watched the smoke curl up toward the ceiling.

"I don't know. I might have. No, I guess I couldn't have.

You were very hard on Dad, Tess. You didn't have to say what you did."

"Neither did he."

"It's different for him."

"Different, hell. Did you ever really look at that picture they had taken right after they were married, the one where Mom is sitting on a bench and Dad is standing behind her with his hand on her shoulder?" The red tip of her cigarette waved through the air. "There's a photograph like that in every single apartment in the building, thousands of them all over New York City. If you took a picture of any one of those women today, you wouldn't recognize them. Where does it get you, Abby?"

"They were in love."

"So they got married and then the kids started coming and the money ran out. You know why I got fired from all those jobs, Abby? You really know why?"

"You can't type, you can't file, and you can't get to work on time."

"A few measly dollars a week wasn't the gold in the streets, that's why."

"That's hindsight, Tess. You were glad enough at the time."

"I was just waiting, Abby. Just waiting for something better to come along."

"And now it has?"

"Maybe. If Sammy Rosen spent as much money and time on me as he has on you, I'd know it had. What are you going to do about him?"

"What do you mean?"

There were some things about which Tess was very smart, and one of them was men. "I might not have a job after all if Mr. Rosen decides to give up on you."

"Don't be ridiculous."

"Don't be an idiot. I know for a fact that he's never taken out any girl who worked for him."

"I don't work for him."

"But you will. I know it, you know it, and so does Saul Gruber. The only one you haven't told is Sammy himself. I don't understand why you haven't. Time's running out, Abby. The contract from Paris came in yesterday. All signed and legal. I heard Bette on the phone ordering the tickets. First-class passage to Paris. What more do you want? You could learn the routines in half the time it's taken me." The cigarette was burning Tess's fingers. She put it out. "Are you in love with him, Abby?"

She was glad the darkness hid her face, glad her sister couldn't read an answer to the question Abby had been pushing to the back of her own mind. She didn't know what being in love felt like, but surely it couldn't be this confusing succession of delight and dread. Sammy Rosen wasn't a boy, bore no resemblance at all to the handsome young Irishmen who tended to treat the Holy Rosary girls with a mixture of poignant shyness and sly, brief touchings. He was a man, and she'd had no experience with men, none at all.

"Go to sleep, Tess," she said wearily. "I can't keep my eyes open any longer." But it was hours and hours before they finally closed.

"Jesus God, you scared the life out of me," Bette Blumfeld said. It was ten o'clock in the morning and she'd almost dropped her cup of coffee and Danish on the floor. The stagnant air in the office smelled of cat and indecision, two suitcases blocked the way to her desk, and Abby and Tess Sullivan were staring sleepily at her from beneath their coats. "What the hell are you doing here? How did you get in?"

"You gave me a key," Tess said logically. "We fought the Battle of the Boyne last night and lost."

"Am I supposed to know what that means?" Bette Blumfeld asked.

"We were told not to come home again, Bette."

"Jeez, I'm sorry, kids."

"Forget it. It was bound to happen sooner or later." Tess was breezily indifferent, as unruffled this morning as if last night had never happened. "Can you help us find a place to stay?"

"Sure. No problem. Let me make a few calls. Wash up and go get yourselves some breakfast at the deli. I'll have beds for you by the time you get back. I've got a few things to do for Mr. Rosen, but they can wait. Jeez, you girls look terrible."

"We didn't get much sleep," Abby said. Even wearing couch-wrinkled clothes and with dark smudges in the hollows beneath her eyes, she still managed to exude that elemental dignity that made her so different from every other showgirl who had stood at Bette Blumfeld's desk trying to wheedle her way into Sammy Rosen's office.

"Don't worry about a thing. Believe me, this is nothing compared to some of the messes I've taken care of. Go on, get yourselves something to eat and let me work a couple of miracles. And listen, put the suitcases in Sammy's office before I break a leg on them."

She waited until they left before making the call, swearing quietly under her breath as she dialed the number. She'd done a lot of things for Sammy Rosen, learned to close her eyes and turn off her conscience about some of them, but this was close, very close to the invisible line she'd drawn a long time ago. Whether or not anything came of it was strictly up to the people involved. Up to Abby, actually. Sammy Rosen never pushed; he never had to.

"Mr. Rosen? I'm sorry if I woke you up, but we've got a problem down here."

"Down where? What's going on?" He sounded sleepy. "Wait a minute." She heard a soft sliding sound as he cupped his hand over the mouthpiece of the receiver, heard him say something to someone, answer a question. She waited for him, tapping ashes off the end of her cigarette until he came back on the line. "Okay, go ahead, I'm listening."

Sure you are. I wonder who else I woke up, she thought. "I'm down at the office. I came in to get a few things ready for Monday, and guess what I found?"

"Saturday morning is no time to play guessing games, Bette. I got robbed?"

"Better. You're running a hotel. Two of your girls spent the night on the couch. They got kicked out of their apartment." She waited for him to ask who, but he didn't, waited for him to tell her to take care of it herself and let him go back to bed, but he didn't do that either. "Tess Sullivan and her sister," she said finally. Playing games and smoking cigarettes this early in the morning made her tired. "I thought you'd want to know. They need someplace to stay." She heard his hand slide over the receiver again, heard him speak sharply to whoever it was he was telling to get up and get dressed. "I've been looking for someone to share with me since my sister got married. The rent's gone up again. I was going to ask for a raise." Nothing comes free in this world, Mr. Rosen. You ought to know that.

"Look, I was going to come in later anyway. I left that contract from Louvier on my desk last night and I want to go over it a few more times. The frog made a couple of changes. Sit on the girls until I get there. I don't want Tess changing her mind at the last minute and running home to Momma. She's not crying or anything, is she?"

"She's upset." Tess had practically tap-danced out of the office, singing like a bird; whatever had worn out her sister obviously had not touched her at all. "She'll be all right, I think. I sent them out to get some breakfast."

"I'll get a cab and be down there as soon as I can."

"Okay, and I'll call a couple of the other girls and see if anybody else has a spare bed or couch or something." Raise or not, she wasn't going to make it too easy for him.

"They need their beauty sleep. Give it a couple of hours." He hung up without giving her a chance to argue.

Too bad Bobby Stein wasn't around, but on second thought he probably wouldn't give her any odds on this one. She wouldn't give them herself. There was no contract lying on Sammy Rosen's desk. She hadn't expected to find it there, but she looked anyway, just for the hell of it.

"I brought you some more Danish and coffee." Tess had sticky pieces of icing clinging to her lips and a cardboard box in one hand. She kicked off her shoes and curled herself into a corner of the worn leather couch where so many girls had sat, feeding bits of sweet dough to the greedy cat between huge bites that spilled crumbs down the front of her dress. She could eat twice as much as Bette Blumfeld ever dared to, with no damage to her clear skin and apparently none to her hips either. "Do you want to hear about it?"

"Sure, if you want to talk. Where's Abby?"

"She went to Mass."

"On Saturday morning?"

Tess shrugged her shoulders, sending a cascade of sugary morsels onto the top of Banquo's white head. "She's got a problem."

"I know." And he's going to be here in less than an hour. "You can stay with me if you want. My sister got married last month."

Tess licked her fingers and put the cardboard box on the

floor. "Here, kitty," she crooned. "God, I hate that cat. He snores."

Bette Blumfeld lit another cigarette. She tossed the pack to Tess, and leaned back in her chair. If it were me, she thought, I'd at least say thank you. She wasn't sure how dense Tess was and how much of it was an act.

"Have you got room for both of us?"

Not dense at all.

"Sure, if it works out that way."

"How long is it before we sail?"

"Three weeks. I called for the tickets yesterday. Mr. Rosen is coming in to look over the contract again, but I'd say that everything's set."

"What about the costumes? Don't we have to get fitted?"

"The frogs are taking care of them." Costumes, hell. Feather headdresses and body stockings with a few sequins sewn on in strategic places. She'd seen the sketches.

"We promised Mom we'd try to see her before we left. She's going to need some money."

"Who doesn't? Tell Mr. Rosen you want an advance on your salaries." Abby hadn't spent a single minute with Bobby Stein, but they were talking about her as if she'd always been part of the act. And hadn't she? Hadn't it just been a question of time and the right words at the right moment? Hadn't Tess figured it out too?

"It was worse than we thought it would be, Bette. Not for me, but for Abby. She's really hurt. I don't think she's made up her mind what she's going to do."

"What about you?"

"Me? I should be so lucky."

So she did know. And it wasn't bothering her in the least.

By the time Sammy Rosen walked in the door, Bette Blumfeld had heard the whole story, and she wasn't as sure as she'd been earlier that things were going to be as easy as they usually were for him. She wasn't even sure why he was going to all this trouble. Abby Sullivan didn't sound like the kind of girl who gave herself away with no strings attached, and beautiful as she was, she wasn't the only redhead in New York City.

* * *

Sammy Rosen didn't know either. Once or twice before he'd waited this long for a girl to make up her mind, but the circumstances had been different. They'd been more or less committed, seeing other men, trying to decide whether he was worth taking a chance on. And they hadn't been in any of the shows he was connected with. None of them had been in love or looking for anything permanent, just a good time and another step up the ladder. Some of them had turned him down, with no misunderstandings or hard feelings on either side. Professionals, all of them, even if they were just getting started. He couldn't remember the last time he'd taken out an amateur.

Bobby Stein had seen the potential. "I can work her in anytime," he'd said. "But the line is good enough without her."

"Good maybe, but I want something special this time out."

"We'll pull it off with a little makeup. These girls already look enough alike to make anybody think they came from the same litter."

"Onstage yes, but I want them seen other places too. I want every paper in Paris talking about the girls Sammy Rosen brought over. There are going to be so many Frenchmen wanting to meet them that it'll make Ziegfeld's girls look like nuns."

"I still don't see what's so special about one girl."

"Just keep looking at their feet, Bobby. Believe me, this one isn't like any of the others."

Bobby was right about the line and Sammy Rosen knew it. He was as sure of the success he was going to find in Paris as if he'd already read the reviews of the show. With or without Abby it wouldn't make any difference. But he kept remembering the night he'd taken her to see Laurette Taylor and the way people had looked at her when they left the theater. Showgirls got stared at all the time, enviously by ordinary-looking women, hungrily by men who knew they were available for a price. But very rarely did you see that kind of admiration mixed with what he could only call respect.

It had to do with the way they hadn't jostled her, the way they'd stepped aside as though she had a better right to the pavement than they, the way lips hadn't smacked and eyes hadn't narrowed with jealousy. It had to do with the girl herself, with the vulnerability you sensed behind the delicacy of her features, the way she trusted him to order for her in restaurants when most chorines could be depended upon to want the most expensive item on the menu no matter what it was, the way she could sit for hours without impatiently tapping her foot or drumming her fingers or making little pyramids out of sugar cubes. More than once, sitting beside her in a taxi, he'd wondered how she would react if he drew her closer to him, ran his hands over her face and body, kissed her until the blood pulsed and she begged him to stop. He hadn't done it, but only because the profile at which he looked during those silent rides hadn't seemed to expect that anyone would intrude on the thoughts she was thinking. Maybe that was it. You could always tell what a woman wanted, what she expected, how far she was willing to go. Something about the smile, the way she held herself, some indefinable invitation in the air. But with Abby Sullivan there was none of that. No invitation, but no putting off either, just an odd neutrality that had no fragrance to it at all, as if she were walking around while one part of her lay sleeping elsewhere.

There were no late-morning Masses on Saturday, but the votive light beside the main altar burned steadily under its red glass bulb, and banks of smaller candles twinkled a remembrance of the petitioners who had lit them. It was a small church, a chapel really, a sanctuary into which theater people could escape for a few minutes or an hour. It had its own mystique of dark wooden pews, painted statues, and curtained confessional boxes, a mystique as powerful as that of the world from which its parishioners came.

Too late for Mass, too early for confession, Abby Sullivan knelt alone. Her mind was tired and quiet, her knees stiff and aching. She sensed that it was past time for praying. What could she ask? She didn't want the type of strength that would turn her into another Bridget, didn't want to renounce the world Sammy Rosen could give her for that of Sean Fitzgerald, the Democratic party's menial jobs, and the bed of a man who would think it a sin to take precautions against pregnancy and the crying mouths he would never earn enough money to fill. You couldn't plead to be allowed to enjoy the sin you were contemplating.

A priest came out onto the altar, genuflected, glanced

toward the pew where she knelt, waited a moment or two as if expecting her to call to him, then turned and went back into the sacristy. The skirt of his cassock swished softly against his legs and she smelled the clean odors of soap and shaving lotion. The sponge soaked with holy water was cold on her fingers when she dipped them into the font, and instead of crossing herself, she shook the droplets off as though they contained no power at all.

Outside, pacing back and forth on the pavement, with smug pigeons waiting until the last second to scuttle away from his feet, waited Sammy Rosen. She saw him as soon as she pushed open the heavy wooden door carved with apostles and gargoyles. In spite of the cold his hands were warmer than hers, his face less pinched and wan, his body more relaxed and easy.

"Tess told me where you'd gone," he said.

"I don't know why I came."

A taxi skidded to the curb, and he bundled her into it, almost picking her up off her feet as though she were a child. "I'm taking you to lunch," he said, "and afterward there's a ship I want you to see."

They went to the Plaza, a place that seemed devastatingly public after the dim corners and small tables of the other restaurants to which he had taken her. Everything about the hotel dining room exuded a richness and an opulence that was as seductive to Abby's senses as the rising of a theater curtain. The table linen was thick, immaculate, stiff with starch and ironing, the silverware heavy and polished to a high gleam, the bud roses in their graceful vase hothouse creations. The room was warm and quiet; soft carpeting and deeply cushioned chairs absorbed the sounds of serving and eating, muted the voices of the men and women who were seeing and being seen, gave the impression that waiters and busboys were soundless, incorporeal beings wafting between the tables on currents of fragrant, steamy air. After the coldness of the church, the wet damp of the streets, and the frigid, stuffy air of the cab, the atmosphere beneath the chandeliers of the Palm Court was as intoxicating as champagne.

Sammy Rosen lit two cigarettes, passed one of them to her. It was a gesture that she'd seen many times, a trick to establish intimacy between a leading man and his lady, a bit of business that went easily from stage to restaurants. He'd never done it before, and for a moment, before she put the cigarette to her mouth, her fingers lingered on the spot his lips had touched.

"The contract came back from Paris, Abby. One or two changes, but nothing I can't live with. We sail on the tenth of March. Are you coming?"

"Did Tess tell you what happened at home?"

"Bette called me. I came right down."

"I don't want to talk about it, Sammy."

"You don't have to. I'm only asking you a question."

"I don't have a job anymore. Or I won't in a few days. That's how they found out."

"You don't have to tell me anything. You don't have to explain."

"If I could do it without hurting them. It's too much all at once. Both of us, I mean."

"If it helps, Abby, you're not the first girl whose parents have reacted like yours did. Do you know what the Jews do when a son or daughter steps outside the Law? They sit shiva, they say the prayers for the dead, and the child's name is never mentioned again."

"We get excommunicated."

"For going into show business?"

"No." She could feel the ghost of a smile tugging at the corners of her mouth. "For not getting married by a priest, for divorce. For other things."

"Have I asked you to do any of those?"

"No, you haven't." She waited, but he was playing with the silver rim of his ashtray. She knew then, as clearly as if he had told her so, that the thought of marriage had never so much as crossed his mind, that what he was not proposing so much as leaving open for her to guess at was something entirely different. "Why do you want me to come to Paris, Sammy? You've never told me."

"When was the last time you looked in a mirror, Abby? Really looked, I mean. I don't think you have any idea what you look like. Everyone in this room knows how beautiful you are, every place I've ever taken you, people have stared at you. You're the only one who isn't aware of it. I know a little something about Catholic girls. I've heard about the sins of vanity and pride. I've seen nuns with faces so exquisite that they take your breath away. The only crime, the only sin is in wasting that kind of gift, in wrapping yourself in black skirts and pious guilt and believing that beauty and pleasure are evil. They're not. There isn't any hell and there isn't any devil except the one you make up in your own mind."

"That's not an answer to my question."

"I want things to happen for you, Abby. I want them for you and I want them for myself. Coming to Paris is just the first step, and it's the easiest one of all to take. You dance, you sing, you wear beautiful clothes, you meet people, you learn. We're not talking about the rest of your life." He reached for her hand, and she let him take it. Behind her, a cart was whisked back into the kitchen. The Plaza's headwaiter was the embodiment of discretion. Food, even that superbly prepared by the best chef in New York, could always wait. "All I'm telling you is that you have the opportunity to begin to make choices. The chorus line is a dead end for a lot of girls because they're not smart. They think they'll never get old and their looks will never change. They're so busy having fun that they don't notice the years nipping away at them. You won't make those mistakes. I won't let you. Take acting lessons if that's what you want to do, and if you're any good, I know people who'll at least give you a chance to prove yourself. There are other ways to go too, but you won't find them in the pew of a church or keeping Saul Gruber's books. Money makes life very pleasant, and there are a lot of rich men in this world who enjoy spending it on beautiful women." He felt her fingers twitch and the curling of her nails as she tried to pull away. "You can name your own terms, Abby, not with me because I already know what I want, but with men who will see you and send you flowers and jewelry and let you dictate the rules of the game. Do you think I don't know what it's like where you live? I came from a street worse than that, from a building where the tenants were so poor there wasn't any garbage for the rats. You can have lamb chops or you can have cabbage. You have to pay a higher price for lamb chops, but they taste and smell a hell of a lot better."

She ate the food put before her mechanically, chewing and swallowing without savoring the perfection of what Sammy had ordered. Later, when this strange paralysis of sensation had worn away, her body would remember and she would finally taste what now seemed as bland and unappetizing as sawdust. Sparks of light scintillated at the periphery of her vision; they were the diamonds in women's rings, the brooches pinned to their dresses, the stones set in their ears and around the faces of their watches. Points of brilliance dancing just beyond her grasp, just far enough away to make her think she could reach out and touch them. What was it Sammy had said? Something about Paris being the first step and the easiest one of all to take? With the coffee came determination to make him spell it out, to force him to say the words. Nothing was ever as bad once it had been named.

"How will I travel, Sammy?"

"With me. On the ship I'm taking you to see as soon as we leave here. The *Katrina.*"

"What else do I have to do, Sammy?"

"You've got a lot to learn, Abby. About understandings and leaving space between a man's back and the wall." He watched her eyes change, the blue and the gray disappear behind a harder green that looked like light reflecting off the polished surface of an emerald. "I've never asked a woman for more than casual intimacy, and I'm not promising anything else, but I want you. I don't want marriage or children, meals you've cooked or slippers by the fire. I want you beside me when I walk into a restaurant, I want to see heads turning when we stroll together down a boulevard in Paris, I want to watch my creation on a stage, and I want you in my bed. What else did you expect to hear?"

"Nothing. Nothing at all."

"Life is business, Abby. Somebody sells and somebody buys. As long as both parties are satisfied, the bargain is a good one. And there's always an end to every contract. Remember that."

"I have an excellent memory, Sammy. I never forget anything." A rose petal had fallen onto the tablecloth. She picked it up and held it between her forefinger and thumb, rubbing the delicate, still living thing gently, squeezing it finally until her sharp nail had cut it in two. "I'd like to see the ship, and I'd like a little time to think," she said.

"Don't wait too long."

"I won't. She felt eyes follow her as she walked from the Palm Court with Sammy Rosen's arm guiding her through the tables. Everything he had said was true, and since it was she who had forced him to say it, she would never be able to pretend that it wasn't.

It was windy and cold on the docks. A light, sleeting rain had begun to fall, and as soon as she stepped from the taxi Abby felt the sting ¬f it against her face. It wasn't enough to peer through the fogged-up windows of the cab at the huge bulk of the *Katrina*. She had to get as close to the ship as she could, needed to stand beside it, imagining the roll of the Atlantic under her feet and herself a passenger on its decks. Sammy Rosen protested, but the cabbie, inured to driving crazy people all over the city in all types of weather, produced a battered umbrella from beneath the front seat. She moved away from its shelter, out into the wet that was colder than snow, walking alone because that was how it had to be, up and down, studying the lines of the vessel, the smokeless stacks that stretched upward, the ropes that held it fast. Sammy Rosen watched her pace. Not this trip, but the next, he had told her. One of those first-class staterooms somewhere above her was reserved in his name—a suite, not a cabin.

She knew that he believed he was reading her mind as he stood there in the rain waiting, patiently, it seemed, for one life to fade away and another to begin. He was wrong, and for once she felt that she, not he, was the cat crouched beside the mouse's hole. The cab had driven by Grand Central Station on its way to the docks, and although neither the cabbie nor Sammy Rosen had so much as glanced at the people scurrying toward the trains waiting in its cavernous depths, she had seen them all, backs bent, parcels clutched against their chests, feet dirty with the city's filth, hurrying through its doors and down its stairways. It was the feet she continued to see, not the backs or the faces, feet that left grime and mud as they ran, bits of paper and gum and cigarette butts mangled and mashed into soggy lumps, the pools of urine and vomit those feet sidestepped or tracked into the greater slime. Late, very late at night, a platoon of women with pails and mops and brushes inched their way across those floors, cleaning up the careless detritus of people who were sighing and dreaming and making love in the warmth of their beds. That was the job Sean Fitzgerald had gotten Bridget Sullivan because he had always been able to count on Patrick's vote. And never once had she complained, never expressed anything but gratitude for the few dollars she earned as cleaning woman to the thousands who weren't even aware of her existence.

It was amazing how quickly you could lose the conscience you had nurtured and obeyed all your life, how swiftly it could die and how little regret you felt for its demise. Maybe it would have protested more strongly, fought back, lingered, had it been spring or early summer, with the sun shining warmly, strangers sparing an occasional smile for one another, and that ridiculous hope that things will somehow change for the better that always surfaces at the end of winter. But it wasn't spring yet, and Abby knew that her mother had never tasted a lamb chop in her life. She made her decision right then, as the traffic light changed from red to green and the clicking of the meter sounded like seconds of pain being totted up on some invisible ledger page.

She could have told him simply by taking his hand or leaning her head against his shoulder, but she didn't. There were things she had to be sure she could hold on to before surrendering, bits of herself she knew he didn't want, knew she would be foolish to offer. She was dividing herself up as she walked in the rain beside the *Katrina*, allotting this portion for what Sammy could give her; that piece for Bridget and Patrick and the boys and the money she would be able to send to make their lives less hard; another, bleaker, lonelier spot for the work she would have to do against the day when the affair ended. At last she slipped her fingers through Sammy Rosen's arm, pressing herself against him, shivering, not, as he thought, with cold, but with anticipation and only the faintest tremor of fear.

"Which portholes will be ours? Can you point them out to me?" she asked.

3

*I*t didn't happen that night, not even that weekend. Sammy Rosen managed things, and he managed them to no one's standards but his own. Bette Blumfeld could have told Abby that he was best at shuffling people around, that it was her lesser talent that dealt with timetables, correspondence, and the paying of bills, but why bother the girl with details this early in the game? She made chicken soup for them Saturday night, chicken soup for whatever ailed you, and taught Tess and Abby to play gin rummy and wrestle with the new vogue of crossword puzzles. Tess moved into the bedroom from which Bette's sister had escaped into the security of marriage, and Abby, the length of her stay a question to which she had no answer, lay awake for another night on a strange couch.

It rained again on Sunday, a cold, miserable, silent day. Tess slept until noon, then wandered aimlessly around the apartment in her bathrobe, borrowing cigarettes from Bette, drinking cup after cup of coffee, watching Abby wait for the phone to ring. "I don't talk to anyone until I've read the *Times*," Bette growled at no one in particular; she was incommunicado until late in the afternoon. By the time she threw aside the last section of the paper and faced the fact that the best part of Sunday was over, Tess had finished her unpacking, throwing everything she owned into the first few empty drawers she opened and shoving the suitcase under her unmade bed. Abby was stiff-backed and tight-lipped, beads of sweat on her forehead and upper lip, ironing clothes in the tiny kitchen as though her life depended on erasing every wrinkle.

51

"He hasn't called," Abby said, moving the iron back and forth over the same smooth spot that was so thin you could see the individual strands of cotton thread. Sammy, when he dropped her off at Bette's apartment, had said that he had things to attend to. "What kind of things?" she had asked. He'd only smiled, kissed her lightly on the cheek, and told her he would call. Bette hadn't seemed the least surprised to find a soaking-wet, thoroughly chilled Abby ringing her doorbell, and somehow she'd managed to cut off Tess's excited questions. Abby hadn't confided in either of them, but both Bette and her sister were acting as if they knew all about it. They'd talked. She sensed that they had worked it out for themselves, and that knowledge suddenly made her decision appear less a turning point in her life than a slow drift toward a situation that had been inevitable from the very beginning.

"Look, put the iron away," Bette said. "We'll go out for Chinese. I'll bet you've never been to Chinatown, have you?" She knew what was keeping Sammy Rosen busy today. Phone calls of the type you can't rush through, maybe a few drinks with somebody, a little good-bye roll-in-the-hay, a key to retrieve, some cleaning out of the kinds of things girls like to leave behind when they know they'll be coming back. He had a gentlemanly streak somewhere in the midst of all his other qualities, and when he made an arrangement that looked like it might last awhile, he liked to make the newcomer feel that she could open any closet without fear of finding her predecessor's clothing hanging there. It was the extra bit of trouble to ensure that old lovers remained permanent friends.

"Could we send out instead?"

"Sure. That's better anyway, even though the food is lousy. You're tired, I'm getting the cramps, and Tess would need half a day to start looking human. Go take a hot bath. There's some oil in the cabinet that smells like Paris. Use as much of it as you like."

"Thanks, Bette."

"Chicken soup and a hot bath. My mother thinks they cure everything except spinsterhood."

Sammy Rosen didn't come into the office on Monday, didn't call for messages, didn't send any, didn't answer his phone. At two o'clock Bobby Stein took an angry, sputtering

Tess out to lunch. Bette Blumfeld made do with aspirins and a carton of rice pudding from the deli. She called home once, but hung up in the middle of the first ring. Abby was there, still waiting, alone. If they talked, one of them might start to cry, and Bette wasn't sure she could get through the rest of the afternoon with a lump in her throat too big to swallow.

By the time Bobby Stein and his eighteen girls were halfway through their rehearsal in the studio, only a thin wall away from her desk, the pounding in Bette Blumfeld's head was louder than the sound of their tap shoes. Shuffle, tap, kick, shuffle, tap, kick. Over and over, a fight between their feet and the rhythmic banging of the piano. She poured herself a healthy glass of bootleg Scotch or something resembling Scotch from the bottle at the back of the contract-file drawer, locked the office door behind her, and walked down the hall to where she could at least see whether the noise meant anything like dancing was going on.

All the girls were beautiful, and some of them, the ones with a little experience, were not bad dancers either. The studio smelled of sweat and wet coats, cheap perfume, and stale food. Half the girls were tapping and counting out loud to themselves at one end of the room, the rest, with drooping, sadly faded feather headdresses tied to their heads, were gliding, swooping, and twirling, climbing up and down a set of wooden steps in the center of the studio.

"Don't look at your feet, don't look down," Bobby Stein shouted at them. He held a long wooden cane in one hand, the kind that Russian émigré dance mistresses were fond of using, and as the girls came within reach it flashed out to tap sagging backs, arms that weren't fully extended, legs that weren't straight enough. "Chins up. Let's see big smiles and a lot of teeth." They looked like a flock of absurdly plumaged chickens on parade. In Paris they would have the audiences thinking they were birds of paradise. "All right, ten minutes," he called. "Stay warm or your leg muscles will cramp." They groaned and collapsed against the walls, massaging their sore shins, reaching for coats and cigarettes.

"They don't look too bad," Bette said. She handed Bobby the glass of Scotch. He emptied it in a single gulp, swaying slightly and grinning like a monkey. "Jeez, what time did you start today? I think you're a little drunk, kid."

"Me? Take a look at Tess."

She was still counting to herself in one of the corners, tapping and puffing and bouncing up and down like a child who confuses skill with noisy energy, half crouched over as if by staring at her feet she could force them to move faster.

"At least she isn't falling down."

"Give her time. She's got the longest hollow leg I've ever seen, but I can hear the booze sloshing around in it even from here."

"That's all we need in this group, another lush."

"Come on, take it easy, Bette. She's a good kid, and she's putting in the hours."

"Has she got any talent?"

"Not a bit." Bobby Stein grinned again. "Not for dancing anyway. But believe me, when she takes her clothes off, she's going to knock their eyes out."

"Somebody's eyes." Bobby Stein's private lessons were rumored to be something else. At least you always knew what a dancer's body looked like. Some men, when they got their suits and shirts and ties and belts off, were all hair and blubber. Bobby had good bones, long muscles, a face that was all angles and smooth skin, brown eyes that twinkled at you, and thick blond hair that made a halo around his head when he danced. They saw a lot of each another, and Bette had known for a long time that all she had to do to see even more was suggest that she wouldn't mind it. But she rarely looked in a mirror nowadays. There was too much of her—too much solid flesh and too many pocky dimples on her thighs. Even in the dark you could feel the sliding layers of fat. She didn't want to be screwed by somebody who would confuse her with his mother.

"Sammy wants them to have all the basic moves down and a couple of simple routines to show the Frenchies before we leave."

"Is there enough time?"

"No problem." He turned his back on the studio's mirrored walls and lowered his voice. "What about Abby?"

"I need another drink. Come on back to the office with me."

"You want me to let them go for now?"

She shrugged her shoulders. "Who's to know?"

She heard his cane banging on the floor for silence, then the clapping of hands and the moaning and groaning of the girls getting to their feet. That was another thing about dancers—they always complained, no matter what kind of shape they were in. There was only an inch or two in the bottle, but she wasn't shy about hitting Sammy Rosen's private supply. She figured she'd earned it.

"So what's going on?" Bobby said. "Tess talked a lot at lunch, but she didn't make much sense. Most of the time she was too busy drinking." He was lying down on the couch with his feet propped up and his glass balanced on Banquo's broad back. "Don't move, cat. This stuff could singe you bald."

"She's in. In every way."

"She tell you that herself?"

"Not in so many words. All she said was that she'd have to talk to you about catching up to the rest of the girls and that she didn't need a place to stay anymore."

"That's clear enough."

"That's what I thought. But listen, Bobby, as far as I know, she's still at my apartment. Saturday night she showed up in a cab with her suitcase, and last night she slept on the couch again. Nothing from the great lover, not a call, not a word. He's not talking to anyone, and the doorman at his building has orders not to let anybody up."

"How do you know that?"

"I checked. The kid's going crazy. All day yesterday she ironed clothes. I was going to take her to Chinatown, but she wouldn't go, wouldn't leave the phone in case he called."

"Christ, what's he doing? Or maybe I ought to ask what she did to put him off."

"I don't know. I can't figure it out."

"Maybe she made some kind of deal. Like money in the bank before she lays it out."

"You know what I think? I think he's mounting some kind of big production, dressing the set up real good so she can feel like nothing like this ever happened to him before, maybe making a few promises. It's not going to hurt anyone but Abby when he doesn't keep them."

"Jesus God." He sat up and held out his glass.

"You got it. Virgin territory. Untouched by human hands. I'd bet a month's pay on it." She filled his glass and then her own. It was very quiet in the office.

"Tess passed out," he said. "I don't know how the hell you're going to get her into a cab."

"Same way I'm going to get myself in. You can pour. Did you know he bought a car and hired a chauffeur? I tell you, Bobby, he's building a whole new image for himself."

"That takes real money," he said, glancing around at the dingy office and its battered furniture.

"Did he ever tell you about the tenement he grew up in? Not enough garbage to keep the rats alive? He's got plenty of money, Bobby. The old man gave up orthodoxy in favor of bars when Sammy was just a kid. Mrs. Rosen suddenly got very delicate and ladylike before she died, and when his father went too, Sammy got everything. He's got four speakeasies that I know of, and his own trucks running back and forth to Canada. Believe me, his accountant is going to be a millionaire before it's over."

"I need another drink and I think I'm going to ask for a raise."

"Forget it. His right hand doesn't know what the left one is doing, and that's the way he likes it. Anybody pokes around and he can show them books you wouldn't believe."

"I've got a sister he should meet. My mother would kill for a son-in-law like that."

"From what you've told me about your sister, she's going to have to."

"I'm a lot drunker than I was an hour ago."

"It gets better." The phone rang, but neither of them made a move to answer it. Bette Blumfeld lit her last cigarette and threw the empty package at the black beast whose ringing went on and on. "We're closed for the day," she said, "there's nobody here." She suddenly realized that she'd been talking too much, telling Bobby Stein things that very few people knew about Sammy Rosen, things a secretary picks up because she's too unimportant for her boss to make much of an effort to hide them from her. She could lose her job for having a loose mouth. This latest affair was getting to her like none of the others had, and it was a mistake, a bad mistake, to let herself get too emotionally involved in it.

"I've got to go stir Cinderella's ashes," she said, hauling herself out of her chair, clumping the keys of the typewriter all together when she lurched against it for support. "It's time to pour, Bobby."

*   *   *

Bette rolled both back windows of the cab down as far as they would go; the cold air cleared her head. Tess lolled against her shoulder, but her eyes were open and her teeth were chattering. Whatever it was she and Bobby had drunk for lunch, at least it hadn't been poison. By the time Bette propped her up in the elevator, Tess was remembering why she'd gotten drunk in the first place. "Don't tell Abby," she whispered as she leaned against the doorbell, watching Bette Blumfeld fumble in her purse for the key. "She's got enough to worry about."

The apartment was immaculate—swept, dusted, polished, cleaner than Bette had ever seen it. A lamp had been left lit on the hall table, and a note was propped up against it. "I called, but nobody answered," Abby had written. "Don't wait up for me."

On the couch were two long white boxes and inside one of them were layers of tissue paper and an empty oblong case lined in deep-blue satin. Saks and Cartier, what else? There were two dozen red roses in the sink in the kitchen, and in one corner of the room that now belonged to Tess stood Abby's suitcase. All the clothes she had washed and ironed the day before lay neatly folded inside. She had taken nothing with her.

"I think it's about time I taught you how to drink, kid," Bette Blumfeld said, taking a bottle of something marked "vodka" out of an otherwise bare kitchen cabinet. "We're going to feel like hell tomorrow, Tess, but so will everybody else. Believe me, there's nothing worse than a champagne hangover."

The roses had come first. No card, but there wasn't any need for one. She'd taken them from the florist's box one by one, laying aside the damp ferns that had hidden the long, thornless stems, a little dizzy with the spicy fragrance that poured into the room. She'd arranged them into a bouquet and walked slowly into the kitchen, vaguely aware that she ought to find a vase to put them in, water to keep them alive. No one had ever sent flowers of any kind to Bette Blumfeld; there was nothing in any of the cabinets to hold them. She ran water into the sink and stood over it, thinking how absurd it was that things of such beauty should have to lean against chipped enamel.

Sheila Cohen had called, her voice thick with what she said was a bad head cold. "He was counting on a couple more days, Abby, but don't worry about it. I can handle things."

"How did you know where to find me?"

"Tess, how else? She talked for an hour, so I guess she's not doing any more work in Mr. Rosen's office than she ever did here."

"Has he hired somebody else yet?" Sheila knew, of course she knew. Let Tess give her all the details, there was no way to stop her, but Abby didn't have to do it herself.

"A couple of girls are coming in later."

"I didn't think he'd have any trouble finding a replacement."

"He never does, but it won't be the same around here."

"Sheila, I'd like to talk, really I would, but I can't right now."

"Sure, kid, I understand. I've got to blow my nose again anyway." Too bad all this good acting wasn't being seen by anyone who could appreciate it. "I'll call you for lunch sometime. Or you call me. And listen, if we don't get together before you leave, send me some postcards from Paris."

"I will. I'll write you, too."

"Sure. And I'll let you know when I make it big. Or I'll invite you to the wedding, whichever comes first."

"What wedding? What are you talking about, Sheila?"

"Nothing. Nothing. This cold is making my brain go soft." Another fifteen years and you wouldn't be able to tell her from Bette Blumfeld. For the first time in her life she'd begun finding excuses not to go to auditions. "Arnie Gruber's started to make serious noises all of a sudden, that's all. Every night at dinner my mother reminds me how he's going to be a big lawyer someday."

"It's something to think about." Abby said it as softly as she could.

"That's just the problem. I'm starting to think about it." She cleared her throat, but her voice was still thick and a little shaky when she spoke again. "It's second best, but sometimes it looks pretty good, Abby." Then she hung up.

Poor Sheila. She was the one who had wanted it, worked her heart out for it, kept trying, kept smiling, kept believing for so long. If she did eventually marry Arnie Gruber, she'd go on hoping—for a daughter who might be dark and slender and alive with the flame that no one had ever seen in her.

The box from Saks came in the early afternoon, brought by a uniformed messenger boy who looked curiously at her when she answered the bell. She was wearing her oldest dress and had a towel wrapped around her head, a dust rag in one hand, and smudges of dirt on her face. She had nothing to give him for a tip, not a cent left in her purse. She could read on his face what he was thinking. Cheap. Or maybe he thought she was the maid. It didn't matter. She forgot about him as soon as she closed the door.

I need to wash my hands before I open this, she thought, setting the box carefully on the couch she had just finished brushing. She'd opened a window for a while to let out the dust and the smells of polish and soap. The apartment was cold, but it was spotlessly clean, even the bathroom tile had turned white again. She didn't know whether she'd worked so hard as a penance or simply to keep busy, but it was over now, all the waiting and wondering. First the roses and now this.

She'd never seen his handwriting before. It was firm and authoritative, as easy to read as printing. "Wear this for me tonight. Eight o'clock." He hadn't signed it, the word "love" appeared nowhere on the card. Her name wasn't even on the envelope.

The dress was made of white silk. It shone in its cocoon of tissue paper and shimmered as she lifted it out and held it up against her. It would slip over her shoulders with just the whisper of luxury, leaving her arms and back bare, her throat exposed, its soft folds molding themselves to the shape of her breasts, its narrow skirt flowing over her hips, moving like a second skin when she walked. It was the simplest gown she had ever seen, cut as perfectly as the sculpted draperies of a pagan goddess, not a bow or button or frill anywhere to mar its line or distract the eye from the body of the woman wearing it.

For a moment she thought that was all. It was enough, but beneath the tissue paper lay a narrow, velvet-covered case only as long as her hand. She laid the dress aside, her fingers lingering over the material that was finer than the silk of a priest's vestments. The catch released itself as soon as she touched it. Diamonds and emeralds. A thin bracelet of precious stones winking against satin the color of the bluest sea, waiting for her to warm the coldness of it against her skin, waiting to be brought to life the instant she fastened it around her wrist. Diamonds to reflect off the white silk, emeralds to match her eyes and extinguish the traces of soft blue and uncertain gray.

She ran water into the tub she had been scouring only an hour before, poured in the scented oil that Bette had said smelled like Paris, stood naked with her clothes fallen around her feet watching the steam rise and frothy bubbles form. She didn't think it at all strange, as she soaped and rinsed and felt the water gradually grow lukewarm and then cold, to see diamonds and emeralds on the arm that held a cake of soap and dipped and scrubbed.

He came at seven-thirty. She'd been ready for half an hour, standing motionless in the very center of the living room where Bette read the *Times* and spent her lonely Sundays. "I couldn't wait any longer," he said when she opened the door. He was dressed in black and white, in clothes she'd never seen him wear before, as formal and far more handsome than any of the famous rich young men whose pictures appeared in the newspapers. "May I come in?"

She stepped aside, the silk rustling against her legs. The silver shoes she had found in Bette's closet, shoes worn at somebody's wedding, made her nearly as tall as he. A thick set man in a gray chauffeur's uniform stood behind him in the hallway, carrying a bottle of champagne in one hand, another long white box beneath his arm, very carefully looking nowhere in particular. "We'll be down in thirty minutes," Sammy Rosen told him. "I can manage those now."

She waited for him to kiss her, to touch her, to tell her to turn so he could admire what he'd created, but he only smiled. She took his hat and coat and gloves, led him toward the fireplace that was empty and cold because it had been bricked up years ago. What did you say to a man who had already clothed you, bought you jewelry, sent you roses, was preparing to feed you, dance with you, amuse you, and make love to you? If there were rules and customs to this game, Abby didn't know what they were. The only rule she knew was that by keeping silent you never made mistakes.

Bette had wineglasses, dusty and probably never used, but long-stemmed and tinkling like real crystal when the stones on Abby's wrist brushed against them. "I didn't think I'd find my roses in the kitchen sink," Sammy said. He broke off one of the buds and held it to his nose. "They always smell like pepper and ginger. You expect them to smell differently, but they don't. Put the glasses down for a moment, Abby."

Her fingers seemed to have forgotten how to let go of what they held. He took the wineglasses from her, laid them on the counter, encircled the fragile wrists with strong, guiding hands. The cloth covering his shoulders was smooth, there were hollows into which her palms fitted. Her chin was being tilted upward, her waist enclosed by arms that were powerful and demanding. For a fraction of a second she looked into the deep-brown eyes that hung above her own, then she was pressed against him, her lips tasting his, bruised as they opened, hungry as he began teaching her.

It was Sammy Rosen who broke the embrace, letting her go as definitely as he had reached out for her, kissing the palms of her hands before he relinquished them, waiting for the pulses beneath his fingers to stop their erratic hammering before he stepped away. "We have champagne to drink," he reminded her. "It's supposed to calm the senses. Are your senses calm, Abby?"

He was laughing at her, and she didn't answer him. She hadn't said a word since he had entered the apartment. She picked up the dusty wineglasses and held them under a stream of water that splashed heavily on the beautiful roses and the lacy ferns, dried them with a dishtowel that was ragged at one end. He was watching her every move, seeing a kitten who plays nervously with a ball of twine, aware that the hand of its master will soon reach out to scoop it up, cradle and tame it.

"Aren't you even curious?" he asked. The champagne was French and so was the design of the dress she was wearing. From this moment on, everything would have a purpose—to mold her for Paris. The dancing and the singing, whatever other lessons she wanted to take in the next few weeks, all of them were of only secondary importance. It didn't matter to him, it had never really mattered whether she appeared in the line or not. What did count was that the men with whom he would be doing business recognize her for the exquisite creature that she was, and accord him the respect that possessing her entitled him to enjoy. He wasn't entirely cold. She excited him, her innocence delighted him, her body clamored to be explored and conquered; whatever other emotions he had, the stirrings he called love because the word was easy to say and conventionally pleasing, those other feelings were familiar ones he had felt many times before, familiar and unthreatening. Popular songs had nearly deified the losing of one's heart, but Sammy Rosen found the sentiments they expressed trite and foolish. No one had ever touched his heart, and no one ever would. "Aren't you even curious?" he repeated, gesturing toward the box that lay half hidden beneath his coat.

"How many gifts are you going to give me, Sammy?"

"As many as you'll accept. As many as I can find that I think are worthy of you. Open it."

It was fur, white fur that was long and thick and glossy, a coat that nestled beneath her chin and reached to below her knees, a wrap to be worn behind the bells of a Russian troika rushing over smooth-packed snow, skins so perfectly matched and invisibly linked to one another that they seemed to have come from a single animal.

White was what she should wear, what she should always wear, he told her. There were women who were washed out by it, whose skin was yellowed by it, whose hair lost its sparkle and seemed drab by comparison, but she wasn't one of them. The white did strange and lovely things to her eyes. When she stroked the fur, the emeralds on her wrist seemed to leap into the pupils; when her hand fell away again, much of the green disappeared, and the blue and gray it left behind were so pale that the eyes seemed capable of more than normal sight. Sammy Rosen's unerring instinct for the theatrical had worked a magical transformation, almost obliterated the Abby of flesh and blood, turned her into a creature remembered from misty midnight dreams, a presence rarely realized and never to be forgotten.

In the morning he gave her a checkbook. "Whatever you want, Abby. You never have to ask and you never have to explain." The account was in her name, the register for recording deposits and withdrawals blank. She had no idea how much money he was telling her she could spend, no hint of the value he had placed on her. "The only thing I want you to promise me is that when you buy clothes, they'll be sent here on approval."

"You don't trust my taste?" He was lying beside her in the huge bed where he had made love to her, his dark, unshaven face almost that of a stranger, the eyelids puffed with recent sleep, the lips swollen where she had bitten them.

"We agreed, didn't we, that you were the pupil and I the teacher?"

She shivered and nearly drew away as his hand caressed the soft skin of her breasts and his forefinger drew unbroken circles around the nipples. He had begun gently last night, as though not hurting her in any way were more important than arousing her to respond. It had been dark then, and the champagne she had drunk had made it seem as though some other girl were uncovering her pale body and slipping between sheets that were softer and silkier than the dress in which she had danced. But this morning sunlight was pouring through the bedroom windows and there was nothing she could not see, nothing she could pretend was happening to someone else.

She didn't know how long she had slept or when he had extinguished a last cigarette and rolled away from her. She had seen the red glow of it in the darkness, smelled the smoke and heard the sounds of him savoring it. Thinking, what had he been thinking then? Her skin had been hot where he had touched her, hot and alive against the coolness of the sheets. It had rippled beneath his fingers like a summer pond when dragonflies skim across its surface, and she had heard herself sigh and knew she wanted to moan out loud with the pleasure of it. But she had kept silent, letting him stroke her, gather her into his arms, kiss her eyelids until they ached. Her mouth had come alive beneath his lips, she had tasted champagne and tobacco on his tongue, the sharper tang of the cologne he had splashed onto his cheeks. Her hands had played in the crisp curls of his hair, massaged the hollows in his neck and the strong muscles of his back, but there they had stopped, not knowing what else was expected of them, what would give pleasure, fearing to make an awkward, ignorant mistake. The breath had caught in her throat when he penetrated her, and her teeth had wanted something, anything, to bite down on. She had bitten him, and then herself, tasting blood and the air from his lungs, feeling the pain in her lips and between her legs grow suddenly sharp and tearing, the palms of her hands moist with the fine sweat on his back. He had moved inside her, hammering against her spine, and then he had shuddered and his mouth on hers had sucked like a baby's emptying a breast. Afterward, he had seemed to forget that she was there, one hand lying absentmindedly on the damp hair between her thighs, the other mechanically raising and lowering his cigarette. He didn't say that he loved her, didn't say anything, and she, not knowing how to ask if it had been good or even if that was all there was, had fallen asleep.

Now a checkbook lay on the bedside table and he was drawing invisible patterns on her body, creating whorling designs that spun around pinpoints of nerve endings so sensitive that they sang and screamed like the taut strings of a violin. "Don't close your eyes, Abby," he whispered. "There's more to it than just feeling. There's seeing and touching and tasting. There's nothing to hide and nothing that should remain hidden." He drew the sheet away, uncovering her. "Not a mark, not a freckle, not a blemish anywhere," he said. "Look at me, Abby. Don't you want to know what a man looks like in the daylight?"

Black curly hair grew on his chest, a mat of it touched here and there with silver, so thick and so dark that she couldn't see the olive skin beneath. She remembered that last night she had been surprised at the furry feel of him; she smiled and tried to straighten one of the curls that wrapped itself around her finger. He wasn't muscular in the way that she was used to. On a hot summer evening the men sitting on their stoops and the older boys playing stickball in the street sometimes took their shirts off. Their arms and shoulders told of the kind of work they did; their biceps bulged like those of prizefighters or weight lifters. As they got older, the muscles turned to fat or grew thin and stringy, but they were beautiful when they were young. Sammy Rosen was compact, tight, strong enough, but not the well-developed workingman of the docks or the building trades.

"Don't be afraid," he said, guiding her hand, spreading out the fingers that had curled involuntarily in upon themselves. "I want you to. If I touch you somewhere, it's because I want you to do the same to me." His tongue flicked against her ear, and the moist warmth of it made her dizzy. She found what he wanted her to touch lying in a nest of coarser hair, and as she stroked in rhythm to the darting tongue, she felt its wrinkled skin grow smooth, its oval, lipped head distend, and the limpness of it stiffen and fill her hand. Last night she had felt it against her thigh, between her legs, pushing through her flesh, but she hadn't even then been able to picture what it was that beat at her so insistently. It was ugly and it was odd, a heavy, erect growth that hung from an already finished body like an afterthought, and beneath it were sacs that rolled between her fingers as if they contained two giant marbles.

Last night she had been dry and tight when he entered her; this morning she could smell her own wetness and feel it for a moment when she guided him to the spot she had never touched with her own fingers. He hung above her, supporting his weight on his arms, then lowered himself slowly, his hands slipping beneath her, fingernails digging into her skin as he kneaded the soft flesh of her buttocks and lifted them, drove himself in deeper, began to rock with a motion that made her legs spread themselves wider, try to twine themselves over his back. The sensation began as a teasing something she could not identify, a feeling of heat and then ice, a burning, itching, twisting call that was unlike anything she had ever felt before. She thought for a moment that there must be animals in the room; she could hear the grunting and the panting as they rooted for food and fought with one another. Something burst within her, something heaved itself out of darkness and scattered sparks and fire over her whole body. She cried out and tried to hold it, tried to touch the flames that licked at her, raised her head to see it and fell back onto the pillow, sweaty-wet with the effort of meeting it.

Cool lips brushed her cheeks, a hand pushed the curling red hair from her forehead, lingered for a moment, pinched the lobe of her ear. Suddenly she was as light as air, the creature above her had gone back to its lair, leaving something of itself behind, something that was pearly smooth and cooling on her skin. When she could speak, when she could remember how to move her lips and form the sounds in her throat into words, she asked him, like a child, what had happened. He laughed and pulled away the sheet she had clutched to her, slapping her on the place where the marks of his nails were like red crescent moons.

"It's called a climax, Abby," he said. "Did you think there was no pleasure for women in making love? If it were all duty and gritting your teeth and putting up with it once a week, no one would bother with an arrangement like ours."

She wanted to ask him about the babies, but she didn't. She had never known a married woman, a woman who did *this*, who didn't fear or want a pregnancy, but she could remember the look in his eyes when he had told her that he wasn't after children or slippers by the fire. There were ways, and whatever they were, whatever you did, he would know about it. She ought to be tired, ought to be exhausted, but she was more awake and alert than she had ever been in her life, hungry and wanting to feel hot water sluice over her body, a cold wind reddening her skin. Somewhere someone was brewing coffee. Surely that was coffee she smelled, and meat, ham or bacon, filling the apartment with its odor and a faint sizzling noise.

"Take your shower and put on a robe," he said. He was standing beside the bed, naked, just inches away from her face. "I can hear Mrs. Doyle in the kitchen." He bent over and kissed the tip of her nose. "Much as I'd like to spend the rest of the day in bed with you, Miss Sullivan, I can't."

"Sammy, wait." She followed him into the bathroom, trailing the end of a sheet she'd wrapped loosely around her. Water was already running in the shower and the room was steamy. "Sammy, what do I do now? I mean, what do I say? What do I do?"

He was lathering his cheeks and chin, humming to himself, rubbing a clear spot on the fogged-up mirror. Her face wore a woebegone look; she was hesitant and already drawing away from him. "No one is going to ask you any questions," he said, remembering that this girl hadn't had time yet to grow the scaly armor that other women seemed to have been born with. "Nobody except Tess perhaps. Tell her as much or as little as you want; it doesn't make any difference to me." Knowing Abby as he thought he did, he was sure there would be few confidences. "You can spend your days until we sail exactly as you please. Bobby Stein will teach you what the other girls are learning, if that's what you want. You have your own money, and you don't have to account for how you spend it. Mrs. Doyle comes in every day to cook breakfast and clean. She's been doing it for years, and I don't think she'd welcome either help or interference. I don't care how you spend your days, Abby, as long as your evenings are with me." Remember that you've been bought and paid for, that the leash is a loose one, but that it can be unsnapped whenever I want.

"I want to work, Sammy."

"Fine. You'll be paid the same salary Tess is getting."

He stepped into the shower and pulled the curtain across. She could hear the water splashing over his body and the thud when he dropped the soap into the tub. All of that money I can give to Mom, she thought. Honest money. The closets in the bedroom and the drawers of the wardrobe were full. He'd opened them for her last night, before he had slipped the silk dress from her shoulders. White, everything white. As though he'd spent most of Monday's hours searching New York for costumes in which to dress her. There wasn't a thing she could ask for that he hadn't already provided. And now, if she wanted to, she could go to a bank and draw out more cash than she had ever held in her hands at one time. The strings by which he had bound her to him were slender and light, either one of them could break them, but Abby knew, as Sammy Rosen cleansed himself and whistled and sang in his shower, that she would neither test them too severely nor be the first to sever them.

"The car is downstairs, Abby. Are you sure you don't want me to come with you?" A waiter pushed open the swinging door of the kitchen, then backed out again, the empty glasses on the tray he carried tinkling against one another. He'd give them a few more minutes in there, then try again. The way this crowd was drinking they'd probably never notice whether they got clean glassware or not. "At least let me get Tess."

"I'd rather you didn't, Sammy. I'll be back in an hour, and you have guests to entertain." It would only hurt Bridget to see him. She wasn't even sure how much her mother knew, what she was pretending not to know. Abby slipped her arms into the white fur coat he was holding for her, leaned against him for a moment, feeling his breath against her neck as he held her. "Tess isn't in any condition to go anywhere."

"Tess is Tess. She just doesn't think. And you'll never be able to change her." There was very little he couldn't predict about Tess. He'd typed her the first time he'd seen her, and she'd run true to type ever since. It was Abby who had surprised him, who had transformed herself more quickly than he had suspected she could, whose last moments of uncertainty had seemed exorcised in the plaintive cries for direction the morning after they had become lovers. Looking at her now, he could hardly remember the red-haired child she had seemed to be, the waiflike girl wrapped in a bed sheet who had wanted him to tell her what to do and what to say. She had money in the silk evening purse lying on the kitchen table beside her gloves, an amount that would have frightened her a month ago, that she would have sewn into her clothing or strapped into a money belt around her waist the way poor people always did, but whose possession tonight did not appear to trouble or worry her. Withdrawal slips were sent to his office as soon as the bank had processed them. Never very large until a few days ago; he'd wondered just how much she would decide to give her mother. She had been scrupulously honest, somehow managing to let him know, without the embarrassment of naming figures, what she had spent on lunches, the lessons he had urged her to have, the cosmetics she bought, the trips to the hairdresser's, cab fares. But she had said nothing of this last withdrawal, knowing he must be aware of it, treating it, in her own mind at least, as some sort of test. Two thousand dollars. More than some workingmen earned in a year. Much less than he'd spent on the first piece of jewelry he'd given her.

"Don't worry," she said. "I'll take Peter inside with me." The chauffeur doubled as a bodyguard and had already received both his orders and the means with which to protect her. She picked up gloves and purse, lingered for a moment to touch his cheek. "You're very good to me, you know," she whispered. Then the door to the service hallway opened, he caught a glimpse of the chauffeur's gray uniform, and she was gone.

Most of New York lay sleeping. Cops walked their beats, cabbies napped outside nightclubs and speakeasies, a few delivery trucks with the morning's milk and newspapers cruised the streets, but the sidewalks were deserted and only in the lobbies of the better apartment houses did lights burn. It was almost too warm a night to be wearing the white fur, but Sammy was particular. It didn't matter that a coat like that had never been seen where she was going; the role he had assigned her fitted so comfortably that she was hardly aware of the playing of it anymore.

Tess should have been sitting beside her. She had promised, blue eyes wide with sincerity, not to drink too much too quickly, to fill a glass with water and ice cubes and pretend that it was vodka. Abby shouldn't have trusted her to remember. She should have taken Bobby Stein aside and told him what Tess had to do tonight, told him how important it was that her sister say good-bye to Bridget. But she hadn't, and because she'd let the moment slip by, her sister had forgotten.

Except for an occasional sip of the beer that Michael Murphy brewed and carried up to Patrick Sullivan in a tin pail every Saturday night, Tess had never touched alcohol until she'd gone to work for Sammy Rosen. Even the Irish themselves called it a curse, and no one ever knew for sure which among them would fall under the spell of the first drop to pass their lips. It was usually the men, hardly ever a girl as young as Tess, blessed with beauty and promise, and not alive long enough to feel the crush of the world, but she had the thirst now, a thirst that the liquor seemed only to deepen, and when there was music to dance to, her legs needed constant refueling. Yet it wasn't entirely Tess's fault; it was never purely and simply the fault of the drinker. Bred in the bones, people said, understanding the waste and the sorrow of what they lamented. Taking the pledge was the only way out of the pit, but Tess hadn't even recognized the depth of the chasm into which she had stumbled.

"I've got some money for Mom," she had said, screwing up her face at the coffee Abby was trying to persuade her to drink. "There would have been more, but I had to give Bette something toward the rent. Tell her I love her and that I'll write. Jeez, I feel sick. This room is making my stomach turn."

They were in Abby's bedroom, the room she shared with Sammy. It smelled of perfume and powder, the bags of sachet attached to every clothes hanger, shaving lotion and the musky cologne he wore, leather polish and the tang of lovemaking. Tess had pushed herself off the bed, leaving a crumpled wad of bills where her hand had lain, lurching with a sideways dance step toward the door and the living room where sixty people had gathered to launch the new venture and get a good look at Sammy Rosen's redheads. "You always know what to say, Abby. Tell her I'll go to Mass at Notre Dame and light a candle for the family."

Maybe it was better that Tess hadn't come. She was so transparent that even the fondest of mothers could read her face and know precisely what sins she had joyfully, eagerly committed. You could never tell when Tess would want to pick a fight. Or with whom. One of the best things about Bobby Stein was that he didn't care enough to fight with her, or perhaps he just didn't know how. He had a way of turning his back on her, feigning deafness, that defused her most volatile moods. They got along, and if Tess thought it was because he had fallen in love with her, no one, not even Abby, was willing to attempt to open her eyes. This little affair couldn't last very long anyway. It would end whenever Bobby Stein decided it had gone far enough. He was ambitious. Everyone but Tess could see that.

There was something about the city late at night that induced introspection. Tess was too simple, too unchanging a personality to engage her thoughts for long, Sammy too far removed in the safe place to which she had relegated him to want to probe. She had kept the vows she had made to herself on the dock, in the rain, a lifetime ago. They had been clear in her mind then, and they had remained so—points of stability, promises that guarded the future and could make it secure and safe. Without the necessity to work, she had had hours and hours to fill, days that stretched blankly before her from early morning until midafternoon, and she had used them well, calling on reserves of stored-up energy that were almost frightening in their intensity.

She had no friends with whom to pass idle days, but with Sammy's money she had bought herself teachers and the temporary companionship of some of the brightest and most talented people in New York. Sheila Cohen, sallow face alight at the mere mention of their names, had told her who was most sought after, who most demanding, who most successful in molding and launching pupils, whose phones rang when a fresh young face was wanted. It was easy to get appointments when you could tell a hard-voiced secretary that Sammy Rosen had suggested you call, easier still when he himself dropped a word or two in the little world that revolved around itself and swept away outsiders in the current of its backwash. Abby had worked hard, methodically applying herself to the mastery of skills that came naturally to only a very fortunate few. She hadn't been born to it, didn't possess talent in her genes, only good looks, but she had other qualities that could prove to be more lastingly valuable than talent. Determination, the willingness to continue to work long after she had reached the point of exhaustion, a commitment that grew stronger every day, and a fear that no matter how polished she became, time would catch up with her before she was ready to stand on her own.

Her speech was nearly accentless now, and she'd learned to pitch her voice low, to breathe from an invisible core of power centered in the diaphragm. Ballet poses, so different from the dance steps Bobby Stein taught, had straightened and strengthened her back, trained her in the beauty of immobility and a taut, proud line of shoulders and jaw. Her singing voice was weak and uncertain, but she knew what pitch was, and her ear had been sharpened so that when the high notes were impossible to reach she could talk her way huskily through the sentiments of a song. The most difficult class, the one for which Sheila would have cheerfully paid the devil whatever he asked of her, was the acting workshop where the name of Stanislavsky was revered only a little less than that of God. It was a painful experience because all of Abby's instincts cried out against revealing herself, fought against submerging her identity in that of a character who was always vulnerable, flawed, struggling in the vast sea of tortured humanity. She did her best, marveling at the way in which other students managed to change themselves from normal, ordinary people into men and women who transcended a playwright's written words and stage directions, leapt into his vision. Only she remained stick-like and awkward, as if her bones had calcified and all her muscles stiffened with old age. The others didn't like playing with her, she could read it in the impatient way they moved around her, but she was quick to memorize her lines and business, and didn't linger to discuss a scene when it was over. She was resented in that class. She occupied space and used up energies that a more promising, less well-connected aspirant would have turned to flame.

There had been physical changes also. She'd gained no weight, but her flesh had shifted, rearranged itself as if Sammy's hands had communicated more pleasing patterns. Her breasts were higher, fuller, rounder where they swelled from the bones of her chest, her waist nipped in more distinctly, her hips and thighs were an unbroken fluid line beneath the skirts of the white silk evening dresses. She was the same height she had been since the age of sixteen, but she moved more gracefully, appeared taller, as if an invisible puppeteer's string were centered in the top of her head. Her skin and hair shone with the vitamins coursing through her veins, and her fingernails, once short and easily bent by repeated soaking in hot, soapy dishwater, curved now like the hard talons of a she-cat, buffed and brilliant, but unpolished because Sammy had said that red paint would destroy the pale fragility that was more attractive than deep, vivid color.

On her dressing table stood a bouquet of white roses, delivered that evening before the first of their guests had surged into the quiet of the apartment. She held one of the flowers in her lap, careful not to touch the petals that would begin to turn brown at human contact. Patrick might have gathered wildflowers from the meadows in Ireland, blue and yellow and pale pink, but she was certain that he could never have given Bridget a blossom as fragile as this one, so lush and fragrant that it was as far removed from nature as blown glass from sand. Why it was so important to see the white rose in her mother's hand she could not have said. The money, after all, was what would buy food, pay the rent, purchase new pants and shirts and underwear for the five brothers, but the flower, destined to fade before the *Katrina* had cleared the harbor, was for Bridget alone to enjoy. Patrick could nurse his pride and his ill-knit bones, wait for Sean Fitzgerald to toss him crumbs, pretend that he'd never fathered two daughters; all of that removed him from the world that daily snapped at his wife's ankles. But Bridget, awash in scummy suds and sour rags, deserved a breath of beauty at which to marvel, a fragrance to linger in her nose and kill for a moment the smell of lye and oily dirt.

"Mr. Rosen doesn't expect you to do anything more than

keep me in sight, Peter," she said. "There won't be any trouble here."

He touched his cap to her, but didn't answer. Burly, heavily muscled, broken-nosed from a fight that hadn't gone his way, he knew that the bonus he had been promised depended on the safety of this young woman whose crazy notion to visit Grand Central Station at two o'clock in the morning was all the proof he needed that the rich enjoyed flirting with danger and would always need men like him to rescue them from actually meeting it. The right-hand pocket of his gray jacket bulged over the gun Mr. Rosen had given him, and he fingered it lovingly, enjoying the clean coldness of the barrel and the warmer wooden stock, scored and ribbed to guarantee a sure grip. The worst he expected to encounter was a wino or two crouched in a corner or staggering along a wall. Harmless, despised failures, but once in a while a half-sober anger would burst forth in cursing, and a shaking hand would be thrust out in a threatening demand for money. Men could ignore or abuse them with impunity; women were their preferred targets. He stayed within a few feet of Mr. Rosen's girlfriend, his eyes sweeping the passageway, his face contorted in a deliberately belligerent scowl. The surest way to avoid trouble was to show that you were well prepared to best it.

Her footsteps echoed through the empty station, and the heels of her shoes clattered on the filthy floor. Her skirts, barely an inch above the unswept tiles, created a tiny breeze that stirred bits of paper and rippled the iridescent pools of greasy water tracked in by the day's travelers. The whiteness of her coat was dulled to pale yellow by the dirty bulbs that illuminated the gloom, many of them burned out or broken by vandals bored with school and embittered by jobs that paid little and led nowhere. So crowded during the daylight hours, the station was a funnel, drinking in great drafts of human beings, channeling them in ever more tightly packed streams toward the narrow train tracks that exited from it and fanned out to all parts of the city. At night it rested, while the scum on its walls trickled downward and a handful of women scrubbed it to a reasonable cleanliness that would be soiled again before they had washed its grime from their bodies.

They moved across the vast expanse of the central waiting room like a company of ants, their knees sliding along on pads of rags, their backs bent, shoulders and arms stretched out, making sweeping motions that left thin lines of soap film where one hand overlapped the parabola of another. It was cold in the station, and the scrubwomen had pinned hand-knitted shawls around their upper bodies and slipped their arms through old, footless socks that were beyond their powers to mend. They wore scraps of scarves tied around their heads to cover their ears and keep their hair from falling down. Their hands were bare, red and knobby around the wrists and knuckles, broken-nailed and cracked with old sores whose scabs were never dry long enough to heal fully. None of them was young or slender. This was work that coarsened bodies already thickened by childbearing, a job that was sought after because there was no fear of layoff, a kind of reward given to widows and wives of disabled Democratic voters. Above them arched the high dome of the ceiling, kiosks were shuttered behind iron gratings, buckets clanged and wet brushes slapped rhythmically. To one who cared it was a cathedral of sorrow.

She wouldn't call out her mother's name, nor would she pick her way across the wet floor to her. There had always been dignity and reserve in every action performed by Bridget Sullivan, and patiently Abby waited as first one woman, then another glanced toward where she stood. At last Abby looked into eyes as changeable as her own, saw a fine-boned hand brush back a strand of hair and dry itself on the hem of a black shawl, watched as a figure got painfully to its feet and began walking toward her. Her mother's form filled the whole of her vision, occupied acres of space, blotted out everything else. Of their own accord her arms opened to embrace the woman she might have become, but Bridget, though she grasped the hands held out to her, would not draw her close, would not soil the magical white fur against the wet stains of her dark clothing.

"You look fine, Abby. Like gentry," she said, and a smile lit up the shadowy fatigue in her eyes. That's what they called them back in Ireland, the ones who owned the land and hired the daughters of the poor to wait on them. Gentry.

"Can we talk, Mom? I've come to say good-bye before the ship sails."

"We'll sit together on one of the benches. I'll have my dinner now." Later, when it was time for the crew to rest and eat, Bridget would work to make up these minutes. "Who's this you've brought with you?"

Peter touched his cap and stepped away from them, seeing suddenly the bone structure and the height that was so like that of Mr. Rosen's doxy, guessing that the woman did not recognize his uniform for what it was and was thinking that so finely dressed a man could only be her daughter's friend. She nodded politely to him, waited expectantly for a moment, then, with a sigh of disappointment, led her silent daughter toward the wooden bench where a small bundle wrapped in newspaper lay beside her coat. He didn't know whether Mr. Rosen would question him, but he couldn't take his eyes off the pair of them, one so white and rich, the other so dark and poor.

"I knew you'd come to see me tonight," Bridget said, carefully unwrapping the package that contained her food, smoothing out the sheet of newspaper so that it could be used again. "Mrs. Goldbaum even told me the name of the boat. The woman has a way of finding out everything."

"Tess sends her love, Mom. She wanted to see you, but at the last moment . . ." Abby stared down at the dinner that would sustain her mother throughout the night, through the hours of scrubbing, through the clattering journey home and early Mass at Holy Rosary, until she could make herself a cup of tea and get the boys' breakfast before they went to school. The heel of a loaf of bread wrapped around a slice of onion and two tiny wrinkled boiled potatoes. In Sammy Rosen's apartment there were platters of catered hors d'oeuvres drying out and spoiling because the women there were afraid of getting fat and the men preferred liquor to food.

"Are you hungry, Abby?" Bridget's hands were already reaching out to share, as though what lay on the newspaper had been prepared by an expert chef and served on a linen napkin.

"No, Mom. You go ahead." She could have brought a feast for them if she'd only thought of it.

"So you came all by yourself."

"Tess said to tell you she'd go to Mass at Notre Dame and light a candle."

Bridget laughed. "The only times she's seen the inside of a church since she was fifteen were when I made her come with me and held on to her arm all the way down the street."

"How are things at home? Dad and the boys?"

"The same. Growing like weeds and Thomas after me all the time to quit school. Mrs. Goldbaum shakes her fist in his face and sends her Leon over to talk to him about college and night school. He went to see Sean Fitzgerald about working a short shift, but he got no promises."

"Don't let him give up. He doesn't have to. Not now."

"Where's the money going to come from, Abby?"

It was a different Bridget who asked her daughter that question, a mother who'd had time and more than enough time to consider each of her children's futures, who'd accepted what had happened to two of them and made a quiet decision to use it to save the others. It was plain that she hadn't talked it over with Patrick, a man who was no good at seizing opportunities and making the best of them.

"From me," Abby said. "As much as you want and for as long as you need it." She unlatched the pearl clip of the silk purse. The white rose, its stem snapped in half and jagged, pricked the palm of her hand. Amazed to find that she had forgotten it, that she was still holding it, she laid the flower on her mother's lap and then placed beside it the envelope containing both the two thousand dollars and the nearly three hundred that Tess had somehow, miraculously, managed to save. The shape of the stack of bills, cash in denominations that could be doled out without causing comment from merchants who were unused to seeing large amounts, bulged against the thick paper.

"How can I take your money, Abby?"

"Just open your hand." She closed Bridget's fist around the envelope, and the scrape of her skin against the roughness of her mother's fingers was a pain in her heart. "It's not tainted, Mom. There's no such thing as tainted money. And it's from Tess too. She didn't forget."

For a long time they sat without moving, and all the things Abby had meant to say her mother read in her eyes. When she turned away to fumble for the worn old handbag that usually held her package of food and subway fare and very little else, Bridget's shoulders sagged just the slightest bit, and before she straightened them she looked as old as the mother of the world.

"I can't tell your father now," she said, when both the money and the rose were safely hidden away. "But he'll find out eventually. Some of the heart's gone out of him, Abby. In time the anger will go too."

"I'm sorry, Mom."

"It's not your fault. You didn't cause it. He's a man who's never had the luck that comes to some others without their asking or praying for it. The night that you and Tess . . . that night I heard him crying in his bed, after he thought I'd fallen asleep. No one else would ever think it, but I know him as well as I know the state of my own soul. He's tender inside, he's been raw and hurting since the day he was born, but too proud to show it."

She's changed too, Abby thought. She's learned what the world is really like and stopped pretending that it had ever been any different. Or maybe the pretense had been to keep up the courage of her husband and children. Maybe she'd always been like this with just the veneer to keep her from breaking apart. She suddenly realized that she knew very, very little about Bridget Sullivan the woman, while believing that she had known everything about the mother and wife and that that was all there was to her.

"I wish I weren't going. I wish I could stay here with you."

"Did I stay in Ireland with my mother? Patrick was all I wanted then, all I could think or dream about. One of my brothers bloodied his nose the day he came to ask if he could marry me. They didn't believe it was serious until then, you see. But I'd known from the first moment I laid eyes on him that I'd never want anyone else." Bridget's thumb drew a tiny cross on her daughter's forehead. She held Abby's face between her two hands, then stood up, settling the shawl more tightly around her shoulders, brushing the folds of her skirt. "God bless," she said. A minute later she was back on her knees on the floor of Grand Central Station, but this time with a difference. Loudly enough so that the other women could pick up the tune, she was crooning the words of a song she hadn't sung in twenty years.

Peter's hand beneath her elbow guided Abby back out onto the street, helped her into Sammy Rosen's polished automobile. She found a handkerchief in the pocket of her coat, a wisp of lace that smelled of Paris and felt like spider's web against her eyes.

It would come. Bridget was right. Perhaps not for several years, but eventually Patrick would understand. It had comforted Bridget to believe that her daughter was deeply in love with the man who was taking her away, and perhaps that deception would touch Patrick also. The truth of it was too hard a thing to ask either of them to endure. She had heard all her life that old people got soft, and had seen the worn-out mothers and widows who reached such a point of loneliness that they forgot what had ever made them vindictive and hard in the first place. Patrick would forgive, more quickly than most because his passions were hotter. In the meantime she could wrap herself in the surety of Bridget's love and warm the cold places of her heart with the sound of her mother's singing.

4

*I*n Paris, in early April, the chestnut trees began to blossom and it rained lightly every evening, bathing the city
in a cool gray mist that washed its streets and fed the
flowers in its hundreds of parks. Leaving their hotel early
every morning during the first weeks of rehearsal, Abby and
Tess and Bobby Stein walked the few blocks to the theater
arm in arm, their feet as light as the clean, sparkling air, their
blood racing faster each day as the show began to fall together
and opening night drew closer. The girls were working harder
than at any other time in their lives; their legs had developed
the hard muscles of dancers, and the cocky walk they practiced for hours and hours on stage sped them along the
sidewalk with an insouciant grace that turned heads and
earned appreciative stares.

The Americans in the company were lodged in a small
hotel within a few minutes of the theater. They had begun to
pair up on the boat coming over, and within a few days of
reaching Paris had settled into the friendships that would last
for the run of the show. None of the girls, for obvious
reasons, made any overtures to Abby.

It didn't bother her to be excluded from the laughter and
the chattering in the crowded dressing room where cosmetics, clothing, and secrets were exchanged with equal freedom
and generosity. The place had a hot, intense atmosphere that
tired her as much as it invigorated the others. Loose powder
floated in the air, swirling like motes of white dust in billow-
ing clouds of cigarette smoke; perfume was slapped on as
liberally as handfuls of facial cream; the pitch of all their
competing voices was high and shrill; and the fussy com-

mands of the wardrobe mistress and her assistants added to the confusion as both the Frenchwomen and the American girls yelled louder and louder at one another in the ridiculous conviction that shouting would make their different languages understood. Tess was the loudest and the happiest of them all, Abby the first to slip into street clothes and the only one to whisper a quiet *"merci"* as she left.

There was never a question about how her evenings were to be spent. Sammy's car came for her promptly at seven. Usually she could hear voices and laughter coming from his suite as soon as she stepped off the elevator onto the fourth floor of the Georges V. The first time, entering the room where conversation stopped, heads turned, and men rose from their seats at sight of her, she had the odd feeling that she had somehow been transported back to Saul Gruber's showroom. Her head had lifted in the old, automatic gesture of the model on parade, and she had paused in the doorway as once she had held a pose before stepping out onto the runway. Sammy's hand beneath her elbow, his light kiss against her cheek had been momentarily unsettling. He had seen the confusion in her eyes and laughed, leading her forward as solemnly as he would a duchess. She had grown to like that moment, to look forward to it as she sweated through the rehearsals that became more and more frantic as opening night approached.

At the theater she was just one redhead among many. She had insisted to Sammy that she wanted no special concessions, and none were given her. She was cursed at just as often as every other girl in the line, and, like the others, she had learned to keep on moving while tears coursed down her cheeks and her stomach churned with the humiliation of being screamed at. Only when she stepped into his suite did she become someone special, was she able to recapture the confidence and the easy poise that he had fostered in her in New York. The magic worked every time. When a man lifted your hand to his lips—and none of the men to whom Sammy introduced her failed to do so—it made you undeniably different, it set you apart from the girls who were drinking cheap wine in Montmartre and worrying about finding a late cab to beat the rehearsal period curfew imposed by Mr. Rosen and strictly enforced by Bette Blumfeld.

She thought her situation puzzled some of the French,

but only Georges Louvier had questioned her about it, and then not until she had nearly yawned in his face one evening and he had noticed the blue shadows beneath her eyes. If this gamble with Sammy paid off, both men were prepared to expand the scope of their limited partnership. They were already discussing the possibility of sending not only a French line to New York, but big-busted blond Germans and the incredibly rose-complexioned English also. Well married and happily mistressed himself, Louvier was curious. No French-woman would have been as satisfied as the charming Abby seemed to be with so little.

"Why do you work so hard, my dear?" he had asked. "Surely it isn't necessary."

"I have so much more to learn than most of the others." She liked his quiet way with her, the absence of the electric tension that leapt at her from other men. He was old enough to be her father and, for whatever private reason, had apparently decided to treat her with the same gentle grace he must surely show his own two daughters. "I'm very new at this, and I have a long way to go."

"That's not an answer to my question. Unless you have ambitions. Are you ambitious, Abby? I wouldn't have thought so."

"Everyone has ambitions." She looked around the salon, at the expensively gowned women whose every gesture she knew to be carefully premeditated, at the men so much older than they who could afford to keep them in style. Not one of those women, she guessed, worked at anything but being beautiful, available, and accomplished in conversation and lovemaking. You couldn't read their faces. Not a wrinkle, not a trace of fatigue, not a hint of thoughts any deeper than the layers of perfect, rouged skin.

She had striven to make herself like them, believed, until now, that she had succeeded well enough to fool herself, Sammy—anyone with a less perceptive eye than Georges Louvier. Yet he had said he would not have thought her the ambitious type, and now, lawyerlike, he was waiting for her to speak and explain. Impossible to tell this so kind and honest man about the Abby Sullivan who had wanted nothing more than to escape a life of duty and obligation, who had worn a mask of resigned acceptance because the truth of her desires was too raw to be revealed even to herself.

But perhaps the ambition he claimed to find wanting in her and the yearnings she knew she possessed were not one and the same. Was this room, these people, this life she was leading what he meant? If so, then he was right, she was not ambitious in this way, to come this far and go no farther. It had never been enough, not even at the very beginning. For Tess perhaps, who made every moment entirely past, present, and future, but not for the Abby who had always, always wanted something better, who had reached and reached until it seemed her shoulders would be torn from their sockets, who longed for every ounce of every fine thing the world had to offer, and who had had to be practical and pretend that second best was good enough.

"You must have sad dreams, little one, to make you smile so wistfully."

"My family is very poor, monsieur. They will depend on me for a very long time." Her own frankness startled her. She hadn't realized how deeply tired she was, how much of an effort it took to avoid the giving away of confidences. The frown on Georges Louvier's face told her that he understood the meaning as well as the sense of her words.

"The French are a practical people, Abby, not at all sentimental as foreigners like to believe we are. I think you must be a little French yourself, to know so young that the only thing constant about life is that it is always changing."

He had patted her hand then, asking no more questions, only suggesting to his mistress later on that night that it would be a good thing to befriend the young American. The girl did not seem to realize yet that Sammy would be traveling soon. She would be lonely in Paris without him, working every night, going straight from the theater to an empty hotel room, visiting museums to fill up the hours of each long day when the company rehearsed only as often as necessary to sharpen up routines or introduce new ones. She would be faithful to him even after he had begun to deceive her. The fidelity and the deceptions were both inevitable because Georges Louvier knew that Sammy Rosen was not in love.

They opened in the last week of April, after a final dress rehearsal that ran nearly twice as long as the timed length of the show itself. Everything that could possibly go wrong was bungled, broken, or forgotten that day. Costumes ripped, heels snapped off shoes, musicians unaccountably misplaced their scores, spotlights beamed onto empty sections of the stage while performers stumbled around in the dark, scenery stuck or flew down from the lofts with deadly speed, singers lost their voices, and dancers were clumsy and out of step. Nerves grew taut, tempers became volcanic, friendly camaraderie disappeared; every member of the cast was convinced that every other member was engaged in deliberate, personally vindictive sabotage.

In the dressing room, brandishing a clipboard with pages of special notes for Sammy Rosen's girls, Bette Blumfeld's eyes sparkled and she lit one cigarette from the half-smoked butt of another, ashes and sparks flying as she yelled into the confusion. The more disastrous the dress rehearsal, the better the show. It didn't make sense, but what in that business did? Zombies, they all looked like zombies out there. One or two of the girls cried, faces bloated and smeary, nails bitten down to the quick. Most of them just stared at her, angry and sullen or too exhausted to care anymore. The only time they laughed was when she commanded hot baths and early to bed for everyone. The hotel plumbing creaked and groaned, spitting out tepid water on the best of nights, and legions of hungry bedbugs had them all scratching like dogs.

Smiling, slapping fannies, tweaking a naked breast, kissing a dozen cheeks, Bobby Stein sauntered from girl to girl all down the row of starkly lit mirrors. No one had heard his knock; he registered, if at all, as a warm hand, a brief embrace, heavily blacked-in eyebrows and a bronze face that was cut off at the neck where the makeup ended abruptly. He had a dirty towel around his neck and three or four times he flicked it at bare legs, a locker-room antic that brought few smiles.

"I've seen livelier morgues than this place," he said to Bette Blumfeld.

"Amateurs," she scoffed. "I told them a hundred times the worst thing that can happen is a final dress that goes like clockwork. Nobody believes me. Half of them are trying to figure out how to get drunk tonight without being fired, and the rest are ready to pack their suitcases and take the next boat home." She lowered her voice. "Tess is going to eat her way back to New York if she's not careful. She's ripped out more seams than anyone else, and it's not wardrobe's fault.

You've got to put a stop to that, Bobby. It doesn't take much before it starts to show."

"She only learns things the hard way. I can't hold my hand over her mouth all day. Weigh her in like a fighter and start docking her pay for every extra pound. That she'll understand."

So Tess didn't wear very well. Not surprising. She already had a reputation for playing too hard, not knowing when to stop, pushing the limits and enjoying the hell out of it when they broke. Too quick to pick a fight. Undependable over the long haul, when it really counted. Too bad about Tess. She was going to miss the gold ring and not even realize it until she could no longer reach high enough to graze it with her fingertips.

Abby sat staring at herself as if trying to identify the gaudy stranger staring back at her. It had happened as suddenly as the click of a key turning in a lock. Bobby Stein in the dressing room, half dressed himself, wandering like a pasha through his harem, touching, stroking, caressing bare flesh as casually as if the intimacy of his gestures meant less than nothing. Costumes were removed and handed over to the wardrobe people just as soon as each girl came offstage, but Abby was seeing herself clearly, her memory as sharply focused as the lens of a telescope, the figure on which she concentrated far away and very tiny, yet vivid in every detail. The legs were long and bare, ending in gold shoes with startling red heels. Strut, turn, stretch, kick. The body compensated for the unnatural angle, breasts thrusting out, hips moving with wide swings that snapped and twisted provocatively. Scarlet and gold scales rippled and flashed, the flimsy net to which they were sewn a second skin that hid almost nothing of what lay beneath. She remembered the deft fingers of the seamstresses, the dry, quick touch of them and the prick of their needles and pins, the way the back of someone's hand had crushed her breasts while with the other the stranger took long stitches to outline the areas the sequins would brilliantly accentuate. On with her clothes, off with her clothes, with not even a screen behind which to conceal herself, standing naked for minutes on end during the last fittings. They were flaming goddesses in one number, peacocks in another, taunting and tantalizing with sweeping feather fans, bird plumage arching over their buttocks, crowning their heads. So many changes of costume that one blended into another, leaving only an impression of glitter and vivid color that drew the eye to probe for a glimpse of what was being touted, what was being flaunted more obscenely than had the girls been frankly naked.

A mask had slipped onto the silvered surface of the mirror, mouth as red as blood, skin powdered and rouged, eyes elongated, shadowed, eyelashes bristly with black paint, eyebrows plucked thin and redrawn, two parentheses in search of a sentence, red hair frizzed and curled, brilliantined so it would crackle like fire under the lights, dusted with flecks of gold that sifted down and caked in the sweat of her scalp. The hand that appeared beside the mask was tipped with curving scarlet nails, only the bone structure familiarly human. In all these long weeks she had thought only of the work, of the effort to master what was demanded of her, responding to the drive to be perfect, not realizing, never thinking what she would look like in the end.

The sight sickened her. She reached for cream, lathering it like soapsuds over her face, smearing the heavy, resistant makeup, rubbing viciously at the colors until they ran together like the mess on an artist's palette. They came off in greasy streaks that clotted on the towel, leaving uneven smudges behind. More cream, applied slower, worked into her hairline, across the fold of her eyelids, around the base of her nose, scrubbed into the red dots that were supposed to make her eyes seem larger and looked like bloody moles. When she was finished her skin burned from the scratchy towel, but the mask had disappeared. In its place was shiny baldness, a face made nearly featureless by the glare of the harsh light, a jaw tight and stern, a pale, set mouth, and tired, very tired eyes.

Only the star of the show had any privacy, and Abby thought of her now, removing makeup and donning ordinary clothing in the dressing room that was hardly larger than a closet, but private, blessedly, gloriously private. She'd watched her work, but never spoken to her. There was hierarchy and there was protocol in this little kingdom, for all the talk of closeness and shared effort. But tomorrow night's audience would fill the theater because of the pull of her name, the established reputation, the years and years of successfully selling herself, the elusive spark of genuine, heartstopping talent.

Léonie Martin was a tiny slip of a woman, a slender black moth lost in the butterfly swarm of chorus girls. Yet when the spotlight hit her, when she lifted one arm as if to beckon you closer, when she began to sing, you forgot everything but the enormous voice carrying you off into her dreams and her nightmares. No one was sadder, no one more desolated by love, no one touched your heart as deeply as Léonie Martin. She made you cry and she could make you laugh with bittersweet pain, at the absurdity of falling in love, at the good and the bad memories, at all the hopeful beginnings and wrenching partings. She wasn't even young or very pretty anymore, but the face and the voice were unforgettable. You wondered how she could have lost the lover she was lamenting, and remembered all the men who'd ever wooed and then abandoned you. It was pure illusion, but so close to life and love that the applause tomorrow night would sound like thunder.

The click of a key turning in a lock. Brittle and final. Abby knew quite suddenly that she could work until she dropped, but she'd never stop a show, never be strong enough to step out of the line and assume center stage. All the lessons in New York—what had they given her? A few tricks, a little polish. Just enough to let her get by for five or six years in this meat market, auction block, sequined playground. Until younger, fresher faces and bodies pushed her aside. And with that certainty came also the memory of how hopelessly inadequate she had proved to be in the acting classes, how day after day she'd burned with embarrassment and heard herself speak lines with such flat artificiality that not even she could believe them. She hadn't the passion to fashion herself into another Laurette Taylor, hadn't the soul for it, hadn't the talent, would never be able to create magic. Two of the worlds in which she'd imagined she could live slipped away from her, and she was left with the one she most despised, the quasi-respectable shadow land where the rings you wore were never wide and made entirely of gold and the clothes that were bought for you had to be earned in bed.

It was too late to back out, to expect to find the you that had been discarded waiting patiently with the same comfortable skin and bright eyes. She owed too much to too many people, could drown in her debts if she missed a single stroke. There wasn't even time to stop and think it through, no time to do anything but go on working—smiling and turning, whirling and strutting, preening dyed feathers, flashing beads and sequins and flesh, pretending to herself, to Sammy, to audiences and co-performers that the glitter was warm and the future promising. She wondered how many candles Bridget had lit to bring her to this.

Paris adored Léonie Martin as usual, and fell in love with the beautiful American girls who swept across the stage like titian-haired nymphs. Halfway through the show everyone knew it could run forever. The final curtain came down to the pop of champagne corks, the cast laughed and cried and hugged one another, and the first of many men appeared with cards in their hands and thousands and thousands of francs to spend.

It had to be Maxim's for Sammy, silver buckets encircling his table, tomorrow's investors congratulating him, the heady perfume of success unmistakable and intoxicating. For Abby there was an emerald ring glowing against a bed of white satin. The stone was larger than the knuckle of her thumb, square-cut, set in prongs of platinum so that it floated above her skin like a concentrated beam of weightless green light. He said nothing when he slipped it onto her finger, and a moment later he was gone from the table, threading his way across the room to where Léonie Martin, all in black like a widow or a nun, stood searching for him, alone as always, the sad eyes like ebony coals at the bottom of a burned-out firepit. So different from Abby. So much older and wiser. Georges Louvier watched as Sammy, a courtier to his queen, bent over the fragile hand that needed no wand to summon illusions. Léonie Martin had never sung in New York, but the legend had traveled. She'd turned down offer after offer, waiting for the right moment, the right man to smooth her way, patient because the sadness of her songs was nothing when compared to the weariness of her heart.

"You were beautiful tonight, my dear," Georges said, taking Abby's hand in his, feeling the effort with which she brought her mind and her eyes back to this table, this cele-

bration that suddenly had an uncertain, bitter taste to it.
"You've captured all of Paris."

She smiled at him, and at Marie-Claire, kind Marie-
Claire who was unconcerned about the wrinkles around her
mouth and the wings of gray above her ears. As secure as a
wife, just as well provided for, she lacked only children in her
life. Twice she had invited Abby to lunch at her apartment,
serving simply prepared, delicious food and light, delicate
wines. Her conversation was as discreet as the good taste of
the paintings on her walls, but the protecting wing had been
spread, and Abby was grateful for its warmth and its shelter.

They poured more champagne and sipped it slowly,
quiet until Sammy and Léonie Martin joined them. It was an
occasion when the city's premiere chanteuse appeared in a
public restaurant; waiters hovered and the most blasé of
Maxim's habitués found their eyes drawn to the table like
flies to honey. Léonie Martin had a young son, an illegitimate
child whose father was rumored to be a well-known member
of the government. Like the most ordinary mère de famille,
the woman whose feet had been covered with roses only an
hour before spoke of measles and teachers, First Communion
and bruised knees, nursemaids and the price of winter over-
coats. It bored Léonie Martin to talk about her work; since
the birth of her child she had sung less and less frequently,
only when she needed the money. Now she was thinking
about buying a house in the country, a place to grow a garden
and keep horses, where the air would smell of ripening
grapes in the summer and the boy could run through the
fields. Unfortunately, such a property would be very expensive.

Sammy Rosen smiled at her. She lifted her eyebrows,
shrugged her shoulders, pursed her lips, not ready yet to
commit herself, but thinking, already adding up sums in her
head, allowing him to move her from "perhaps" to "why not."
She was twice as old as Abby; she had had lovers whose
names and faces she could no longer remember. None of
them had advanced her career, none of them had stayed
through the hard times, all of them had bled her dry and left
richer than she, carrying away the expensive gifts with which
she had filled their hands. She hadn't known how not to fall
in love, over and over, never learning to shield and protect
herself. But now she had a son, and his life and his future
were serious matters. It was sad to have to calculate, a loss

not to be able to offer everything anymore, to open heart and purse as though both were bottomless.

She had never been a very good businesswoman, but for the sake of the child she was prepared to become one. The American girl was so lovely it took your breath away. She was sorry to have to wound her, and for a brief moment she remembered the first young man, and how she had sung her soul out over him. What had seemed like a death blow then had become the beginning of her legend. She had been so poor that she had sung and sung, night after night, in every boîte that would give her a free meal and a few francs, until finally all of Paris had heard her and the siege had ended. So poor then, all those years ago, and not very much better off now, for all the adulation and the hard work. She looked at the ring on Abby's finger, at the dress that was finer than anything she'd ever bought for herself, at the yards and yards of white fur cascading over her chair. Sammy's mistress wouldn't suffer in that way; not for a minute would she lie awake at night too hungry to sleep, wondering if she would ever taste meat or drink decent wine again. Americans were generous with their women; like small boys, they were always conscious of being a little guilty, always paid well to buy the freedom to play again with someone else. She would make sure that it happened slowly, that there would be time for the girl to choose the moment of letting go, time to learn that she must. More than anything else, Léonie Martin despised greedy people, the ones who grabbed and ran away and never looked back to see what damage they had done.

"I must go," she said. "Jean-Paul drinks his chocolate in bed with me every morning, and you know how early children wake up." She refused the offer of Sammy's car and avoided Marie-Claire's level stare. They had talked about her son, had they not? So, the other woman wasn't blind. She understood the way of things. She laid a hand lightly on Abby Sullivan's shoulder. "You are very beautiful, my dear," she said, so quietly that no one else heard. "Life will treat you gently." She kissed the girl's cheek, the cool smooth skin that was so much tighter than her own, so much fairer, so like a child's. Then she left. The taxi would be cold, the long ride lonely, the apartment dark when she let herself in, but a night-light would be burning beside Jean-Paul's bed, she would tuck the blanket more securely around his warm body, and fall asleep knowing that his arms tight around her neck and his breath against her face would wake her in the morning.

It was hard to believe that people had once lived here, slept and eaten, washed and relieved themselves in rooms as splendid as these. The Sun King had died in that bed, nearly eighty years old, dimmed at the end and dominated by a woman who convinced him that hell was real and even monarchs could spend eternity aflame. Marie Antoinette's skirts had swept that staircase; she had romped her careless way to the guillotine in the park that was so peaceful now and in the palace that was a museum.

"It overwhelms you, doesn't it? I never tire of coming to Versailles," Marie-Claire said. Her arm was loosely linked in Abby's, her affection as sincere as that of an aunt for a favorite niece. In the past few weeks there had seldom been a day when the two had not passed an afternoon together. Paris was the most charming history book in the world, and Marie-Claire one of its most appreciative readers.

She hadn't set out to instruct Abby, merely to amuse and distract her, but the little American was so quick to learn, so hungry to learn, that it had been impossible not to give lessons. She was a marvelously apt pupil, with a good ear for language and a memory that effortlessly absorbed the dates and names associated with the cathedrals and châteaux through which they wandered. She had lit candles at Notre Dame and Sacré Coeur, folded her hands and knelt in the side chapels that were so much more personal than the huge central naves. It touched Marie-Claire to see her pray, always with a wan, bleakly confused expression on her face and a sigh that stirred the yellow flames and was more pitiful than tears.

The affair with Sammy Rosen wasn't over yet, but it was cooling, the tempo had slowed, and Marie-Claire's intuition told her that it could not last much longer. Sammy was absentminded these days, as if his thoughts were being continually pulled in another direction, as if part of him were engaged elsewhere. One or two of the investors, sensing ambiguity and opportunity, had held Abby closer than the dance required, nearly embraced her while Sammy looked on and apparently either did not notice or did not care. It would have been amusing had not Marie-Claire grown fond of the girl, or if Abby had shown that she was ready to make a new alliance, if she had demonstrated the resilience of other women in her situation who cut their losses without a qualm and chose a new lover as carefully as they did any other investment. But you were seldom as cautious with the first man as you later became; it wasn't the kind of lesson you could learn in any way other than by living it. You did learn it eventually, and from then on life was easier, though never again as carefree or innocent.

"I have a fitting this afternoon that I'd almost forgotten," Abby said. "We'll have to hurry back if I'm to be there on time." But she lingered on the gravel path, looking toward the man-made lake and then at the long gallery of the Hall of Mirrors. An artificial world, to be sure, but far, far removed from the tawdry, dusty, splintery backstage corridors that surprised her every night because they were always the same, always crowded, smelling of humans who sweated excitement, anticipation, ambition, and fear of failure. The only defense against them was to remember places like this, to lift yourself up and away while the body did what it was trained and paid to do.

"Not everyone was happy at Versailles," Marie-Claire said, knowing that it was both imprudent and dangerous to let one deception replace another. "Most people, in fact, were probably miserable. It was terribly crowded and not very sanitary, and one had always to be jockeying for position, currying favor, worrying that a frown might mean disgrace or banishment. Life was hard, and often very short. The more important you were, the less freedom you had. Even the king was a prisoner."

Abby smiled and took her companion's arm again, her face beneath the sunlit red-gold hair almost as serene and young as it had been troubled and old only a moment before. "You always say the right thing, Marie-Claire. I was thinking how much I might have preferred that time to this, but then I would have been a chambermaid emptying slops and sleeping in an unheated corner somewhere, certainly never allowed into the park or anywhere but the garrets or the kitchens."

"And instead of ordering a dozen new dresses, you would have had only a change of linen and a clean apron to wear on Sundays. No one ever remembers that many of them never bathed at all. Just imagine the stench! *Imaginez l'odeur!*" She held one hand delicately over her nose.

"*Épouvantable!*"

"*Bien, Abby, très bien.* Every word you say in French makes the next one easier."

"I love Paris, Marie-Claire. It's going to be very hard to leave it."

"But why talk of leaving, my dear? Georges believes the show could run for a year at least. You could stay for as long as you like, even after it closes." She hailed a taxi, giving the dressmaker's address in syllables too quick for Abby to follow. "Many Americans have found themselves more truly at home in Paris than in the United States."

"I should like that. I could very happily be one of them." Again the wistfulness, the tone of voice that acknowledged defeat before the battle had even been declared. "But I'm afraid it's impossible."

Now was the moment to plant the seed, to make the delicate suggestion that she had read in Léonie Martin's mind the night of the opening. It would take time for Abby to accept it, perhaps even to consider it, but Marie-Claire did not know how many months or even weeks were left to her before the older woman would force the issue. "Simply because Sammy feels he must go back does not mean that you must also. With him it's never anything but business; he is obliged always to look for a new challenge, another success. This trip of his to Germany. Do you think he will take even one moment to realize that he's in Berlin? No. Hotels, night-clubs, theaters, he hardly knows one from the other. Always he's searching for something to package, as he calls it, something to sell. For him it's always tomorrow, never today." She had spoken critically, even harshly. For Abby's own good, not for any other reason. Actually she respected Sammy Rosen's ability to maneuver his way through the world, to take only what he wanted and not miss the rest of it. She possessed some of those same qualities herself, and she valued them. "You are not married to him, after all." Occasionally it was best to say a thing baldly. Americans always boasted of their frankness, though privately she thought it a rather childish trait.

"No, I'm not."

Stiffly said, but firmly. Voiced for the first time perhaps, but accepted in the mind and heart, where alone it was important to know the truth of things. "Never mind. There's time to decide. Tomorrow I am going to take you to the Louvre. We will buy a guidebook and appreciate the Great Masters as seriously as though we were both still schoolgirls."

"I liked school," Abby said. "I even liked the nuns."

"Then you must have been a saint, my dear."

"I think I was in those days. I was a very, very good little girl." She stared out the window as the taxi sped them back to Paris.

The dressmaker fussed and clucked, pins in her mouth, a tape measure around her neck, adjusting seams and hemline to flatter her client's slim figure and long legs. She had very lit.e English, certainly not enough to follow the conversation between the woman before whom she knelt and the one who sat sipping a coffee, watching every movement with a critical eye. She thought they were speaking of love, of men, or a man, at least. The words were foreign to her, but not the long pauses, the tentative quality of the questions the young American was asking and the compassionate, gentle way Madame was answering them.

Twice a year she created beautiful clothing for Madame Guérin, designs copied from the great houses, carried away from the showings in Marie-Claire's excellent memory. Everything that she had sewn for the American girl had been suggested, even sketched out, by Madame Guérin. She had chosen as carefully for her inexperienced friend as she always did for herself, and the results would transform Mademoiselle Sullivan. The dresses she wore to her fittings were often striking, and certainly there was nothing cheap or shoddy about them, but they were unmistakably American; they lacked the subtle perfection and exquisite lines that Frenchwomen demanded. Any pretty girl could have worn them and looked exactly like anyone else.

Madame Thérèse's gift was to tailor each garment to its owner in such a way that an impression of uniqueness was created. She never used the same material twice, nor did she repeat the same style, popular though it might be. And if a client chose a color that was wrong for her, she simply refused to make the garment at all. For Mademoiselle Sullivan it was shades of off-white, the palest beige, a blue that matched her eyes on sunny days, and a gray-green tone to wear in the misty spring evenings when the skies above Paris wept softly. You were not often fortunate enough to dress a young woman whose eyes changed with the sun and the rain, and perhaps also with the thoughts she was thinking.

"One week, madame," she said, standing back to make certain that every pin was where it should be. "I will have Mademoiselle Sullivan's wardrobe completed in one week. I will let you know. More coffee perhaps? It tires the legs to stand so still."

An assistant began to gather up the garments that already had the air of belonging to no one but Abby, while Madame Thérèse herself removed only enough pins to allow her client to slip out of the dress on which she had been working. Marie-Claire looked at her wristwatch and shook her head regretfully. "Perhaps the next time," she said.

"I could stay here forever," Abby murmured. *"Toujours, madame, ici."* With a sweep of her arm she seemed about to embrace the small room that resembled no other place in which she had ever selected clothes. "It's more like a boudoir than a fitting room," she said to Marie-Claire. "It seems more perfect every time I see it." Heavily carpeted and draped in complementing blues and grays, the room encouraged the feeling of being nestled in a velvet-lined jewelry box. There were a chaise longue on which to stretch out one's legs, satin-covered chairs with curved, gilded legs, spindly, marble-topped tables, a fireplace inlaid with blue and gray tiles, paintings of elegantly garbed women from the past. Two full-length mirrors set in carved, polished oak reflected your image and framed you as if you were one of the painted ladies. It was impossible not to believe yourself beautiful in such a setting.

"You see, Abby, how well Paris is seducing you. You have nothing like this in New York, no?"

"There's never enough time. We're always in a hurry."

As Marie-Claire translated the English, Madame Thérèse's eyes began to snap and she thrust out her bosom like an angry pouter pigeon.

"She says to tell Mademoiselle Sullivan that in Paris there is always time to create beauty and that without beauty one cannot live, one only exists."

"Tell her, please, that I agree." She knew the look of horror that would appear on the dressmaker's face were she to see her client an hour from now, a befeathered, painted Kewpie doll like those hawked on street corners by men with dirty fingernails. The longer she stayed in Paris, the more time she spent listening to and learning from Marie-Claire, the harder it was going to be to go back to New York with Sammy. She was already aware that the white silk evening dresses she wore for him every night were only more expensive versions of the costumes she wore in the theater. The effect they created was the same. She heard it in the applause and the catcalls from the audience and read it in the eyes of the men who joined them in his suite or watched her enter a restaurant. It was a world from which she now wanted desperately to escape, but there were moments, moments like today, when she wondered if she would ever find any other.

Sammy Rosen stayed three weeks in Germany, conferring every few days by telephone with Georges Louvier.

"We arranged that he would always call at eleven," Georges told Abby. "He said it's impossible to get through to you at the hotel late at night and that the concierge is too stupid to take a message during the day." He thought that with this creation Marie-Claire had surpassed herself. He had paid enough of Madame Thérèse's bills to know that the one sent to Sammy Rosen had been enormous. But worth the expense, well worth every franc. Abby's dress was exactly the color of the finest sandy beach along the Côte d'Azur, her shoes and handbag of supple leather dyed to match, her linen gloves cut to the precise length of her fingers. She wore no jewelry but the emerald ring, her face had been so skillfully made up that he could not tell where nature ended and artifice began, and her perfume was the faintest suggestion of roses and lilies. She looked every inch a Parisian, chic and cool, reserved and yet enticing. "Will you take an aperitif while we wait?"

"Yes. Thank you, Georges. Has he found what he was looking for?"

"Not yet. He says the girls are too hard and all the shows too frenetic, too desperately gay for New York. I told him that before he left, but he had to see it for himself. Germany is a strange place nowadays. The war has not been over long enough for anyone to be able to forget it. Least of all the Germans."

She sipped the drink he handed her, looking curiously around his office, trying not to keep glancing at the silent phone. She thought the room suited him; it was what she had always imagined a gentleman's private study would look like. Wood-paneled walls, hundreds of books behind glass-fronted shelves, a massive desk with silver inkstand and ornately framed pictures of his family, leather-cushioned armchairs, a rug patterned in tones of light and dark burgundy, faded just enough to let you know it must be very old and very valuable.

"I was trained in the law, you know," he said. "A family tradition. I represent only a few clients now, personal friends who will let no one else manage their affairs, and three or four charming widows inherited from my father."

"He was a lawyer also?"

"Six generations of lawyers, my dear. One son to each father, and every one of them obedient. I often wonder what my ancestors would have done if any of them had refused. None did, however, and each one increased his son's inheritance. I shall be the last." His eyes twinkled as he said it. "The renegade. It's the fault of all that scheming and saving and good management of property."

"Don't you enjoy the practice of law, Georges? The drama of a courtroom and the battle of wits with an opponent?"

"You're thinking of criminal law and saving some poor wretch from the guillotine he richly deserves. I merely shuffle sums of money around and dictate documents whose wording hasn't changed since Napoleon's day. In fact, Abby, I will admit to you that I was very, very bored until Sammy came to Paris last year. There's no challenge in keeping what you've got. It's the gambling of it that's exciting."

This was a side of him that she had never suspected, yet it was the only logical explanation for the partnership that seemed so accidental and contradictory. "I thought you told me once that the French were a practical people."

"We are. We're the most practical people in Europe. My daughters, my wife, Marie-Claire, they are all well provided for with incomes I could not touch no matter how badly I wanted to. Even the gambling I spoke of is as safe as speculation ever is. I never buy more than a share of a horse, many different horses, and Sammy, of course, may be depended upon to turn whatever he touches to gold."

You had to have money to make money, that was what

he was telling her. Investments, horses, trusts, the acquisition of paintings such as Marie-Claire's, treasures handed down from one generation to the next, all these things and the kind of life they represented were incomprehensible to her. Her mother had called people like that the gentry. In only one way did she resemble them, and that was in the clothing she was wearing and the ring she was twisting around on her finger. Even Sammy Rosen didn't belong to that class. His money was too new, his education too limited, his ways still too quick and hungry. But he amused them, he made their blood run a little faster and their hearts beat more loudly. Ultimately, because he earned a profit for himself, he made someone like Georges Louvier even richer.

The telephone rang, a shrill double peal that seemed out of place and presumptive. Abby lit a cigarette, picked up her drink and waited. She could hear a crackling, static noise as Georges held the receiver to his ear, a tinny-sounding voice that faded away, then was suddenly very loud.

"Abby is here. Abby," Georges repeated. "Yes, yes. All right. Thursday then." He held the apparatus out to her, and she leaned across the desk to take it.

"Sammy? Sammy, are you there?" More of the crackling, as if branches were breaking across the line as it snaked through Germany's dark forests. "I can hardly hear you." There was an explosive pop, then the connection cleared.

". . . thinking you must be bored," he was saying. "I told that Englishman, Anthony Osgood, to amuse you while I was away. You remember him, don't you?"

"Yes, of course." Insolent hands and hot breath in her ear on the dance floor. "I think he's gone home to London. When will you be back?" She could hear him as clearly now as if he were in the next room. Georges was pouring himself another drink, his back turned to her, politely pretending he wasn't there.

"I don't know. It may take longer than I had planned. Are you sure Osgood hasn't called, Abby? Your concierge is an idiot."

"I'm not bored, Sammy, and there haven't been any messages at the hotel." Why was he talking about Osgood when there was so much else he could be telling her? "Is it important?"

"Just a question of money. Let me speak to Georges again."

"I do miss you. And I've run up a terrible bill with Madame Thérèse." The crackling noise began again and she couldn't tell whether he answered her or not. She wanted to say so much more to him, but she would have had to shout the words. "Georges?" She handed the phone to him and lit another cigarette. When had Marie-Claire arrived? Abby hadn't heard her come into the room.

"We have reservations at a little northern Italian restaurant just off the Champs-Élysées. Cream sauces with a hint of lemon," Marie-Claire whispered. "It goes well in Germany?"

"I think so. The connection fades in and out. I couldn't understand everything he said."

"The taxi is waiting, my dear." She blew a kiss at Georges, who was listening intently to whatever Sammy was saying, the auxiliary receiver pressed against his other ear. "After lunch we are going to the Sainte Chapelle, and you must recite the names of the queens of the Louis to me."

She had the impression that Marie-Claire was hurrying her out of the office, drawing her away before she could begin to wonder what Sammy was saying to bring such a strange, almost embarrassed expression to Georges' face. And Georges himself, so easy and relaxed with her a few minutes ago, speaking of his family and his personal life as he had never done before, looked angry now. She had never seen him pursue a quarrel with Sammy, never known him to do more than shrug his shoulders and let the subject drop when discussing a point on which they disagreed. She had thought him a man whose control of emotion was as much habit as inclination, but perhaps she had judged too quickly. There was no mistaking the brusqueness with which he nodded at them, nor the tension in the hand that held the phone. So cordial before, welcoming her as warmly as if she were the wife or daughter of a cherished friend, he now wanted her gone.

She hardly touched the Cuscinetti di Vitello, played with the leaves of her salad as though the oil glistening on them had mesmerized her, and finally, when Marie-Claire's bright, chirpy efforts at conversation had died away into the busy noontime clatter of the restaurant, pleaded a headache. Just before her taxi sped away into the traffic that whirled suicid-

ally around the Arc de Triomphe, she looked back toward the
corner where Marie-Claire had kissed her on both cheeks as if
this parting were somehow different from all the others, almost
as though she had been trying to strengthen her for a long
journey. It may have been a trick of the light, but she thought
the older woman's eyes were unusually bright, as though the sun
had found two pools of unshed tears in which to reflect itself.

There was mail for her at the hotel, two envelopes which
the concierge handed her even before she asked for her key.
One had no return address, no stamp, and the writing on it
was unfamiliar, the other was from her mother. Bridget wrote
with a child's arduously formed loops and curlicues, a style of
penmanship taught by the nuns in cold stone schools all over
Ireland, never forgotten, as much a part of her as the prayers
she had laboriously copied out to learn it. The letter was
short; Abby read it standing at the desk while the concierge
looked on and smiled. She had sold many stamps to this
American, assured her that yes, every letter she handed to
her was safely deposited in the postman's pouch that very
same day. She approved of a young girl who wrote so frequently to her mother. One of the natural functions of a
concierge was to know everything that went on within the
walls that enclosed her entire life.

> We are well, and pray that you are too [Bridget had
> written]. Your dad has been to see the doctor last
> week, and now he has a set of leather braces to
> make the walking easier. The boys are healthy,
> thanks be to God, as I am myself except for a chill
> because of the rain. Father Phelan says our Tom
> has the makings of a priest, very good on the altar
> and with the Latin and never missing Holy Mass or
> Communion. It's a blessing to be proud of, he says,
> and the education at the seminary is free. Mrs.
> Goldbaum's son is graduating college next month.
> Say a word to her when you write. She keeps your
> letters for me and always asks how you are doing.
> Your loving mother who prays for you every day
> and may the Blessed Mother keep you safe.
> P.S. Mrs. Goldbaum took me to a bank. She said
> it wasn't smart to keep it in the house.

It was as though Bridget stood beside her, pouring tea and telling her the news of the day. But Thomas a priest? She was amused by Father Phelan's duplicity, and she wondered how many other bright Catholic boys he had sponsored, knowing full well that they hadn't true vocations, just brains and talents that would be wasted without the education to sharpen them. Theoretically the seminary was a first serious step toward the priesthood, but she knew that many who attended it never went any further and there was no disgrace when they changed their minds, nothing like the stigma attached to those very few she had heard of who left after ordination. She thought she detected a hint of Mrs. Goldbaum's pragmatism in her mother's comment about the schooling being free. "So what could he lose?" Leon's mother must have said. "A college education for nothing? A Jew should be so lucky."

"*De bonnes nouvelles, mademoiselle?*" the concierge asked.

"*Oui, madame.* Very good news."

"*La famille?*"

"Yes, from my family in the United States." She smiled at the thin little woman who was always at her desk no matter what time of the day or night Abby entered or left the hotel. Their conversations were always short, always punctuated by gestures and smiles that filled in the gaps left by the American's faltering French and the concierge's scanty English. How could Sammy have called her an idiot? The headache suddenly became very real, and with it came a question, a suspicion that perhaps he had never tried to call her here. But why would he lie?

"*Coups de téléphone?*" she asked. What was the word for Germany? "*De l'Allemagne, de Berlin?*"

"*Non, non. Rien. Pas de coups de téléphone.*"

Nothing. No calls. "*Hier?*" Yesterday? She ran through the days of the week, ticking them off on her fingers as she had done when Marie-Claire taught them to her. The concierge shook her head. No, she was certain that Mademoiselle Sullivan had not received any calls. She pantomimed writing. She would have written down a message if there had been anything of such importance.

"*Merci.*" Abby refolded Bridget's letter, creasing the two sheets of paper over and over again until finally they tore and the pieces fluttered to the floor. The other envelope still lay on the concierge's high desk, bearing only her name in a starkly black, almost illegible scrawl.

She picked it up, holding it away from her as though it were wet or soiled, reading the note quickly, turning as white as if someone had slapped her across the face. The concierge watched her enter the tiny glassed-in elevator, listened to the creak and the protesting hum of the old machinery and stepped out from behind her desk to pick up the pieces of Madame Sullivan's letter to her daughter. She was certain mademoiselle would be grateful later to have them.

"What does it mean, Bette?" Abby hadn't waited for her knock to be acknowledged, hadn't asked if she could come in, had offered no explanations, simply appeared in the doorway with a letter in her outstretched hand and that question, asked in a voice that was flat and far too loud for the square little room where Bette Blumfeld had been sleeping off a magnificent lunch and too much wine. "Read it," she said, "and then tell me what it means."

Jesus H. Christ, not today. Not with a show to do tonight and probably another fight with wardrobe afterward. It wasn't like Sammy to handle it this way. Some bitch in the line must have picked up on the gossip backstage and rushed right off to find out for herself how true it was.

"It's an invitation," Bette said, reading the note, trying to remember what it was Sammy had told her about the English lord with the prematurely bald head and sun-freckled complexion. He played polo and kept an apartment in Paris for weekends away from London and his wife. "Nice. I'd like to have somebody ask me to spend some time at a château in the country. What's the problem? We're dark one night a week. You can go anywhere you want as long as you're back in time for the next show."

"You know exactly what I'm asking, Bette. Sammy set this up before he left, didn't he? I talked to him a few hours ago. He wanted to know whether Osgood had called me yet. He said he was thinking I must be bored. I need some answers, and you're the only one who can give them to me."

"You better sit down, kid. This may take a while, and I don't think I know any way to make it hurt any less than it has to."

"It already hurts," Abby said softly. "I just want to make

sure I really understand what he's doing. I don't want any mistakes about it. I need to hear it."

"It happens to all of us," Marie-Claire said. "Often more than once. But the first time is the worst because we don't expect it, we don't have any defenses built up yet."

"You're not surprised, are you?"

"No, Abby, I'm not. Experience has taught me to read the signs and believe in them."

"Do you know what he thought would happen, what he was arranging so carefully? His own replacement, another lover. No scenes, no explanations, no chance even to ask why. Everything tidy and neat and settled by the time he got back. And he would have stayed away until it was, until I had gotten the point of it all and backed out of his life gracefully. Those aren't exactly the words Bette used, but they're close enough." She remembered that she hadn't interrupted Bette Blumfeld, hadn't cried or cursed or even gotten angry. And she'd thanked Bette at the end, thanked her, gone to her room, lain down on the bed, gotten up again to go to the theater, smiled through the show as if nothing had changed, walked the few blocks back to the hotel alone, lain down on the bed again, not bothering to turn on the light, staring into the dark until morning, as stiff and unfeeling as a block of wood. But now the numbness had worn off, and she wanted, she needed to talk, to tell it no matter how badly it hurt, tell it, get it over with and begin to pick up the pieces.

"Once, in New York, he told me that life was very simple, a series of business arrangements between a buyer and a seller, and that as long as both parties were satisfied, the bargain was a good one. He even reminded me that every contract ended sometime. I told him my memory was good, that I wouldn't forget." Never forget that lunch at the Plaza, her forcing him to say more than he had intended.

"What are you afraid of, Abby?" Marie-Claire's voice was so soft, so gentle. She might have been a wise old priest hidden behind the screen of the confessional.

"I don't know. I'm not sure. Of so many things someone like you can never understand. My mother scrubs the floor of a train station at night, but no matter how hard she works, there's never enough money. She was beautiful when she was young, but she's an old, old woman now, worn out and with nothing and no one to turn to but the Church."

"Don't you believe anymore?"

"No. I don't believe as she does, as I was taught to, but I still pray. I can't help myself."

"Sammy," Marie-Claire prompted. "Tell me about Sammy. You're not really in love with him, you know. Was he the first?"

"The only one. He said that he wanted to give me the opportunity to make choices, and that coming to Paris was the first and the easiest one."

"And so you did."

"I shared his apartment in New York. He gave me things—clothes, jewelry, money."

"Was that so bad?"

"They weren't gifts, Marie-Claire. I *earned* them."

"Of course you did. That was part of the contract. And when an arrangement burns itself out, you keep whatever you've earned. That's also understood. I've watched you, Abby. You haven't the right sort of temperament for this game. In fact, if you had known how to do it, you would have ended it yourself weeks ago. I think it was just ignorance of the rules that kept you hanging on so desperately."

"You make it sound like such a cold, passionless thing, Marie-Claire."

"Sometimes it is."

"Not for me."

"Be honest with yourself, my dear. And be fair to Sammy. When we're very young, as young as you are, and especially if it's the first time, we want to believe it's love, that it can't be anything but love. And so it is, in its own way. But, believe me, if you are ever fortunate enough to encounter the real thing, your first passion soon becomes a never quite forgotten but harmless little joke played on you by a hungry body and an inexperienced heart. I don't think you Americans perceive this as clearly as we do. You don't want to make allowances for nature, you make life a battle between sin and virtue. It's so much more realistic to see it as a playground, and to believe that we are all as innocent as animals obeying their instincts."

"That would be chaos, Marie-Claire."

"Of course. So we draw up a few rules to make the game

run more smoothly. For myself, I've always accepted the rules and they protect me. You, I think, must go back to the beginning and realize that they were there even though you pretended not to acknowledge them. When I say that you never really loved Sammy, that you're not in love with him now, I'm not wrong, am I, Abby?"

"No. I wish I could tell you that you were."

"Wake up, little one. It's been a good dream, but if you refuse to learn from it, it could turn into a nightmare."

"There was never time for anyone before I met Sammy. Never any hope. They were all boys, and when I looked at them, I could only see the defeated men I knew they'd eventually become. He was so different. He lived in another world."

"You see? Already you begin to understand."

"The lovemaking, Marie-Claire." Even now Abby could feel the blood reddening her cheeks.

"It feels good, *n'est-ce pas?* The nuns didn't tell us that, did they? Good women, most of them, but so terrified of breaking their vow of chastity that they tried to turn all of us into reluctant virgins. Many a young girl has found her husband disappointing because she was taught that duty is a hard taskmaster. She discovers herself only with a lover."

"I thought there would be more than that."

"Marriage? Would marrying Sammy make it all come right somehow? Would it absolve the guilt, as though you were a bride hiding a pregnancy with her bouquet? That makes you laugh. I don't believe you're as deeply hurt as you thought you were. Your pride is suffering, and that's only natural. You've been replaced a bit more quickly than usual. And Sammy himself is being awkward about it. He seems to have forgotten that you're too new at the game to catch all the signals."

"Tell me about Léonie Martin, Marie-Claire. Bette said that she's bought her quiet house in the country. Everyone in the company seems to know that the money to pay for it will be earned in New York."

"It's little enough to compensate for all she's lost over the years. She's nearing the end of whatever pleasures are left to her, Abby, while you're just at the beginning. I'm a few years older than she, and I remember when she was singing in cafés for less than the price of the dress you're wearing. She's not cruel and she's not rapacious, whatever you may think. She looked at you and saw what I'm seeing now—a young, very young and very beautiful woman. If you sold the emerald ring, Abby, you could live off it for a year. Comfortably. She looked at you and she looked at herself and she listened to Sammy. He's what she needs, what her son needs. She's always chosen badly until now, always loved without counting the cost. We adore her and we weep with her because of that, because we're too cautious to make those generous, tragic mistakes. She makes them for us. She said in a newspaper interview once that she didn't dare step onto a stage to sing unless she was in love. She's fragile. She makes love to her audiences with her voice, but audiences leave a theater before a performer has his makeup off. She has to have a man nearby when she works, someone to reassure her before the curtain goes up, someone to be waiting in the wings when she finishes, someone to sit with her and make love to her while the little boy sleeps. She didn't choose Sammy, he chose her. It would have been the same even if you had been married to him. This is *her* time. There's nothing you can do to change that."

"And you think I should be practical?"

"I think you know you have to be. For the mother who scrubs floors and the brothers you told me about."

"I'm going home, Marie-Claire."

"Wait. Work and sleep and take long walks in the rain. Give yourself a chance to heal before you decide."

"I already have. I knew it this morning. I'm not a prostitute and I won't let Sammy Rosen pimp for me."

"She won't change her mind," Marie-Claire reported to Georges a few days later. "She's been to Cook's to book a ticket, and last night she didn't go to the theater. They've already replaced her."

"It doesn't matter. Sammy knows. Lord Osgood was confused, and in the way of the English he blundered into Germany via telephone. He's gone to Monte Carlo to recoup his loss at the tables."

"How easy to watch a wheel spin and know the little black ball will bounce the way it should for a lord."

"Sammy thought he was being kind, to arrange things for her."

"She was too young to understand arrangements, Georges."

"And now?"

"Now she feels too old to believe in them."

"When does she sail?"

"Another week."

"And in the meantime?"

"She walks. Along the river, across the bridges, along the river again."

"I have a horse running at Longchamps next Thursday."

"How could you have remained a lawyer for all these years, Georges? Lawyers are not supposed to have hearts."

"The horses are as beautiful in their way as the cathedrals she's seen. Prayers are cold, but no one forgets his first race. We will give her something nearly as good as love to remember from Paris." Could anything replace the bad memories? "If nothing else, it will distract her."

Her favorite walk was along the Quai de la Mégisserie, Notre Dame beckoning from its island in the middle of the Seine, the wooden stalls of the *bouquinistes* hinting at treasures to be found in their piles of secondhand books. Watercolors of Paris fluttered from the roofs of the stalls, barges on which industrious wives hung out lines of blue washing plowed the Seine, the peal of Notre Dame's great bells sent pigeons swirling into the air, and everywhere she looked, lovers strolled hand in hand, pausing in the cool, leafy shade of chestnut trees to kiss, to press close to one another, to whisper and make promises. This section of Paris breathed peace and antiquity. She thought it must not have changed in hundreds of years, the cathedral, the river, the pairs of young men and women made beautiful by the light that shone on their faces.

She had come here every day for a week, drawn to this spot as to no other, strolling from stall to stall, sometimes sitting for hours on one of the iron benches watching the life of the river, wondering what it must be like to be constantly traveling the waterways of France, how it felt to lean one's back against the smooth bark of a tree and taste last night's passion in the lips exploring your own so gently now in daylight. It soothed her to be surrounded by happy lovers, by the aproned women and the stout men in berets who kept the stalls and had begun to greet her familiarly. She brought sausages with her when she came, cheese, bread, and wine, in one of the string bags used by housewives doing their daily marketing. She ate the food slowly, sharing it with the plump, cooing pigeons, letting the wine lead her thoughts wherever they chose to go.

She had had to tell Tess and Bobby Stein, and she had done it brusquely, expecting her sister's anger, the hands balled into fists, the explosive Irish rage that rained down curses on Sammy Rosen's head. Bobby Stein's eyes had been pitying, and he had held her hand in his until she pulled away. Léonie Martin's name wasn't mentioned; she cut off Tess's first question rudely and refused to answer any others. She was leaving the show and going back to New York. It was over, by mutual consent. Period. She knew they didn't believe her, knew that sooner or later they would guess the truth, but by then she would be gone and the story would have the same flat impact as last week's news. She left the hotel before they were awake, and when they came in at night it was late enough to pretend to be asleep, to ignore Tess's knock on her door and the voice calling her name. She wanted to live these last days in Paris in silence.

"Use my apartment, kid," Bette had said, pressing the key into her hand. "The rent's paid, the phone's still connected, all you have to do is turn on the refrigerator and you're in business. I'll write a note to the super so he doesn't call the cops."

"Thank you, Bette. I hadn't really thought about where I'd stay. That's funny, isn't it? Get in a cab and then suddenly realize you don't have an address to give."

"You're welcome to stay there as long as you like. I don't know yet when I'll be leaving. Not for a few more months anyway."

"I'll have found something else by then."

"No hurry. Good apartments don't come cheap. I wouldn't mind having someone to split the rent."

"I couldn't, Bette. I really don't think I could do that." Sooner or later she'd pick up the phone and hear his voice again. Even if, as she now admitted to herself, even if she'd used him as much as he had used her, he was still the first and she'd never be quite able to forget that.

"So what are you going to do with yourself after you get back? You ought to be able to get into another show without any trouble. I can give you some names if you want, people to call who owe me a couple of favors."

Abby shook her head. "No more. I'm quitting while I still can, before I get in so deeply I start believing in the magic all over again. At least I've learned something. The looks don't last long enough, you can't count on luck alone, and I don't have even a fraction of the ambition that Sheila Cohen did. So where does that leave me ten years from now?" Bitterness was corrosive; she would not let it feed on her as it had on so many of the Irish she had watched reaching out for the drink, hating so hard they ate up their own souls.

Sammy had been generous, had played by the rules, just as Marie-Claire had predicted he would. The jewelry he had given her was in Georges Louvier's safe. In New York she would find a bank vault. She wouldn't wear a single piece of it ever again; the stones represented money, nothing else. Money and time. She didn't know how much of either she was going to need. She only knew that after Paris, New York this summer was going to be very cold and very lonely.

"He's a beautiful horse, Georges. I've never seen an animal like him. May I?" Her hand was inches away from the long, proud head, the huge brown eyes that reminded her of the mournful gaze of Italian children sitting on their stoops beside their parents on a summer evening in sweltering New York.

"Of course, Abby. He's not as skittish and temperamental as most racehorses. Not now. But after the race, and especially if he wins, you won't be able to get near him."

He held very still while she scratched the bony place where an irregular white star grew out of short, silky brown hair. She crooned his name, "Bravo, Bravo," delighting in the alert prick of his ears and the spark, she thought of recognition, in his eyes. "He knows his name."

"He likes the attention. You have to give them love, like children," Georges said. "Some horses need companions to keep them company, often a goat, a pony, or a dog. When they retire to stud, they have herds of mares, but the companions who shared their stalls when they were racing go with them."

"You make it sound almost like a romance." She stepped

back from the stall, and after a moment Bravo shook his great head and began to paw restlessly at the ground.

"You see. He begins to sense what's coming and to prepare himself. He scents the crowds in the stands and the excitement."

There were more people in the paddock area than when they had arrived, owners greeting one another and conferring with trainers, jockeys pacing and slapping their high boots with short, flexible whips, working themselves into a state of controlled tension and anticipation, elegant women in pastel dresses laughing and lightly embracing one another. It was an intimate world where everyone knew everyone else, where even the language was a kind of code and great sums of money were won or lost with casual, nonchalant grace.

Abby was glad she had come, glad that Marie-Claire had insisted when she would have refused the invitation. The *Stella Maris* was sailing tomorrow afternoon; she had visited the *bouquinistes* for the last time yesterday and found an exquisite leather-bound volume of poetry which the concierge at the hotel had accepted with tears in her eyes and an unexpectedly warm embrace that had touched her deeply. It seemed that everyone in Paris, and even the city itself, smiled at her and wished her well. She had worn one of Madame Thérèse's loveliest dresses today; the fabric was as sheer as a fine batiste handkerchief, and the color, a subtle blend of tones of gold and apricot, exactly matched her hair and made her skin seem sun-kissed, like the pale spring flowers that she had seen young lovers carrying beside the river. She thought that the Paris she had discovered had made her nearly whole again, more expertly than a physician, more lastingly than a priest. She smiled at nothing, at no one, almost drowsy, lifting her face to the sun, breathing in the rich meadow smell of this place, turning once around as if caught in a languorous ballet.

Someone was watching her, staring at her, eyes pulling at her, urging her to find and meet them. Confused, vaguely troubled by someone's urgency, a stranger's unvoiced command, she felt as if she were being tugged out of a deep, drugged sleep. The sunlight suddenly seemed uncomfortably hot, the odor from Bravo's stall so pungent and overpowering that she put a hand up to cover her nose and mouth. Twenty feet away, Marie-Claire and Georges stood talking to a dark-skinned man, a man as slender and tightly muscled as any of the diminutive jockeys, but tall, a figure glimpsed from far away, a shadow against the sky. Hawk-nosed, burning black eyes beneath straight, heavy brows, a stillness about him that made her think of the sudden hush backstage in the few seconds before the curtain opened. Sicilian? No, more like an Arab; desert sands and flowing white robes would be as natural to him as the Seine and the misty Paris evenings had felt to her.

"Abby," Georges called. "Come here. I want you to meet another of Bravo's owners."

They seemed miles and miles away, the group of three, Georges' arm beckoning to her, Marie-Claire's puzzled, questioning face, the dark man who was drawing her to him as though he had sent out a cord that had wrapped itself around her waist. Slowly, very slowly, she moved toward them, one hand still veiling the lower part of her face, the green eyes above it enormous around the pinprick pupils.

"Are you all right?" Marie-Claire asked.

"Yes, of course." She was. The giddiness had passed, and the odd feeling of walking in a dreamworld, of inhabiting a body that was not her own.

"I want you to meet a friend who will be joining us in the owners' box," Georges said. "Mademoiselle Abby Sullivan, Monsieur Joseph Kelemen."

Lips against the skin of her hand, the eyes she could not read never leaving her face for an instant.

"Abby is sailing for America tomorrow," Marie-Claire said. "I have tried to persuade her that she must not leave us, Joseph, but . . ." She left the rest of the sentence dangling in the clear air.

"And your ship, Miss Sullivan?" His English was nearly perfect, his voice very deep.

"The *Stella Maris*." He had taken her arm in his, matched his stride to hers, was leading her away from the paddocks, toward the stands where she could hear the rumbling, wavelike noise of the crowd.

"You will enjoy the voyage, I'm sure."

"You've sailed on her?"

"Many times."

He left her side only once that afternoon, not to place a bet, because runners came to the box before every race.

When he returned, it was to smile and order champagne and touch his glass to hers. "It seems that we shall be fellow passengers, Miss Sullivan. I find the North Atlantic suddenly more attractive than Paris."

Surprised, not understanding at first what he meant, then catching a glimpse of Marie-Claire's quickly suppressed smile and Georges' satisfied nod, Abby flushed and raised binoculars to her eyes. The horses below leaped into magnified life; she could almost feel the shudders along their flanks, smell the warm breath, read the hot desire to run and win. She thought confusedly that the man beside her was very much like these blooded animals held barely in check at the starting gate. There was about him the same aura of danger, of excitement, of hidden forces waiting to be let loose. Of control also, and something else, secrets and a past that would not easily, perhaps never, be revealed. But with all of that, she felt no fear of him, no sense either that there would ever be cause to fear him. And, oddly, when she finally lowered the binoculars, turned, and allowed herself to meet this stranger's compelling eyes, she thought she detected a look of recognition, of old hunger suddenly appeased. It was as if he knew her already, could read her mind, heard and welcomed the sudden skip of her heart.

Bravo thundered around the Longchamps track, dark and swift and determined, running so passionately that all the others in the race seemed hardly to be moving at all. The champagne that Joseph Kelemen and Abby Sullivan drank became a river, and when the next day's sun rose to gild the spires and twin towers of Notre Dame, its rays found them too, she leaning against the cool, damp trunk of a chestnut tree, he bent over her, drinking in the light from her green eyes as thirstily as a man who has just stumbled out of a barren desert, down sloping hills of sand, into the waters of an oasis he has nearly despaired of ever finding again.

PART TWO
Joseph
January 1912–1914

5

A dog howled in its sleep somewhere in the cluster of
mud-brick houses huddled around the oasis that had
given Fort Bel Nama its name.

The only noise Joseph Kelemen made as he turned his
body to face the direction from which the sound had come
was the oily clink of the three-foot chain securing his rifle to
his wrist. He waited. Then, satisfied that it had been neither
a signal nor a warning, he reached for the pail of now tepid
coffee that had been boiling hot when he first came on duty.
Thick and brutally shocking to the nerves, it would have been
considered swill in any café of the reasonably civilized world.
Yet perversely, proudly, because their very existence was a
slap in the face of weaker, more fastidious men, legionnaires
thrived on it, commenting laconically to the *bleus*, the recruits who spat it out at first taste, that unless the brew was
viscous enough to float a bullet, it was too weak to satisfy
anyone who wore the white kepi and had left Europe behind
when he signed his enlistment papers.

Criminals, political exiles, runaway husbands, disappointed
lovers, drunkards, and veterans of other armies were common in the Legion's ranks, but there were also dreamers,
adventurers, poets, the disenchanted, and always a fair sprinkling of youths who had enlisted on a bet, a dare, or simply
because they had failed their university examinations. Background meant nothing at all in this army from which only
Frenchmen were excluded.

In Europe the now twenty-five-year-old Joseph Kelemen
had been good-looking in quite an ordinary way, but here in
the Sahara the sun had tanned his skin to a deep-golden olive

115

and the arduous marches of the Legion had pared away every ounce of fat from his bones. He was as lean and lithe as an animal that lives by its wits and its speed. His eyes were hooded, as they had not been before, a habit born of the necessity to spare them the worst of the sand's glare. His nose was sharply aquiline, his clean-shaven face an oddity among the mainly bearded men with whom he lived. His own parents in far-off Budapest might not have recognized him in a crowd. With a few strokes of a borrowed pen on the document that was more binding than a marriage certificate, he had chosen what he had known was the only possible way to win the final argument with his father, and after four and a half years of service he had become more Bedouin in appearance than was entirely safe for any legionnaire to be.

The long-standing quarrel had had no single beginning, no truces, and because Julius Kelemen was the master of his house, the son had lost skirmish after skirmish. Joseph had never discovered precisely what it was that set them at one another like dogs meeting on a common pathway. He knew only that the struggle had gone on for years and years, that his successes in school were proof that he could do better, his musicianship a demand for longer and longer hours of practice, his love affair with books the sign of an academic but undisciplined mind, the daydreams into which he fell an unproductive, Bohemian vice, the drawings with which he covered the pages of his notebooks dangerous follies that could lead him into the dissolute life of an artist. Julius Kelemen's practice left him little leisure; patients consumed his energies and interests, leaving for the son only rules and schedules and thirty minutes a day during which to gauge progress and berate the boy for failing to achieve the perfection no child could.

Joseph had not been opposed to the study of medicine. In time he could have become as famous and honored a physician as his father, and he would have been happy either in a laboratory or at the bedsides of the sick. But he had wanted to travel that summer during which his trunks were being packed, to visit Italy and England and France, to walk through museums about which he had only read, to hear the Divine Sarah declaim on a Paris stage, to laugh and sing and drink and court pretty actresses in the company of two other young men who were also destined for the Vienna Medical Faculty.

The scheme was both ridiculous and unthinkable, he was told, a squalid waste of valuable time. Medicine was not a career for which one prepared in beer halls and cabarets. Until mid-July, when a celebrated Viennese researcher had agreed to take him into his animal laboratory to wash glassware, sweep floors, clean out cages, and transcribe notes, he would make rounds with his father every day. By the time he attended his first lecture, he would know more than any other first-year student. Without money of his own, it was useless to argue and too humiliating to plead.

It was a hot summer. Illness stank, and no matter how often Joseph washed his hands or changed his clothes, the smells of dying people clung to him. He was always tired; at night, when he couldn't sleep, he reread letters and cards from Bologna, Venice, Rome. His friends, traveling on liberal letters of credit, expected to reach Paris on the very day that he was scheduled to enter the stifling, fetid atmosphere of the animal laboratory. He grew paler and more listless as the weeks dragged on, pleasing Julius Kelemen less than at any other time in his life.

He didn't plan it, didn't even know he was going to do it until he saw his trunks piled on the quay in Vienna and heard behind him the sounds of the Orient Express gathering up steam for its run to Paris. He had enough Austrian money in his wallet to buy a ticket and live frugally for perhaps a week, but he knew he could borrow more. The train was already moving when he swung himself aboard; later, after he had seen Paris, he would begin to worry about the consequences of defying his father.

At the Georges V he was told that his friends had stayed only two nights, making new reservations for late August, when they expected to return from London. They had left no forwarding address, but if monsieur cared to give a letter into the care of the manager, he would see that it was kept for them. There seemed little point to it; he hadn't enough funds to last that long in this city.

The women strolling on the Champs-Elysées were exquisite creatures, the lacy steel of the Tour Eiffel as graceful, as breathtakingly beautiful as every other structure in Paris. He visited them all, wandering from the wide, tree-lined

boulevards of the beau monde to the twisting alleyways of
writers and artists, subsisting on cheap wine, bread, and
plates of steamy pot-au-feu bought in restaurants so tiny that
only a handful of workingmen could be served at any one
time. Tickets to the museums cost practically nothing, the
cathedrals were free, and by sleeping in the Latin Quarter, in
a room no bigger than a closet, he saved enough to see
Bernhardt, not once, but twice. Sometime during that week
he picked up a newspaper left lying on a café table in the
Boulevard St. Michel. Nine European workmen had been
massacred in Casablanca; French forces were being rushed to
the city. It was feared that the unrest in Morocco would
spread to the border, would reawaken the tribes that the
Legion had only begun to subdue in westernmost Algeria.
And because there was such contradictory information coming from Casablanca, the correspondent had filled out his
story by retelling the history of the Foreign Legion, by
listing, one after another, its successes in the Sahara. They
weren't welcome on French soil, but in the colonies legionnaires were irreplaceable.

With the few coins remaining in his pockets, he had sent
a telegram to Budapest, that much and no more. No explanation, just the stark announcement that his trunks could be
collected in Vienna if anyone wanted to reclaim them from
the pension where his board had been prepaid for a year. By
the time the piece of flimsy yellow paper had been delivered
to the decorous and unostentatiously rich house on the
Tabakgasse, he had been processed through Vincennes and
sent clattering through the night to Marseilles and quick
embarkation to Algeria. The Legion did not surrender those
who had turned to it—not to parents, not to lovers, wives or
mistresses, not even to governments. It was a land and a life
all its own, fiercely protective of those who chose it, promising only a minimum of five years of concealment and French
citizenship to any who survived and cared to claim it.

There were no surprises in a Legion fort of the type to
which Joseph Kelemen was ultimately assigned. The design
was repeated without variation in dozens of isolated locations.
Remote and chronically undermanned, built as often atop a
natural outcropping of rock as on the shifting sand itself, they
were supremely functional, efficient, and cheerless. A company of one hundred men and three officers could raise the

three-foot thick walls of mud and stone within four weeks of pacing off the foundation. Barracks, infirmary, storerooms, stables, and officers' quarters took longer to build, but the fort became a manned garrison from the moment that its heavy wooden gate was hung and its bolts secured.

Everything needed to support life at Bel Nama was hauled in on the backs of camels and mules. The gate was brought in pieces and reassembled, as were the wooden frames of the hemp-strung cots on which the men slept. Not a scrap of lumber was wasted in the treeless desert. The barracks floors were hardened mud strewn with clean white sand, the latrines open trenches that boiled in the hot sun, the washing facilities a common trough, a legionnaire's closet the wooden peg above his cot and the tin trunk that stood at the foot. Macaroni, rice, flour, dried beans, figs and dates, coffee, sugar, salt, wine, preserved fish and meat lay stacked to the ceiling of the locked storeroom. To pilfer from these provisions was a crime only a little less serious than desertion; the supply trains seldom came more than twice a year. Changes had been made in many places along the frontier; larger, stronger forts built at strategically important points, garrisons from which the commander of the southern region could order hundreds of men into the desert. But Oran, administrative center of the northern sector, had been reluctant to abandon forts like Bel Nama. Sixty men were considered sufficient to man it; troops were rationed as closely as the supplies with which to maintain them.

Dennis O'Brien lay awake in Bel Nama's six-by-five-foot disciplinary cell. His feet were flattened on the door of his prison, his head butted against the opposite wall. Staring at a tiny, barred square of star-flecked sky, he measured off the long hours of darkness as he had done every night for more than a week. He slept by day, rousing to eat the food that was handed in to him and to make the twice-daily walk to the latrine trench that was the only exercise he was permitted. His leg muscles had begun to knot every few hours with painful, stinging cramps; he massaged them, kneading the flesh with the huge, powerful hands that had encircled the wiry little Italian's neck and snapped his spine as effortlessly as a small stick of firewood.

Every night he expected to be released, every morning

he cursed his lover's cowardice, never knowing if that would be the day on which the march to the disciplinary battalion at Colomb-Béchar would begin. None of the dozen or more witnesses to the crime had been able to deny the simple facts of what had happened. One moment Abruzzo had been leaning into his face, droplets of tobacco-stained saliva wetting his lips and spraying through the gaps in his teeth, slyly, lasciviously whispering that a man of O'Brien's size and stiffness must surely be too much for young Erich's mouth to hold; the next he was crumpled on the floor, his head at an absurd angle, the eyes bulged out and staring, the foul tongue lolling from the even filthier mouth.

O'Brien could not remember the act of killing. He had done it all right, but between Abruzzo's last words and the sight of the body sprawled at his feet, there existed moments, whole minutes of his life that he would never recall. His arms and his hands had not forgotten; they tingled and the fingers curled toward his palms whenever he thought of Abruzzo. And think of him he did, not of the corpse or the living vermin he had exterminated, but of Abruzzo, the fate that had been awaiting him, the incarnation of the devil pitilessly riding his soul.

It had begun so long ago, so quietly, so insidiously. Perhaps the inclination had always been there, tucked away beneath a fold of skin or lodged in a spot from which he was helpless to pluck it out. He had come to believe that it was so. Once his soul had been filled and shining with the love of God and the desire for self-sacrifice, but as the seminary tried to pound obedience and a sense of his own unworthiness into him, the love of God shrank to a cold, forced striving, and the empty corners of his heart cried out to be filled. By the time the candidates for ordination were practicing in earnest for the celebration of their first Masses, he had already had several lovers. All of them priests-to-be, all of them prepared to hold the Body and Blood of Christ between fingers that had delighted in the ultimate impurity.

Parish work was every young priest's crucible. Prying, sharp-eyed, knife-tongued old women, hordes of dirty little boys and scrubbed-faced girls who had to be taught their catechism, honey-voiced young women looking at you from eyes that teased, young men who drank too much and had the spirit leached out of them by having to live on the dole, married couples who fought constantly and produced a baby every year, sodalities and altar societies whose members bickered and pulled you into their intrigues, nuns in the parish school who caned their pupils and dared you to interfere, the worn-out pastor who was jealous of your youth. Sins that you thought you would commit no more came back to tempt and torment you. There were hours and hours of drudgery and nights spent remembering when you should have been asleep.

It was a boy who did it finally, who stole Dennis O'Brien's vocation, a boy very much like his younger self, intelligent, handsome, his only ambition to be a priest like Father O'Brien. He was seventeen and very malleable. He brought his Latin books to the rectory, stayed to eat dinner sometimes when the pastor was called out to comfort the sick or administer the Last Sacrament, walked the lanes with his mentor talking of the saints and what little theology he knew, gave up seeing lovely Maggie Flynn since it would lead nowhere, and one day, when the fish were biting and his eyes shone bluer than the Irish sky, shyly disrobed down to his shorts to swim in the cool water of the River Liffey.

His mother found him the next morning hanging from a beam, his bare toes inches above the overturned stool onto which he had climbed. Widow woman that she was, with no other children to console her, she begged and pleaded with Father O'Brien to allow the lad to lie in consecrated ground. But suicide is mortal sin, and he had written no note that might have proved him to be of unsound mind. Dennis O'Brien left the parish, left Ireland, after having walked in a plain black suit, his cassock forever put aside, behind the coffin that had not a single flower on it to soften the lines of the box. He was twenty-eight years old that summer, guilty of the damnation of one soul and of the loss of one life, wholly incapable of taking his own in expiation.

He did the next best thing. He found the Legion and dropped into its obscurity, the closest he could come to living hell. In North Africa he discovered a culture in which women played so insignificant a part that boys and men loved one another without shame. He chose his lovers carefully and treated them gently, accepting only those who were no longer initiates. After seven years in the Legion he was neither soft, nor was he young.

Strangely enough, though he had come here to claim the

death the Legion promised its recruits, he found that he had attached himself more strongly than ever to life. The devil and God shared his soul, sometimes one, then the other gaining ascendancy, and Dennis O'Brien, possessed by a black sense of humor, grimly watched the combat. This round would go to the Prince of Darkness. Abruzzo had been his minion, the only murder he had committed with the strength of his own hands. Long, long ago, that first time in the seminary, he ought to have known that a forbidden passion once unleashed becomes a demon. He ought to have read his future, ought to have known there was no evading it.

There were pools of blackness in the corners of the compound, long shafts of darkness along the porches that fronted the barracks and the commandant's quarters. The flagpole was a deadly fencing foil reaching upward to rip the fabric of the sky. The mules in the stables shifted in their sleep, blowing a bellows breath of air through their nostrils. Several times each hour the sentries turned their faces toward the disciplinary cell built along the west wall, their separate thoughts pulled as if by a magnet to the man who lay within, knowing that he too was awake and surely wondering if the crime had been worth what lay ahead of him. The reputation of Colomb-Béchar was enough to make them break out in a sweat even on a night as cool as this one.

The six weeks of training exercises, which began as soon as recruits stepped onto the docks at Oran, quickly dispelled any illusions picked up in romanticized novels or the popular press. Joseph Kelemen never forgot the shock of the first few days, the agonies through which his body had suffered, the feeling of hopelessness that had washed over him when he first realized that he and every other *bleu* in their company were considered fair victims for any cruelty a sergeant cared to inflict on them. Three or four men in every new group committed suicide before the six weeks were over. The casualties were expected and surprised no one, certainly not the dedicated taskmasters whose job it was to drive the men until the weak and flawed among them broke.

The rock pits of Colomb-Béchar were a ten, no, a hundredfold intensification of the bleakly harsh life and torturous punishments that the recruits had endured and that were, depending on each commandant's degree of sadism, routinely meted out at large encampments and small outposts alike. Though he had sworn that he would do nothing, say nothing to deserve any one of them, Kelemen had experienced them all, even the crapaudine. For Dennis O'Brien, the man who had served with an exemplary record well into his second enlistment, Colomb-Béchar would be an eternity of suffering. Major Allard had given him five years, a light sentence because the Italian had been drunk on stolen wine when he deliberately provoked the Irishman, but extra days, weeks, months, or years could be added on to his term almost at will by the administrative officer of the punishment battalion. Escape, except through suicide, was so rare as to be commonly believed impossible. Kelemen thought it likely that even a body as strong and fit as O'Brien's would eventually collapse in the pits or under the lash of a guard. He was haunted, as was every other legionnaire at Bel Nama, by the knowledge that any one of them could be lying in Dennis O'Brien's place. They all drank up every franc of their pay, all played the game of pooling their daily wine to allow one of their number to get wonderfully, uproariously, suddenly drunk, and they all fought, using fists, teeth, feet, and whatever weapon lay at hand.

Kelemen had liked the Irishman, had respected his easy skill with rifle and bayonet, his ability to read the commandant's mind and predict the orders for any given day. On a long march it was always O'Brien's voice that had first broken out into song, always he who had sung as if he needed no breath to lift his feet through the sand. He sang the Legion's own chants well, but even better were the sad, haunting melodies that came from his throat when the column halted for the night, built its protective breastworks, cooked and ate its beans or macaroni. Lying on the sand around a tiny campfire, their heads pillowed on their packs, rifles beside them, warming their hands with tin cups of coffee, O'Brien's *copains* listened to him sing. He brought them the sweetness of longing, the beauty of love and tragic death, the misty green grandeur of the island where he had been born. Spells are easily cast in the desert, but none ever wrapped itself so tightly around Joseph Kelemen as those woven by O'Brien's singing.

The worst of it was that no one knew when O'Brien would leave, whether an escort party would be sent out from

Colomb-Béchar or if Bel Nama itself would have to provide one. If O'Brien had not possessed that wonderful gift of song, if he had not developed an aura of mystery about him by refusing all promotions, if it had been the ratty, weasel-faced Italian who had been condemned, the garrison would have given the prisoner up gladly, even with some measure of relief that one in whom *le cafard* lurked would be safely out of their barracks. You were vulnerable to the madness that could derange the man next to whom you slept. But this case was so different, so puzzling, in fact, that many of the witnesses to the murder asked themselves afterward if it could truly have happened or if it had been a dream. The mound under which the Italian lay was their answer, but even that, except for the cross erected above it, could have been part of the illusion.

No one at Bel Nama except O'Brien himself envisaged a sucessful escape. Only one man, the very young, very blond Erich, a Bavarian with the deceptive face of a choirboy, might have been driven to set his lover free, to give him at least a chance at freedom. He was watched, but not interfered with, by a garrison who knew that if O'Brien were given the opportunity to kill himself wandering in the desert, another man, and he only a boy, would take his place at Colomb-Béchar.

He had not sung in ten days. Neither had he spoken a single word to any of the men who came into brief contact with him. As silent as if his tongue had been cut out, Dennis O'Brien lived in a cell that was hardly more than a pit. He had a blanket to pull over his shoulders during the coldest hours of the night and a slop jar in which to relieve himself between sorties to the latrine trench. His uniform stank; it was not thought necessary that he be given water in which to wash. His boots were scuffed and dulled with layers of fine sandy dust, and the full beard he had once trimmed every few days grew ragged and unkempt on his face. He had withdrawn himself so completely from any semblance of normality that the walls of the cell were hardly more substantial than the invisible walls he had erected around himself.

He fell asleep at sunrise, willing himself not to dream of the wasted years, but every day, while the sweat poured from his body and flies buzzed around his head, he walked again in the damp mists of Ireland. Faces that had once smiled at him and asked for his priestly blessing now cursed and turned away from him, the low stone walls over which he had vaulted with ease as a boy rose to tremendous heights, twisting and turning their way across the countryside so that he could see only a few yards of the road he had traveled and nothing at all of what lay around the next bend.

When he awoke, more tired than if he had not slept at all, his skin encrusted with salt and the flecks of the flies that had crawled on it, it was as though Ireland, the seminary, and the parish of Saint John the Baptist had never existed. He couldn't remember the dreaming. He was too tall by a foot to be able to stand upright in his cell, but he did what stretching exercises he could, combed his beard with his fingers, used his spit to wash the grit from his eyelashes, and lay down again to await supper and the tantalizing taste of freedom when he was taken out to empty his bowels.

When the post grew quiet and the occasional footstep of a sentry or the rattle of his chain were the only sounds breaking the deathly stillness of the desert, he forced himself to think of Colomb-Béchar, to recall every tale he had ever heard of the place, conjuring up the faces of men who had lived through their sentences and returned to the ranks of the Legion, searching their pitted eyes and cadaverous faces for some clue to their survival. You never walked at Colomb-Béchar; you quick-marched or ran everywhere. You wore the same clothing, scrubbing the dirt from it every day, until it was reduced to rags that fell from your body. You hacked hundreds of tons of rock from the pits during your time there, broke it up into the gravel used for miles and miles of Legion-built roads, hauled it in baskets strapped to your back up the slope that became harder and harder to climb the deeper you dug. You were fed slops, and never, never tasted good wine. Your skin burned and blackened in the sun; your hands and feet bled day after day until finally they grew callouses as thick as those on the knees of a camel.

If that had been all, it would still have been unendurable. But the population of Colomb-Béchar was made up of the most desperate, the most vicious men in the world, and the measures taken to control, subdue, and break them to the Legion's authority were equal to the subjects on whom they were inflicted. Daily beatings with rifle butts were as certain as the desert sunrise, vicious kicks in ribs, groin, and face as common as the dead insects floating in your soup. You trotted in a never-ending circle with hundred-pound packs of sand or sharp stones lashed to your back, crawled on your elbows until you left streaks of blood on the ground, slithered through the muck of latrine trenches. You dug your own grave and lay on your back staring up at the golden orb of the sun while they shoveled sand over your body until only your face was exposed, crouched in a funnel-shaped hole called a silo while your own urine and excrement rose above your ankles. Most terrible of all, your hands and feet were trussed behind you in the crapaudine, the toad position, cutting off the blood supply to arms and legs; the agonizing pain spread from your bound limbs to engulf your whole body, and you were entirely at the mercy of those who had bound you. You screamed and screamed in the crapaudine until your closing throat could no longer make any but the most piteous of mewling sounds. You had had a taste of all this long ago as a recruit, but it took the thickset, heavily muscled German sergeants who were the camp's most efficient personnel to realize its full horror. It was no wonder that many men condemned to Colomb-Béchar killed themselves by any means possible to avoid transportation to its barracks.

Dennis O'Brien, fully aware of what awaited him, rejected death at his own hand. Night after night he concentrated his energies on Erich, attempting to pierce to his lover's soul with all the ferocious force that he had once directed to entering the mind of God. All that stood between him and the open desert were two wooden bars across the door of his cell, an iron plate whose lock would be no match for the Bavarian who had once made a good living from his thin, skillful fingers, the wall itself, and the sentries in their watchtowers. He rated his chances of survival in the Bedouin world outside the fort as an even bet; the odds in that game suited him better than the ones dealt out by the Legion.

The stars and the moon grew dim halfway through the night, their pellucid silver glow turning pale yellow, then a murkish tan as the sands, picked up by a wind that began as no more than a sigh, began to blow steadily. Joseph Kelemen wrapped his neckcloth around the lower part of his face, breathing dust and the dry, dead-tasting air that preceded the full force of the approaching storm. Within minutes his visibility was cut by half, by three quarters, then reduced to the sight of his own hand held before his eyes. He continued to stand his watch, a useless task, his shoulders stinging as minuscule bullets of sand hurled themselves against him. There would be no patrols of any kind sent out tomorrow, no inspections to stand, no drills to perform. When the Sahara blew itself to hell, the Legion, the Bedouins, every living thing that lived in its wastes sought shelter, curled limbs in the fetal position of sleep, and waited, suspended in a whirlpool of mingling earth and sky, for the fury of Allah to pass.

The whisper came with the sand that blew through the barred window.

"*Dennis, mon ami. Réveille-toi.*"

"I'm here, Erich. Quickly. Don't speak."

A fist was thrust between the bars. Fingers searched, found and clasped O'Brien's hand. One brief, convulsive pressure, and they were withdrawn. Tiny, scratching sounds of metal on metal, a slender, delicate probe testing the intricate workings of the lock, the hiss of exhaled, long-held breath, the blessed, scarcely believable click as the lock was released. A moment later the bars thudded softly against the ground and the door of the cell opened just wide enough to allow the Irishman's body to squeeze through.

He felt Erich's arms around him, the body pressed to his own, the kiss on his neck just below the ear, the moisture of flowing tears on the young man's face, the swift, reluctant letting go. In silence O'Brien's lover gestured toward the ground at his feet, then replaced the wooden bars and relocked the cell door. When he turned to face him, the Irishman had already gathered up the coil of rope, shoved the package of food into his shirt, attached the water-filled *bidon* and knife to his belt, and slung the rifle over his shoulder. Erich had forgotten nothing that was essential.

They were late in discovering O'Brien's escape; the sandstorm had slowed the life of the fort to a crawl. Reveille was blown at 5:00 A.M. as usual, but from then on every simple task became a herculean effort performed against the force of the swirling wind. There was grit in the morning coffee, grit in the bread, layers of powder-fine sand on every face and every rifle. The two guards assigned to bring the prisoner his food and empty his slops did not open the cell door until nearly midday.

Erich was sent for and interrogated. The Bavarian said not a word during the questioning, standing before the commandant with eyes that stared straight ahead at a point somewhere above Allard's head, wearing a thin-lipped smile that told everything. The men who escorted him to the disciplinary cell and locked him into the darkness reported that he went without protest or pleadings, almost gladly. In less than an hour, every legionnaire at Bel Nama knew what had taken place during the night, knew also that the commandant had neither struck Erich nor allowed any of the three sergeants to use their rifle butts on him. What was the use? He would be tried and punished later, when the sand ceased to blow. Most of the garrison hoped the storm would last for days.

O'Brien was lucky. Allah or his own Christian God gave him twenty-four hours of good wind, most of which he spent crouched in a hollowed-out burrow within hailing distance of the fort. He began to walk as soon as the light of the stars broke through the clouds of dust, feeling the still moving sand slide into the indentations left by his feet. Not for many hours would he begin to leave footprints, but between the fort and where the tracks began would lie miles of glassily smooth desert. Only a very few Bedouins could match the speed and the endurance of a legionnaire on foot. March or die, sergeants told the *bleus*, and whatever else he had or had not learned, Dennis O'Brien could march.

The search party that set out to recapture O'Brien more than two full days after his disappearance was composed almost entirely of men who doubted that he could be found. The storm had erased all trace of his passing and recontoured the landscape so subtly yet so completely that there were no longer any familiar landmarks to guide them. Seemingly immovable mountains of sand had shifted position by a few degrees, the sun that had once risen over a series of undulating dunes now flared above a deep depression, the date palms that grew on the outskirts of the village of Bel Nama, even the village itself, could barely be seen from the watchtowers.

There were only two possible directions in which a sane man would go, only a few routes he could follow that would lead him from water hole to water hole. One of the beauties of desert service was its simplicity. Water was everything, and though it always appeared to uninitiated *bleus* that you could easily lose yourself in unchartable sands, experienced men knew that caravans of desert travelers had long ago established tracks to which they kept as faithfully as Europeans to their roads. It was a question then of putting oneself in O'Brien's place, of reasoning as he had done, of choosing the single destination that must now be his goal. If Major Allard guessed wrong, the Irishman would never be seen again.

To the north lay the Mediterranean coastline of Algeria with its heavy concentrations of population in the port cities of Oran and Algiers. It took money to buy a hiding place in the Arab sector of a town, more money than any legionnaire possessed who had lived as O'Brien had done. Unless he owed his life to the Irishman, an Arab could be depended upon to take his coins until the last one had been spent, then betray him. The Legion paid well for the service. Neither recently arrived colonials nor *pieds-noirs*, Algerians of European descent, would give him refuge on their farms or in their homes. Almost all of them, while valuing the protection of the Legion's presence, despised and feared the individual legionnaire. He was an animal, a ferocious, ill-tamed guard dog to be penned up or let loose only on a chain, never considered safe enough to turn one's back upon. A lone man, traveling as O'Brien must be traveling, would be immediately suspect.

To the west loomed the Atlas Mountains of Morocco, a kingdom so divided, so filled with warring Berber tribes, so weakly governed by a succession of ineffectual sultans that it was like no other place on earth. The European presence was minimal, even in such fabled cities as Fez, Marrakech, Tangier, Casablanca, and Rabat. In all the history of these mountains, in all the years that renegades, fools, and adventurers infinitely bored with the safety of ordinary living had attempted to penetrate them, only three or four had succeeded. Major Allard, in one of the few astute moments of his career, concluded that Dennis O'Brien, outlaw, a man of unusual silences for whom at least one other human being had been prepared to sacrifice himself, was one of those outcasts for whom no other choice was possible. He had turned mercenary soldier by joining the Legion; it was only another swift turn to exchange its secrets and his skills for the sparing of his life.

Bel Nama's senior noncom was the man directly charged with the pursuit. He ordered that each of the four men who had been standing watch during the hours when it was presumed O'Brien had dropped over the wall be assigned to the patrol, not because there was any suspicion of complicity on their part, but simply as a reminder to others that hard, onerous duty was always a consequence of even the most unavoidable mistake. Kelemen he would have taken in any case. The young Hungarian who could pass for a native by his looks was the only man at the fort whose knowledge of Arabic was expert enough to question the Bedouins Sergeant LeClerc expected to encounter during the trek. It wasn't enough to be able to speak the words; Kelemen also understood the nuances of the language. The man he was interrogating would know that this foreign devil could smell out a lie. The others he would handpick, choosing the fastest, the most tireless marchers, and from among them only those with the keenest eyesight. They would be a reluctant group at best, but none would dare to slacken his pace or deny what he was capable of seeing. LeClerc was a bull-strong man who never tired and who could read the desert as well with his one remaining eye as any perfectly sighted legionnaire.

It was settled then, everything discussed and planned out as carefully as possible, the manhunt orchestrated with all the precision that Major Allard had seen the English devote to their sport of hunting the red fox. But the desert was as much a land of contradictions as it was of samenesses. The key to finding O'Brien alive was the speed with which LeClerc could march his men from one oasis to another, always moving westward toward the Atlas range, banking on the menace of other Legion garrisons to buy them safe passage, hoping that the Moroccans' chief interest lay in killing one another, that if O'Brien approached one of their camps they would regard the Irishman as probably insane and therefore reasonably harmless. It was just as likely that Dennis O'Brien lay within less than a day's march from the fort, his throat cut and his body mutilated by the sharp, genital-seeking knives of the veiled women who were more skilled than their men at prolonging pain.

Five days after leaving Bel Nama, when the searchers were weary, bored with their task and the unvarying diet of boiled rice, beans, macaroni, and coffee, Sergeant LeClerc led them over a sandhill toward a tiny water hole almost lost in a small grove of palms. The trees were stunted but healthy, the miniature pool filmed over with dust, the only signs of life a single mangy camel and three black-robed figures squatting around a fire that was hardly more than a glimpse of orange flame in the blue light of early dusk.

Lying prone on the slope of the dune overlooking the oasis, Sergeant LeClerc held his men back for more than an hour. His one good eye searched the horizon while the empty socket under the black patch burned with the memory of the bullet that had splintered bone and spilled the jelly of sight over his cheek. He watched the woman below him stir up the fire and saw her fade back into the shadows when a man stepped out from behind the camel he had been tending. The husband ate first, using his fingers to scoop up food from a circular flat pan, taking his time about it while his wife and the two smaller women who were probably his daughters squatted at the edge of the circle of light thrown out by the flames. The legionnaires smelled tobacco and the fumes of boiled coffee before the Arab signaled that his women might help themselves to what remained in the pan lying beside him in the sand. They ate quickly, as if afraid that what they had labored to prepare might be snatched away from them, and only when the tallest of the three began to scour the empty dish with handfuls of sand while the two others spread carpets beside the fire did Sergeant LeClerc decide that this oddly isolated group posed no threat to him or his men.

The women clustered together as the legionnaires slid down the sandhill toward them, and the man moved toward the camel where he had presumably left whatever weapons he possessed. Dressed in white robes and headgear that seemed almost clean in the dim light of the stars and the fire, he drew the fabric of his headcloth down to his eyes and across the lower part of his face as though to protect himself from blowing sand. Many desert dwellers did so upon meeting Europeans, fearing that their souls would fly out of their mouths or be contaminated by speech with unbelievers.

For several minutes neither side moved. The Arab had returned to stand in front of his women, blocking them from sight. One hand was tucked into his sleeve, the other hung empty at his side. He had no rifle, but there was surely a knife clutched in the hand that could not be seen. Outnumbered as he was, he would not use it unless an absurdly foolish legionnaire attempted to communicate in any way with the women he was protecting. His camp was made for the night, but as with most desert nomads, he was capable of slipping noiselessly away from the oasis before the sun awakened those with whom he might be forced to share it. The confirmed desert wanderer shunned the company of strangers; he was born as suspicious as his animals and as hostile as the physical world in which he lived.

All these thoughts ran through Sergeant LeClerc's mind as the fire of dried palm fronds and camel dung smoked in the fast-cooling air and the hobbled camel swayed restlessly with the unfamiliar smell of Europeans irritating its nostrils. The only thing he could sense that was in any way out of the ordinary about this group was its size. One man and three women traveling alone could only mean that they had been left behind by a larger party, a tribe whose members were bound by ties of kinship and intermarriage. Wary, because there were sicknesses from which Arabs sometimes recovered but Europeans did not, he motioned to Joseph Kelemen to come into the light.

"Assure them that we come in peace, then ask them how long they've been here. Find out, if you can, when the others left and where they're going."

Other than to blink his eyes and nod his head once or twice, the Arab did not respond to the long speech which courtesy required among his people when strangers met for the first time. No matter how urgently one needed information, it was extremely impolite to question a man before the preliminaries had been completed. Such a slight could result in a refusal to say anything at all, and, if a man's temper was hot and his pride great, in the type of serious misunderstanding from which feuds were born.

"Why doesn't he answer you?" Sergeant LeClerc demanded. "Do you think he understands what you're saying?"

"He understands. He's weighing his words before he speaks."

The Arab hunkered down on his heels, and his women fluttered to the ground also, pulling their robes tightly around them so that not even their bare feet showed. He turned his head slightly and exchanged a long stare with the bulkiest of the three black-robed figures, then motioned the smallest and presumably the youngest girl to creep forward until she was so close beside him that they appeared to melt into one another. He seemed to be waiting for something.

"Sit down," Kelemen whispered. "We must not look down on them or we'll get nowhere." He was puzzled by the man's silence, confused by his apparent consultation with his wife. Arabs always ignored females when other men were present.

"Tell him that we're searching for a legionnaire who has committed murder, that he must be found so that he can be punished. Describe O'Brien." Sergeant LeClerc fidgeted impatiently with the hammer of his rifle. "Ask him again what they're doing here."

Joseph Kelemen translated the questions into Arabic, using his hands to indicate the direction from which they had come, speaking slowly and clearly. The Arab listened to him impassively, showing no inclination to reply, but the girl at his side began to tremble and her eyes widened like those of a startled animal.

Quite suddenly the Arab raised one hand to point to his mouth and then made gabbling noises deep in his throat. He pushed his wife's head forward, bending it down so that only the top of her veil could be seen. She said something quick and low, her voice quivering with the fear and the embarrassment of being obliged to speak to a man other than her husband.

"The woman lost the child she was carrying. The others apparently could or would not wait for her to recover. The husband cannot speak. He's either a natural mute or has had his tongue cut out. She didn't say which."

"What about O'Brien?"

"She claims they've seen no one."

"Can we believe her?"

"We'll have to. I don't think I'll be allowed to question her any more than I already have."

As if to confirm what Kelemen had said, almost as though he could understand the legionnaires' French, the Arab and his family stood up, all together, like puppets manipulated by a single string. The wife and her elder daughter rolled the carpets they had so recently spread and relaid them in the dark shadows beneath the farthest palms, abandoning the warmth and security of their fire. They were well-trained women who moved soundlessly, obeying a nod from the equally silent man who ruled them. When he appeared satisfied that the legionnaires would not prevent their withdrawal, the Arab inclined his head courteously and turned away from them. The youngest child stuck like glue to his side, taking two hopping steps to each of his long strides.

"Maybe tomorrow," Sergeant LeClerc muttered. It was not Kelemen's fault that these Arabs had provided no clues to O'Brien's whereabouts, but he was angered nonetheless. The longer the fugitive remained at liberty, the less likely they were to recapture him, if indeed they found any trace of him at all. Shortly after midnight they would set out again, marching through the bearable heat of early morning to make up the lost hours. He ordered his men to build up the fire, to boil coffee, and to set beans and dried meat to simmering. It was in just such a place and on just such a night that the Irishman's plaintive songs would have been most welcome.

The moon rose and gilded the desert with a wash of silver. Stretched out around the banked fire like spokes radiating from the hub of a wheel, the legionnaires conversed quietly among themselves, dozed fitfully, and then drifted off into a light sleep. They had lain down fully dressed and fully armed, loosely rolled in their blankets, their heads pillowed on their arms, their packs encircling them like a miniature stone wall. In two hours Sergeant LeClerc would shake them awake. By that time they would be cramped, cold, and reluctant to stir, all of them more fatigued than if they had never rested at all.

Joseph Kelemen had the watch, as much a tangible proof of LeClerc's displeasure as if the sergeant had bluntly told him to use his eyes and his ears since his tongue had obviously failed them. One or two others had offered to walk the perimeter of the camp with him, but Kelemen had merely smiled and sent them back to the fire. The only time a legionnaire ever knew any privacy was when he stood sentry duty, and to Joseph Kelemen the periods of being apart from his comrades were never frequent enough. They were in no danger that night. For once the desert and all its creatures seemed to be held in a peaceful dream.

He studied the stars as he paced, picking out the constellations, giving them the different names by which the Europeans and the Arabs called them. There was a whole world of human and animal behavior frozen in the void above him, for man seeks to tame what he cannot conquer, reducing the splendor he cannot imitate to crude diagrams of his own experience. He sees himself as a hunter in the skies, surrounded by the animals who most challenge him on earth, imagines the story of his own yearning heart in stars that are drawn to one another yet may never touch, distinguishes a fiery masculine brilliance from a steady female glow, and reads portents of great events in the fall and swift extinction of a star that has consumed itself. The sky is as truthful a teacher as the planet over which it arches, and for a man seeking wisdom its chief lesson is the vast expanse of what is to be learned.

Absorbed in his own thoughts, retracing his steps so exactly that one footprint fell neatly into its predecessor, Joseph was unaware for a long time that he was being watched. "Keep a close eye on the Arab," Sergeant LeClerc had ordered, and alert to the command that was no more than a sensible precaution, he had glanced toward where the Arab family slept every time his circular route took him past their camp. No sudden movement beneath the trees caught his eye, no rustling of garments told him they were awake, and the camel's unmistakable shape cast a dark, still shadow in the moonlight. The women were pools of black in the deep gray of the outlined palms, the man a pale, rocklike shape massed against them. Only after Joseph had looked more than a dozen times in their direction did he realize that while the women were lying prone on the sand, the man sat upright, as still as though he had died in the midst of a conversation, his muscles locked forever in his last pose. One hand was still hidden in his sleeve, the other lay across the body of the small female who had never left his side since her father had gestured her there. The headcloth remained secured over the upper and lower parts of his face, but above its whiteness his eyes stared at the sleeping legionnaires, and the stars twinkled a reflection in their depths.

Kelemen made two more circuits of the camp, his mind just on the edge of grasping a suspicion so ridiculous as to be beyond belief. But as he continued to walk in sands he had not dreamed of until four and a half years ago, beneath stars not seen in Europe, breathing air that was unscented and so pure that it hardly seemed substantial enough to sustain life, bits of the puzzle that had earlier disturbed him winged out of the darkness and settled themselves into a mosaic as easy to read as the symbols with which the sounds of a language are expressed.

He checked the horizon one last time, stood for a moment to gauge the depth of the sleepers' breathing, then walked toward the clump of palms and the eyes that were neither heavy-lidded enough to be called hooded nor wise enough to be resigned.

He sat down opposite O'Brien, close enough to whisper and yet be heard, his rifle cradled in his lap, the muzzle pointed at the man's heart.

"So you've figured it out." O'Brien's hidden hand moved a fraction of an inch, enough to show the blade of the knife pricking at the thin cloth of his sleeve, a slow, deliberate movement toward the throat of the child whose head lay across his knee.

"I was stupid not to have guessed it immediately."

"It was a good bluff, the best I could think of under the circumstances. The rest of this charade depends on you now, doesn't it?"

"They've put Erich in the hole."

"I'm sorry about that." It was true; a spasm of pain wrinkled the skin at the corners of O'Brien's eyes. He loosened the cloth over his face until it hung down beneath his chin. His teeth clenched together with a grating sound that sent a shiver up Kelemen's back. "They won't get him as far as Colomb-Béchar. You can count on it."

"Allard hasn't made his mind up yet."

"He will. You can count on that too."

For a few moments they sat without speaking. The camel chewed steadily on its cud; a vagrant snore came from the direction of the legionnaires' camp; the Bedouin woman sighed and turned over in her sleep.

"Where are you going?"

"Where am I going?" O'Brien smiled, a quick, broad grin that showed the whiteness of his teeth. No one but an Irishman could switch moods so suddenly, could so obviously relish the night, the situation, and the question that proved he'd won the first part of his bet. "Deep into Morocco, to the Atlas Mountains. I wouldn't stand a chance anywhere in Algeria. They'll be watching every ship and counting every rat that goes aboard."

"Will you take the women with you?"

"I wouldn't go without them. It's a game I'm playing, Kelemen, and time to change strategy, add a few more pieces to the board. I'm finished in the Legion, but there are other armies, there will always be other armies."

The knife was still a finger's width from the Bedouin girl's throat. "Won't she betray you as soon as she can? The mother, I mean."

"They're queer creatures, these desert women. She's frightened now, but already she's got more than a thought or two in her head for her future. My Arabic isn't half as good as yours, but I got the gist of what happened out of her. She was pregnant, all right, but not by any husband, and that didn't sit well with the father-in-law. He'd a few new prospects lining up in the wings, so he beat her until he was certain she'd abort, then persuaded the others to go on without them. For an old man he put up a hell of a fight. She wouldn't touch him, wouldn't even help with the burying, wanted to leave him out for the jackals to find."

The dirty stains on O'Brien's robes were blood then, rubbed over with sand to work them into the fabric and keep it from stiffening. The blood that had burst from Abruzzo's ears had been shoveled off the barracks floor with the sand that had absorbed it.

"How old is the girl?" For an instant Kelemen imagined he could see blood pouring from her throat, running down the blade of O'Brien's knife onto his fingers, pooling around his feet.

"Twelve or thirteen, I imagine. Old enough to be married according to these people, pretty enough so that the mother's already jealous. She wants sons, that woman does. She's desperate to have them. They all are."

"And you've promised to give them to her?"

"Not yet, but I will. I told you the rules of the game were changing. I'll have her pregnant again before we reach the foothills of the Atlas. She's an outcast too. She understands the way of things."

O'Brien drew back the girl's veil. She was as fair-skinned as a European, her eyelashes long and feathery against the roundness of her cheek, the nose arched and thin, the mouth slightly open in sleep, the teeth small and even, the tip of her tongue dark red between wind-chapped lips. She reminded Kelemen of his sister; she was, in fact, a slightly younger Magda, without the comfort of a doll clasped in her arms.

"You'll need a rifle. You won't last long without one."

"On the camel. I've plenty of ammunition." The knife stood between them, buried up to the hilt in the sand. "I could have slit her throat before your bullet killed me. And I would have. Make no mistake about that, Kelemen."

"I know."

"I gave you no choice in the matter."

"You're growing a conscience, O'Brien."

"The Irish are born with them. That's more than half of what's wrong with us."

"*Bonne chance*. Good luck."

"I owe you a life. If there's ever the chance to repay it, I will. And if you've a mind to come into the Middle Atlas someday yourself, I won't be hard to find."

Joseph Kelemen touched his right hand to the brim of his kepi and got slowly to his feet. He guarded his sleeping companions throughout the remainder of the watch and told no one that the fugitive Irishman would never be recaptured.

The Arab had lain down beside his women, his knife resheathed and his dreams undisturbed when Sergeant LeClerc led his twenty legionnaires out into the desert again.

6

Two months after O'Brien's disappearance, five weeks after the chase had been given up, headquarters at Oran finally reacted to the incident. Allard received a bluntly worded official reprimand which, coupled with his past lack of distinction, would freeze him forever at the rank of major. LeClerc, slapped only lightly on the wrist because experienced noncoms were more valuable than officers, read between the lines commending him for the thoroughness of the search and the clarity of his report, and understood that the fact of its failure was the one significant point that outweighed all others. Both men knew the Legion well enough not to be surprised. But in the messenger's pouch was another order, one that mystified the commandant and infuriated the sergeant.

Very seldom was an ordinary soldier singled out from the anonymity of the ranks. The only way, in fact, that such a man could work his way up from obscurity was to receive a battlefield commission, and this was a rare reward for exceptionally heroic valor. Somehow Joseph Kelemen had attracted Oran's attention; something the fair-minded LeClerc had said about his skill in Arabic had reminded someone at headquarters that, whenever possible, Europeans were preferred to untrustworthy native interpreters. Kelemen, as much a part of the O'Brien debacle as anyone else, was coming out of it with a plum, a new assignment that was ordinarily reserved for a very few, very specially trained officers: Fez, the northern capital of Morocco. He was to be attached to the small military mission already established there, to work on the staff of the local commandant as official interpreter. No change in rank, but that, given the circumstances, would have surpassed the limits of the tolerable.

Once the shock of it wore off, LeClerc discovered that he was glad to be rid of the Hungarian. Something had happened out there in the desert, something to which the sergeant could put no name, but which had left him with a peculiar ache in the gut that he had felt no more than once or twice before, a suspicion of having been duped. And Major Allard, really noticing Kelemen for the first time when he informed him of the odd order, considered the man's looks and his unnatural, uncanny ease in a language that baffled most Westerners, and found that the combination made him acutely uneasy, as if he had left his back unguarded and vulnerable to attack.

Joseph Kelemen heard the news of his transfer without comment. He had less than six months left to serve, and one too many secrets weighing on him to make Bel Nama an easy place to finish it out. It was mentioned nowhere in his records, but Bel Nama had been a punishment tour for him, and although bitter at first, he had eventually accepted and lived it as such, not because he was guilty of a punishable crime, but because cold, unrelenting indifference and pride were his sole defenses against the injustice he had no other means of fighting. They had kept him sane, kept *le cafard* at bay, done more than anything else to turn him from a youth into a man. They were almost second nature to him now.

He was detailed to the first supply train traveling north to Oujda, there to join an artillery detachment for the final leg of the journey to Fez. Not once did he look back as Bel Nama dwindled to a dot of gleaming white mud on the horizon. The slow rock of the camels and the steady, shuffling pace of the mules set the cadence of the march. Joseph, as well as every other man on foot, adapted his stride to theirs, and except for the mounted scouts who periodically fanned out from the column, each man retreated into a private place, a spot tiny and dark where the rays of the sun could not reach. Few of them fought their pasts during a march as long as this one; the effort of remembering to forget used up too much energy.

Joseph Kelemen had realized within four months of his arrival in Algeria that the Legion had tapped him for a career he would never have dreamed of choosing by himself. During the first six weeks he was treated no differently from any other *bleu*, but he was watched more closely. When the boys and men who had stumbled off the ship with him were dispersed to forts deep in the desert, he alone remained behind in Oran. For a month and a half he worked as a clerk. From time to time, and always without warning, he was called away from his desk and plunged suddenly into the role of simultaneous translator. He was being tested, always by a native Englishman, a native German, a fellow native Hungarian, and the speed, accuracy, and fluency with which he turned their speech into accentless, colloquial French was judged by a native Frenchman. The first time it happened, he was amused. He hadn't chosen the Legion in order to hide; his true name was on his enlistment papers, as well as an almost complete catalogue of the languages he spoke. German and Magyar were the tongues of his nursery days, French and English added later, when private tutors came to live in the Kelemen household. Back there in Paris, Joseph had almost added a fifth to the list, but some memory of his father's hand pressing against his shoulder on his thirteenth birthday had intervened. It was a small omission, but an enormous denial.

Without the distinctive looks that turned heads even within Oran's huge headquarters, he might have remained a clerk, one of the few relatively easy jobs to be found in the Legion. But the beaked nose, the deep-set eyes, the black of his hair, and the skin darkening every day in the sun set him apart. He was told nothing and he wasn't asked to volunteer, but the officer who had spied him out, who had initiated this clandestine recruitment, reckoned without Balkan familiarity with intrigue. Hungary's history was so checkered with betrayals that her sons had come to be born suspicious, and among the varied peoples living within her borders none were more wary than Joseph's. He guessed at the future being prepared for him by the end of his first month under the tutelage of Hamid el Kader, but he thought it wiser to pretend to be as ignorant of it as when the project had begun. As time passed and Hamid el Kader's lessons took him deeper and deeper into Islam and the Arab mind, he thought less and less about the purpose of them, forgetting finally the exquisite paradox of the nascent spy learning to love what he was being trained to betray.

It began with language lessons, Joseph still in uniform, Hamid el Kader forcing him to repeat words, phrases, passages from the Koran for ten, sometimes twelve hours a day, until his throat was raw and his tongue as swollen as though he'd been chewing on sand. Only when he could understand the whole of a long conversation and answer Hamid el Kader's questions without making a single mistake did the holy man take him out into the streets. When it happened, the stored-up knowledge coalesced very quickly, as enlightening as the brilliance of sunshine let into a hidden courtyard by the opening of a door. They returned to Legion headquarters at night, each knowing that both were virtual prisoners and one hostage for the other, but during the day they mingled with the crowds in the markets, Kelemen observing, absorbing Arab smells and sounds and ways of acting, his tutor whispering that this or that man came from another region, naming tribe and dialect, imitating differences in speech until his pupil caught the nuances.

Hamid el Kader was one of a legion of impecunious, ragged holy men wandering from city to city throughout the Arab world, saints who were to be found in the courtyards of every mosque, and he did not question the design of Allah in bringing him to his present task, did not, although the thought of it was repugnant, deny that the foreigner might someday bring harm to his people. That, too, he left to heaven, only occasionally comforting himself by speculating that a holy jihad might arise out of the French victories his pupil would help to guarantee.

"Your people are an ancient race," Hamid el Kader once said, "even older than mine. We honor many of their prophets." By this, without the word ever being spoken, Kelemen knew that his teacher had picked him out as a Jew. It seemed to make no difference to the saint, except perhaps, and Joseph could in no way be certain he was right, that Hamid el Kader must have found it easier to deal with a Jew than a Christian. Dog of a Christian. The word was hardly ever said without an accompanying epithet. He even picked up the habit himself, a little trick of usage that never failed to make the holy man smile.

The blow, when it came, was unexpected and devastatingly final. They were reaching the end of their time together; both of them knew there was very little still to be learned. Hamid el Kader's last lesson was, of all the hundreds he had given, the one that most captivated his pupil. He described the mountain fortresses of Morocco where he had been a guest, the fierce, proud, bloodthirsty chieftains for whom he had recited the Koran in dim, smoky palaces, the battles he had witnessed, the piles of headless corpses that enticed jackals and lions from their dens.

Tents on the Sahara mingled with mosques; mosques with Moroccan bandit lairs; veiled women with those of tribes that were freer; more primitive, black slaves from the Sudan with blue-eyed, fair-skinned Berbers; whitewashed tombs of saints with the lost caverns in which legends claimed hills of precious gems lay, guarded by ghosts and evil spells no man had ever dared to challenge. Kelemen listened to it all, dreamed that final night that he tasted all of it, lived a thousand lives of adventure and danger.

In the morning, when he awoke, Hamid el Kader, his pallet, his sandals, the bowl from which he ate and the cup from which he drank, all were gone. A dust ball behind the door had trapped several of the long white hairs that fell out whenever the holy man removed his turban. If it were not for those feeble signs, Joseph might have believed his tutor part of the dream in which he was still more than half caught.

Later that day, standing at attention in the uniform that was prickly and hot after the loose robes he had grown accustomed to wearing, Joseph Kelemen heard the name Bel Nama for the first time. A sergeant he had never seen before gave him his orders, brusquely refusing his request that he be allowed to talk to the officer who had promised nothing but hinted at so much. No point to it, and the sergeant had his orders also. The legionnaire's gear was already packed up. All he had to do was load it on his back and report to the supply-train sergeant. The convoy was already moving through the gates.

He figured it out somewhere between Oran and Bel Nama, at some unidentifiable furnace-hot point in the desert. An older or a better Jew would have expected it, but Joseph Kelemen was neither. The final outcome of the Dreyfus Affair had convinced almost none of France's military men that it wasn't extremely dangerous to have Jews occupying positions that gave them access to information for which other countries were prepared to pay handsomely. You especially couldn't trust a Jew in North Africa, where the chances for selling one's services to the enemy were at least a hundred times more likely to occur than in Europe. The officer who had smelled promotion through creation of a spy whose appearance was already perfectly camouflaged by nature had had no choice but to get rid of his mistake. A career could be ruined by that kind of error in judgment.

What or who had betrayed him? He would never know. Perhaps it had been Hamid el Kader himself, unable, in his holiness, to plumb the depths of blind prejudice in a people who claimed reason as the most precious jewel adorning the crown of their accomplishments. An unguarded word, a slip of the tongue would have been sufficient. Joseph was still young enough then, still naive enough to hope that his path would someday recross that of the saint. Only long after reaching Bel Nama did he admit to himself that though his teacher had gone quietly, he had certainly not gone unknowingly. There must be beggars and orphans aplenty in Oran who wondered why he had abandoned them and prayed for his soul.

The city lay in a bowl-like depression ringed by bleak hills atop which crumbled the foundations of ancient fortresses and palaces. Above the walls girding this settlement that dated from the early ninth century rose hundreds of slender minarets, and on either side flowed the sparkling waters of the river that had given it life through all those generations. Ninety thousand people lived in Fez, crowded into streets so narrow and overhung with latticework that from the vantage point of the hills it seemed there were no thoroughfares at all.

To the desert dweller, it was as deceptively beautiful a sight as his own familiar sands, but the Fez that Joseph Kelemen first saw shimmering in a bright April sun was a seething caldron about to boil over. Morocco had been a French protectorate for less than two weeks, but already there were reports that Berber tribesmen so fiercely independent that no sultan had ever been able to control or subdue them were joining forces, setting aside old hatreds and rivalries, converging rapidly on the northern capital to demand the death or expulsion of all foreign devils. Sultan Moulay Hafid trembled in his palace, terrified by the specter of a jihad of his own making, a jihad he was certain he would not long survive. Yet day after day the diplomats from Paris had to be entertained and feted with a seemingly endless succession of lavish banquets and ceremonial meetings. They seemed unconcerned, these powerful foreigners, and strangely blind to the raw power about to be unleashed against them.

Posted as translator and clerk to the office of the military commandant of Fez, Joseph Kelemen was perhaps the one European in the city who was capable of understanding the full folly of what was planned for the morning of April 17, and almost certainly the only one who could have predicted its outcome. He was never asked his opinion, of course, never made privy to the decisions reached at the top level of command. Had he been the Arabic-speaking officer Colonel Gansard had requested, the situation might have been different. As it was, however, his first assignment was an insignificant one, the commandant's angry reaction to having been sent a translator of virtually no rank at all and dubious background. Let him clean out the files, bring some order to the bundles of newly acquired court documents tied up in goatskin, left lying in empty cabinet drawers, stacked in smelly heaps in storerooms that could be put to better use.

The study fascinated Joseph Kelemen. Time after time the kingdom's records detailed services that certain Jews had rendered their sultan, the easy access to him that many enjoyed, the very real part they played in the life of the country, and the very substantial taxes they paid. Once refugees from Isabella's Inquisition, there were now perhaps as many as ten thousand Jews living in Fez, clustered and crowded together behind the high walls of a quarter known as the mellah, a ghetto whose gates were locked every night at sunset. Even more interesting was the fact that long, long ago, a fair number of those elegant Spanish Jews had converted to Islam. Their descendants, faithful followers of the Prophet, were to be found in the ranks of the most important families in Morocco.

Colonel Gansard's instructions were carried out to the letter, his schedule to the minute. Nothing was allowed to interfere with the European discipline, the European efficiency, about to be imposed on Sultan Moulay Hafid's army. Its new French officers cursed the rains that delayed the ineffectual ruler's departure from the city, but did not read them as a sign from heaven that he should remain, nor did they interpret that day's solar eclipse as Allah's clear reminder that darkness and foreign domination had fallen upon Morocco at one and the same hour. Logical men, they saw no deep shame in burdening the Moroccan soldier with the full kit customary in the French army, nor did they consider the substitution of French for commands formerly given in Arabic an intolerable insult. The Moroccan units standing stiffly at attention before them looked to the empty hills over whose brows would surely come the Berbers whose spies had already slipped into the city, looked at one another, and read the will of Allah in each other's eyes.

It happened so quickly, so unexpectedly. Swarms of Moroccan soldiers from the bloody, nearly destroyed barracks raced through the city, calling to the Fassis to leave their homes and courtyards and join the massacre. And they did. By the hundreds and then the thousands they poured into the streets, brandishing long-hidden firearms and gleaming, lovingly polished blades. There was no organization to it, no plan, no leaders. None were needed. The riot was simplicity itself. Any European who showed himself was fired on or chased down to his death. There was an air of vicious sport about each encounter, a terrible anger that could not be satisfied with quick and merciful slaughter.

When the heavily armed and expertly defended European quarter held fast against them, its gates slammed shut and extra men set to guard them within minutes of the first frenzied cry that something unbelievable, some irreversible horror had broken out of the military compound of the Qasbah Cherarda, the mob wheeled and seethed in the narrow, serpentine streets, the rioters trampling one another in their fury, surging through the labyrinthine mazes of the city, hungry for the European victims denied them by the rapid fire of French rifles.

The mellah, undefended by the French because no one really knew whether the Jews who lived there were Moroccans, Jews, or some hitherto unknown combination thereof, suddenly took on an allure nearly as attractive as that of the European quarter. There was no reasoning to it, again no plan, no single rallying cry, no directive given, no thought to what was to be done once the gates had been forced open.

The mob simply turned in that direction, picking up speed as those in front began to run through familiar streets, the realization of where they were going dawning on them only gradually.

The runner who brought the news to headquarters was whitefaced, plainly as unsure now whether Moroccan had turned against Moroccan as he had earlier been certain that it was his own kind who were being attacked. Jews in the thousands were fleeing from the mellah as best they could, some who waited too long being flung from the roofs of their homes, others who had blundered directly into the path of the mob being viciously cut down as they ran, many more fanning out into streets that paralleled but never intersected with the main body of Fassis snaking through the quarter. He had seen whole families run past him clinging to one another, the children tied onto their parents' backs, the old people being led by the hand, falling and stumbling to their feet again. They were only Jews, but in the confusion of the crowded streets, with eyes that looked like anyone else's eyes mutely pleading for help, the runner had nearly forgotten the difference.

Almost before the runner had finished his report, a courier delivered a message from the palace. Joseph Kelemen was called to translate. The sultan, besieged by Jews who had instinctively turned to him for protection, was opening his garden, indeed all two hundred acres of the palace compound, to as many Jews as could reach it. Once within those walls, they would be safe. Although it was inconceivable that any Fassi, any Moslem, would condemn his soul to eternal hell by raising his hand against the anointed of Allah, reinforcements were urgently needed, as many of the deadly expert French marksmen as the commandant could spare. A squad of twelve men from headquarters was dispatched, among them the translator, Joseph Kelemen.

Above the muted thunder of thousands of running feet, louder than the wailing of mothers whose children's hands slipped from their grasp, almost as frightening to the Jews as the Fassis who were looting their homes, shops, schools, and synagogues, came the roar of the sultan's lions, restlessly pacing their cages and leaping against the steep walls of their pits. Other animals in his private menagerie caught the scent of fear and the urgent frenzy of humans seeking to escape from one another, adding their howls, their piercing screams, their trumpetings to the cacophony of sound rising from the immaculately tended palace grounds. Shepherded into the gardens by servants and soldiers who shouted at them to hurry, hurry, the Jews of Fez collapsed beside fountains that sprayed cool, sparkling water over them, pushed past helplessly protesting guards to throng by the hundreds into the public rooms of the palace, even, so tightly were they packed within the compound's walls, squeezed themselves into cages from which exotic birds and harmless animals had been released. And still they came, the last to arrive confirming that many who had tried to fight the mob had died where they stood, many others been wounded. The mellah, they reported, was very nearly a wasteland already; the crowds had quickly turned from murder to thievery and destruction of what could not be carried away. There were Fassis who had detached themselves from the looters, who had continued to stalk the weak and the unarmed, but except for the unfortunate few who might still be wandering the streets or who had foolishly chosen concealment rather than flight, the lives of the city's Jews were safe. Practically nothing of what they had labored to create during the four hundred years of their exile in Fez would survive the greedy fury of the rioters, but was anything of greater value than human life? Here and there, as stunned men and women regained their senses and comforted the crying children, prayers of thanksgiving for their deliverance mingled with the calls of the animals and the shocked, sympathetic murmurings of the servants who moved among them offering cups of water and handfuls of dried dates.

The legionnaires who had spread thmselves out thinly on either side of the palace's main entrance, funneling the Jews through the central gate while never taking their eyes off the farthest-visible point from which they came, withdrew into the compound. Their faces glistened with sweat, and a very few, very young men, having met the violence of North Africa for the first time, wore the same dazed, unbelieving expression as many of the children who had been carried past them. Climbing onto the parapet of the wall, they stood among the sultan's brilliantly uniformed guard, looking over rooftops toward the mellah, turning to stare briefly down into the now slowly milling, exhausted crowd below them.

One of the gates remained open, swung inward on its hinges just enough to allow a slender body to squeeze through. It could be barred in two or three seconds if necessary, but for a few more minutes it would offer hope to any Jew who might still be alive to reach it. A very tall, very slender man stood in the gap, the rifle of a guard holding him back. There was an eloquent tension in the way he held his shoulders; he was like a man straining against the barrier that separates him from a train he is about to miss.

Another man joined him, an imposing, dignified figure whose flowing white robes were immaculate, whose right hand, resting on the Jew's arm, glittered with flashing stones set in gold. Not until he reached the gate could Joseph Kelemen hear what was being said. The Moroccan's voice was pitched very low, his tone that of a physician obliged to forbid entry to a room where a loved one lay dying in the pain of a contagious disease.

"You may not leave, my friend. Your life is too valuable to the city to be risked or thrown away."

"I have a child somewhere out there, Ahmed ben Sussein. My youngest daughter."

"I, too, have children whom I cherish, Abraham ben Jakob. But Allah has hung their fate around their necks and even a father cannot change it. The sultan will need you when this is over. Your people are already crying out for those to whom they have always looked for guidance. Holy men such as your rabbis will comfort their souls, but even they will depend on others like yourself to see that they are fed and sheltered. The sultan will be generous, as will every Fassi honorable enough to acknowledge his part in the shame of what has been done, but the rebuilding of the mellah, the recreation of the community that has been destroyed, these things must be led by Jews. Look behind you, Ben Jakob. You are father to many thousands of children."

It was true. Kelemen could read it in the Jew's eyes, eyes that swept the compound with infinite compassion, lingering for a fraction of a second whenever they encountered the slim figure of a girl ministering to the needs of her mother or cradling a child on her lap. Ahmed ben Sussein's hand never moved from the arm of the man he had addressed as friend; the touch was strong and as firm as the words he had just uttered, but as there had been no hint of pleading in his voice, so there was no weakening of his grip. Ben Jakob was not to be allowed to endanger himself. Power radiated from the two men, power locked in conflict with its own kind. The Arab, already the victor, waited patiently for surrender to be acknowledged and accepted.

Only an arm's reach away, half turned to go he knew not where, Joseph Kelemen felt the Jew's eyes bore into the back of his head, knew a moment of sharp, physical pain at the base of his skull before he turned. Ben Jakob was indeed looking at him, saying nothing in any language but that of the heart, every proud feature of his thin, aristocratic Spanish face as composed as those of the stone effigies of Isabella's grandees. It was a strikingly colorless face, pale with no tint of olive or rose beneath the skin, illuminated by green eyes that had the transparent sheen of spring grass. For a moment, startled by the remarkably similar body and facial structure of the two men, both of whom now seemed to be waiting for him to speak, Kelemen thought that he was looking at a pair of brothers. But no, Ahmed ben Sussein's skin was darker, though not as brown as Kelemen's, his eyes a strange light mixture of blue and hazel, his beard nearly black, with only here and there a scattering of reddish hairs.

He knew, even before the question formed itself on his lips, what he would ask.

"How old is the child?"

"Rahel is eighteen." It was the Arab who answered, stepping away from Ben Jakob to link them all together in a half-circle. On his face Joseph could read what, for the agony it would bring, could not be said. Though to her father she might be a child, Rahel was a woman, already many years beyond marriageable age. If she had been caught by the men rampaging through the mellah she was probably already dead, killed as surely by repeated rape as by any knife.

"She's wearing a litham and a haik. There was time enough for that before the mob came." Ben Jakob's control was nearly perfect. Only the hard light in his eyes and the chalk whiteness of his nostrils revealed that he was a dead man struggling back to life. "We saw a few women running with the men. She may be mistaken for one of their own."

Until someone looks into her eyes, Joseph thought. They

would be as green as her father's. He was unreasonably certain that the girl was a diminutive feminine replica of Abraham ben Jakob. Impossible for her to be anything less. The haik, a long straight robe without which no Fassi woman ventured from her home, would make the girl's body as shapelessly anonymous as any other female's, the litham, a head covering worn low on the forehead, folded into square peaks like a nun's coif, supplemented with a veil secured across the bridge of the nose, would hide her hair, almost all the face except for the eyes. Those eyes and the red-gold brows above them would betray her.

There was no point in asking where the girl had become separated from her father. Ben Jakob could not know. Such a man would never have continued once he became aware that she was missing. The only answer was that he had not discovered her loss until well within the palace grounds. But how, how could he not have known?

"My son is a cripple," Ben Jakob said. The eyes that compelled could also read as well as speak. "I strapped him to my back in the kind of frame water carriers wear. All I could see as we ran were the stones and the dirt beneath my feet. I prayed that it was Rahel who ran beside me, and for a time, who can say how long, it must have been."

Just before he eased himself through the gate, Joseph was given a promise very much like another he had received in an utterly different place. "My life is yours if you find her," Ben Jakob said, his voice almost a whisper. "Go with God. Salaam." They had all three, the Jew, the Moroccan, and the legionnaire, been speaking Arabic, and more like an Arab than a Jew, Ben Jakob had offered the desert gift of a life for a life. The green eyes widened and a shadow darkened them when Joseph Kelemen, raising his rifle to the level of his shoulder, replied, "Shalom."

The flight of the mellah's population was an easy one to retrace. The streets through which they had come were littered with the debris of their passing. There had been no time to stoop to retrieve a lost shoe, a veil that had slipped from a woman's head, a toy that had fallen from a child's hand. Bundles containing bits of food and cherished possessions snatched up at the last possible moment littered the ground. Too heavy or too awkward to carry for long, they had been flung away in the scramble for safety, or perhaps they had simply slipped from fingers grown too numb to register their fall. In places the stones were as slippery underfoot as though an oily rain had coated them. People had bled as they ran, voided their bladders without realizing it, sweated like oxen plowing a field.

Kelemen was cautious, moving soundlessly from one recessed doorway to another, flattening himself against the curving walls of archways that hid what lay beyond, watching for shadows that stirred, listening for steps other than his own. Within a few hundred yards of the palace gate it was as though he had entered a city of the dead. Every door was tightly closed and bolted, every window shuttered fast. Not a single scavenging dog barked, no child, if there were any hidden behind the blank facades of the houses, dared to cry out or laugh, even the cats who usually sunned themselves on doorsteps had crept away to darkness. The possessions of the Jews lay untouched, the unrifled contents of the bundles spilled out just as they had fallen. If there were people about, only the most terrible of fears could have blunted their greed.

He found the first body crumpled on the steps of an alley leading steeply upward. An old man, white beard reaching halfway down his chest, he must have died within minutes of crawling from under feet that would have trampled him. There was no mark on the corpse, not even a look of surprise on the still face. He had seen death approaching and welcomed it. There were others, three so covered in blood that it seemed impossible that they could have come even this far, one tiny child whose broken neck lolled heavily on his hand. Where was the mother? Gone, swept along, perhaps even now walking despairingly through the sultan's gardens, begging strangers to remember if they had anywhere seen a curlyheaded child wandering lost in the crowd.

Thirty minutes, an hour. He judged the time by the dryness of his mouth, the rivulets of sweat on his back, the pounding of his heart as he went farther and farther from the palace. When he could smell the mob and hear individual voices above the tumult, he knew that he had gone as far as he could. Looters with an eye to keeping what they had stolen would soon be creeping back to their own quarters and they would tolerate no living witnesses to their thefts. The law decreed the cutting off of hands that took what did not belong to them.

He kept to the streets through which he had already passed. Their emptiness was less menacing for having been explored, the bodies no more than familiar signposts marking the way. As he walked he tried to find the words with which to tell Ben Jakob that he had failed. None came. The call to prayer pealed out across the quarter, as shrill and insistent as though the day were a normal one. Somewhere inside the closest mosque a muezzin had climbed faithfully to his tower, years of obedience to Mohammed's dictum to pray five times a day driving him upward. What could he see from his vantage point high over the city? Were there orderly ranks of men touching their foreheads to the tiles below him? Could anyone be living an ordinary day anywhere in Fez?

He had halted at the muezzin's first call, his train of thought abruptly broken, his body, in reflex action, pressing itself against the nearest wall. Behind him, to his left, came the unmistakable soft slap of babouches on stone. Whoever was coming was approaching quickly, the steps were hurried but light, like those of a slender boy, a woman, or a child. He listened intently as they climbed the short flight of stairs on the far side of the arch. No more than one, a hesitant individual, an indistinct gray form hugging the deep shadows along the curve of the arch. The street ahead would appear deserted; coming from the darkness into the full brightness of sun reflecting off white walls, his pursuer would be blinded. But only for a moment. Very, very slowly, Kelemen removed his right hand from his rifle, wiped palm and trigger finger against his tunic, found his grip again, and waited, a tiny pulse leaping alongside the knuckle of his forefinger.

The hem of a garment fluttered from the gloom. He was in the middle of the street, feet braced, weapon raised to his shoulder, eye sighting the length of the barrel, trigger finger aching to release the tension. Ten feet in front of him stood a woman, veiled from head to foot in a linen haik the color of desert sand at twilight. Without lowering the rifle he beckoned her to come closer. Holding one hand above her eyes to shade them from the glare, she walked toward him, the backless babouches that were several sizes too large for her slender feet stirring up little puffs of dust, flapping against her soles with the distinctive rhythm that had given her away.

"Why were you following me?" His grip on the rifle did not loosen, his finger remained on the trigger. He was as wary as she, taut and ready to fire at any sudden movement.

"For help, monsieur. For protection. I couldn't stay where I was any longer. If you hadn't come back down the street again, I would have tried to reach the palace alone. I know the way." Her French was accented with liquid Spanish vowels.

"Rahel? Rahel, the daughter of Abraham ben Jakob?"

The hand she had held to her forehead reached out to clutch at his arm at the same instant that he jerked his forefinger from the slippery, tightly sprung trigger.

"You know my father? Is he safe? And Avrom, my brother?"

"Both safe. Come now. Quickly."

Whether she caught hold of his hand or he of hers he didn't know. The coolness of her fingers and the feel of the thin bones that were as delicate as those of a bird held him irresolute and as if turned to stone. But only for a moment. He heard voices, male laughter, the clattering babouches of five or six, perhaps as many as a dozen Fassis. Only armed men, confidence bolstered by their number, would make no attempt at stealth.

Someone else had heard them also. A door creaked to the right, Kelemen saw a dark eye peer through the crack, cut off the hiss of surprise with the flat of his hand against the wood and before the Arab could turn to run, twisted his fist in the folds of the man's djellabah, slamming him against the interior wall of the tiny passageway. Rahel, moving only a fraction of a second later, slipped through the doorway, closing and barring it behind her.

"Not a sound," Kelemen ordered, the black hole of his rifle barrel shoved so deeply into the Arab's throat that a ring of white flesh formed around it.

The voices seemed to come from both sides of the street, from men who walked unhurriedly, stopping now and then, calling excitedly to one another. Without releasing the pressure of the rifle that held his prisoner immobile with fear, Kelemen glanced quickly over his shoulder. Rahel's green eyes were as hard and bright as emeralds, their angry fire cutting through the dimness of the passageway. The veil had slipped from her nose and now she wrenched it entirely from her face, crumpling it within a tiny, white-knuckled fist. Scavengers prowled a few feet away from where they stood, more dangerous and more cunning than the lions that still roamed Morocco's plains and mountains. There would be jewelry in the hastily tied-up bundles that lay in the streets, candlesticks of gold and silver, cups and salvers engraved with Hebrew lettering.

In the black pupils of his captive's eyes, Joseph saw two Rahels, each one no bigger than a mustard seed. Each tiny face was a perfectly shaped oval, each nose straight and thin as only aristocratic Spanish noses grow to be after centuries of careful breeding, each mouth slightly open, softly curved lips parted, drawn tightly over white teeth through which came the panting breaths of a child who is resting from his play. The skin over her cheekbones was flushed the color of a damask rose, her forehead damp and pearly. The scent of her perfume filled the air, stronger than the smell of the acrid fear sweat emanating from the nearly senseless Arab, sharper in its peppery sweetness than the legionnaire's soaked and steaming uniform.

Not until the last shout had echoed into silence did they dare to speak. Not a rustle or a murmur broke the stillness of the street, but even so they whispered, bending their heads so close together that faces and lips nearly touched. The Arab, his hands and feet securely bound with the torn cloth of his own turban, watched them curiously, Allah having providentially made the foreign soldier too soft to kill him. He was a fat man, happy with the wives who fed him well and the children they produced from his seed. The shops he owned, well managed by prudent sons who had boarded them up long before the first crazy ones had surged into the souk, were in no danger. The property of Ali ben Mustafed, well liked, well respected in this quarter, would be safe.

"Where does this passage lead, effendi?"

Ben Mustafed could not believe his ears. This legionnaire, this dog of a Christian, had addressed him as politely as if they had met by chance on the steps of a mosque. He peered more intently at the man whose face was so dark that it was difficult to tell his nationality. Until the rifle had been lowered from his throat, he had seen nothing but the eyes that threatened a bullet through his neck. Surely no Moroccan would want to join the ranks of the Legion, even if such an abomination were permitted.

"Where does it lead?"

"To another passage."

"And that one?"

"To the courtyard of my home, effendi." Always return courtesy for courtesy. "The gate to the second passage is locked from the inside. A precaution, you understand." Almost, but not quite, Ben Mustafed ceased to regret his own recent lack of caution. Because there were no windows cut into the street wall of his house, he had spun his prayer beads so often and so rapidly that blisters had formed on his fingertips. Finally, with the tearful faces of his three wives bitterly reproaching him, he had stalked from the courtyard to see for himself what was going on outside.

"Monsieur." Rahel's hand on his arm pulled urgently.

"Joseph. My name is Joseph Kelemen."

They will fall in love, these two, Ben Mustafed decided, forgetting for a moment the ache in his wrists where the cloth bindings cut too tightly. They will not be able to help themselves. His youngest wife was very beautiful, but no more than a pale star beside the bright moon when compared with this girl. He sighed for the many years he had already lived and the few joys that could be suitably relished once a man had passed his prime.

"Joseph . . ." She seemed to be having difficulty pronouncing his name. "I think I recognize . . ." His finger touched her lips, trembled there as the words were cut off against it. Was there the suggestion of a caress before it fell away?

"Speak Hebrew. Slowly, so I can understand you."

Two Jews. It was inevitable then. Both hearts would be broken. Ben Mustafed had caught the extraordinary gleam of Rahel's eyes, and he was confident now that he had nothing more to fear from the legionnaire. He knew Ben Jakob well, personally and also by reputation. In the largest of his shops and in Ben Jakob's home the two men had sipped mint tea at the close of every business transaction. Their association had begun well before this child had been born. Over the years they had gravely congratulated one another as their families grew and prospered. Ali ben Mustafed was blessed with many sturdy sons, many lissome daughters; Ben Jakob's wife had borne three girls and the crippled, shy little boy who was intellectually brilliant but of such poor health that most of his life was spent lying in the shade of his father's garden or shaking in the arms of the sisters who nursed him through recurrent bouts of fever. Ben Mustafed had seen him only once, when the then twelve-year-old Avrom had asked to be allowed personally to thank the Arab who had sent him the little monkey that perched on his shoulder by day and slept in a box beside his bed at night. A daughter, this Rahel, he thought, had brought medicine into the garden. Except for one quick glance, Ben Mustafed had kept his eyes from straying to her face, extremely uncomfortable to be in the presence of an unveiled woman. But he remembered the sound of her voice and the way she had laughed at the monkey's antics. The mother was dead, and Ben Jakob had never remarried, though for a Jew to remain without a wife was nearly as unheard of as for an Arab to confine himself to only one when he could afford to support others as well. Allah had mixed sorrow into the prosperity he had allowed the Jew to enjoy, but in spite of that, Ben Mustafed had sensed a deep wellspring of love and happiness in Ben Jakob's home.

"I told you before that I thought I knew this man. Now I'm certain. I've seen him with my father many times. He gave my brother a pet monkey. We can trust him, Joseph. See, I think he recognizes me."

She smiled at Ali ben Mustafed and whispered his name aloud, her voice lilting upward in less a question than the beginning of an apology for the way he had been treated.

"Is it true? Are you acquainted with her father?" Let the Fassi prove himself by supplying the name. Joseph would reveal nothing, would make no mistake that might cost them their lives.

"I am, effendi. Abraham ben Jakob honors me with his friendship. We have done business together for more than twenty years. I pray that Allah has spared him and his family, and I rejoice because my house will shelter his daughter."

"Untie him, Joseph. Please."

The anguish and the uncertainty in the legionnaire's eyes were as easy to read as the pages of the Koran. He would gladly die if by so doing he could prevent any harm from touching this girl. Stories of deathless, immediately blooming love abounded in Arab song and literature, seldom encountered in real life, but all the more believable and precious for being so rare. Ben Mustafed would not be the one to tell the legionnaire what he must soon enough learn about Abraham ben Jakob's daughter, nor would he put the father on his guard, friend though he was. Allah held these two in the palm of his hand. Let them rest there for as long as it was ordained that the one should believe there was hope and the other forget that she was bound. Many Jews must have died in the wreckage of the mellah. Perhaps Tomas ben Torres had been one of them. Ben Mustafed wished no man's death, but he decided that he would make inquiries as soon as possible. As a youth, and for a short time after being married to his first wife, he had written poetry. Not for years had he thought about those early verses, but now the words and the feelings they evoked stirred in his brain and heart. He could remember them as clearly as if they had just flowed from his pen.

Ali ben Mustafed's eldest son, shocked to see his father return accompanied by an unveiled woman and an armed and dangerous-looking foreigner, fumbled with the lock as long as he dared, rattling the key and the gate, cursing his obviously deaf brothers for not sensing that something was wrong, not rushing to his side.

"It is enough, Omar. The daughter of Abraham ben Jakob must not be kept waiting outside our home like a stranger." Ben Mustafed turned to Joseph Kelemen and salaamed as gracefully as his bulk permitted. "I beg you to forgive the discourtesy, effendi. My humble dwelling is crowded with women and children."

Rahel, the corner of her litham drawn across her face so that only the astounded, instantly admiring Omar caught a glimpse of her beauty, was led immediately to the harem. Nothing could be seen of the women within, but their sympathetic voices rose in a questioning chorus that was abruptly cut off as the door closed behind her. Ben Mustafed's wives, female children, and daughters-in-law would smother Rahel with kind concern while undoubtedly wringing from her every last detail of what she had observed and suffered.

"I will send one of my sons to inform Ben Jakob that his daughter is safe. I share the sorrow of his father's heart."

"It would be better if I were to go, Ben Mustafed. Your sons are not soldiers."

"As you wish, effendi. But not in that uniform, I think. After you've rested and eaten with us, Omar will find clothing less conspicuous. Somewhere in my house there must be a djellabah so old and worn that no one would suspect it hides a person of as great value as yourself."

Ali ben Mustafed seated Joseph Kelemen in the place of highest honor at his table, noting how quickly and easily the legionnaire folded his legs beneath him, something most Europeans could manage only with the greatest difficulty. Whoever had taught him the excellent Arabic he spoke had not neglected instruction in manners. As each of the sons and several of the older grandsons was presented to this strange guest, the foreign soldier salaamed with perfect aplomb and exactly the right mixture of dignity and deference. The younger boys frankly stared at him, hoping to see some display of the uncivilized behavior they believed common to all Westerners. Terribly disappointed, but unable to tear their eyes from his uniform, they squatted down on their heels along the walls, whispering excitedly to one another as soon as the conversation of the adults grew loud enough to let their own pass unnoticed.

Only part of Joseph Kelemen remained in that room, registering the opulence of its rugs and cushions, the exquisite carving of the doors and ceilings, the scent of the rose water poured over his hands in the ritual of washing, the smells and the tastes of the food he scooped up with the curved thumb and first two fingers of his right hand. Somewhere deep within the house Rahel might also be eating and drinking, her haik discarded in exclusively female company, her own clothes perhaps replaced by a daughter's pastel gown, eagerly lent jewelry flashing on her arms, around her neck, in her ears as she braided the red-gold hair and bent her head to laugh.

Ben Mustafed's sons peppered him with questions, but after he had told them all he knew of the origins of the rioting and its extent throughout the city, they fell into a silence as brooding as his own, sending the little boys off to be fed in the kitchens, dismissing the older ones to their tutors. How much longer would the French allow the madness to continue before they retaliated? Kelemen shook his head. Would they use the big guns that had so quickly cowed the inhabitants of Casablanca? Everyone knew there was artillery in the camp outside the city. Again Kelemen shook his head. The answer would come soon enough, he was certain, but not to this quarter, so close to the palace and the European sector. Looking about him, hearing the singing of birds in wicker cages and the splashing of the fountain in the shady courtyard just beyond this room, Kelemen was almost tempted to deny the sights he had seen outside this house. Were it not for the purpling bruise at the base of Ali ben Mustafed's throat, it might all have been a dream.

He saw Rahel once more before he left. They stood together in the courtyard, so close to the fountain that no casual eavesdropper could have heard what they said. Flowering jasmine trailed from baskets above their heads, the milky-white flowers cascading all around them in a fragrant waterfall.

Joseph had not asked for her; she had simply and without warning appeared in the courtyard, standing motionless amid the jasmine sprays until Ben Mustafed, too experienced in the ways of foreigners and too full of good food to be shocked, sent him out to her. The sons pretended to see nothing, ignoring the open, arched doorway and the man and woman whose hands met one another's though their bodies did not touch. She was veiled in the light, diaphanous haik and litham worn only within doors and only in the cruelest heat of summer, garments that stirred in the light, cool breeze lifting off the fountain, molding themselves to what they were supposed to conceal. He was a proud figure from the high desert, all in white, darkly tanned face and arched nose the equal of the fiercest, most handsome Berber warrior. Something of fat Ben Mustafed's newly reawakened romanticism communicated itself to his sons. Without quite knowing why, one by one they left their rapt father who could not, would not tear his eyes from the scene in his own courtyard, and stole off to find their wives.

"Tell him that I'm in no danger here. That Ali ben Mustafed will gladly keep me for as long as necessary."

"I will."

"Joseph, no harm came to me in the streets. No one touched me." The green eyes above the nearly transparent veil looked steadily into his, but her fingers tightened convulsively and a stain of color flushed her cheeks as blood rushed to the surface of her skin. "He'll want to know that also."

He would have killed any man who had even thought of touching her, hunted him down through all of Morocco, all of North Africa, killed him slowly and with relish.

"I'll be back in a few hours."

She shook her head. "They won't let you. Ben Mustafed will eventually remember that my father kept his daughters almost as closely confined as any of the women or girls in a Fassi harem. It's the custom here. The Legion will need you, Joseph. Will you be sent out to fight in the city?"

"It doesn't matter. I'll come back."

"For your uniform? Of course you'll have to retrieve it." She was teasing him lightly now, the way a girl plays with her lover when she is being wooed.

He dared not kiss her and did not trust himself not to, not if he continued to hold her hands in his, to breathe in the scent of her perfume and the heady fragrance of the cloud of jasmine in which she stood, to gaze into the eyes that belied the teasing voice. The skittering, irregular pulse in her fingers told him that he had wound himself as tightly around Rahel's heart as she around his. For the moment, until Gansard tamed the city and he was free to find her again, that would have to be enough.

7

More than two thousand of the rioters, survivors of the French bombardment of the Qasbah Cherarda and the Bou Jeloud, surrendered on the evening of April 19. Reinforcements had been sent from Meknès, and nine additional infantry, cavalry, artillery, and rifle companies commanded by General Moinier returned by forced marches from Tiflet. A week after the massacres had begun, the city was proclaimed in a state of siege, an indemnity of a million francs levied against it, the population disarmed, martial law proclaimed, and the first of more than a hundred summary executions carried out.

The mellah had been nearly totally destroyed, the Qasbah Cherarda quarter virtually leveled; many hundreds of Fassis were killed, scores of Jews dead or wounded. Much of Fez was a city in mourning; other sections, frightened but still defiant, lay quiet under the French fist, knowing that perhaps half a thousand deserting Moroccan soldiers had managed to find sanctuary in the hills, where their knowledge of French defenses would surely be welcomed and just as surely acted upon. No one believed that the final battle for control of the city had yet been fought.

The streets of Fez were crowded with French soldiers. In their official capacity of forces of occupation they were in every market, at the entrance to every holy place, standing guard at the gates of every quarter, patrolling every street and alley. General Moinier's orders to stop, search, and arrest any suspicious Fassi were carried out ruthlessly. Better a hundred innocent Fassis locked up in jail than one rebel spreading sedition. Already there were divisions between

162

military and civil authorities, Eugène Regnault, diplomat and civil governor, believing that harshness would lead to new rioting, Moinier convinced that iron control was the only effective means of dealing with the situation.

Homeless Jews were scattered throughout the city, fed and sheltered by wealthy merchants who had contributed generously to the sum of money given for their relief by the sultan. The work of rebuilding the mellah had begun even before the last of the rubble was cleared away. Moroccan and French engineering companies worked side by side, directing gangs of Fassis and young Jews in the reconstruction. What could have been a thoroughly modern, sanitary quarter of the city gradually arose on the ruins of the old, its streets just as narrow, its houses just as high and tightly crammed together as they had always been.

Ben Jakob and his family had been provided with a gracious, jewel-like mansion near the sultan's palace. The rooms were spacious, the floors and arched doorways brilliantly tiled, the tables inlaid with scented wood, the deep cushions and low Moroccan sofas covered with silks embroidered in gold and silver thread. Fountains splashed in courtyards and hidden gardens, orange trees perfumed the air, and dozens of caged birds sang during the daylight hours. At night, sweet white flowers opened their petals to the moonlight.

"There is no way a father can repay the saving of his child's life. My home is yours, my family forever in your debt." Ben Jakob's handsome face had grown gaunt; it was marked by lines of anguish that would never be erased. The old horror of the days of the Inquisition haunted his eyes, the new proof that there was no safe refuge anywhere in the world darkened them. Yet he poured Spanish sherry into Joseph Kelemen's glass with a steady hand. Only for those he loved did he fear death, and then not the release of life, but the manner in which it might be taken.

"Ali ben Mustafed sheltered both of us until the worst danger had passed."

"He is an old and valued friend, one of many Fassis who hid Jews in their homes that day." Ben Jakob sipped at his sweet amber wine. He had sent a servant to the headquarters of the French military mission more than a week ago, but not until today had the legionnaire been free to come to him.

Now they were seated face to face, the wealthy, scholarly merchant who could claim a personal friendship with the sultan and the young man who was among the lowest-ranking soldiers in the French army. It was a delicate moment, one for which Ben Jakob was surprisingly unprepared. A small brass coffer filled with gold coins stood on a low table beside him. He thought that he could have offered them to any other legionnaire in North Africa, but not to this one. Now that he had studied the face he had been too troubled really to see before, he knew he was looking at a man whose pride equaled his own.

"My servant reported to me that you work as a translator."

"I was trained by a holy man in Oran. He tutored me as carefully as any pupil could wish."

More than anything else, Joseph wanted to see Rahel again, wanted to hear the sound of her voice, touch the slim fingers he had held in his hands, watch sunlight play in her hair and dance in her eyes. But he had been warned, and he was cautious. Ali ben Mustafed had explained the difficulty of the problem. "Ben Jakob will thank you personally, effendi, may even allow his daughter to do so also, since their customs are not as strict as ours. I doubt it, yet all things are possible. But Rahel cannot leave the harem again while she is under my protection. My honor demands that I act as her father would wish. Yesterday was a day of calamity, a day when laws and customs were forgotten. Today, effendi, things are beginning to return to normal. You must remember where you are." He had not been discourteous, but he had been firm. Mint tea and the uniform he had left behind, freshly laundered by Ben Mustafed's servants, were all Kelemen was given. The fat little man had come to his senses. The spark he had seen ignited, which he had foolishly believed could flame, he now attempted to extinguish.

"Will you eat the Sabbath meal with us, Joseph? We have much to be grateful for."

It was an unplanned invitation, one that might never have been offered had Ben Jakob been able to think of a graceful way to conclude their awkward conversation, had he not suddenly remembered that Rahel, although she said little else about the legionnaire, had remarked that he was a Jew, and a very lonely seeming one at that. Now that he had asked the question he saw that the only reward that came truly

from the heart and that was instantly perceived as such, was
the one contained in the words he had just spoken. To mingle
with Ben Jakob's family as an honored guest made as welcome as a true son of the house was the way one Jew thanked
another. And if this young Joseph could sing and pray with
them in Hebrew, he would already be revealing much about
his past.

"I'm not a good Jew, Ben Jakob. It's been many years
since I've celebrated Shabbos."

"But you will join us?"

"With great pleasure."

Ben Jakob clapped his hands, summoning a servant from
beneath the arched colonnade that enclosed the garden in
which they sat. "Bring my son to me," he said, the command
soft and courteous. In everything he did this man demonstrated respect for those who served him and those who
sought his friendship. "Avrom is a curious child. As you will
see, he cannot get about like other boys of his age, so whenever possible, we bring the world to him. He will weary you
with his questions."

"I have a brother in Budapest, Miklós, and three younger sisters. I'm used to answering questions." In almost five
years Joseph had never spoken Miklós' name aloud. Once,
months ago, an Arab girl had reminded him of Magda. But
for the other sisters and the mother and father, nothing, a
mental silence as total as the physical reluctance to speak
about the past that was so common in the Legion.

The boy was carried to his father gently cradled in the
arms of a strong young man too finely dressed to be a servant.
A monkey scampered along beside them, darting in and out
of the shadows, leaping to the fountain edge, scolding the
water that dampened its paws, slipping between the feet of
Avrom's bearer, perching at last on the table, chattering gaily
as it explored the contours of the brass box. Both the man
and the boy were laughing as they came, one heartily, health-
ily, the other with frequent catches in his throat, as though
his lungs could not contain enough air to breathe and express
enjoyment of life at the same time.

"This is my son, Avrom," Ben Jakob said when the child
lay propped up on cushions beside him, "and my son-in-law,
Ari ben Benjamin."

"Did you kill many Fassis?" Avrom asked. "They tried to murder us, you know."

"I'm not that kind of soldier anymore. I work in the headquarters of the military mission, where reports are filed and the commandant plans what must be done next."

"You saved Rahel when she was lost. Didn't you have to kill any Fassis to rescue her? She said you carried a rifle and pointed it at her."

"It's wrong to take a human life, Avrom. Joseph would not use his gun unless his own life or that of another were in danger." Ben Jakob scooped the monkey off the table, quieted its protests, and deposited the nervous little animal in his son's lap.

"Then why is he a soldier, Papa?"

"Avrom, do you ever read stories about great adventurers who travel all over the world just to fling themselves into dangerous situations? Men who are drawn to war and faraway places and can't help themselves?"

"I've studied history. I know about Alexander and Julius Caesar and Napoleon. Is that what you mean?" The child's eyes were bright in the paleness of his face. His thin body, wasted legs utterly useless, strained with the desire to move freely. All of his thirteen years had been spent in a confinement that was as much a prison as the wicker cages where the songbirds lived out their days, wings clipped to keep them from injuring themselves against the bars. Abraham ben Jakob's son, precociously bright, inquisitive, who studied history in an innocence and simplicity he would not live long enough to outgrow, was no bigger than a seven-year-old and had the physical strength of an infant.

"That's part of it. When I was a boy in Budapest I used to hide stories about men like that in the pages of my schoolbooks. Our teachers were very strict with us; we had to memorize dates and battles and lists of kings, but I was always dreaming, and always in trouble. I made up stories in which I was the hero, but I knew people would laugh at them and punish me because of it, so I wrote them secretly, at night, when I was supposed to be asleep, and hid them in an old trunk in the attic of our house. You know what the Legion is, don't you?"

The boy nodded, so intent on what Joseph Kelemen was telling him that it seemed he had almost forgotten to breathe.

"As I got older, I thought the Legion was the most exciting and the most romantic army I'd ever heard of. A lot of young men do. When it was time for me to do something I really did want to do, something that would have made my family very proud of me, I rebelled. I had a very good life, very loving parents, but my head was filled with dreams, and one day I simply ran away from it all. I joined the Legion, not to kill people, not to be a real soldier, but because everything and everyone I'd known suddenly seemed dull. And I've learned, Avrom, that what seems thrilling to someone who only reads about it can also have its dull moments."

Even the monkey sat as if turned to stone. Ari ben Benjamin had forgotten to stroke his beard, and Ben Jakob, one hand on his son's thin arm, knew that he had been right to bring this stranger into his family. He was an accidental legionnaire, of the same stamp as the young men who fidgeted on the benches of the yeshiva and angered their fathers by talking too much about the colonies of European Jews who were attempting to farm in Palestine. It was good to have dreams when you were young, necessary for some men to do more than dream. How many years did you have, after all, before you married, begot children, and found you could no longer afford to dream?

"Shalom, Joseph Kelemen. Welcome."

She was even more beautiful than she had been in Ali ben Mustafed's garden. Her hair was uncovered, twisted and loosely bound up in thick, shining coils that framed her face in a red-gold nimbus of light. A long-sleeved, low-necked jacket, apricot silk embroidered with gold thread, molded itself to her body, and a full, flounced skirt of the same shimmering silk curved out from her waist like the bell-shaped bud of a new rose. Her feet were encased in yellow slippers stiffened with more of the precious gold thread. She was smiling at him, what might have been only a combination of courtesy and gratitude softened by her love for the crippled Avrom with whom the legionnaire had dealt so gently and so honestly.

Beside her stood two other women, a few years older and almost as beautiful as Rahel. Their dangling gold earrings and filigreed necklaces broke the sunlight into a hundred tiny rays so that they seemed to be a trio of candles aflame in the sanctuary of their hidden garden. One of the women was expecting a child. Close behind her a handsome young man in a long dark robe was standing guard over the precious treasure she carried. When she took a few steps forward to hand a goblet of frothy, newly pressed orange juice to her brother, he moved also, matching his step to hers, following the awkwardness of her body with his eyes. Another young man accompanied them, a youth of about sixteen, no trace of a sprouting beard on his cheeks, tall and thin, bonyknuckled hands hanging loosely at his sides. He had a bandage wrapped around his head, black hair curling in the warm dampness of the day, skin so white that it looked as though he had been dipped in flour, large black eyes in which could be read the continuing ache of his head wound.

"My daughters and their husbands," Ben Jakob said. "Estrella, Zorah, Isaac ben Marco, Tomas ben Torres." Each name was spoken with so much love and so much pride that it was as if Ben Jakob had reached out to caress his children.

"What you said about the Legion was interesting, Monsieur Kelemen. One always hears that all legionnaires are criminals trying to hide from justice." Zorah, the pregnant sister, seated herself beside him, acting the hostess, already, even though her child was unborn, the mother of this family. She was in her mid-twenties, Joseph guessed, her hair a shade redder than Rahel's, her features not as sharply defined, a little plump, probably to grow slightly more rounded with every child she bore.

"Many of them are, but no questions are ever asked, so there is no way to know what a man was before he enlisted."

Rahel had found a place on a cushion at her father's feet. Her face was in profile to him as she held up the glass from which Avrom had taken only the tiniest of swallows. Joseph dared not look directly at her; it was taking immense concentration to answer even simple questions. He had the sensation of being engulfed by Ben Jakob's family, of being pulled into their midst before he had had a chance to sort them out.

"We've heard that General Lyautey is totally unlike Moinier, that in Algeria he often dressed in Arab robes and favored conciliation whenever possible. Is it true? Will he be lenient with the Fassis?" Ari ben Benjamin's question was one that was being asked throughout the city. The personality of the new resident general who was soon to replace the

departing Eugène Regnault was the key to the future of the
protectorate, and would influence the life of every Moroccan.

"He has the reputation of being a visionary as well as a
very practical and determined military man," Ben Jakob said.
"The sultan hates and distrusts Moinier and has repeatedly
told Regnault that he wants to abdicate. Every morning he
wakes up with a new plan of action. Yesterday it was to slip
out of Fez, place himself at the head of the tribes, and
proclaim a jihad; today it was to blackmail the French into
giving him a fortune in exchange for cooperation and eventual
exile. The ulema is already talking about a successor."

"And what will become of us in the midst of all this
chaos? Are we also to be driven from Morocco by the French?"
Isaac ben Marco's question was the anguished and bitter plea
of a young husband soon to be a father who sees the safe life
he had planned for his child dissolving into uncertainty.

No one looked to Joseph Kelemen for the answer. Ben
Jakob was much more than the head of this family, he was
also one of just a handful of important Jews whose ties to the
palace ensured that few secrets would be kept from them.
This house had been put at his disposal by order of the sultan;
he had only to request an audience and it was granted.

"Within a year from now all trace of what was done in
the mellah will have disappeared. We've made ourselves too
important to this country to be ignored, set aside, or ejected.
We've become a part of its lifeblood. Almost every economic
tie with Europe has been made through us. No one can
control the rabble or the Atlas tribes. There's never been a
sultan capable of doing so, and the French, no matter how
many troops they station here, will have only slightly better
success. The rabble and the tribes have never been the whole
of Morocco. The type of man who could conceive of and build
this palace is the same one who has grown used to the
mechanical marvels we import for him, the same good Moslem
who cannot say 'Jew' or 'Christian' without also saying 'dog,'
but who has nonetheless cultivated a taste for fine wines."
Ben Jakob smiled. Moulay Hafid was known to be one of
those who had developed a delicate and demanding palate.
He turned to Joseph Kelemen. "You are an outsider," he
said, "a European, a Jew who by his own admission has
removed himself from his past. Do you see things any
differently?"

Joseph couldn't match Ben Jakob's quiet eloquence, nor, with Rahel's eyes now fixed on him, could he bear to contemplate a future that would bring harm to her. But he had found anti-Semitism in the Legion, and he knew that it infected the entire French army.

"There are Jews living in all the cities of North Africa," he said slowly, remembering how often Hamid el Kader had told him of them. "Lyautey, if he has his way, will not try to interfere with Moslem law, and he will certainly protect the Europeans already here, but I cannot say whether he will concern himself very much with the Jews."

"He'll want us safely back inside the walls of the mellah," Ben Marco said. "In every country in which we've ever lived, walls have been built around us. We're easy to find when a scapegoat is needed."

Avrom's eyes were very wide. He dreamed every night that he was on his father's back, being carried through streets he could never negotiate on his own, the bloody hands of screaming Fassis reaching out to drag him toward their knives. Now Zorah's husband was saying that it could all happen again.

"Our new homes will be finer than the ones we lost," Ari ben Benjamin said, frowning at the intense young man, warning him by his look that talk such as this frightened women and children and was best reserved for a time when men could be alone. "Where else would any of us want to live but in the mellah near our synagogues and schools?"

"Avrom, you've hardly drunk any of your juice," Rahel interrupted, getting up to hold the glass to the boy's lips. "Don't you think the bandage on Tomas' head makes him look as if he's wearing half a turban?"

Her laugh broke the tightness with which they had all been holding themselves. Estrella and Zorah excused themselves to see that the Shabbos table was being properly laid, Ben Jakob took Isaac ben Marco aside, talking so quietly to the young man that the splashing fountain drowned out what he was saying, Ari ben Benjamin poured more sherry into the empty glasses, dipping his finger into the wine so that the monkey could have a taste. The creature wrinkled up its nose, sneezed, shook its head, sneezed again, and scrambled onto Avrom's shoulder. The boy laughed, and a trace of color came into his cheeks.

"Were you badly hurt?" Joseph Kelemen was not certain who this Tomas ben Torres was. He had said nothing to anyone during the course of the conversation, nor had he touched his wine. He had the slightly dazed appearance of a person who has suffered a concussion, a wandering look in eyes that he seemed to have difficulty focusing. Perhaps the bright colors of Rahel's dress were all he could see clearly; until now he had never once looked in any direction other than where she sat.

"I fell somewhere and struck my head. The last thing I remember before I woke up in the sultan's gardens was Rahel bending over me." Torres' voice had only begun to deepen and change tone. He put a hand to the bandage and rubbed gently, worriedly, at a spot just above his left eye. "I still feel half asleep sometimes."

"You didn't fall, Tomas," Rahel said. "Someone pushed you from behind." She guided the hand that held the glass of sherry to his lips, watching to see that he swallowed some of the liquid, as assiduous in her care of him as she had been with Avrom, who was now coaxing the monkey to take a date from between his teeth. "Ari was able to pick him up, thank God," she went on, "and that's how I was separated from them. I was very foolish, Joseph." The gold embroidered cloth over her breasts scintillated as she sighed in mock derision of her own stupidity. "Tomas was carrying the best of his mother's jewelry in a bundle he'd stuffed into his robe, and when he fell, the bundle became untied and the jewelry spilled out onto the ground. I stooped to gather it up and all those people running behind us nearly trampled me. I am a very stubborn person, as my sisters will be happy to tell you. Once I have set my mind to something, I do not give it up easily. So I crouched in a doorway until everyone had gone by and then I ran into the street. I thought, you see, that I could find the jewelry and run after them and still be safe. But it was ground into the dust, most of the pieces broken and scattered. And then I heard Fassis coming, and I had to hide behind some hay stacked in a corner of an alley. Do you remember that day and how it was? This necklace is the only thing I managed to save."

She bent toward him, the fingers of one hand twisted in the intricately worked collar of gold and chips of precious stones. He could smell her breath, the scent of warm brown sherry and yellow roses, the spicy heat of her hair, the pungent fragrance of ginger that seemed to come from her skin. She was almost as close to him as she had been in Ali ben Mustafed's garden, and her eyes, more gold than green in that light, looked into his. What was she trying to tell him? What message was she conveying, what secret knowledge was she attempting to pass on to him with those eyes that were at once pleading, demanding, moist as if with tears she dared not shed, hard as if warning him that she had triumphed over disappointment and so must he, melting as though from the same flame that was consuming him?

"Tomas' mother wore this on the day of her wedding," she said, straightening as Ari ben Benjamin, a puzzled frown creasing his forehead, looked from Avrom and the monkey to his sister-in-law, who was closer to the legionnaire than she needed to be, "and so did I. You can understand why I couldn't bear for it to be lost."

"A necklace doesn't make a marriage, Rahel." Ben Jakob touched the circle of gold around his daughter's neck. "Even one that has been worn by a family's brides for as many hundreds of years as this one has." There was anger and exasperation in his voice, as though this youngest and most beautiful of his daughters was also the most difficult to teach and mold. "Zorah and Estrella both lost jewelry given them by their husbands, but neither of them risked her life to save it. Ask them what they value most in the world. Ask Zorah if any amount of gold would make her endanger the life she carries." Isaac ben Marco, not at all appeased by the quiet talk beside the fountain, had obviously stirred up feelings that the normally self-controlled Ben Jakob kept hidden. He sighed, and let his eyes rest on the young man whose head was swathed in bandages. "Tomas himself will tell you that the necklace would have been a curse to him had it caused your death." Estrella beckoned from beneath the colonnade. "When I've built the house in which you and Tomas will live, you will learn what it is to be married. Until then remember that you acted like a child, not like a woman, and thank God in your prayers every morning and evening that He sent this legionnaire to preserve your life and give you a second chance at acquiring wisdom."

Ari ben Benjamin picked Avrom up in his arms and Isaac ben Marco handed the noisome monkey to a servant. Ben

Jakob, having chastised his daughter, led the way to the songs and prayers and good food of the Shabbos table. Beside him walked his guest, a young man so stunned by what he could not believe he had just learned, so deafened by the phrase, "Tomas' mother wore this on the day of her wedding, and so did I," that his feet moved as disconnected from his brain as they had in the worst moments of the Legion's training exercises.

Rahel's eyes, so full of the secret she had known she could no longer keep from him, burned into his soul. She had said, in Ali ben Mustafed's garden, that she was untouched, that she had come through the peril of the streets unscathed. The sixteen-year-old husband to whom she had been married for God alone knew how many years was certainly as innocent as she. But how much longer would it be before Ben Jakob decided that the time had come for them to be bedded? Until the house he planned for them was built. Until the mellah breathed life again, until the rabbi could gather his pupils on the benches of the new yeshiva. Tomas ben Torres, scrawny, brains addled by the blow to his head, with hands that would be awkward and rough instead of gentle, a body that would bring shame, embarrassment, and pain instead of love and pleasure, could never be allowed to possess Rahel. Ali ben Mustafed had tried to interfere; Rahel, Joseph did not know how, had somehow seen to it that her father had been unable to end it all with speeches and a box of gold; Ben Jakob himself, a man upon whom many burdens had been laid, had unknowingly opened his house to the man who would steal his daughter from him. There was time, not much time, but weeks and perhaps even months in which to hope.

Rahel, her arm solicitously aiding Tomas ben Torres' faltering steps, looked at the legionnaire's stiff back and knew every thought that passed through his brain, felt every leap of his heart, shared every hope that rang in his voice as her father led them in song to greet the gladsome Sabbath.

It was the worst, the longest meal Joseph Kelemen had ever tried to eat.

They met in the crowded souk of the pottery workers, amid bowls and jars and cups and whirring potter's wheels. She wore a purewhite haik and litham, and he a djellabah and hooded burnoose. French soldiers glanced at them, passed by, Fassi workmen pointedly ignored them.

"Why did you let me find out like that?"

"How else could I tell you, Joseph? You had to know. My father isn't blind. You mustn't come to us again, no matter how often he invites you." The green eyes above the veil would not look into his.

"Tell me about it, Rahel. I have the right to know." He couldn't touch her, not here in this market with its hundreds of spying eyes that only feigned lack of interest. Whenever a man and a woman spoke together in these streets, ears listened and eyes watched. The haik concealed the female body, but it also shrouded it in a mystery that was more sexually arousing than naked flesh. "I have the right to know," he repeated, challenging her to deny it.

"Joseph, please. It can't matter. After today we must never see each other again."

"Tell me." He thought he heard a sob choked off before it could break. She looked straight ahead as she walked along the rows of brightly decorated clay pots. Her breath stirred the veil and muffled her words, but they were clear enough, and every one of them was as difficult for her to say as for him to hear.

"I was ten when we were married, Tomas barely eight. The feasting and dancing went on for three weeks, but we were too young for most of it. Afterward, when it was all over, we went home and picked up our lives as though nothing had happened. When Tomas' parents died, he came to live with us. We've grown up together, Joseph. We know each other as well as brother and sister."

"You're not really married, Rahel. How could you be? You were a child. You couldn't give your consent to this match."

"But I did. My father gave it for me. It's our custom, Joseph, and a good one. Moslems are often strangers who meet for the first time at the wedding ceremony. Tomas and I have had years and years in which to learn to love one another. When the time comes for us to begin our real married life, we'll slip into it easily and without fear. My sisters were both married at the same age. You've seen them with their husbands. Did you think they looked unhappy?"

He stepped in front of her, forcing her into a tiny shop

where a man looked up from his wheel, then hurried to greet and serve them. Pots lined the walls, the floor was damp with the water dripping from the wheel, the smell of moist clay was like that of a flooded riverbank.

"Fifteen minutes," Kelemen said to the surprised potter, dropping coins into the man's outstretched hand. "Fifteen minutes in which to rest your fingers and drink a glass of tea." The man ducked past them, pulled a scrap of curtain across the open doorway, peered once inside at the couple who were certainly planning adultery, then hurried away. It wasn't every day you were paid the value of five good pieces for doing nothing.

"Do you love him, Rahel?" He reached for the veil, but she put her hand on his, pushing it away before he could expose her face. He held the fingers, carried them to his lips, forced them open, kissed the soft, tender palm. "Do you love him? Look at me when you answer."

She could not escape him, could not, for both their sakes, fail to convince him of what was not true. "I do love him, Joseph. I love him very much." Her eyes filled with tears. They cascaded down her cheeks, soaking the veil behind which she hid. She could not look away, could not break the spell of that awful moment. Like the helpless, tamed snake who weaved to the hypnotic music of its master's pipe, she was caught, trapped, unable to do anything but stand within reach of his arms, weeping with the pain of it.

"Don't cry, my love. Tomas is still only a boy. He'll find himself another wife when the time comes that he needs more than a playmate."

"No, Joseph. I couldn't hurt him like that. Why won't you understand? My father. My father would cut me out of his heart, would read the prayers for the dead and never, never say my name again. Go back to Europe. I'm married and nothing either of us can do will change that." She had said the words over and over again as she walked to meet him, repeated them a thousand times since he had whispered that he would be waiting here for her. Go back to Europe. I'm someone else's wife. Forget what has not even had time to bloom between us. It's madness to continue. She hadn't slept in two nights, remembering every word he had said to her, the scent of the jasmine in Ali ben Mustafed's garden, the terrible, wrenching shock of seeing him beside her father. Now she was so blinded by tears that she could hardly make out the features of his face, features she had planned to engrave on her heart for all the long, empty years to come. Dizzy with fatigue, she swayed, the potter's shop swirling around her. A moment later she was in his arms, the veil fluttering to the floor, her lips raised for his kiss, her whole body straining to become one with his, all her senses betraying her, sharpened and hungry, no thought at all in her mind of how this would end.

It was Ari ben Benjamin who destroyed their hopes, made them furtive, guilty lovers. He did it out of kindness and duty, prodded on by a worried, suspicious Estrella.

"He comes too often, Ari. When he knows that Papa will be at the palace or in the mellah. He sits in the garden with Avrom, brings him books and tells him long stories about Budapest and a tutor he once had who taught him to dress and think like an Arab. The boy loves him and is only happy when Joseph is amusing him, but something is very wrong. To look at them when they're laughing together, he and Rahel and Avrom, you would think they were married and Avrom their child. Tomas senses it. He follows Rahel everywhere she goes, and I've heard him plead with her to tell Papa that it's time to begin building their house." They were in bed, Estrella braiding her hair for the night, pulling angrily at the strands that curled themselves around her fingers. "Nothing has happened yet, and nothing must. For all we know, he could be lying to us. Good Jews don't join the Legion, Ari. Have you ever heard of one who did?"

She was lovely when she was angry, aroused like this, flushed and so impatient that she hadn't taken the time to button the yoke of the thin white gown she wore at night. She had been his wife since the age of ten, but only for the past four years had they lived together. It was puzzling that they had no children yet; both had learned that duty could also be pleasure, had forgotten by this time that the act of coming together had ever bewildered them. Ari ben Benjamin was a passionate man, a man who badly wanted to see his wife's body swell and bear healthy sons and daughters. He took the comb from her hand, undid the thick plaits, and kissed her into silence. His need for her was so strong that night and his release so explosive that he was sure she had become fertile at last.

The question and the problem were still there in the morning, more worrisome because she had smiled at him in a way that told him she too had experienced a new depth to their lovemaking. She was fussy and distracted, as though half attuned to a growing miracle within her, more determined than ever that the husbands and wives beneath Ben Jakob's roof should regulate their lives. "Tomas is right," she declared. "He and Rahel have waited long enough."

"A dozen years, the rabbi says. We're not Arabs to push a girl into womanhood too young."

"Rahel is eighteen. Tomas is man enough to learn to be a husband."

Ari ben Benjamin, loving Rahel almost as much as he did his wife, knew what it was that Estrella feared. It didn't happen very often in their closed, tightly controlled society, but there had always been girls, young women, who disgraced themselves and their families when the needs of their bodies became too clamorous to be ignored. They had partners in their sinning, but inevitably it was the girl who was discovered, who tried to end a pregnancy with drugs or a pointed stick, who pretended illness to hide the evidence of what she had called love, until the sharp eyes of other women discovered it and their determined hands dragged her out to public humiliation. There had been times, Ari remembered them well, when he had whispered into Estrella's ear and slipped his fingers beneath her skirt, teasing her and himself into trembling, shaking spasms of a wanting that had to be denied. And that was when they were already married, waiting out the years from sixteen to twenty, their parents' and the community's eyes constantly watching, gauging the time, forcing them to learn that what is long forbidden is all the sweeter and the stronger for having been withheld. They had brought their marriage customs with them from Spain centuries ago, and in the even hotter climate of Morocco their ways had flourished alongside the similar practices of the people among whom they lived. With one important difference. The girl who became a bride at eight or ten did not become a wife until her body was mature enough to stand the strain of childbearing. In this the Jews were wiser and kinder to their women than the Arabs.

"I'll speak to Rahel," he said wearily, dreading what would be an uncomfortable, certainly an unpleasant task. "She cannot understand how foolish and dangerous it is to be so often in this man's company."

"I think she knows very well what she's doing, Ari. She *wants* to fall in love with him."

Husband and wife looked at one another. Slowly Estrella laid her head on Ari's chest. His hand stroked her hair, and against his heart she whispered, "Poor Rahel."

"He will speak to my father if I don't obey him," Rahel said. Avrom had fallen into a light, shallow sleep, his hands resting on the soft fur of his monkey's back. The child's lips were faintly blue in color, his fingertips cold and also tinged with blue. The heat from his pet's body no longer warmed them. "He wasn't angry, Joseph. He was kind, and once I thought I saw tears in his eyes when he told me of how he and Estrella had come to love each other. He said that I would be the one to blame if you fell in love with me." There was such desolation in her voice that it was as if generations of disappointed lovers spoke through her.

"Tell him I won't be coming here anymore. Tell him I came because of Avrom, but that with Lyautey arriving any day now, I won't be able to get away from headquarters. Rahel, tell him that I talked to you about a girl in Budapest, a girl I'm going back to find and marry when my enlistment is over. Tell him, if you like, that you pity me."

"Is there a girl in Budapest, Joseph? Was there one?"

He shook his head. She was so thin it made his heart ache to look at her. There were blue shadows beneath the fine green eyes, and the rings on her fingers slipped around the bones from which loving him had seared off all the flesh.

"Avrom is dying, Joseph. We all know it. Whatever happens, I cannot leave him."

"When you need me, go to the potter. He has five children and a wife to support. I'll pay him well to carry messages."

"My father has changed his mind about the house Tomas wants. We're all to live together, in one enormous place that will also contain his offices. He's already bought the land and shown us the designs. He wants Avrom to die in a Jewish home, and he wants grandchildren around him. He's never talked about death before. The only time he smiles now is when he asks Zorah if the child has begun to move. Joseph, I'm so terribly afraid."

They sat in the sunlight beside the fountain until Avrom stirred and opened his eyes. He didn't weep when Joseph told him he would come only once more, to say good-bye, but after the legionnaire left, he reached out his hands to Rahel. Silently, because neither of them could speak, they comforted one another.

Joseph Kelemen went through the files at headquarters meticulously, searching, since he could not remember the name of the officer who had penned the report that had caught his eye, for the name that stood out from all the others. It was the only possible solution to the dilemma of having fallen in love with Rahel. "He may be a deserter, either from the Spanish sector of Morocco or from the Legion. The natives call him the Dark Foreigner. All we know of him is that he appears to have turned bandit, taken over a fortified village in the Middle Atlas, and set himself at the head of a gang of cutthroats whom El Hiba has not been able to recruit into his coalition of tribes. It seems clear that all of these men are outlaws, and as such, pose no immediate threat except to the local peoples on whom they prey." O'Brien had said that he would not be hard to find.

Kelemen removed the pages from the file, memorized the sketchy information they contained and the name of the informer who had reported the existence of the Dark Foreigner, then burned them. It was unlikely that anyone but he would read significance into the unedited notes, would even remember O'Brien among so many legionnaires who managed to desert every year, but he was taking no chances. If the plan that was forming in his head was to succeed, there must be nothing in the headquarters of the military mission that might betray him. More importantly, when Rahel disappeared, no one must wonder whether he and she were somehow linked. Some friendly spirit had placed an incompetent captain named Moreau in the office of adjutant, and for that he was grateful, but the recently arrived General Louis Hubert Gonzalve Lyautey and his insistence on superior officers worried him. The new resident general was far more knowledgeable about North Africa than anyone but Keleman and perhaps one or two officers skilled in Arab affairs suspected.

No one denied any longer that the city would once again become a battlefield. The Berbers who had proved to be no more than phantoms in April were reported to be massing again, in far greater numbers than before, and this time animated with the holiest of sworn oaths not to abandon their cause. With the legendary Lyautey to lead them, Keleman was certain the French would hold Fez, preserve it nearly intact. And afterward, as soon as it became safe to venture into the Atlas range, he would take the first necessary step to a new life with Rahel.

The attack began at 10:00 P.M. on May 25. Ten thousand Berbers poured from the hills surrounding Fez, each tribal unit concentrating its assault on a particular section of the city's wall. In the darkness the French fired at anything that moved beneath them, any piece of fluttering white cloth, any flash of flame from unseen rifles. The streets behind them were unnaturally quiet and empty. Spies had been slipping into Fez for days, passing the word in markets and mosques that when the battle was joined, it was the French and only the French who were to be killed. The city's inhabitants and its sultan were in no danger from the tribes. General Moinier had left the Fassis weaponless; they crouched in unlit rooms within their houses, listening to the man-made thunder all around them, waiting for what the dawn would reveal; many of them fashioning sharp, killing knives from kitchen tools, anticipating a breach in the wall, an invasion of their co-religionists, another chance to destroy the hated French.

At noon on the twenty-sixth the guns fell silent. Fourteen hours of continual fighting had exhausted both besiegers and defenders, and among the Berbers the casualties were enormous. Bodies littered the ground beneath the wall, the stench of gunpowder and spilled blood was stronger than any of the nauseating smells that clogged the air of the tanners' quarter, a layer of black smoke hung like an evil cloud above the domes and minarets. The French had sent for reinforcements, but no one knew how long it would take them to arrive. The tribes withdrew to the hilltops, regrouped, rested, sent burial parties out to retrieve the dead and dying. The French, trapped within the city, cleaned and reloaded their guns, wiped the soot from their faces, bound up their wounds, and waited. Lyautey held back the officers who wanted to lead suicide squads out into the hills. Every hour that passed meant that more French troops, more artillery drew a few miles closer to them.

The second attack was launched on the morning of the twenty-eighth, and this time there was a new and more murderous violence animating the tribes. The coalition was a tender thing; it would fall apart, perhaps never to be reborn, if Fez was not taken. They had only a few miserably out-of-date pieces of artillery, not enough shells for effective or sustained bombardment, a handful of men who could aim and shoot them. All they really possessed were numbers, the potential for sending down from the hills a human wave that might, just might, engulf and overwhelm the more vulnerable parts of the wall. A few breaches were made; groups of ten or twelve bloodied attackers were shot down in the city streets; almost none managed to escape. The artillery from Dar Debibagh swung around to savage the Berber flanks, the decimated units that had held together for so long broke apart, and by late afternoon Lyautey ordered limited pursuit. The artillery, against which rifles were virtually useless, had broken the back of the jihad. There were still those who resisted, who hid behind boulders or stood screaming in the open until their last bullets were fired, dying with the promise of heaven animating their eyes, but the real danger was past. Fez remained in French hands.

That night, with garbled reports filtering in, contradictory accounts claiming that the Berbers were both retreating and preparing for yet another massed attack, with all the important French documents piled in the courtyard of the hospital, cans of gasoline ready to be poured over them and ignited, locked in darkness again, waiting again, General Lyautey sat with a few of his officers, all of them fully armed, all of them prepared to execute whatever orders he might give them. And he asked one of them who was both a soldier and a poet to recite some verses of Alfred de Vigny, to read his own most recent work. The young officer, whose voice was strong and deep, whose oral mastery of his own language was as great as that of any actor who ever toured the provinces, declaimed for more than an hour the poetry of the man who had begun his military career imbued with the ideals of honor and arms, who had passed through periods of romanticism and ended embracing a solitary stoicism. It was poetry particularly well suited to the complex Lyautey, and the story of how he had spent that fifth evening of his command in Fez became another of the legends that he wore with grace and dignity. Four thousand Frenchmen lost in a city of ninety thousand Fassis, the remains of an army of ten thousand Berbers somewhere out there in the night, and the general soothed himself with poetry.

By June 1, the hills had been swept clean of insurgents by the reinforcements from Meknès. Papers were found that confirmed the worst of what Lyautey had suspected. More than twenty tribes, some of them hereditary enemies, had acted together to besiege Fez. There were hints that the sultan had encouraged them; Moulay Hafid was no longer to be urged not to abdicate. As soon as Lyautey found a royal successor less erratic and more controllable, the machinery for a change of ruler would be set in motion. Fez was the heart of northern Morocco. Now that it could be forced to beat in a rhythm set by the French, the pacification of the rest of the country could begin.

On August 1, 1912, Joseph Kelemen served his last day in the Legion. Fez was a changed city, Regnault and his mission of French diplomats had escorted the sultan to Rabat on June 6; Lyautey had remained only long enough to conciliate the wealthy and merchant classes and promulgate a series of orders that did much to return control of internal affairs to the traditional ruling bureaucracy, then he too had gone to Rabat. The native affairs bureau was in the charge of a brilliant and compassionate Arabic-speaking officer under direct orders from the resident general; Moinier's enormous fines had been canceled; pardons and amnesties had released the prisoners taken during and after the April rioting, and the French troops, except for a token force, had been withdrawn to camps outside the city. By giving Fez back to the subdued, defeated Fassis, General Lyautey had bought peace in this one small corner of Morocco.

The life of the city was its universities, its mosques, and its markets. While the rest of the country continued to seethe, while Moulay Hafid vacillated over signing the document that would place another brother, Moulay Youssef, on his throne, the markets of Fez began to bustle again, holy teachers gathered their students around them, wealthy men looked forward to a new influx of European luxuries, and the work of rebuilding the damaged quarters of the city proceeded faster than anyone had dreamed possible.

Colonel Gansard personally ordered Kelemen's file closed, an easy task in the new order of things. The former civil governor, had he remained in Fez for more than five days after the end of the siege, might have complicated matters, being an impossibly honest man with a passion for detail. But the care of Moulay Hafid had totally occupied him. He had had no time in which to remember the young man whose services to the family of a prominent Jew had momentarily interested the palace in mid-April. The legionnaire's discharge papers were processed promptly; the colonel's adjutant did not suggest that he should reenlist.

"I have already written to my family, telling them that I plan to take up my studies again." Kelemen scrawled his signature on the final document. "Probably in Vienna."

"You'r not tempted to remain in North Africa? Not in Morocco, of course, things are too unsettled and the general is discouraging colonists, but perhaps somewhere in Algeria?"

"No, Captain. I want to be on the next ship crossing the Mediterranean."

He really was an easy fellow to read. Life on the farms in Algeria was difficult and lonely; how like a Jew to want to scurry back to safety to learn a profession in which he could make his fortune. The adjutant made a neat packet of the copies of everything that separated Kelemen from the Legion and pushed it across the desk. The originals would remain in the permanent records, buried with thousands of others.

"You're entitled to transportation to the coast and passage back to Marseilles. After that, you're on your own. Good luck."

"Thank you, *mon capitaine*. I shall not forget the Legion."

Was there something cryptic in the way he said that? It was a phrase wrung from every departing legionnaire, sometimes spoken bitterly, sometimes with a catch in the throat. Kelemen's face was impossible to read, too dark and too foreign-looking to show emotion or reveal his thoughts. The adjutant rose to his full height, straightened his tunic, accepted and returned the Hungarian's last salute, and then shook his hand. He could not bring himself to give the traditional embrace which many officers bestowed on men who had served the Legion well. Keleman turned and left the office, already a free man. His final act would be to remove the insignia from the uniform he would never wear again.

"It's done," Moreau reported a few minutes later. Colonel Gansard, to whom the Jew was only a very minor matter, glanced over the papers.

"Good. We want only loyal Frenchmen in Morocco." On his desk was a memorandum from the officer in charge of the native affairs bureau, asking him to provide the names of any men who spoke Arabic and had demonstrated an ability to work with the population. Lyautey had an idea that some among them might, even as civilians, be useful to the job of rebuilding and the consolidation of French interests. Kelemen certainly qualified, but it was also unspoken policy among certain ranks of those assigned to the task that by discouraging the Jews from establishing close ties with Moulay Hafid's successor, the uneasy Jews and the ruling Arabs could be played off against each other, more deftly controlled and manipulated for the distance maintained between them. He put Kelemen's dossier underneath a stack of old reports in one of his desk drawers. Eventually it would be filed; eventually someone from native affairs might find it and regret that the man had been lost to them, but by then it would be years too late. Kelemen belonged back in Europe, where everyone who mattered understood how to deal with his kind.

Ben Jakob's home was one of the first constructed in the new mellah. Patterned after the small palace in which his family had lived for half of April and all of May and June, it was on a larger, grander scale than anything ever built by a Jew living in Fez. From the street its walls were blank, plastered, sun-dried mud, washed with many coats of white. Within lay a central, almost public-sized courtyard, in the middle of which a tiled fountain sprayed cool water into the sunlight. Two stories of arched colonnades surrounded the courtyard, and beyond them were other, smaller squares, each with its fountain, its orange trees growing in tubs of cedarwood, its cages of singing birds and baskets of cascading flowers. There was much work still to be done; it would probably be another six months before the placing of mosaic tiling in the floors and door frames was completed, but it was a living house, already home to the daughters and sons-in-law who had settled into the rooms that bound them together and yet allowed each man and wife absolute privacy.

Estrella welcomed Joseph Kelemen, calling for mint tea to be poured, fruit set out, delighted to see him again, sorry that he was on the point of leaving Morocco forever, secretly pleased that Ari's intervention had resulted in weeks and months during which only Avrom had occasionally mentioned his name. The boy would join them. He had not forgotten his legionnaire. Rahel also must be found and told that he had come to say good-bye. Lately she had been so busy that Estrella hardly knew where to look for her. Zorah had given birth to her first son in a room that still smelled of wet plaster, and she herself had been obliged to restrict her activities. She who had always worn her skirts tightly cinched in at the waist now favored garments that were looser, more flowing. She blushed prettily when he gravely congratulated her. Wasn't he going back to Budapest, perhaps to be married? Rahel had mentioned something of the sort, not betrayed any confidence, but hinted that a girl was waiting, that Joseph had begun to think of becoming a husband and a father.

Avrom, little more than a wasted, skeletal figure with alarmingly blue fingers and lips, huge, bruised eyes and a voice that was almost a whisper, was pitifully glad to see him. Without the chattering monkey clambering over him he was so small, so still.

"He ran away, Monsieur Kelemen. Or was stolen. Two days after we came to live here. I woke up in the night because I was cold, and reached out for him. But he was gone. I don't want another monkey. There isn't time to learn to love someone else."

Rahel, when she came, behaved like a stranger, almost impolitely, Estrella thought. She didn't bother to remove the haik she wore so often now that much of her time was spent in the markets of the city searching for delicacies that might tempt Avrom's failing appetite. Whatever spark had seemed to be catching flame between these two had been buried under the ashes of their brother's long dying and the legionnaire's absence. Except for Avrom's whispers and Kelemen's attempts to make him laugh, the conversation was stilted, with long silences that the splashing of the fountain and the sounds of the tilers' small mallets did not fill. Finally Estrella rose.

"My father will want to see you before you go," she said. "I will tell him that you're here." She walked like a pregnant woman, feet a little wider apart than before, pelvis tilted slightly forward.

"Rahel."

"I know that you love her, Monsieur Kelemen, and that she loves you. I'm sorry that I can't disappear and leave you alone, but I cannot." Avrom's voice was so feeble that both Rahel and Joseph bent over him. "Will you be free after I die?"

"No."

"Yes."

"I'm not afraid to die. I don't want to, but I must. Tomas doesn't make Rahel happy. Sometimes he makes her cry. Are you really going back to Europe?"

"No, Avrom, I'm not. I'm going into the hills to find a place where Rahel and I can live together until everyone has forgotten about us. Then I will take her away from Morocco. But that's a secret, the most important one any of us will ever have."

"I won't tell anyone, no matter what. You don't have much time before Father comes."

They left him lying on his soft couch, huddled beneath a brightly patterned wool coverlet, shivering on a day that was so hot the flowers drooped and the birds were too exhausted to sing. Rahel's face, framed in the folds of the veilless litham, was strained and pale.

"When are you leaving?"

"Tomorrow night. At dark, when they close the gates. I've left my things at the potter's."

"It's so dangerous, Joseph. Anything could happen to you out there."

"But nothing will. I have a donkey loaded with pots and pans, nothing worth stealing. Peddlers are safe in the hills, Rahel."

"What if you don't find him? Or if you do and he turns out to be another person entirely?"

"It's O'Brien. It has to be. The description couldn't fit any other man. He told me, remember, that I should look for him in the Atlas. I've read other reports written by the same informant. There are women and children at the fortress, many of them. He mentioned one in particular, one woman who arrived with the foreigner and no longer bothers to veil herself. I'm as sure of what I'm doing as I am that I love you."

"Joseph." Rahel's eyes widened and she set her mouth as if to force herself to tell him something that would devastate both of them. "Joseph, I didn't keep my promise. I was so afraid for you that I . . ." She couldn't go on. Her hands twisted in the depths of her long sleeves and her shoulders sagged as if all the strength had gone out of them.

"What did he say?"

"Both of them. I pleaded with both of them to allow a divorce. Tomas first. I told him that I could never be a real wife to him, that no matter how long we lived together or how many children of his I bore, I would always be thinking it was someone else who was making love to me. I didn't tell him your name, Joseph, only that if he didn't give me my freedom I would hate him for as long as I lived." She pulled back her sleeves. Her wrists and forearms were encircled by purpling bruises, the marks of fingers that had twisted and gouged the tender flesh. Crescent-shaped cuts were evidence of fingernails that had clawed through her skin.

"I'll kill him for this, Rahel."

"No. No, he's powerless. He can't hurt me anymore. I frightened him, that's why he tried to force me. Afterward he wept like a child and begged me to believe that he loved me. He does, Joseph, but all the love I ever felt for him I've given to you. I pity him, that's all."

"Your father also knows?"

She nodded her head, miserably aware that she had misjudged the man she had revered since childhood. "I thought my happiness meant everything to him, and that if I explained, made him understand that I loved you as much as he loved my mother, he would give us his blessing, would agree that this time, at least, an arranged marriage could bring nothing but bitterness."

"But he did not?"

"He wasn't angry at first. He was like Ari was, saddened and gentle. He said that although he owed you a life, it was not mine, but his."

"Where were you yesterday? I waited for more than two hours."

"I was here. My father is having me watched. He said that I would learn to love Tomas, that he promised me, but also promised that I would not have his trust until you had left Morocco. I tried to leave the house, but I can't go anywhere alone. Even today, when I went to the market to buy fruit for Avrom, the woman stuck so closely to me that I could feel her breath on the back of my neck. Joseph, he doesn't really know about us. He's convinced that I've almost made a fool of myself but that you know nothing of my feelings. He said that many girls on the eve of becoming wives think they have fallen in love with someone else. He said it's natural for a bride to be afraid."

"I want you, Rahel. Tonight. I want to leave this place knowing that you're my wife, that nothing and no one will ever be able to take that away from us."

She turned away from him. "Do you see that basket of roses, Joseph? The white roses hanging beside the blue tiles? And the door to the right? Not even my father would imagine that I would leave it unbarred."

When Ben Jakob hurried through the colonnade to the courtyard, he saw a scene that slowed his footsteps, made him smile to himself, though with very little joy. Rahel, his beloved, impetuous, husband-shy daughter, sat demurely under the shade of a fringed palm. Her eyes were on the legionnaire, who was talking animatedly to Avrom, but she was so far away from the young Hungarian that private speech between them was impossible. He could read the look on her face, a fond, almost hungry yearning, but Joseph Kelemen seemed to be unaware that he was being watched. Young girls, particularly those about to know their husbands for the first time, were often skittish; Ben Jakob believed that Tomas had only to woo her with as much tender passion as he could to drive all thoughts of this stranger from her head. He could not blame the legionnaire for the romance that attached itself to him. Never, not even from Rahel's own lips, had there been any suggestion that he guessed what she imagined she felt for him. Nevertheless, because he was a prudent man, Ben Jakob resolved to speak to the rabbi as soon as possible. He was glad now that when Ahmed ben Sussein had suggested that it might please Ben Jakob if the sultan offered

Joseph Kelemen a commission in the Moroccan army, he had been too preoccupied in the mellah to do more than shrug his shoulders and reply that time would reveal the most suitable reward.

The night was moonless, so dark that sentries on the city wall felt they were staring into folds of black velvet. Joseph Kelemen, blending into shadows, hidden and hooded in a dark-blue djellabah, walked barefoot from the potter's shop where he had earlier spread a pallet and paid handsomely for the privacy of the shop floor. Soundlessly he padded through the streets of Fez, slipping through shuttered market squares, past silent, empty teahouses, stopping when the growl of a dog threatened to turn into a bark, gliding on again through unlit streets beneath stars that were dim and far away.

How many times had they met at the potter's shop and walked together through the quarter that smelled of mud and dyes and baking clay? Two dozen, three dozen? His hand had surreptitiously sought hers among the folds of the garments that encouraged clandestine contact. They had talked, he telling her of Budapest, Paris, and nearly everything that had befallen him since then, she speaking of the mother who had died, of the loneliness that care of Avrom only deepened, of the heartbeats that had suddenly accelerated when she had looked above the rifle pointed at her to the eyes that were so soft and deep.

"Joseph," she had said, "I began to love you at that very moment, and later, at Ali ben Mustafed's, even though I thought I would never see you again, I knew I would dream of you every night."

"I smelled the jasmine everywhere I went. Even in my sleep I smelled it."

"Not hay and dust, Joseph? When you first saw me I was covered with the hay and dust of that alleyway." She could tease him because the happiness of being alone with him in the midst of a crowd fostered the illusion that they were hiding nothing. "When did you first love me?"

"I loved the idea of you all my life, and when your father sent me out to search for you, I knew the face that I would find."

It was foolish, light bantering, words and phrases such as lovers have always exchanged, thinking themselves the first couple to say so much to one another in a code as old as speech itself. Sometimes they were silent, Joseph burdened by the knowledge that there was no easy escape from this city and no hope for them if they remained, Rahel aching and drained from a sleepless night at her brother's side, her heart sick with wanting to keep all that was being taken from her. In the farthest recesses of the potter's shop they kissed and held one another, finding forgetfulness in hands that stroked, caressed, and yet denied themselves the intimacies both craved. Each parting was more difficult than the last, each meeting a new risk of discovery. Joseph had fought like a devil on the walls of Fez, every Berber he killed, every shot he fired buying a moment of safety for the girl whose life he would rather take himself than surrender to the maddened tribes whose treatment of women he understood too well. And Rahel, knowing that he was fighting, with no comforting woman god or saint to hear her pleas, had prayed to darkness that, if he fell, she might also die. When they had met again after those terrible days at the end of May, neither had been able to speak, and they had never left the clutter of the potter's workroom, wanting only to be reassured that each was safe, unhurt, and loving still.

The wooden doors that sealed off Ben Jakob's courtyard from intruders were unlocked, unbarred. Sometime during the night, after everyone within had fallen asleep, Rahel had crept down and removed the barriers that would have kept her lover from her. Now she waited for him deep in her father's house, beyond the fountain that made music in the night, behind a curtain of white roses and blue tiles. Had he been as blind as an eyeless man, he could have found his way to her.

Her skin was cool and infinitely smoother than the silken cushions on which she lay, her lips, opening at the first touch of his mouth on hers, like the firm, waxy petals of a night-blooming flower. She did not whisper his name; her heart sang it. Red-gold hair, hanging loose to her waist, enveloped him in a net of web-fine tendrils, flowing beneath his fingers as she pressed herself against him and then drew away so that his hands could mold her body as if she were a woman made of clay.

He made love to her with agonizing slowness, sometimes

motionless for minutes that seemed to stretch into infinity, arousing her, teaching her, fitting their bodies together with a passion barely held in check so that what was achieved was a perfection neither would ever forget. If these few hours were all that was ever granted them, they would be as worthy of remembrance as the lives of lovers celebrated in song and legend.

They never slept and they never spoke. They drank no wine but the nectar of each other's lips, lit no candles, wasted no precious moment listening for the footsteps that would mean they had been discovered. Like creatures in a timeless place, they existed only for the moment, each utterly lost in the other, each unable to cease loving even when it seemed that both were satiated.

He left before dawn, drawing a white coverlet over her, smoothing the tendrils of hair from her forehead, kissing the eyes that were tear-drowned jewels in the darkness, not looking back once his fingers rested on the door, slipping out of that room, out of that house, before his will weakened and his body betrayed them both, wandering through the streets like a man caught in a dream. At the potter's shop he rolled up his pallet, loaded the packs onto the donkey's back, left money concealed in their agreed-upon place for the man to find, and before the sun had risen, before the first call to prayer went out, had passed through the gates of Fez and up into the hills. Then and only then did he look back. If every man's and every woman's fate was written, as the Fassis in the city below him believed, then all he could do, all he could hope to do, was trudge onward to meet it.

8

His progress toward the mountains called the Middle Atlas was slow, sometimes no more than ten miles a day. The disciplined step of the Legion, a pace that ate up the roads with a speed unmatched by any except Roman soldiers, would have been a death sentence for Joseph Kelemen. Instead, he shuffled beside the plodding, heavily laden donkey, pretending a stoop-shouldered fatigue and a weariness that were more taxing to maintain than any forced march across the Sahara.

Now that Fez was inching toward normality again, the countryside that supplied the city's markets breathed a new vitality. Everywhere he looked the fields were under cultivation, the irrigation ditches flowing with laboriously diverted river water. In the pre-dawn hours he met farmers hauling produce toward the northern capital, and in the afternoon he was often caught up by men returning homeward with empty wagons. The nature of peddling is to move slowly, to greet every stranger as a potential customer, to sip tea and pass along the gossip of the region, to spread out one's wares a dozen times in a day, to take the time to bargain before reluctantly accepting an offer, to welcome the hospitality of food and a bed for the night, to linger in a spot and promise to return. It was too soon for Kelemen to begin asking questions. He maintained the guise of a poor merchant who hoped his journey would be short. But he had chosen his new profession very carefully. A good flat pan or deep stewing pot could last more than one wife's lifetime, and he made very few sales.

He was moving steadily southward, his mind fixed on

the location where the Dark Foreigner was reported to be living, and every night, checking his position by the stars, he knew that he was drawing closer. He made better speed once he had left the immediate environs of Fez, pushing the donkey along with few stops for water or feeding, leaving the farming villages behind, tasting a difference in the air as the elevation increased, the blue mountain peaks loomed larger, and the land began to slope perceptibly upward. The unfertilized soil was thinner, untouched by plows, broken by rocks that had heaved themselves through its surface thousands of years ago. At last there were no more palms, even at noon he was cool beneath his robes, and he could hear the sound of wind sighing through stands of pine trees and tall cedars.

Now when he stopped in one of the clusters of mudbrick dwellings clinging to the side of a mountain or nestled in an unexpectedly lovely valley, he disarmed the suspicious hill people with an almost simpleminded garrulity, bringing to vivid life the week-long siege of Fez about which all of them had heard but none had experienced at first hand. These Berbers were too independent, too fiercely devoted to their private little wars to have been enticed away from their mountains by El Hiba and his suspect plea that each tribe forget its grievances against another and join together for a common purpose. They had lived for generations swooping down on one another, raiding, stealing, taking captives whose executions were sometimes prolonged by torture, their scope of the world limited to a night's ride and a day's battle. They spoke their own language, Berber, a tongue with many dialects and no written form, but the Islam they practiced, although in many respects not the purer faith of Arab sections of Morocco, had also ensured that the men could converse in Arabic. The Koran existed in no other language. Hamid el Kader had trained Joseph Kelemen's ear well. In Fez he had heard Berber spoken in the markets; in the Middle Atlas both languages poured over him and he forced himself, often late into the night, to repeat conversations, to make sense out of the rush of syllables, resorting less and less frequently to Arabic, speaking a mixture of the two that often brought tears of laughter to the eyes of his listeners.

He was harmless, unarmed, a wanderer who threatened no one, whose store of tales was seemingly endless, and when he judged that the stars above him were in the right position, he began to dare to demand story for story, to exchange a pot here or a basin there for information about a man he had heard mentioned in another, unnamed settlement, one who had been given a title that must surely be an exaggeration, for how could any foreigner, any infidel, penetrate into these hills and carve himself out a domain that was reputed to be as impregnable as that held by his audience? It was true, they told him, but perhaps he wasn't really a foreigner but only called so because he had once lived among them. Four long days away, then three, then two. He was a giant of a man, black-haired, black-bearded, his eyes as deep a brown as the bark of a winter pine, but, and this was strange, so fair-skinned that he might have been one of them. The peddler, no insult meant by the remark, looked like an Arab, but the Foreigner, whoever he might really be, was neither distinctively Berber nor Arab, but something in between.

Looking into the blue and gray and hazel eyes that reported this, he himself much darker than the lightly tanned, brown-haired, or almost blond Berbers with whom he sat, Joseph Kelemen knew that O'Brien's black Irish looks both puzzled and intrigued them. The informant had been wrong about one important point. O'Brien was not the leader of a renegade bandit group; in these mountains every strong, marauding chieftain was only the ruler of a fortress or a village that mixed halfhearted agriculture and herding with the pleasure of raiding. If the little Kelemen knew of ancient Irish history was correct, there could be no other place on earth where O'Brien would feel more at home.

Three weeks after leaving Fez, he gazed upward at the fortress he had sought. Hidden in a stand of pines, he watched it for a day and a night, adapting himself to its rhythms, seeing traces of Legion training in the way the guards were changed at regular intervals, the careful mending of walls that showed signs of having once crumbled and fallen outward, the clearing of ground beneath them so that no force could approach without being seen or heard. In no way could this place be compared to the strongholds that Hamid el Kader had visited in remoter, more rugged mountains. The walls were not high enough, nor extensive enough to enclose more than a hundred inhabitants. But it was snug, secure, tucked into the folds of the hills so naturally that it might have grown there without human help. Sound carried for extraordinary distances in that thin air, and by the melodic hum and the rise and fall of voices he judged that O'Brien's enclave rang with life and a security that was all the more prized for being only slightly less precarious than that of any other Berber settlement.

He approached cautiously, at dusk, a time when cooking fires were lit, stock was being settled for the night, women were feeding their children, and men were thinking about the food that would soon fill their bellies. Crossing the open ground below the fortress's walls, the pots and pans banging against one another so that there was no pretense at stealth, he hummed a tuneless song to himself, deliberately playing the fool while his eyes and ears remained alert for a rifle bolt slammed back or a sudden quiet that would mean aim was being taken while others watched to see how he would fall. Ten paces from the central gate he halted, stood motionless so that they could study him. The minutes dragged on. The sentries searched the surrounding peaks for the quick flash of dying sun on other rifles, watched the outline of his robes blown against his body by the wind, concluded, as he had hoped they would, that he traveled alone and without firearms, opened the gate finally, and waved him through.

Inside, he was surrounded by armed men, curious women behind them, children who peered past their elders and laughed at the tired, sweating donkey whose muzzle was foamy and lax. Hands patted him roughly, darting into the folds of his djellabah, snatching the turban from his head, unwinding it, flinging the long piece of cloth back at him. He bore it all as impassively as a statue, seemingly oblivious to the insult of being touched and searched. Single-story dwellings with flat roofs of split pine leaned into the central avenue in which he stood. Like the walls, they looked to be old, abandoned at some time in the past, reclaimed and patched up with new brick atop the old. Directly opposite the gate was the fortress itself, a sprawling, sharp-angled building partially carved out of the mountain, not quite a castle, but far larger than any other structure he could see, reaching upward with exterior staircases, a stepping-stone arrangement of rooms and halls, a series of rooftops and open beams that suggested courtyards within courtyards.

And striding toward him, black robes whipping around his legs, a black turban on his head, an ebony-handled knife and a scabbarded sword hanging from his belt, came the man he had traveled all these miles to see, Dennis O'Brien, worth as much dead as alive to anyone who could return his body or just his head to the Legion. The women and the children fell back as he swept past them, the men, eager to share the powerful baraka he possessed, pressed as close as they dared. The essence of his magic was so strong that it could be transferred merely by the touch of his garments. They were explaining to him the precautions they had taken before admitting the peddler, the thorough way in which he had been searched, even the packs stripped from the donkey, as he could see. Pots and pans littered the ground; a few women had already begun to finger and exclaim over them.

Fifteen paces from the peddler, O'Brien stopped. He stared at Joseph Kelemen as though at a long-lost brother, his eyes lighting up and a broad grin spreading across his face as recognition became certain. An instant later he had seized both of Kelemen's hands and then crushed him against his broad chest, laughing aloud, slapping him on the back, stepping back to laugh again, shouting out to his people that this peddler was flesh of his flesh and heart of his heart. He snatched a rifle from the man nearest him, fired it exuberantly into the air, and before the reverberation of the second shot had died away, rifles were being fired all around him. His baraka was intense, never more so than when he was animated by joy and the power poured out unchecked. With no need to be told that tonight the fortress would be a place of feasting and celebration, boys ran off to cut out from the herds sheep to be slaughtered, roasted and stewed until the aroma of their cooking filled the valley with the heavy smell of mutton and crackling fat. Towering over his guest, O'Brien led him into the core of his fortress, a hall large enough to hold every soul living under his command, a dim, smoky place where enormous pillars of carved cedar held up a roof blackened long ago, a room on whose walls goatskins hung to keep out the cold, whose earthen floor absorbed the sound of their steps, in whose corners were heaped dozens of brightly hued pillows and piles of sheepskins.

"How long has it been, Kelemen? Half a year since we met in the Sahara?"

"Seven months, I think. How did you do it, O'Brien? Acquire all this, all these people?" Kelemen looked out over the hall, settling himself into the yielding support of the pillows that had been quickly spread for him, seeing even by the poor light of the torches burning against each pillar that the fine fabrics were stained with grease, worn thin, crawling with vermin. He pushed them aside, crossing his legs underneath him, hunching over as desert men do when they meet to talk beneath the stars. O'Brien handed him a clay cup, filled it with a white, translucent liquid that gave off a penetrating odor of alcohol and spoiled milk.

"To us, *mon brave*," he said, raising his own cup to his lips, "and a pest on the Legion."

The first taste was like a cauterizing iron applied to a fresh wound, searing and burning the flesh, the few drops of liquid Kelemen swallowed eating away at his throat, sending up fumes from his stomach that blinded his eyes from behind and seemed to singe the hair in his nostrils.

"My God, what is it, O'Brien?" he gasped, turning red and then redder stfil as he realized that the laughter he could barely hear was directed at him.

"Fermented sheep's milk. This batch is flavored with a bit of dung to give it more of a bite."

Kelemen sipped it cautiously through lips that were absolutely without feeling. The fire spread through his body, hot and then merely flowing; a wave of light-headedness gave way to a surge of well-being. He managed to laugh and then smile crookedly, wondering if he looked as foolish as he felt. All around the hall men raised their cups to him and he to them. When he turned back to O'Brien he had managed to down half the liquid; his face no longer had a rubbery feel to it and there was no trace of soreness in his muscles, none of the sodden fatigue that he had fought during his night in the pines. After their initial salutes, O'Brien's men ignored them, talking quietly among themselves, only a quick glance now and then piercing the polite reserve that allowed their leader and his guest to converse as privately as though they were entirely alone.

"Who are these people?"

"My people now. When I came here, there were only fifty of them still living in this fortress, the men killing each other off one by one because none of them was strong enough to lead, the women squabbling and the babies dying of filth and malnutrition. They had no baraka until I brought them mine."

"How did you do it?"

O'Brien touched the knife at his belt and held out his hands. "With this and with these," he said, his teeth gleaming through his beard. "I led the best of the lot on a raid with their rifles pointed at my back the whole way and their fingers itching to pull the triggers, but when it was over we had the beginnings of a good herd of sheep and no casualties. After that, others started drifting in from wherever they'd managed to hide and from villages where they were barely tolerated, bringing their guns and their families with them. I must have fought twenty men in hand-to-hand combat before the challenges ended, and once they did, I ordered the rebuilding. We raid at night, and once in a while I perform a little magic to remind them that without my baraka they'd all be homeless. I've never met a people like these before, Kelemen. They make the Arabs seem like weaklings. Look at them. They may be the last free men to be found anywhere."

Whether truly free, or willing captives of O'Brien's baraka, they were without exception handsome men who held themselves arrogantly, whose fine-featured faces were set in proud, defiant lines, whose limbs were straight and strong, whose eyes were clear and light in color, gray as the rocks or blue as the sky, eyes that never fell away in confusion or shame. The women who had begun to move about the hall, bringing in platters of oil-coated vegetables and steaming grain, basins of hot water and towels to cleanse the fingers of those who were about to eat, were as handsome and as fierce-looking as their men. Unveiled, wearing their husbands' wealth on their bodies, chains of gold coins woven in their hair, framing their faces, dangling around their necks, bracelets and rings on their arms and fingers, tight jackets outlining their breasts, baggy trousers gathered at waist and ankles, head veils that floated out behind them as they walked, they were like creatures liberated from the dream of a harem. But only Joseph Kelemen seemed aware of their presence. Wife-stealing or open lust could destroy the security of this fortress more surely and more quickly than any enemy from the outside. Here the Prophet's injunction against intoxication might be ignored, but the separation of the sexes, except in the privacy of each man's bed, was a sensible and binding way of life. Watching them, Kelemen remembered the woman whose husband O'Brien had pretended to be, the desert widow so shrouded in black robes that he had glimpsed only her eyes. At the right moment he would tell the Irishman why he had come, remind him of the debt that lay between them and name the price of its payment, but not yet. He had to be sure of O'Brien, had to be convinced that Rahel would be safe here, had to know without a doubt that the fortress would not fall, that the men who raided from it were truly loyal to the one who led them, had to know whether the wives and daughters would welcome his beloved or whether she would be condemned to the lonely life of an outcast.

"What happened to your bloodthirsty widow, O'Brien, the one who wanted her father-in-law's body left for the jackals?"

Annoyance flickered across the Irishman's face, disappointment that was almost disgust. "She miscarried again. A month ago. Another daughter. This one was too small to live." He waved his hand to cut off any compassionate remark, his eyes hard, white lines streaking around his mouth. "I took a second wife the day the girl was born, and I'll take a third and a fourth if I have to. The baraka must be handed on."

Kelemen guessed that it was less a question of needing a woman than proving his seed could produce male heirs that made O'Brien determined to beget a son. Even the Koran said that a man who fathered only daughters was both unlucky and cursed. Magic, whatever tricks the Irishman passed off as magic, might enthrall and mesmerize his followers, but soon, if he remained without a son, they would begin to wonder at the baraka that was useless to its possessor. Once the doubt set in, it was only a question of time before the challenges began again, and there must be a man, or two or three or four, who would not scruple to work in the dark, to sharpen his knife or seek out a witch.

"Tell me why you've come, Joseph Kelemen." O'Brien's fingers scooped up food, his beard sparkled with oil, the muscles of his huge body were relaxed, but his eyes, dark in the whiteness of his sun-resistant skin, were curious and alert. "I know it wasn't for the scenery."

It hadn't been two hours since he had entered the fortress, but already the Hungarian's status had changed from that of enthusiastically and joyfully received fellow European to that of specter from the past, legitimate claimant of a debt on the one hand freely contracted, on the other carelessly accepted, now so important that demand for payment must be pressed. Joseph Kelemen was a threat to O'Brien, a threat to be explored, reckoned with, and neutralized. Only the presumption of honor had led the legionnaire into the Middle Atlas, and he could wait no longer to find out whether his gamble would pay off.

"I'll send a half dozen men back with you," O'Brien promised. "But even though I ask them, order them as much as anyone can order these people, you'll still have to prove that you're worthy to fight beside."

It was nearly as dark inside the hall as it was outside. Most of the torches had guttered out, the remainder gave off weak, flickering flames. The meal was long since over, the sticky, sweet cakes that ended it consumed or cleared away. Only unmarried men slept or reclined amidst the cushions; husbands lay beside their wives in the houses that clustered around the central fortress, a few of them still awake, telling the inquisitive women that both foreigners had spoken all night in their own tongue, that no one knew who the stranger was or where he had come from, only that he was cherished by the leader whom most of them had begun to call the Lion. Cuffing or stroking their wives into silence, they too eventually fell asleep.

Joseph Kelemen had no more secrets from O'Brien. The fermented sheep's milk and the atmosphere of closeness, of trust, of having somehow come home to a place he had never visited before, had seen to that. He was as drunk as he could ever remember being, the kef in the pipe that passed back and forth between them heightening the effect of the alcohol, enlarging the hall, sharpening his senses so that he seemed to float out of his body without sacrificing the awareness of being. By morning he would have forgotten much of what had been said, but some part of his brain told him to hold on to the strange story O'Brien had recounted, the tale of the priest who had abandoned God.

They lay close together, their bodies touching at hip and ankle, torsos half raised against the cushions, eyes looking upward toward the faraway, smoke-begrimed roof of the hall.

Once, only once, O'Brien had spoken Erich's name, saying again, as he had seven months ago, that the rules of the game had changed, almost, but not quite confiding that there were young men here in the mountains whose bodies reminded him of the Bavarian's. A woman had approached them, gliding quietly out of the shadows, thin and dark, her face moving in spasms of apprehension and anger when she looked at the guest, her lips curling derisively as her nose caught the fumes of kef and alcohol. O'Brien threw a sheep's bone at her and she melted away, a black figure hung with gold and silver ornaments.

"A month, and still she bleeds," the Irishman said, shuddering at the uncleanness. "The other women are afraid of her. How many men have you killed, young Joseph?"

"None whose faces I've seen."

"The only ones who really count are the ones who come so close that you can tell the color of their eyes. A man isn't a man until he's taken a life and sired a son. That's elemental wisdom, but not to be despised. I'll make you half a man tomorrow. The rest of it you'll have to do on your own." O'Brien laughed, choking on the smoke he'd drawn deep into his lungs. "We have two prisoners captured in a raid, brave men who fought well. I offered to let them be ransomed, but the time for a reply ran out several days ago. We'll execute them at dawn. The baraka from one of them will pass to me, the other's neck will earn you the little Fassi girl." With a grunt like a satisfied dog that has finished its bone, O'Brien turned over, digging deeper into the pillows on which he lay, molding his body to Kelemen's, falling asleep as soon as he closed his eyes, snoring loudly under the sophoric effect of drug and drink. Joseph inched away from him until they were separated by a hand's width of space. He dreamed of a sensuously dancing Rahel clothed in floating, transparent veils, chains of gold coins tinkling like bells with every movement of her body.

He awoke the next morning to a thunderously pounding pain in his head, legs that threatened to buckle when he stood up, hands that trembled, and a stomach so weak that he didn't dare put anything into it. There was no sign of O'Brien, and except for the spot where he had lain, the floor of the hall was bare, all the pillows and cushions on which men had sprawled the night before piled haphazardly in the corners. It was as gray as twilight outside, the sun had not yet appeared over the mountain peaks, and the air was so cold that his cheeks reddened within seconds. Smoke from cooking fires rose above the rooftops, and from the large communal oven in front of the fortress came the smell of baking bread.

"You're as pale as a dead man, Joseph." O'Brien walked so quietly, so unlike the tall, heavily muscled man he was, that Kelemen started at the sound of his voice.

"You could make a fortune selling that stuff to legionnaires. It's more effective than a sergeant's kick to the side of the head." Joseph smiled ruefully, even that slight movement setting off firecrackers in his brain.

"If I wanted to make a fortune. Is that what you're after, *mon ami?*"

It was amazing. O'Brien looked as sober and vigorous as though he'd just bathed in a mountain stream. His eyes were clear, his skin was glowing in the icy air, one enormous, rock-steady hand idly slipping the ebony-handled knife in and out of its sheath.

"Someday, perhaps." Kelemen spoke without thinking, surprised to have said it, knowing suddenly that it was true. He owed it to Rahel, who had grown up in luxury, who would gladly follow him wherever he chose to take her, but who deserved far more than the mountains could ever give. She wasn't like these Berber women, had not been born with their strength, didn't come from a line that expected its females to work as hard or harder than any man. "Have you ever thought of going back to Europe, O'Brien?"

"Europe is as closed to me as Algeria. Even if I had papers, I'd smother there." The Irishman tore off a piece of the freshly baked bread he was eating and handed it to his guest. "Get this down," he said. "You can't afford a queasy stomach this morning."

There was a secret in his eyes, in the thin stretching of his lips, in the way he held his shoulders and rocked back on his heels. He was watching Kelemen with the anticipatory look of a predator waiting to pounce. And then, with the first swallow of bread sticking in his throat, Joseph remembered what had been said last night. "A man isn't a man until he's taken a life and sired a son. We have two prisoners. I'll make you half a man tomorrow. We'll execute them at dawn." He stood frozen with horror, unable to breathe, incapable of asking the question to which he already knew the answer.

"Think of your Jewess while you're doing it, or better yet, think of nothing at all. They expect to die, their honor demands it, and every man witnessing the act will judge you by the skill with which you make the cut."

"No." The word was no more than a croak, a harsh, explosive sound that savaged his throat.

"It *will* be done, Joseph. By someone. If you refuse, if you so much as turn your head away from the sight of the blood, not a single man here will lift a hand to help you. You may be able to make it back to Fez by yourself, but what will you do then? Alone, without my men, you'll be killed the first time another man covets her. And from what you told me last night, she's not ugly enough to be safe anywhere. Leave now, if you wish, if you think her father will not have you thrown into prison or sold as a slave when you ask him for her, if you believe you and she can hide from him in Fez, if you think they'll watch the ships any less carefully than they did when I was being sought." O'Brien smiled, a death's-head grimace. "There are ways to forget afterward, if your conscience is tender."

They were bringing them out now, men, women, and children stepping from the doorways of their houses, wiping the grease of the morning meal from their mouths and hands, silently gathering together, leaving an open space through which the captives walked, arms tied behind their backs, allowed to march at their own pace by those who were guarding them. Two bearded faces were all that Joseph Kelemen saw, two faces in which the eyes burned and the lips moved, not in fear, not in pleading, but in repetition of the holiest prayer in Islam. They carried their fate around their necks and it was he.

"It can be done either of two ways," O'Brien was saying, "by the stroke of a sharp sword on the back of the neck, or by a knife drawn across the throat. I've given them the right to choose."

Let it be the sword. Dear God, let it be the sword, Joseph prayed. Time slowed, nearly stopped as his vision narrowed, became a tunnel down which he peered at two tiny figures miles and miles away from him. A flash of light, and the ropes that bound their hands fell to the ground like dead snakes. They knelt, touched their foreheads to the earth three times, straightened, remained kneeling. First one and then the other raised a closed fist to the level of his heart, extended one finger, brought that finger across the throbbing pulse in his throat. They had chosen, and the crowd let out a collective, deeply satisfied sigh. This was the harder of the two deaths for being seen as it approached, and therefore the one that was both the more defiant and the more honorable.

"So be it. Watch me, Joseph Kelemen. Do exactly as I do. If you hesitate I'll take the knife away from you. That's a shame you'd never be able to erase. I won't be able to help you if you fail. And one thing more. We believe that a man who proves himself a coward deserves death. I've told these people that you are flesh of my flesh and heart of my heart. If you dishonor me, they will wipe out the stain by killing you. I know them, and I promise you that I speak the truth."

Three long strides brought O'Brien to the kneeling prisoners. With his left hand he reached out, grasped the hair of one of them, bent the head back until the skin of the throat was taut and every muscle stood out like knotted cord. The man's hands hung at his sides, his control so perfect and his courage so great that he had no need to ball them into fists to keep them still. O'Brien looked into his eyes, the condemned man blinked once in consent and acceptance, and then so quickly that it was over almost as soon as it had begun, the ebony-handled knife slashed so true and so deeply that the head was nearly cut from the body. Blood gushed over O'Brien's hand, spurted in a heavy arc to splash at his feet, flowed along the rocky ground. He let go the hair in which he had twisted his fingers, and the corpse fell forward bonelessly. Every eye followed him as he held out the bloodied knife to the peddler whom he had proclaimed to be so much more.

Joseph Kelemen's feet moved, his arm extended itself without volition, his right hand closed on the instrument of execution and tightened around the cold handle. O'Brien's eyes bored into his, dragged him forward, stopped him when he was in position. He could do it if he could look only into those eyes and no others. The second man was younger than the first, and the Irishman, taking a few steps to stand behind him, seemed to be placing himself there to guard the captive's honor, to hold his arms still should he at the last moment, unnerved by the sight and smell of his kinsman's body beside him, attempt to ward off the knife. But O'Brien had read the entreaty in Kelemen's soul, and he knew that only by maintaining the nearly hypnotic trance his eyes induced could he ensure that Joseph would be able to go through with it. Look at me, he was saying, speaking mind to mind and soundlessly, look at me and remember what my hands did. It's my left hand, not yours, pushing back the head, my right hand, not yours, raising the knife, placing the point below the ear, thrusting forward and to the side, digging the blade in with all the strength that can be mustered, slicing cleanly to the bone.

The second dead man fell forward into the pool of his own blood, rifles cracked all around them, and Joseph Kelemen, his right hand redder than it had ever been before, would ever be again, held out O'Brien's knife and wondered why so many faces looked at him approvingly and with new respect. They seemed to be acknowledging that it wasn't always easy to kill a man against whom you had not fought, who aroused no passionate anger, no hatred, nothing but perhaps the quickly fleeting reminder that your fate too was already written.

That day and for many days and nights thereafter, Joseph Kelemen accepted all the kef and all the fermented sheep's milk O'Brien pressed on him. Sometimes, waking in the middle of the night, he reached out for more, fumbling through the pillows on which they lay for the dream-inducing little pipe and the alcohol that burned away memory. They were always there.

"Welcome to my shop. How may I serve you, effendi?"

"Information only." Joseph Kelemen pushed back the hood that concealed much of his face. "Do you recognize me?"

The potter, who had risen from a crouched position over his wheel, sank back onto the short, three-legged stool on which he spent most of his waking hours. He wiped his hands on a bit of clay-stiffened rag, peering up at the man who stood over him. He knew who it was, had expected that one day he would return, even though almost three months had passed without a word since the night the donkey and the stranger who had never revealed his name had disappeared. Nervously, because half the money left behind had already been spent and he had no means of repaying it, he nodded his head.

"Good. Is there a message for me?"

"No, effendi. Nothing."

"The woman never came here? Not once?"

"I swear it by the hair on my children's heads."

"She sent no one in her place? No one who might have left a scrap of paper with you?"

The potter shook his head, raising empty hands, turning the palms up and outward. If there had been any temptation to lie, he had abandoned it the moment he looked into the eyes of the man who had changed so much since the profitable, sinful days when he had used this shop as a trysting place. It was cool in the damp corner where the potter did his work, but the shiver that ran up his back and made his fingers quiver was not caused by the chill in the October air. He thought he had never seen so hard and so merciless a face as that now before him.

The weeks of oblivion in kef and alcohol were long behind Joseph Kelemen. One other time he had been handed a sword with which ceremoniously to end a life, and on that occasion he had had no need of O'Brien's baraka to aid him. The code of the Berbers with whom he rode was so elemental and so intrinsic a part of the life they had carved out for themselves in their bleak, barren, and unyielding mountains that it quickly replaced, for any man who joined them, softer, more charitable or weaker standards. Given that time and that place, it was inevitable that courage was all, that to die well was as important as to live without asking that quarter be given.

He had grown a beard, developed hollows in his temples, his cheeks, and below his eyes. Honed to thin, muscular strength by the Legion, he was now pared down to bone and sinew, his skin so tightly drawn, so weathered by cold mountain nights and the glare of a sun without warmth that the blue veins beneath it showed through. He held himself differently, as still as a wild beast outlined against the sky when there was no need for movement, acutely aware of stimuli that lesser men never felt. When he walked, when he rode, when he fought, he was a dark wraith borne on the wind, menacing, soundless, his body implacably set on reaching the point on which his mind was fixed, whether it be a meeting with O'Brien inside the fortress or a herd of sheep they were stealing from another village. He had killed on those raids, but that was unimportant, incidental to the thrill of the raid itself. He was many times over a man, and none of the faces from which he had seen life ebbing haunted his sleep or disturbed his waking hours.

But the greatest change of all was in his eyes, and it was there that lay the ice which had so chilled the city-bred potter. The hooding of his lids was more pronounced, the folds of skin themselves somehow thicker, the black brows heavier, the eyelashes sooty streaks against the blue-whiteness surrounding irises in which no expression at all could be read. At once flat and compelling, empty and threatening, patient and merciless, they were no longer eyes in which stood the soul of the man. The essence of who he had been and might someday become again, the tender part of him that Rahel had captured in the first moment he saw her standing in the debris-strewn street of riot-torn Fez, all the heart of him that ached for her he had banished to a locked and guarded place that only she could ever touch. It had been necessary. To a great degree he had created himself anew, very nearly in reality what he had begun by pretending to be. The potter had good reason to be afraid of him.

"You'll never see me again. It would be wise, in fact, to forget that you were ever in a position to render me any service at all, no matter how insignificant."

"Yes, effendi."

"Close your ears to any gossip you may hear in the markets, and make sure your tongue doesn't wag." One by one Kelemen dropped a handful of coins into a jar. The potter's eyes blinked at the sound of his new wealth. For that much money he could arrange not to remember the name of his own father. "I have ways of finding out if you are foolish or careless."

The hood drawn over his head once more, the stranger paused in the doorway of the shop, a shadow against the brightness outside. The potter hadn't stirred from his wheel, and Kelemen knew that even after he had left, the man would be too busy retrieving and counting his bribe to think about following him. He paused nonetheless at the farthest corner of the souk and stood for a few minutes looking back at the shop. The curtain over the doorway never moved. The little man's curiosity was not nearly as strong as his greed and his instinct for self-preservation.

Hussein was waiting for him in the outer courtyard of the Karaouyine mosque, inconspicuous in the crowds of students and worshipers passing in and out of its arched entrances. The Berber was unimpressed by the size and splendor of the holy building. It had, after all, been built by man, whereas the mountains could only have been created by Allah.

"There was no message from her," Kelemen said quietly, hardly moving his lips as he spoke. "That means she's safe and she's here in her father's house. Nothing has changed, or she would have managed somehow to leave word for me."

He smiled, the genuine warmth of it startling his companion. El Elemen, as he had come to be called, did not waste his emotions, did not often display them except when he drank with the Lion and both of them argued until long after moonrise in tongues that had never been heard until he had arrived. They were different, the two languages they used when they signaled that they wanted to be left alone, more different even than Berber and Arabic; the one melodic, nasal, almost a song, the other full of stops and starts, less liquid, somehow stronger and more definite. It was good to see El Elemen happy, good to know that his fate would soon resemble that of other men, that the rooms the Lion had given him close by his own sleeping quarters would have a woman in them and children as the years went on. He was a brave man, the craftiest raider and the best fighter among them except for the Lion, and perhaps now that he was claiming his own, there would finally be some peace for the fathers of unmarried girls. Hussein, the parent of two virtuous, hot-blooded maidens, had been convinced from the beginning that their hopes should be directed elsewhere, but stubborn as were all females, they had never believed him, not even when El Elemen let it be known that he had taken a sacred vow to possess no woman until his wife was restored to him. Male and female of all species bedeviled one another; it was Allah's joke on the creatures he had formed. He himself wasn't inclined that way, but he had more than once thought that the Lion's preference for boys was a calmer, less troublesome way of satisfying the flesh. Take a woman for children, take your own kind for peace and pleasure.

"We must be certain," Hussein said, thinking it was more difficult to steal away one woman than a dozen horses or two herds of sheep. "We'll have only the one chance, and if we fail and an alarm is given, her father will not hesitate to have her killed, thinking that she has already dishonored him." El Elemen might call her his wife, and in his heart, perhaps even in the sight of Allah, she might well be, but earthly fathers were not omniscient. A virgin who was not a virgin was an abomination. For the sake of his name and because every other father would expect it of him, Hussein would not hesitate to dispatch any daughter of his who proved herself a wanton. The law was strict, but life was hard.

It was better, Kelemen decided, not to attempt to explain that Jews seldom killed one another. Hussein would think less of Rahel for believing she came from so cowardly a people. But he was right. There could be only one attempt made, and that one must be successful.

"There is a man in Fez who knows the family well, who will have visited their house many times since I left. His name is Ali Ben Mustafed."

"Does he know you by sight?"

"Too well for me to risk visiting one of his shops."

"The beard, El Elemen? Even I hardly recognize the peddler."

"This man would not be fooled. He knows too much, and he would be instantly suspicious. What reason could a Berber from the Atlas have for inquiring about one of the women of this city?"

Both men lapsed into silence, neither of them contemplating giving up, yet neither feeling that any of the tactics that had made them proficient stealers of sheep would be of any use in the narrow lanes of Fez. Suddenly Hussein stopped, one hand dropping a nearly valueless coin into a beggar's bowl. His face, when he turned back to his companion, was that of a devout believer to whom ultimate truth has just been revealed. He prolonged the moment, relishing it, finding no weaknesses in the scheme he was about to propose.

"Have you ever noticed the beggars, El Elemen?"

"They're everywhere."

"And yet no one sees them. No one pays any attention to them."

"It's the lowest profession a man can choose. Many of

their sores are faked. Even the ones who pretend to be crippled can probably walk as well as you or I."

"They must hear everything in the quarter, every bit of news, every hint of scandal, every lie and every thread of gossip, since no one bothers to lower his voice in their presence."

"What are you suggesting, Hussein?" Once more the smile played around El Elemen's lips.

"Seat yourself at the door to this man's shop. This Ali ben Mustafed. In rags and filth and with an empty bowl in your hand. If, as you say, he visits the house we must enter, it is only reasonable to assume that he also speaks about what he has observed there. Every merchant stands in his doorway talking to his customers in the sunshine. Why should our enemy do any differently?"

"He isn't our enemy," Joseph said.

"Any man who is not with us is our enemy. Do not mistake him for a friend, El Elemen. There are lives at stake in what we do."

Several nights later, at sunset, they stood at the gates of the mellah. Joseph Kelemen had learned more than he had dreamed possible when he first squatted beside the shop from which most of Ali ben Mustafed's business was conducted. By now the smallest and least important of his properties, it was also the one from which all the others had grown, and although he sent his sons to supervise grander enterprises, Ben Mustafed himself was too superstitious and too grateful to Allah for what had been given him to abandon it. A beggar outside your store, especially one who appeared unexpectedly and who bore no visible evidence of loathsome disease or disfigurement, was not to be chased away. Who knew but that he might not be one of those whom the finger of God had touched, a holy man who had found his fate outside the perimeters of mosque or school? And so Ali ben Mustafed gave orders that the bearded one was not to be disturbed, was even, since charity was a virtue much esteemed by the Prophet, to be given food twice a day and hot tea whenever the wind blew. Then he promptly forgot about him.

It was entirely due to Ben Mustafed's devotion to the Koran and to Hussein's conviction that no one really saw a beggar that Joseph learned as much about Ben Jakob's family as if he had interrogated the man himself. After the completion of the house that Fassis were already calling "the Jew's palace," Ben Jakob had flung himself into activities that occupied his every waking moment and so exhausted him that sleep, even as his son lay dying before his eyes, was both necessary and impossible for his body to repulse. He had been everywhere as that summer turned into fall, spurring on the construction throughout the mellah, spending hours with Ahmed ben Sussein and the others who were now the true governing body of the city, acting as liaison between them and the French, plunging back into the stream of commercial transactions that had always swirled around him, breathing new life into the cautious banks and trading companies, and expanding the scope of his own house, which maintained such close ties to other Jewish firms in Europe that between them they rivaled an empire in wealth and influence. And Ali ben Mustafed, in an introspective, saddened frame of mind the third day that the beggar sat beside his door, sipping the national beverage brewed from crushed mint leaves, had told his eldest son that there were men whom Allah blessed with one hand and chastised with the other.

"His only son dead, Omar, not quickly, not without the suffering that every father hopes his child will be spared if Allah takes him before he becomes a man, but gasping and wheezing for breath so that the entire house was filled with the sound and there was no need of a doctor's fingers to tell them when life had ceased. The boy's soul has hardly had time to find its way to heaven, and now the youngest daughter hasn't the strength to rise from her bed. My friend is wrung out with grief; he blames himself for what the women are whispering but the girl has refused to allow anyone to confirm. Why else would she keep to her room and turn her head away at the smell of food? In my opinion Ben Jakob is too lenient with all his women; he would not have consented to her husband's demand had she not also been insistent. Tomas ben Torres comes from what was once the best of their line, but it's no secret that he's suffered fits ever since the old mellah was destroyed. Had it been my daughter who was married to him, I would have bought a divorce. How can a simpleton get good sons from his wife?" Sighing mournfully, Ali ben Mustafed had emptied the dregs of his tea on the ground. The beggar over whose bare feet the liquid would have splashed had already taken up his bowl and fled.

The gates of the mellah were swinging shut. Two bored guards who knew that their charge was largely a symbolic one ignored the pair of hooded, dark-robed figures that slipped past them. Threats to the city's security were nonexistent in these days of the French protectorate; there were no challenges to the authority of the third brother to rule Morocco, the new sultan, Moulay Youssef; even the spies and agitators who had once infested the streets seemed to have given up. The only time a man hid his face and walked abroad at night was on an errand of love or lust. And may Allah give him strength and endurance enough to make the journey worthwhile. They settled themselves comfortably for the night, fitting their bodies into niches in the mellah's wall, their rifles a poor substitute for what they would have held had not this job paid as well as it did for next to no effort at all.

Joseph Kelemen and Hussein waited for midnight, watching the stars come out one by one, then by the hundreds. There was only a sickle of a moon, too thin and too far away to do more than turn the whitewashed building opposite them a dirty gray. Sound died away in the core of the house, night-prowling cats stepped lightly within arm's reach, scenting but not obliged to threaten the men who were as motionless as the stones over which the animals walked.

Hussein was calm, his soul at peace with the task he had set himself, the killing that must be done after El Elemen and his woman had left the room in which she now slept beside her new husband. He respected El Elemen, he would never have come this far with him had he not; but something, some excessive prudence had kept him from revealing what he knew the Lion would not have hesitated to request him to do. If the husband awoke, El Elemen himself would slit his throat, but if he did not, if his dreams were so deep that he didn't feel the absence of warm flesh beside him, then the final action, the taking of his life, would be Hussein's to accomplish. He suspected that El Elemen was possessed tonight, that his body had been invaded by the djinn who were the cause of the confusion and the momentary weakness that all brave men suffered periodically. Certainly his plan was sound, his movements no less controlled than usual, his eyes above the blackness of his beard as hard as Hussein had

ever seen them, but there was a fever heat to his skin that
warmed the doorway where they crouched, that emanated
waves of fire as hot as the coals over which the hindquarters
of sheep were roasted. By this heat Hussein knew that El
Elemen was for once capable of rash haste, susceptible to
forgetting the one action without which he could not bring up
his sons in honor. He was thinking only of the woman and
how quickly he could spirit her away to the hills above the
city where five other Berbers waited for them. For fear of the
noise the profaner of her body might make in his dying, he
might elect to spare him. And this Hussein could not allow.

Once before Joseph Kelemen had crept into Ben Jakob's
house in darkness, but that night he had been expected, the
way had been made easy for him. This time there were
smooth walls to scale with the aid of a slippery rope and a
padded hook, rooftops over which to slither, handholds to
find, vines that brushed against his face and tubs of flowers
newly set in the second-story colonnade. The location of
Rahel's room was burned into his brain, but there was no way
of knowing whether Ben Jakob had provided more spacious
quarters now that Torres had successfully pressed his claim.
His mind had played tricks on him all afternoon, throughout
the beautiful hours of dusk, deep into the black time of
waiting, never more vividly than when he felt Hussein's hand
on his arm urging him to go more slowly, more stealthily,
reminding him that caution and absolute silence were even
more important the closer they came to their goal. Did the
mountain Berbers ever fall in love with the women they
bedded? They killed for them, or for their own honor, but
were they ever possessed by the thought of a woman as he
was possessed by Rahel? Had Hussein ever experienced the
torture of imagining a beloved body stroked and penetrated
by someone so ignoble, so much less than a man that he
deserved the death given a beast destined for the cooking fire
or the dung heap? None of them had. There was no one on
earth that night who suffered as excruciatingly as he.

The door was unbarred. Did she slip from her bed every
night in the hope that he would come for her, awaken before
dawn to bolt it fast again with a heart that was close to despair
and a violated body that ached and yet would not forget him?
He hesitated, unwilling to risk the sight of an empty room or
a bed occupied by anyone else. It was Hussein's hand that

pressed against the wood, that caught and slowed the inward swing, that inched it open, then hung suspended in midair at the sight before them.

A huge four-poster bed in the heavy European style dominated the room, its sides hung all around with thin, gauzy curtains. On a low table beside it burned a candle, and beneath the candle, piled two feet high on the floor, lying on the chair over which a night robe had been flung, were stacks and stacks of leather-bound books. A man slept on the right-hand side of the bed, his body an oblong mound beneath covers pulled up to his chin, rumbling snores rising and filling rhythmically. Beside him sat a woman, one hand already laying aside the volume she had been reading, the other parting the curtains that seemed to have entombed her. Before they could enter the room she was at the door, her arms outstretched, lips biting back glad cries and loving words, the fabric of her gown so finely spun and diaphanous that Hussein turned his head away, willing himself not to remember the curves of her breasts and the red-gold triangle beneath the soft swelling of her stomach. She seemed not to be aware of him at all, melting into El Elemen's embrace, lifting her face for his kiss, shaking back the hair that glowed in the candlelight and flowed down her back like a waterfall in sunset. He counted his heartbeats, and when he reached twenty, he tugged at El Elemen's sleeve, never taking his eyes from the man who continued to sleep as if a long, untroubled life lay before him. They made no sound as they left; only by the emptiness of the air beside him did Hussein know that El Elemen and his love were gone.

As he walked toward the bed, Hussein ordered the man to awaken, not risking sound, but repeating the command in his mind, insistent, demanding. He slept on, drops of spittle collecting around his mouth as though he were a toothless old woman. He was young, a boy still, not more than a year or two older than Hussein's eldest daughter, fleshy like a man who spends his days indoors or sitting dreaming in the patch of sun at his doorstep. His skin was pallid and dotted with sores, his breath stank, and his hands were uncalloused. No wonder El Elemen had not killed him, had not remembered that it must be done. You could forget this one even before you turned your back on him.

Hussein's knife made the faintest of hissing noises as he

drew it from its sheath. He waited for the sound to register in the dull brain of the sleeping youth, but nothing happened. He reached down, shook him once, hard, and as soon as the eyes opened he plunged the blade into the soft spot beneath the chin, held it there with his right hand while with his left he seized both the flailing arms and pinned them to his victim's chest. Within seconds the legs had stopped their thrashing, the last breath had gushed from the severed windpipe, the heart no longer beat, and only the stubborn blood continued to flow sluggishly from the wound. It was over. El Elemen's honor was preserved. Hussein would leave it to the Lion to tell him how it had been accomplished. He had never been a man to boast about doing what was only necessary.

Minutes after Tomas ben Torres had ceased to exist, the bedroom in which his body lay was a shambles. Let them believe that thieves had broken in, Hussein thought as he shredded mattress, pillows, books, and clothing, opened chests and flung their contents on the floor, carried away with him Rahel's nearly priceless jewelry. The rings, necklaces, earrings, and bracelets, any one of which his daughters would have happily stolen from one another, he would give to El Elemen as soon as they were a day's ride from the city. It was a husband's right to deck his wife out or withhold jewelry from her as he chose. The last thing he did was to toss an armful of Rahal's clothing over his shoulder, reasoning as he did so that no matter how much they respected him, it was better that the men who would guard El Elemen's bride as they rode into the mountains should be shielded from the sight of her beauty. They were, after all, only men.

Five days later, having ridden day and night, pausing only when El Elemen feared that the woman for whom they had risked so much would fall from her saddle with fatigue, they reined in their horses before the fortress. O'Brien himself came out to welcome them, and in French, so that only Joseph Kelemen could understand him, he asked one short question.

"The slate is clean, *mon brave?*"

"Clean."

Now they were equals.

Her body was different under his touch, firmer, more rounded, almost like a pomegranate swollen to bursting with seeds that dripped sweetness and contained the promises of new life at their centers. Almost angrily, because he could not believe that in only three months he had forgotten the feel of her on the night they had become lovers, he stroked the skin that made his fingers burn with wanting her again, touched the lips reddened by his kisses, played with the damp curls over her forehead, remembered Tomas ben Torres and abruptly turned away. Why hadn't he killed him? Why hadn't he strangled him in his sleep? It was unfinished, he knew it was. With or without the help of O'Brien's men, he had to return to Fez and put an end to the life of the sniveling cur who had forced his way into her bed, usurped the place that rightfully belonged to him, done things to her that he could not bear to contemplate. What was it Ali ben Mustafed had said? "Ben Jakob would not have consented had she not also been insistent." The thought of a yielding Rahel, a Rahel eager for Tomas ben Torres' caresses, was one that nauseated him, that made his blood grow cold. Yet he would not ask her, would never mention Tomas' name in her hearing, would somehow manage to live with a snake gnawing at his vitals and slow poison driving him mad.

"Joseph." Her fingers traced the outline of his spine. "Joseph, don't you know? Can't you guess?"

It was an effort to turn back to her, to take her in his arms again, to unknot the cords about his heart and pretend that it was the exhaustion of their lovemaking that had made him separate himself from her as if to sleep.

"What will you name your son, Joseph?"

"My son?"

"Or daughter. I can promise you only one or the other." She was laughing quietly, teasing him again as she had done in Ben Mustafed's garden, in the potter's shop, in the markets where they had felt safe. She reached for his hand and cupped it around her breast. "Can't you feel the difference? I'm three months pregnant, Joseph. I've been carrying your child since the night you left Fez."

His hand fell away as though singed by a hot flame. He seized her shoulders, and sitting upright so that she could not escape from him, he looked into her face, his eyes questioning, doubting, his fingers digging into her until they met bone, relaxing only when he saw the tears well in her eyes and he realized that he was hurting her.

"Don't ask me if I'm certain, Joseph. Don't ask me if I know without a doubt that the child is yours. That question would kill me, my love, and I don't want to die, not when our baby is dependent on me for its life." She was crying now, her eyes wide open and streaming, her fingers reaching for his beard as if for hope itself, brushing over his mouth, silencing him, dipping into the hollows of his face. "Why else do you think I added my entreaties to his? I knew, Joseph, that it was bound to be discovered. Maids talk, and the woman my father set to guard me was unfriendly, a wizened, jealous hag who had never been loved by a man. I didn't know when you would return. There were nights when I couldn't sleep for imagining you dead. If I had had to wait for you for twenty years or into eternity, I would gladly have done it, but I could not, I would not let your child be born a bastard. Do you know what happens to unmarried women who bear a child? Do you know that by our law bastards have fewer rights than criminals? If you blame me for what I did, Joseph, if you cannot forgive me, it would be kinder to all of us to end our lives tonight. All three of us—or, if you cannot love me, then take only two lives."

The next morning, while Rahel still lay in the bed from which El Elemen had ordered her not to stir until all danger of a miscarriage caused by their forced ride was past, O'Brien told him how Tomas ben Torres had died.

9

The child was born in the first week of May 1913. The heaviness in her back had been with her since before dawn, but not until nearly noon was Rahel certain that this time the nagging discomfort would not go away. She was weaving a piece of striped cloth made from wool she had spun and dyed herself, the skill she had acquired during the cold winter months a source of considerable pride. The wool was so fine and the weave so nearly perfect, Fatima had shyly told her, that it was as good as anything the old women produced, and they had had since childhood in which to become experts. She glanced at the girl sitting beside her, thinking as she always did whenever she looked at Fatima that they were alike enough in looks to be mistaken for sisters. O'Brien's fourth and youngest wife was also pregnant; her ripeness in this her sixth month reminded Rahel of the way Zorah had bloomed, putting on extra flesh and becoming more and more languid the larger the infant had grown. She herself had become thinner, all her strength and energy seeming to flow into her womb, so that although her belly was enormous, her hands, her legs, and her face were nearly emaciated.

It wasn't that she didn't eat enough. She ate all the time, from the moment she opened her eyes in the morning until she closed them at night; bowl after bowl of steaming couscous, bread hot from the stone oven and dripping with golden sheep fat, meat stews simmered for hours over glowing coals, cup after cup of frothy white milk still warm from the animal that had produced it. All the nourishment she took in went to the child and to the breasts from which it would feed. Yet she was never tired. She awoke more ready than Joseph to clamber out from the skins under which they slept, cooked and cleaned, wove her cloth and helped care for other women's children, learned to scrape and stretch hides, even oiled his saddle and the Legion boots he still wore sometimes, until he put a stop to it. She was happy in O'Brien's fortress, more content than she had ever been in Fez, perhaps because the life she was living now was so different from the one she had led in her father's two grand houses that no comparison was possible.

Only a few times since Joseph brought her here had she been melancholy. Once, when a child had died and she had been among the women who had washed the body, the memory of Avrom's death had overwhelmed her and she had wept as she had not done on that terrible night. He lay in the same grave as their mother, so small and frail at the end that even after this short a time there could be nothing left of the flesh that had never been anything but a burdensome prison to his spirit. Whatever belief in God she had lost while he suffered had come surging back, and after her weeping ended, she had prayed. Joseph had understood, as he sensed her every mood and thought with no need for explanations. He had held her very tightly while she chanted the Hebrew words that were a comforting mystery.

When her baby had first kicked, when she had exclaimed in surprise and wonder, when she had gazed proudly around at the women sharing that moment, laughing with them and clapping her hands as excitedly as they, there had been one dark face that stole away a portion of her joy and frightened her.

"She doesn't like me, Joseph," she had whispered that night, her head cradled on his shoulder. "I don't know what I could have done to offend her, but I really think she would harm me if she could. Some of the women believe she's a witch."

"She's more to be pitied than feared." And Joseph told her Arema's story, remembering how broken and cowed she had appeared in the desert, how savagely O'Brien had treated her after their daughter had been born and died, how every man in the fortress knew she had remained unclean and would not let even her shadow fall across his path. In everything that concerned Rahel, and this poor woman's misery certainly did, he displayed a patience he brought to no other part of his life. "O'Brien could divorce her, but he won't. She keeps order among his other wives and sees that everything he asks for is provided. She still believes that one day the bleeding will cease and he'll breed a son on her."

Rahel shuddered. There were no ties between her and O'Brien such as those that linked Joseph and the man she felt was too obsequiously deferred to in this place. She knew some of his history, was even aware, since her husband hid little from her, that the Irishman satisfied himself with women only until they were pregnant, then spent his nights with boys and narrow-hipped young men. His second wife had also become mother to a daughter, but this time the infant lived. They adored him, all these women whose minds and bodies were set on nothing but conceiving his children, and because all of them except Arema were kind and loving to her, she hid her revulsion at their willing servitude and knew herself far luckier for being truly loved. Only Arema spoke harshly to her, seemed to be always waiting for an unguarded moment. Joseph said she was jealous, and being a man, he made light of it. Rahel wanted to tell him that it was more than that, but she had known too many sharp-tongued women, disliked too many of them herself to allow the cutting, uncharitable words to be spoken.

She mourned Tomas ben Torres for part of one day and all of a night, lying beside Joseph while he slept, her body rigid with thinking of other nights she would never forget, recalling the good companion Tomas had been when they were both children, the inadequate, fumbling, bruising husband he had become because she had allowed it. It was she who was the experienced partner when they came together, he the novice, but somehow, because she had wept and held herself stiffly, he had believed that she was what patient, deceived Ari ben Benjamin had promised him, an innocent girl-woman for whom response to his passion would come only after many months, perhaps years, of married life. Tomas had been her husband for barely three weeks before Joseph returned and Hussein killed him. She ought to hate the Berber for what he had done, for the murder that was far more cold-blooded than any death meted out by the old sultan's executioners, but she could not. Fatima was Hussein's daughter, and once, just once, the girl had revealed the

simple honesty of her father's character. "He loves El Elemen
as though he were a son," she said. "There is nothing he
would not do for him." Very, very hesitantly she had continued. "No daughter could have a better father." And Rahel
had understood that her honor was as close to his heart as was
Fatima's.

A sudden pulling, stretching sensation made her pause
in her weaving and hold her breath. She felt no pain, only
the gathering up of muscles readying themselves to expel the
burden they had carried for so many months. It would happen today. She was sure it would be today. "There won't be
time to finish this," she said, laying down the shuttle with its
thread of bright-blue wool. Faima looked questioningly at
her, and when Rahel nodded, catching her lower lip between
her teeth as the pulling sensation began again, the younger
woman reached out to embrace her. Laughing, because only
by leaning sideways could they touch, they got awkwardly to
their feet and left the warm sunshine for the room where
Rahel would lie on the birthing pallet until it was time to
squat and allow the midwife to pull the child from her body.

Other women, seeing the proud way El Elemen's wife
walked, counting the seconds during which she stood very
still, leaning heavily on Fatima's arm before continuing,
called excitedly to one another and wished her well, all the
stories of their own past confinements setting up a rhythm in
which their fingers moved more and more rapidly over the
looms. The old woman skilled in midwifery and the younger
woman who would one day take her place moved off together, pulling the bracelets from their arms and the rings
from their fingers as they went. No hard substance could be
brought into the room where a laboring mother lay, no small,
round, unyielding circlets. The first was the hardest and the
longest birth, the most dangerous because the djinn gathered
when a woman was at her most vulnerable. The midwife
never waited to be called; knowledge of her own kind was in
her bones, and although the ultimate fate of each of her
patients had already been written, she had fought back too
many demons, stanched too much blood, thrust her strong
hands into too many reluctant wombs ever to believe that
Allah was not merciful to those who fought well.

The initial examination was brief. Very quickly and very
gently the midwife measured the extent of the stretching,

palpating Rahel's abdomen, nodding contentedly to herself at the evidence of this very thin young woman's deeper strength. She ordered her to be dressed in a warm woolen garment that hung loosely from her shoulders, to discard all jewelry, to unbind her hair and remove her shoes. "Now walk," she commanded, starting her off with a firm push in the small of her back. And while Rahel paced from one end of the room to another, surprised because she had not expected this, the women cleaned the already clean chamber, brought in an iron pot filled with hot coals, and fresh water to be heated when the child was on the point of coming. All the garments and soft wrappings that Rahel had woven and sewn for the baby were laid out, the boxlike cradle in which it would lie was lined with a tiny lamb's skin, and finally, because the midwife expected the labor to be a long one, she ordered meat to be stewed with herbs, cracked marrow bones, and extra fat. The gelatinous broth that resulted would provide the new mother with strength to walk, to endure, and to push, and later, when the child lay in her arms, to heal quickly. An excited little girl dressed like a miniature woman, clutching a doll made of rags to her flat chest, ran to the open field where the sheep were spread out over the scanty new grass, then, too shy to approach the men guarding them, hopped from one foot to another until finally, unable to contain herself any longer, she burst out the news. It had never occurred to anyone else in the fortress to inform El Elemen that his wife's labor had begun.

The hours passed more slowly for Joseph than any other afternoon of his life. Hussein, too compassionate to laugh at the prospective father's obvious distress, kept him as busy as it was possible to be, but O'Brien, strangely surly and short-tempered, disappeared long before sunset. There were too many women in the fortress to make childbirth an unusual or infrequent occurrence, but somehow, as it had been when the Lion's women labored, this was subtly different from all other births. It was, and every man was intensely aware of it, the slyest of challenges, the tiniest of threats to O'Brien's baraka.

Everyone rejoiced when a male infant came into the world, each man feeling the kinship of their sex even though the child was born to another. There were always too many women in their camps; the lives they led and the raids from which some did not return took a toll among those who fought. The Lion would offer a celebration if El Elemen, flesh of his flesh as he had proclaimed him, became father to a healthy son. How could he not? But also, and there was no need for it to be said aloud, how could he not fail to wonder why Allah had twice withheld the blessing from him? There was much drinking that night as the moon rose and no word came from the chamber where El Elemen's wife struggled silently, as she should, but although Joseph's cup was always full and he raised it frequently to his lips, Hussein, watching him closely, saw that he never did more than pretend to swallow, and he thought it a good thing. There were hours in every life that needed to be obliterated, but there were also those which were very nearly sacred. One hoped to die knowingly, joyfully, touching the essence of Allah before being immersed in His fullness, and as birth and death were merely two sides of the same coin, it was fitting to meet the one as soberly as the other.

Rahel had walked until her legs could no longer hold her and the pains were coming so quickly that she barely caught her breath before the next one began. When it seemed that her body would break in two from the hammer blows across her back and the spasmodic cramping in her belly that was like the slicing of a hundred knives, she clutched the midwife's arm and uttered one deep, sobbing moan, the only weakness she had permitted herself during the more than fourteen hours of her travail.

"Soon, very soon now, my brave one," the woman murmured.

Rahel gestured toward the pallet spread out on the floor. She couldn't speak for panting through the pains as she had been told to do, panting with glazed eyes like the ewes who also stood during lambing. How many times had she been allowed to rest since the infant's efforts to be born had intensified? Not many, and not for long. Sometimes she had felt herself drifting off into a gray limbo of half-consciousness, the pain surely racking some other woman, but the midwife's hands had always shaken her awake, pulled her back onto her feet. With a woman holding her up on either side, she had begun to walk again. Now she wanted only to end it, to lie on her tortured back, give one last mighty push that would either kill her or release the child, and afterward she would sleep and sleep forever.

"You're very close, very close," the midwife said, her right hand firmly probing. She chewed on a piece of meat, as careful for her own well-being as she was for the young mother's, motioning to her assistant to wipe the cracked lips with water and to force another sip of the good rich broth between them. There was nothing wrong with El Elemen's wife, none of the danger signs she had often seen in births that ended badly. You could not hurry an infant into life, any more than you could force the flowers in the meadows to bloom one second earlier than Allah intended. Three or four more good pains and it would be time to get her to the birthing stool.

But that night, for the first time in many years, the midwife was to be fooled. Later she laughed about it and cautioned her helper against ever turning away, as she had done, to check that the sharp knife and the binding cloth were both within reach. "Train your assistant well," she told her, "and then remember that animals chew the cord with their teeth. If it comes to it, you can do the same." No harm had been done; El Elemen's wife had simply known that she had reached the limit of her strength and taken matters into her own hands.

With drops of the viscous broth still trickling down her throat, Rahel struggled onto her elbows, opened her eyes widely, fixed them on a wooden peg jutting out from the wall opposite her, took in air to the very bottom of her lungs, and then bore down harder than she had ever believed she was capable of doing. The veins stood out on her forehead and in her neck, she gulped air one more time, and then with a guttural, triumphant growl, she pushed Joseph Kelemen's son into the world. The midwife, a gleam of admiration in her eyes, caught the child in her two hands and held him up for everyone to see his sex.

"Just like a man," she laughed, praising Allah that he was whole and healthy. "Look at him. The first thing he does is to make water all over his mother!" Attending to Rahel, helping her to expel the afterbirth, deciding that the tear the child had made would heal itself, she washed the blood of life away, rubbed fat into the place that would be sore when feeling returned to it, made a compress of carded wool, and,

ready to interfere if her assistant hesitated, watched with one
eye as the pulsing cord was cut, the infant wrapped in absor-
bent cloths and placed in his mother's arms.

Her back was stiff and aching because she was old, but
there was one more task to accomplish, and this the ritual of
which she never tired. She washed her face and hands in
warm water, stepped outside the hot, stuffy room to put on
the jewelry she had left in a small heap beside the door,
straightened her garments, and then walked as proudly as
any victorious general to the hall where she knew El Elemen
awaited her.

Only three men sat there, two of them conversing in
whispers so as not to disturb the third, the Lion, whose face
was red with drink and whose eyes stared vacantly into some
past defeat or future dream. Arema, that strange, cold woman
from the desert whose daughter had turned blue and stiff
before uttering her first cry, seized hold of her arm before
the midwife could cross the threshold, before she could put
an end to the waiting.

"Is it born?" she hissed, her dark face so close that the
odor of her breath sickened the woman whose stomach never
turned at the smell of blood or death.

"A son," she said, not wanting to touch the fingers that
clutched her, but shuddering because they were so cold and
pinched so cruelly.

"A son." And the midwife knew that she had heard a
curse, knew that what had long been whispered was true.
The Lion's chief wife was a witch. Arema moved quickly, the
gold coins with which she adorned herself jangling against
one another as she whirled away. If she had attempted to run
toward the room where Rahel lay with her child in her arms,
the midwife, for all her age, would have flung her body across
Arema's path, but she did not. It was close to morning, long
past the hour when the djinn began to stir, but Arema,
minion of darkness, did not fear her natural element. The
midwife let her go, watching her as she fled, believing, as she
had never believed before, that powers awaited her in the
blackness of the hills outside the fortress.

Much of the delight with which she had approached this
hall was extinguished, her feet, a few moments earlier as
quick as a girl's, now dragged like the ancient, tired things
they were, but El Elemen's baraka was powerful, he would

know how to protect his son. Gathering herself together, smiling as she entered the hall so as to announce the good news before he had a chance to question her, she went to tell him that his wife had done her duty well, that his son was the most beautiful child she had ever held in her hands and that, Allah be praised, he would live to bring honor to his father's name.

The birth of his son cracked the armor Joseph Kelemen had forged in order to survive in the Atlas Mountains. Had the child been a daughter, the result would have been the same. Not until he held the infant in his arms, drew aside the cloths in which it was bundled, saw the perfect, curled fingers and the toes with their minuscule rosy nails, watched the miraculous, rhythmic rise and fall of the narrow chest, touched the tiny nose, the translucent eyelids, the soft, moist mouth, smoothed the feathery wisps of hair on its head, and cupped his hand over the spot where the bones had not yet grown together, where the pulse of the heart could be felt more strongly than anywhere else—not until he had experienced all these new sensations did he really believe that together he and Rahel had created a new life from the love and pleasure they had given one another.

Night after night through her pregnancy he had lain beside her, his fingers continuing to explore her body even when there was no passion left in either of them, talking in soft whispers while the twisted rag in the bowl of tallow beside them flickered and burned with a yellowish light that turned her hair to gold. They were precious hours, the only ones during which they reverted to European ways and speech. In daylight, and whenever they were outside the room that had become the center of their universe, they observed other customs, so ostensibly at ease in the Berber world that a stranger would never have guessed their origins. Although Joseph had caressed the growing infant every night through the muscles of its mother's belly, had felt it move, had seen the marks its size had made on the skin that stretched and stretched to accommodate it, had even, at Rahel's insistence, played at choosing a name for it, he had had no concept of what a living child would mean to him.

The weight of his son, the feel of him against his chest, the silky smoothness of his skin, the fragility of his limbs, and the angry, demanding wail when he was hungry or wet sent waves of excitement and a fiercely primitive love surging through him, making him feel more a man than he had ever dreamed possible. He had had some vague idea that one day, perhaps after several years, he would leave O'Brien's fortress, take Rahel back to the continent from which her people had fled, make peace with his father, perhaps even pick up and complete the medical studies he had so lightly abandoned. He had always known that he would cherish her, had always planned to make her life comfortable and secure, but in the deceptive isolation of the mountains, free to live together at last, he had drifted into a time that seemed so rich and so full that it had lulled him into forgetting that the essence of life was change, that, unlike O'Brien, an outlaw with a price hanging over his head, he was a free man, an honorably discharged veteran of the Legion, who could, if he desired, claim the citizenship of the country whose interests he had served. All this changed when Emmanuel, barely a week old, opened his eyes one night and smiled as sweetly as an angel at the man who hardly slept anymore for wanting to gaze at the bit of flesh that was even more a part of him than any beloved wife could ever be.

Rahel sensed the difference in her husband, was aware of the restlessness that came on him so suddenly, knew that all their lives were dependent on the decisions that would result from the thoughts he was thinking but not yet sharing with her. Patient because she trusted him, lethargic because she was cosseted and fed so well that her tired body was filling out again and demanding extra hours of sleep in which to heal itself, she allowed weeks to pass before questioning him. They were close, very close, their lives entwined one about the other's and both around the babe's like the tendrils of two plants whose roots draw nourishment from a common soil. Yet if they did not begin to talk of other things again, if they continued to allow themselves to drift, if they ignored the beckoning world beyond the hills, it would soon be too late to attempt to return to it.

"The baby will sleep for a long time, Joseph. He's full of milk, and I fed him a dozen spoonfuls of couscous tonight. Look at his stomach. It's as tight as the skin of a drum." The pull of Emmanuel's mouth on her nipples had aroused her, made her body remember how that mouth had come to be there, made strong muscles between her legs tingle and ache. She would gladly die to protect her son, but she also hungered for the little death that made her writhe and cry out beneath the weight of Joseph's body.

Somehow, in the few instants between turning away from the cradle and stretching out against the muscular length of her husband, she managed to let her clothing fall to the floor. She made no awkward movements, did not struggle with ties or laces or jeweled pins, simply shrugged out of skirts and bodice as easily as from a discarded skin. Watching her, Joseph remembered the night on which she had first given herself to him, and before the soft sheepskins had closed over her, he was ready. Their mouths opened and closed, met, parted, and met again; their hands and their hearts pulsed and fluttered like birds driven from their nests; they forgot to be quiet so as not to awaken the sleeping infant, and finally, when neither could do more than sigh contentedly or nibble at the lobe of an ear, they found that the reawakening of passion had also set free other hungers.

"We can't stay here, Rahel." He was the first to speak, the one whose thoughts were the more completely formed.

"I know that. I could be a good Berber wife to you if that were what either of us wanted. But it isn't."

"I'm not the man O'Brien is. I can make other choices. He can't. He'll die in these mountains, with or without a son to follow him."

She was glad that Joseph had said it, wondering only whether he saw the Irishman's obsession for what it was. Fatima seldom smiled now, too conscious that what Rahel had accomplished she must also not fail to do. All the joy that should have been hers in these last months of waiting for her child to be born had soured. She was afraid, afraid of the Lion's anger if she gave him another daughter. His third wife, barren or simply slow to conceive, had already been divorced and replaced. Hussein's daughter had confided that she would prefer to die in childbirth rather than have her husband berate her or set her aside. The strain of it made her almost hysterical at times; the fear was very real, the imagined disgrace that might be awaiting her something with which she declared herself too proud to live. What O'Brien did to his wives was wrong, terribly, terribly wrong, but

Joseph was probably the only man in the fortress who would agree with her.

"I don't want us to live our lives like this, Rahel. I respect these people, and perhaps if I were alone, I might become one of them, but I don't want our son growing up a thief." He had to laugh. He was a thief many times over, and other things as well: a kidnapper, even though the woman had been more than willing; an executioner; half a Moslem, half a Jew, who believed in neither faith; an accessory to the murder of Tomas ben Torres. Out here in these mountains, none of that troubled him. In each instance he had done only what had to be done, and the very acts that would have made him a criminal in Europe had in this place earned him the respect of men who considered them the proper deeds with which to fill their lives. "We'll have so many secrets to keep once we've left. You as well as I."

"Where will we go, Joseph? And when? And how?"

Emmanuel gurgled and hiccuped in his sleep. Both parents lay still, listening for the child's quiet breathing to become regular and steady again. At least one of Rahel's questions was easy to answer.

"Not before he's a year old. We can't risk taking him through the mountains until then." And while they waited for that year to pass, no other child must be conceived. Joseph would not endanger his wife for all the sons in the world.

"Will you take us to Budapest?"

"Someday."

Now that the decision was made, Rahel wanted all her questions answered, wanted to be able to envision the city in which they would live, begin to learn the languages she would speak if it were Hungary he chose instead of France, imagine the clothing they would wear, the type of food they would eat, the women who would become her friends, and the family that didn't even know of her existence. She pushed at him, tickled him between the ribs, as impatient and as playful as a girl. "Tell me, Joseph, tell me everything you're thinking. Tell me about Paris." She dotted his cheek with kisses and chewed for a moment on the hairs of his beard. If he didn't guess that the capital of the French nation was a magical fairyland about which every romantic little girl dreamed, then he was both blind and deaf, and she knew him to be neither.

"Paris is the most beautiful city in the world, my love, like nothing you've ever seen." He brought one of her hands to his lips. "Frenchmen kiss the hands of women like you, and in the springtime it rains nearly every morning, just enough to make the flowers bloom and the grass turn a brilliant green. In the afternoon gentlemen and ladies stroll in the Bois de Boulogne or sip coffee or wine on the terraces of cafés, watching the world amble past them."

"Are the women very lovely?"

"The most captivating of any country." She was too enthralled with what he was telling her to be jealous, but he reassured her nevertheless, telling her only what was absolutely true. "I never saw a Frenchwoman more beautiful than you."

This time it was he who sought to arouse, she who responded so quickly that afterward they only remembered that the lovemaking had been exquisitely sweet. She fell asleep, her lips moving slightly as she dreamed. The dreams were of Paris, of the Paris that Joseph had revealed to her, and if she envisioned mosquelike cathedrals that no medieval artisan would have recognized as his handiwork, she didn't know the difference and strolled happily in their nonexistent courtyards.

Child of luxury that she was, Rahel could not know that there was one problem above all others which her husband could see no way to solve. She had bargained in markets, haggled over the price of a handful of limes, measured out lengths of cloth that allowed no extra inch of fabric from which to make a garment, seen that tiny scraps of food were reused, even, in her eight months in the fortress, tasted the edge of want that was the constant threat under which the Berbers lived, but neither in Fez nor in the mountains had she ever been denied anything for which she asked. Her father was a wealthy merchant; all her life he had delighted in surprising her with gifts of jewelry, never mentioning the price of the gold that shone on her arms or the worth of the sparkling stones that hung from her ears. Money poured into her father's hands, flowed from his office into the lives of his daughters, but of where it came and how it increased itself she was entirely ignorant. Like a child she trusted that she would always be fed and clothed, that toys would always be placed in her hands, that she would never awaken to be told that her empty belly could not be filed.

Joseph Kelemen had no profession except that of soldier. He had been fodder in the ranks of the Legion, and there was no place for him in the officer cadre of any army in Europe. Unless he were to sell a piece of Rahel's jewelry, he could not, at that moment, have bought them passage on any ship sailing from North Africa. Only the very, very poor lived by selling what a few good years had allowed them to accumulate, one bad one obliged them to sacrifice. It was bitter, a foul taste in the mouth to look at his sleeping son and wife and know that if O'Brien turned them out, he might watch them slowly starve.

He had an unusually receptive ear for languages, a retentive, alert mind, and the eye of a man who instinctively distinguished between what was beautiful in form, color, and line and what was merely acceptable. His father's house had been filled with good art, fine music, enduring works of classic and modern literature. Hours and whole days spent in Budapest's museums had educated and refined his tastes. He could remember every detail of every painting he had ever seen; he forgot nothing. The desert had sharpened his naturally acute perceptions, had shown him the poignant beauty of stark landscapes and empty skies, the hypnotic quality of a living canvas where the absence of vivid color both soothed and disturbed. In Oran, under Hamid el Kader's tutelage, he had come to understand and appreciate the complex designs of Islamic art. Having grown up accepting the Western notion that the human form was every artist's ultimate test, he was stunned and then intrigued by the idea that geometric design could be equally challenging.

Five years of near solitude in the Legion had made the young Hungarian an inward-turning person, a man whose interior dialogue never ended. The silence of the desert had been deeper than that of any monastery; it had tested all his resources, stripped his soul, honed his mind, created in him habits of self-containment he was never to lose. The husband and father who worried now about how he would feed, clothe, and house the two tender, vulnerable beings for whom he accepted, welcomed responsibility, already possessed within him the seeds of his future profession. He would be slow to discover them; tragedy, chance, and another man's obsession would all combine to break them open. In his sleep that night he seemed to hear Hamid el Kader's voice reminding him that his fate was already written and hung around his neck. It was a trick of the mind to pretend to believe it. True fatalism came to him many months later.

"Look at him, Joseph. Look how well he walks." It was good to be outdoors again, good to see the snow melting on the slopes, to hear the torrents of icy water rushing toward the valleys, to feel the sun on dry, chapped skin, to breathe in fresh, clean air. Rahel's eyes sparkled, her hands reached out as if to gather in all the warmth of the day, and when O'Brien scooped Emmanuel into his arms and lifted him high above his head, she laughed to hear her son's delighted squeals. There were other children playing in the sunshine, and babies nuzzling against their mothers' breasts, but no child in the fortress was as beautiful or as perfectly formed as her son.

"He looks like you, like your father," Joseph said. The boy's head was a tangle of red-gold curls and his skin was as fair as Rahel's, but his eyes were a dark gray, nearly the black of Joseph's own.

"O'Brien adores him. I wish that . . ." She left the thought unfinished, the unspoken words haunting the air. Fatima's infant had been stillborn, and a girl. The Lion had not made love to a woman since. One by one he had sent his wives back to their families, all except Arema, who had no father or brother to take her in. Hussein had not allowed his daughter to die. He had slapped her until she wept, force-fed her with his own hands, and bought her a new husband two days' ride from the fortress, one who already had four sons and whose other, older wives treated her like a beloved daughter.

"Walk to the gate with me."

"Emmanuel . . ."

"Will be perfectly safe. O'Brien won't let anything happen to him."

It was true. Since the birth of Fatima's dead infant and his final turning away from women, the Irishman had held Emmanuel in his arms so many times that Joseph's son went to him as eagerly as he did to either his father or his mother. Evening after evening he had held the boy on his lap, feeding him food from his own bowl, tucking him between his legs while he listened to the disputes that were brought to him for judgment, allowing him to chew with his sore, teething gums on the smooth, cold ebony handle of his dagger while raids were being planned. It sometimes happened that a man without male heirs adopted a boy from a family with sons to spare, all children being the gift of Allah, and the women who saw how frequently the Lion appeared with Emmanuel on his shoulders or in his arms looked enviously at Rahel, believing that as soon as she gave her husband a second son, O'Brien would ask for, and she would be honored to surrender him, the first. It mystified them that she who had conceived and delivered one child so easily showed no signs of bearing another.

"We've waited long enough. In a few weeks the trails will have dried out and the nights will be warm enough to sleep outdoors. I'm going to tell O'Brien this evening that we'll be leaving by the next full moon. I'll ask him to buy our herds. He has gold from the sheep taken to Fez last summer."

"Will he do it?"

"I can't think of any reason for him to refuse."

"Joseph, have you thought that he might not be willing to give up Emmanuel?"

"He has no say in the matter. No chieftain can steal another man's wife or child without killing him first. It's the law. He loves the boy, Rahel, and because he does, he must know that the child is too fine and too intelligent to be denied his true heritage. There's a side to O'Brien that you've never seen, that he's revealed to me because he couldn't help himself. He's a king here in these mountains, but only because he failed so utterly in his own country."

There were things about O'Brien that Joseph could not tell her, secrets that festered in the soul of the man. There was a parallel between the drink he brewed and the life he led. Out of decay and rottenness came a product that was fearfully strong and intoxicating. In the blackness of the vats, in the barren, cold place that had once been filled with love, changes occurred that, once begun, were irreversible. Joseph knew too much about O'Brien, knew the full story of the boy who had hanged himself and come back now to dangle eternally from the rope to which the Irishman had driven him. On windy days, seeing from a distance the black robes whipping around O'Brien's body, Joseph could imagine he saw the priest in him, cassock plastered against his legs while he stared at the rocky soil and inhospitable hills of Ireland. It was a fine madness that seemed to be overtaking Dennis O'Brien, a duel he was waging with himself that not even death could end. He was scarred with the old wounds of the fight, bleeding invisibly with new cuts. Only when he warmed himself with the body of the little boy who trusted and loved him with unsullied innocence did he appear to be momentarily at peace. Even more than Rahel, Joseph knew what role Emmanuel played in the Irishman's life, what redemption he saw in the child's eyes.

He counted his sheep carefully, totaling up the worth of their fleeces, the market price of their meat, the swelling sides of the ewes, the health of the younger animals, the continued vigor of the rams. He was a wealthy man by Berber standards, but even if O'Brien was generous with his gold, he would be a poor one by the time they reached Europe. Rahel's jewelry, sold piece by piece and at whatever price he could get for it, would keep them for a while, but it was only a weak dam against the flooding waters of a future that still had no shape.

"You can stay or go as you wish," O'Brien told him. "You're a free man and the equal of any other." His eyes glittered and his hands seemed to be reaching for something. Alone in the hall, sitting cross-legged on a pile of sheepskin rugs, warming themselves at a smoky brazier, they had begun by talking of other things, by sharing kef and the milky alcohol with men who were restless after having been snowbound all winter. The animals in the pastures were becoming stronger and friskier every day, the men within the fortress impatient to feel horseflesh between their thighs and rifles in their hands. Joseph could not speak of leaving while they remained to listen and guess his intention from the Lion's face. It had been a long wait, but at last the words had been uttered. O'Brien had not been surprised.

"You said so yourself the first night you came here. One year was what you asked for, that and a handful of men. We struck a bargain, and I'm satisfied with it." A thin curl of smoke rose from O'Brien's pipe. He waved his hand through it. "Choose your country well. There's going to be a war in Europe. The diplomats in Tangier all know it. France and

Germany will be at each other's throats again. The French won't be able to maintain more than a token force in Morocco, and if they lose, they may never be able to come back. El Hiba is waiting for that. His messengers are all over the mountains. This time he may succeed, this time all of us may join him. Have you considered what could happen? Your wife and son may be safer here than in any of the so-called civilized nations."

"We can't wait much longer. If there is a war, the Mediterranean will be uncrossable. Who knows how long the fighting could drag on?"

"You're thinking France will welcome you, but I know her better. She'll give you citizenship and slap a uniform on your back before you've finished swearing the oath. We're both veterans of her army. Do you believe Saint-Cyr's officers have suddenly fallen in love with Jews? You'll be in the front ranks and in the worst battles. On foot."

"There are ways."

"To buy yourself out of service? In other wars, yes, and maybe, just maybe, in this one too. But with what? The sale of a herd of sheep and the rings from your wife's fingers? Don't be a fool, Joseph."

"We can't go back to Fez. Hussein saw to that. There's no city in Morocco where Rahel could be hidden. She's too much Ben Jakob's daughter."

"Stay here then. For a few more years at least. What difference does it make to a baby where he lives?" O'Brien had known all along where the crux of the matter lay. "He won't grow up to be a savage. Do you think I'd allow that to happen any more than you? Long before he's ready to begin his schooling the world will have reshaped itself. You'll be able to make a wiser choice then. You won't be walking blindly into darkness and confusion."

Everything O'Brien said made sense. Joseph puffed on the pipe the Irishman held out to him, drew the calming smoke into his lungs, drew again, and felt the tightness around his heart loosen as he handed it back. There was only one thing O'Brien had forgotten.

"In three or four or five years, there may be other children. That would make it harder, not easier." How could he explain to this man what loving a woman did to you? There had already been occasions when he had not been able to withdraw in time, weeks of anguished, guilty waiting during which Rahel tried to hide her worry from him and he had not slept for fearing that he might have made her pregnant again. It was like spinning the barrel of a gun that contained only one bullet. Eventually, if you pulled the trigger often enough, there would be an explosion.

O'Brien's face was a mask. Each separate feature had hardened, fixed itself in place. Joseph could no longer read his thoughts; the Irishman was very far away. The coals in the brazier turned to ash, the little pipe grew cold to the touch, and the midnight stillness of the mountains crept into the hall. There seemed to be nothing more to say.

"Go to bed, Joseph Kelemen. Give me your final decision in the morning. No matter what it is, I'll help you in any way I can. There hasn't been an hour since he was born that I haven't loved Emmanuel as deeply as if he were my own. Whatever is best for him will be done."

How could you feel painfully, compassionately sorry for a man who possessed a baraka as powerful as O'Brien's, who from condemnation to living hell had built a tiny kingdom in which he could live just as he chose for the rest of his days? Yet Joseph Kelemen did, and when he left the hall with the thought of Rahel's loveliness in his mind and the promise of his son lightening his heart, he knew that Allah had written a hard fate for the Irishman. Behind him, making not a sound, moving not a single muscle of his body, O'Brien wept.

"I can give you a son," Arema said. With a flaming stick she relit her husband's pipe. Her hands were as black as a devil's; the charcoal she had carried into the hall began to burn and she nudged the brazier closer to O'Brien's feet. "He wants to take them away, doesn't he? I've always known it would happen."

"I told you never to come near me," O'Brien snarled. He would have struck her, would have slapped the dark face, drawn his knife to terrorize her, but the pipe was warm in one hand and into the other she had forced a cup of liquor heated over the coals. Tears had frozen into the hairs of his beard even though the skin of his face felt too hot to touch.

"The boy is strong, and I would be very, very careful." She reached over, drew his knife from its sheath, held it to her neck, pressed the blade against her skin until a thin line oozed blood. "I give you my life on it," she said. "You would take it if I failed. Do you think I don't know that?"

He said nothing, neither agreeing to nor forbidding what she proposed. She was a witch, and once before she had removed an enemy, sent him into a lingering decline that had ended in death. She was more skilled than the midwife, more knowledgeable, less a woman. She had practiced her arts on her own body; she could gauge the efficacy of a poison drop by drop, could ressurrect from apparent death as well as kill. It showed in the brittleness of her hair, in the coarseness of her nails, in the dark mottle of her skin, in the way her bones refused to cover themselves with healthy flesh. The only thing she could not do was change the sex of a child in the womb.

"What would you use if I allowed it?"

She shook her head, raised a hand to cover her smile and hold back the breath that smelled of decay. "If you want a son, if you want El Elemen's child, I can give him to you."

"There's a price on every life."

"I ask nothing."

"A death must be paid for. In blood or in coin."

"No one will know the debt exists."

"Women have no honor. I will know."

"What value does a father dare place on his son's life?"

"I will take him to the cave. Tell him he can choose whatever he can carry away."

"It makes no difference. The djinn who live there are helpless. They will not always sleep, but for a few more years I can keep them quiet."

He despised her, that part of her that remained female, but the devil that rode her was fashioned from the same evil spirit as the one he had lived with since the age of twenty-eight. She saw it in him as plainly as he in her. He laughed to think that they would grow old together, bargaining, always bargaining, pretending to cheat their fates. He wanted the boy, wanted the assurance of the baraka she could steal for him, wanted to taste the immortality a son could give him, wanted him to silence the other one.

"Hussein will have to die also. Others might question, but only he would act."

"His fate is already written," she said. "There may be others too."

"Three or four women. Not too many. One of your daughters, to avert suspicion later."

"Both, if you wish. They are less than nothing to me."

He took the knife from her. When he killed her she would fight him as strongly as a man, would curse him with her last breath. He didn't believe in curses, only in blood and poison.

"One will be enough," he said.

"This is the last raid, Rahel. He asked it of me; one more time, he said."

"You want to go, don't you?"

"If you ask me to stay, I will."

She was dizzy and weak. His face seemed to swim in an opaque white sea. For two days now she had fought back nausea in the mornings, crawled in beside Emmanuel when he napped in the afternoons. The midwife had looked at her oddly today, but said nothing. She couldn't be pregnant, Rahel thought. Even if she was, she would hide it. Joseph would never know until she told him, and she could wait, she knew she could wait until Paris.

"Go ahead, my love," she said, wrapping her arms around him, resting her aching head against his chest. "You don't have much longer to play at being a thief."

Three quarters of the men who lived in O'Brien's fortress rode away with him, the sound of their horses' hooves echoing down the valley. If all went well they would return in eight days, driving sheep, horses, and goats before them. The fortress had only been raided twice since the Lion took it over, both times with no loss of life and few animals stolen. There were villages in the mountains that now paid a twice-yearly tribute in order to save themselves from the raids he led. It was a system under which everyone prospered. But this time, in honor of El Elemen, O'Brien was taking them to a community nearly as strong as their own. The reward could be great, but there might also be casualties. The women carded wool and set the softest mounds aside to bind up wounds; the men on the walls laughed at them, but appraised their work and thought it a good thing.

The first woman to fall sick was Arema's younger daughter. She complained of pains in her head, a terrible dryness in her throat, and griping cramps in her belly. Tended night and day by her mother, she died within forty-eight hours. The baby still feeding at her breast was given to another woman to nurse.

In bad years people said that djinn flew into the wells and contaminated them. By the time a grave had been dug for Arema's daughter, a dozen women complained of the same symptoms, two of the older men could not lift their heads from their pallets, and eight or nine children, most of them infants, were vomiting and passing bloody stool. O'Brien's only wife dragged herself around as if she too were on the point of death, wailing loudly and tearing at her hair whenever she saw her motherless grandchild suckling in the arms of the new mother whose milk was abundant enough for two. Three children died within hours of one another, and the midwife, brewing a bitter mixture of roots and herbs, fell into the fire beneath her pot. The skin melted from her face and arms and the coma into which she lapsed after hours of screaming agony was deep and mercifully short.

Rahel knew very little of what was happening in the fortress, heard only the echoes of the death cries and the grief of the bereaved. Emmanuel was ill, and sometimes, late at night, someone seemed to be helping her change his soiled cloths, someone held a cup to her lips, folded her arms around her son, sat beside her while she slept and dreamed and woke in a sweat and drifted into sleep again. In the morning there was no one there, and while she could, she fed the child and rocked him, memories of a dark angel mingling with a desperate longing to hear Joseph's voice, see his face, and cry out to him that they were dying unless he could save them.

The women whose bodies remained sound tended those whom Allah had smitten, wrapped the dead in white winding sheets and gave them to the men to bury. When the midwife died, charred and raving at the end, the assistant she had trained kept vigil over her body and then labored through a long day to deliver safely a child born prematurely. She was asleep herself, worn out with birth and death, when Arema carried El Elemen's son into the red light of sunset. There were empty graves waiting on the hillside, heaps of earth wet with the spring rain, two exhausted men leaning on their shovels, their feet caked with the mud they had just flattened over another child.

"He looks as if he's asleep, the little one," Arema said, folding the cloth back so they could see the still, white face. "There's another woman to be carried out. Leave the burial of this child to me."

They didn't argue with her. She had recovered, as had many others, but there was a clarity to her dark face, an otherworldliness that was unnerving. They watched her slide down into the grave, saw her place the dead baby on the soil, sprinkle handfuls of dirt over him. She clambered out again, fell to her knees and touched her head to the ground. She was praying like a man, but perhaps what had always disturbed people about this woman was that she seemed to possess a male soul imprisoned in a female body. They left the shovels at the edge of the grave, and when they came out of the fortress again, carrying lanterns because night had fallen, they saw that the hole had been filled in and rocks heaped over it to keep the jackels away. Far off in the distance there was a spot of blackness moving toward the hills. Let her go, they said to one another. Good witches intervened with and subdued the djinn. Bad ones were better off left to wander in the caves where their masters guarded old souls and waited to cast their spells on the unwary.

Rahel died in Joseph's arms. She regained consciousness only once during the night that he held her, smiling up at him now that there was no more pain, only this weariness against which she no longer intended to fight. "He would be lonely without me, Joseph. Even in heaven a child needs his mother." She could make out the figure of O'Brien kneeling beside her. She stretched out a hand, but did not feel him take it. "Thank you," she whispered. "Thank you for keeping us safe and giving us this time together." The green of her eyes matched the emeralds in her ears; they turned to stone, lost their fire and their glow, paled and died while the jewels continued to flash in the firelight.

No one touched her body but her husband. He wouldn't allow the gentlest of hands to wash or dress her. Alone, he did what was necessary, wrapping her warmly against the cold of the ground, tearing his garments, rubbing ashes into his face and hair, bending over her and wailing Hebrew prayers into the night. He wanted the grave where his son lay opened again, and it was done, but O'Brien and two others held his arms and wrestled him to his knees when he would have leaped into the gaping hole and torn away the cloth from the baby's face. One glimpse of the shroud was all they permitted him, one instant of whiteness below the dirt. They lowered Rahel in on a cradle made of rope, then shoveled the grave over, replacing the stones above it, leading him away to the oblivion he had known once before.

Rahel was the last to die. The sickness disappeared as mysteriously as it had come. Of all the men who had ridden away on the raid, only one had perished, Hussein. He had gone more quickly than any of the women or children, alive at the campfire one night, stiff and cold in his sheepskin in the morning. His fate was written, they had said, burying him beneath a pine tree, continuing on to the herds that awaited them, not guessing then what lay behind them and what only he had contracted.

"I don't want to stay."

"I won't urge you. Not now." O'Brien thought he had never seen a man more desolated by grief than Joseph Kelemen. He had already given away his herds, dividing them up between the men with whom he had ridden and fought. Everything that had been touched and cherished by Rahel was in another woman's possession, everything but the jewelry that had lain against her skin. That he wore in a leather pouch tied around his neck, resting against his heart. He slept in the hall, ate whatever was set before him, drank prodigiously every night, but was no longer affected by the liquor he consumed.

"You were right about the war in Europe. There's no stopping it now. By summer every nation will have chosen sides."

"A man could lose himself in a war."

"He could."

"Before you leave, come into the hills with me. Just the two of us. There's something I have to show you, a place I would have taken you anyway. I had a gift to give you, Joseph, a gift for Emmanuel and Rahel. I don't want it, it's of no use to me here. I intended it for them, for all of you, to make your life easier. I knew what your decision would be, that night I asked you to think over what I said."

"If you wish." So little mattered anymore that a few more days or weeks were nothing.

"Hamid el Kader told me there were caves like this. But he spoke of them as legend, as things that men only imagined might exist."

"Hobble the horses. There are inner rooms carved out of the rock."

They were a day's ride from the fortress. The last few hours they had ridden in darkness, O'Brien seeming to know the way even without the guidance of the stars or the light of the moon. The entrance to the cave had been a narrow cleft in the rocks. The horses' flanks had scraped against its sides, and were it not for the rags O'Brien had bound over their eyes and muzzles, they would have whinnied and shied away. After ten yards of twisting and turning, the cleft had widened, ending in an opening not large enough to admit the stunted mountain ponies, just tall enough to allow a man to pass through without grazing his head. A line of skeletons sat propped up before them, their bones resting against rocks piled up against their backs before they died. On either side of the cave walls, more dead men reclined, a gauntlet of fleshless guardians over whose outstretched leg bones they picked their careful way. O'Brien's torch flared on the chalky skulls; they were grinning in its flame.

The roof of the cave receded above them, its walls widened; the marks of picks wielded by dead men shone, smooth cuts in the natural outcroppings of the rock. "It was done for him, whoever he was," O'Brien whispered. He leaned forward, directing the flickering light over a pile of bones that had collapsed and fallen into a skull-topped heap. A rat darted between their feet, his red eyes shining briefly. They could hear his paws scurrying behind them.

"How long ago?" Joseph asked. He touched the skull, amazed at the heat it had absorbed from the torch, then picked up each of the clean bones carefully, almost reverently, and laid them aside. There was an iron chest beneath them, a coffer over which the man had once brooded before he began to decay.

"It could be hundreds of years. Most of the caves like this were looted while their inhabitants still rotted. I don't know why this one wasn't found. No matter how many spells were cast or how many curses proclaimed, even in those days there were robbers who did not believe in them. Open the chest, Joseph. I've been here many times. I think I know what it must contain."

The hinges were rusted, the leather straps that bound it so deteriorated that they were merely scraps. One hand was all it took to raise the lid, one slight push enough to break the threads that had once held it fast. The lid fell back, and Joseph caught it with both hands to keep it from clattering to the ground.

Light flashed from the open chest as though a fire had been lit in its depths. A wide collar of beaten gold that would cover a woman from her neck to the tips of her breasts lay atop the stones of every color of the rainbow. O'Brien lifted it out, let it hang, glittering and turning, from his hand, draped it across his arm like some fantastic scarf. Bracelets, armbands worn by expensive slaves, chains of twisted silver and gold links, rings set with gems the size of a man's knuckle, ropes of pearls strung on gold thread, cut and uncut stones were all mingled together haphazardly, as if impatient hands had scooped them into the chest from some greater treasure, taking time only to arrange the collar before closing and securing the lid.

"I always left the dead man undisturbed when I came here. I took what I needed from those clay jars along the wall, lesser pieces, smaller stones, miniature ingots of gold that were easy to melt down and reshape."

"When did you find this place?" The gems into which Joseph plunged his hands made a noise like pebbles sliding down a rockfall. It was impossible to calculate the wealth they represented, almost impossible to believe that they were anything but pieces of cut glass.

"Arema discovered it. She tried to keep the secret, to buy me with promises to bring me anything I asked for." O'Brien laughed, a bark that bounced off the rock walls of the chamber and echoed over their heads. "She claims to have put the djinn who guard the cave to sleep, and swears that she saw them, that she pitted her magic against theirs and won."

"I can almost feel myself believing her."

"There may be spirits here, but they're only the ghosts of dead men. I don't fear ghosts."

O'Brien fitted the torch into the empty eye socket of one of the dead king's companions. He squatted on the floor of the cave and took a packet of dried meat and thick round cakes of bread from the folds of his djellabah. "Eat some of this, Joseph, and tell me what you'll do with my gift."

If Rahel were alive, he thought, I would cover her with jewelry like a queen. If I still had a son, he would grow up to be richer than a Habsburg prince. If I were not alone I could care enough to be able to answer O'Brien's question. He let the gems fall through his fingers one last time, then sighed and turned away from the chest. He wasn't hungry, but mechanically he ate what the Irishman handed him, not even tasting the difference between bread and meat.

"I stole your child from you, Joseph. I killed your wife. Those are crimes for which you must either take my life or accept reparation. "O'Brien watched him closely. He could take the Hungarian in a fight, he was stronger, taller, alive in places where Kelemen was dead. It all depended on how he interpreted the confession.

"I blame myself for not noticing that she was already sick the day we left. What happened was not your fault. It has nothing to do with you. I wanted that raid, O'Brien. Rahel said it was my last chance to play at being a thief. I was like a boy acting out a great adventure; I wanted to ride a prancing horse one final time, feel the wind whip against my robes, fire my rifle into the air, scream like the savage I was pretending to be, see the proud look in her eyes when I drove a stolen herd into the valley. What is reality to them is a game to us, to me at least. Allah has written our fates, yours and mine. There is a time for boyhood and a time to grow into a man. I confused the two."

"I was your chief. You had to ride with me."

"No. I chose to. Do you remember how quickly and how quietly Hussein died? Every man who helped to bury him grieved, but not a single one disputed the will of Allah. There is no comfort in that, but there is peace."

"Take my gift, Joseph. If you throw it back in my face, you dishonor me. My life is here, and I must live it in harmony with a code you can discard in Europe. Your blood is on my hands, and only by accepting what I offer can you wash them clean."

He couldn't scoff at O'Brien's tortured logic, couldn't

even argue with him. The Lion believed every word he had said. He would probably go mad as the years passed. The sleeping djinn of the mountains would eventually awaken and join forces with the djinn he had brought with him from Ireland so long ago. Quiet madmen lived long lives, protected by the very spirits that possessed them, devils not eager to lose the host on which they fed.

"I'll take what you need to give. Not all of it, not even a tenth of it, but whatever portion pleases you."

"You see, Joseph, in this way I can give you back a life for those I stole. You can buy your way out of war, you can buy all of Paris if that's what you want."

He wanted to be out of that place, to stop O'Brien from talking, to cut off his explanations, to prevent him from speaking of death and the absurdity of ever being able to buy happiness or forgetfulness. Rahel's and Emmanuel's names were burned into his heart; he never wanted to hear them on another man's lips again.

"I'll wait for you with the horses," he said, getting to his feet, brushing crumbs from his fingers. He disturbed nothing as he walked from the cave, neither the bones of the king's guardians nor the djinn who watched him leave. They marveled that any human creature could so easily triumph over greed. They had no power over him.

O'Brien felt them hovering, but he ignored them as he worked, filling a leather saddlebag with the purest, the bluest diamonds, the clearest emeralds, the warmest rubies, the largest pearls. He chose only a few small bars of gold. It wasn't worth its weight when there were so many other, rarer objects for Joseph to smuggle back to Europe. He included only one piece of jewelry, a ring that lay amid the stones of the cave's rough floor, fallen perhaps two centuries ago from a hand losing its flesh. It resembled a wedding band, a thick, undecorated, faintly scratched circle of gold. The value of the metal could not match a single one of the stones, but as he held it briefly in the palm of his hand, he seemed to see its owner twisting and turning it, never without it, his other jewels rubbing against it, leaving their marks, denting its unalloyed softness. It was a memory ring, executed by a very ordinary artisan to commemorate some small personal happiness or sorrow. He didn't think Joseph would sell it as he would everything else. This was a piece that spoke to the heart, and one day the Hungarian would feel his begin to beat again.

Even after the saddlebag was full, he continued to search for more perfect stones, for brilliance and fire enough to buy a son. "There's a price on every life," he had told Arema. "A death must be paid for. In blood or coin." Only when the djinn sighed that it was enough, that diamonds could not cut as deeply as they into the place from which payment would be exacted did he close the bag and extinguish the torch.

Joseph Kelemen waited a long time for O'Brien, watching the stars, reading the constellations, remembering Hamid el Kader, seeing Avrom coax a monkey to take a date from his mouth, feeling Rahel's arms around him, smelling the warm drops of milk that spilled from her breasts onto Emmanuel's hungry lips. When the Irishman touched his shoulder and handed him the heavy saddlebag, he tied it to his horse and led the animal through the cleft in the mountainside, never even looking back to see if the leather had split against the sharp rocks and spilled its contents on the ground.

They parted at the foot of the mountain, within sight of the fortress and the graves that had been dug outside its gate. They clasped hands and then turned away from each other, their farewells long behind them. Within a week or ten days, the first of the unknown king's gems would be sold to a jeweler in Rabat. By the time Arema thought it safe to bring her treasure out of the hills where she had hidden him, Joseph Kelemen would be in Paris, teaching himself to forget.

O'Brien blessed the darkness into which the Hungarian had disappeared. He made the sign of the cross as easily and as cleanly as he slit a throat. The Latin words of absolution stole into his mind and he said them for himself, knowing it was a pointless, empty rite, laughing because life promised to be good and he had cheated his fate.

PART THREE
Paris
June 1936–November 1942

10

A shaft of pale-yellow sunshine stealing through the not quite closed shutters of her bedroom window woke Abby Sullivan Kelemen on the morning of her eleventh wedding anniversary. She let the spot of warmth play languidly over lips, cheeks, and eyes, then reached up one hand to capture the glow before it could creep across her pillow to where Joseph still slept. Turning her head, shielding him from the light, begging a few precious minutes in which to study the beloved face that was never as still, never as vulnerable-looking as in the last moments of sleep, she thought she had never loved him as much as she did today. Smiled then, remembering how many times she had puzzled over the miracle of living with a man who grew more dear to her, more a part of her, with every day and week and month and year that passed.

"It's almost indecent, Abby," Marie-Claire had said yesterday, tears shining in the eyes that were seldom free from pain now. "But I thank *le bon Dieu* that I saw at least one miracle before I died." The ever-skeptical, worldly Frenchwoman had shaken her head in mock despair. "It's nearly enough to make me believe in marriage."

Abby tried to push the thought of Marie-Claire from her mind. What was happening to her oldest friend in Paris had cast a pall over the past few months that Marie-Claire herself declared was not only unnecessary, but in extremely poor taste. "I won't come to Les Roses unless you swear that you will not waste a single good moment worrying over this abomination," she had threatened. "And if I see one frown, one of those so sad smiles that my poor Georges tries to

249

deceive me with, I'll leave." Because Marie-Claire wanted it that way, and because she had promised, Abby would forget, for this one lovely day at least, that for the second time in slightly more than a year, the devil cancer was killing someone she loved.

"Courage deserves to be met with courage, my darling." Even coming out of sleep, Joseph could read her thoughts, see to the very soul of her. He kissed the warm skin beneath the spot of sunlight, the exquisitely sensitive hollow in the palm of her hand, each finger, one by one, lingering over the pulse in her wrist as though he would count with his lips the beats of her heart.

"I wanted to watch you while you slept," she chided.

"Shall I pretend?" He closed his eyes, set the muscles of his face in a preposterously serious imitation of slumber, even managed an explosive snore.

"Joseph, you never make a sound."

"Years of learning to sleep on duty without ever being caught. One of the first talents a legionnaire masters."

"No, don't open your eyes. Shall I tell you what I see?"

"Brave woman, if you tell the truth." But he lay very still, holding the palm he had kissed curled against his cheek, while with the fingers of her other hand she traced the features of his face.

"I see a man I've loved for so long that sometimes I think I must be dreaming it," she whispered. "And the strangest part of all is that he doesn't look any different to me now than he did the first day we met. I can make those few touches of gray disappear from his hair just by blinking my eyes. This tiny line at the corner of his mouth, this deeper one across the forehead. Gone. I hear my name being called, I turn, and there he is again, reaching out with only his eyes to pull me toward him." Then, even more softly, lips brushing his. "If it is a dream, Joseph, I want never to wake up from it."

They made love slowly, each exploring the other's body as if for the first time, each finding the special, private places where a touch of hand or tongue most pleased the other, teeth nibbling delicately, teasingly, fingers stroking with the maddening softness of a feather, eyes open to see as well as feel. When Abby's breasts and thighs shone pearly and damp in the ray of sunshine that now seemed to fill their bed, when Joseph's skin had somehow darkened and the sound of his breathing filled the room, he entered her, and so ready for him was she, so desperate for the fullness of him, that one stroke set them both afire, made them both cry out at the same instant, both strain to hold and prolong the waves of ecstasy in which lovers have always claimed to drown but none has ever died.

They slept again, Abby deeply and contentedly, curled up like the cat he often told her she reminded him of, Joseph lightly and briefly, still, after all these years, attuned to the rustlings of human movement that meant danger in the desert. It was his turn now to look in secret, his turn to marvel at the loveliness of the woman he had pursued across an ocean, so afraid she would change her mind when on the last night of the voyage she had finally whispered yes to the question he had asked her not once, but dozens of times during those eight days, that their luggage had been left in the customs shed and he had persuaded a judge who was both friend and client to marry them while the confetti of docking was still in their hair.

He touched the gold ring she refused to allow him to replace with something finer, the soft gold, dented band he had found among the stones O'Brien handed him. Without quite knowing why, he had worn it himself as a talisman, so that by the time he stripped it from his finger to place on Abby's, it had the sheen and the feel of something impossibly ancient and sacred. A tiny piece had later been cut out by a jeweler, kept for years, then lost, Joseph could not remember precisely when or how. A fragment of his past, a portion of memory excised cleanly and without pain when finding Abby had begun to heal him.

She wasn't alone in being able to remember and recreate at will the moment when they met. It had happened over and over again to Joseph in the eleven years of living with her. A word, a glance, entering a room where she waited for him, even just the sound of her name on someone else's lips. The magic was always there, the vision of her brighter each time he saw it. She had whispered that he was unchanged, then conjured away the gray in his hair and the lines on his face, but he had no need to blink his eyes or murmur incantations of love to recapture the Abby of 1925. She lay beside him, more beautiful, if that was possible, than the girl who had whirled in sunlight in the paddocks of Longchamps.

It wasn't only the loving husband who thought so. Georges Louvier, as fond of Abby as if she were his own daughter, claimed she was the most beautiful woman in Paris. It had become a ritual for him to stand before the portrait painted on the Kelemens' first anniversary, champagne glass in hand, saluting the eternal youth of the woman who grew more lovely with every passing year. Poor Georges, he would be lost without Marie-Claire, was half lost already, knowing she would be dead before the first rains of October.

Very, very gently, so as to bring her slowly from dreaming sleep to wakefulness, Joseph touched the bright red-gold of Abby's hair, not a single strand less vivid than when he had first thought her crowned with light. He stroked the pale, translucent, perfect skin, the delicate eyelids that quivered beneath his finger. One almost invisible line was the only sign of change in her, and that tiny indentation at the corner of her mouth had been imprinted there by years of smiling at him, years of laughing with him, years of giving more joy and love than he had ever hoped to find.

Green eyes in the morning sunlight. Misty green eyes like the hills of Ireland that neither of them had ever seen but Abby had once described in Bridget's words and lilting voice. Soft eyes, heavy with sleep and something else, the so close remembrance of what she was stirring to arouse in him again, what he moved to meet even before her lips could form the words, that it seemed their skin had never cooled, their bodies never fallen apart for a moment. He whispered the words of love against her ear, and she against his. Old vows, so often repeated that they were eternally new. Eleven years of loving, eleven years that had passed so quickly, too quickly, moments that slipped away even as they tried to hold them and make them last forever.

"They can wait," Abby murmured.

"Who?"

"Our guests."

"Tomorrow. Fifty years from now."

"You talk too much, Joseph."

It was midmorning before they left their bedroom, a warm, bright June day that would be briefly hot before the tall pine trees that surrounded Les Roses began to cast their cooling afternoon shadows. The house was filled with the smells of baking and of simmering sauces, while through the open windows drifted the scent of thousands of roses in full bloom. Thirty minutes conferring with the cook, one small crisis to solve over the savory that would end tonight's festive dinner, and Abby was free to enjoy the remainder of the day. Thanks to Marie-Claire's years of careful tutelage and her own gift for inspiring loyalty and good service from the staffs who worked for her both here in the country and in the apartment in Paris, Abby's households ran like clockwork.

An acre of smooth green lawn sloped downward from the terrace, flanked on either side with intricately patterned formal beds of roses, a broad sweep of them leading to the vegetable and herb gardens at the foot of the slight incline on which Les Roses had been built four hundred years ago. She saw Joseph, deep in conversation with Gustave Lebrun, the elderly gardener who had come to this place as a boy of ten and never left; the flashing white streaks of her two West Highland white terriers tearing madly along the graveled paths; Tess's red hair flaming in the sun as she cut yet another basket of flowers to bring into the house; Patrick Sullivan hobbling toward the pond on which a pair of swans floated serenely; Miklós Kelemen, Joseph's younger brother, slowing his step to match her father's. One of Patrick's canes was flourished upward, almost as if he were waving it at her, and Abby sighed. Were they arguing again, these two men who could barely understand each other's English, the only language they had in common? Or was it just a continuation of the political discussion that had been going on now for nearly a week? As long as they kept it to themselves, Abby thought resignedly, knowing it was more than likely they wouldn't.

"Come drink coffee with me, Abby," a voice called out. "Leave them to their foolishness."

Her sister-in-law embraced her delicately on both cheeks, murmuring congratulations and best wishes for the day before she stepped back, seated herself again, and began to pour inky-black coffee and thick yellow cream into two cups. Trust Hanne to while away the morning hours placidly in the only shady spot on the terrace, always composed, always holding herself just a little bit apart from whatever group she

found herself in. She had been married to Miklós for nearly
fifteen years now, but her French was scarcely better than
when she had come to Paris as a bride. "I'll never learn," she
had confessed disgustedly to Abby years and years ago, and
solved the problem by teaching Abby German, a language
her American sister-in-law now spoke as fluently as she did
the French that was so perfect and so accentless that many of
Joseph's clients never suspected she was foreign-born.

"Politics," Hanne sniffed. "The Irish and the Hungarians
lose themselves as completely in them as a Frenchman does
in a woman. I told Miklós he was not to start in again today,
but when has he ever listened to me?"

Shorter than Joseph, grown stout with Hanne's good
cooking, Miklós Kelemen was so different from his older
brother that Abby had often, in the early years of her marriage, found herself looking from one to the other wondering
how two such opposites could have been born to the same set
of parents. Miklós had none of Joseph's ambition, none of his
talent for distinguishing between the merely pretty and the
work that signaled genius. He had studied history at various
European universities for some eight or nine years without
ever earning a degree, and was living in Munich on the last of
the inheritance left him by his father when Hanne changed
his life. Fell in love with him, married him, and convinced
him it was no shame to accept the good job offered by the
brother whose name was one of the most highly respected in
international art circles, whose gallery in Berlin Hanne herself had often visited. Miklós had a desk in the Paris gallery,
and enough work to keep him as busy as the rest of the staff,
but nothing he signed ever left Galeries Kelemen without his
brother's careful perusal, and he could sell no painting, acquire no new piece, without Joseph's approval. Miklós' only
real gift was conversation, and at that he could sometimes be
charming, though it might take him hours and hours to get to
the point that Joseph would have made within minutes. "A
boy who never grew up," was how Joseph characterized the
brother he both loved and was frequently exasperated by.
"Not someone to be taken seriously." Abby thought he was
one of the innocents of this world, and softened Joseph's
tongue whenever possible.

"Georges was down for a few minutes," Hanne reported.
"He's gone back up to have breakfast with Marie-Claire in

her room. He looks almost as bad as she does, Abby. He won't live very long after she goes. I can read it in his eyes. I know, I know. We're not supposed to talk about it. There, I'm finished. Not another word."

The two dogs came jumping and skittering onto the terrace, followed, a moment later, by Tess, scattering roses from her overfilled basket as if she were an aging flower girl at someone's wedding.

"I cut too many, Abby," she called blithely. "I thought that old gardener was going to snatch the shears from my hand, so I decided to beat a strategic retreat. They're just so beautiful I couldn't resist." She scooped up spoonfuls of the thick cream floating atop the coffee Abby poured her, added more cream and drank that off too, managing not to sip the coffee at all.

"Just wait until you see the public gardens in Berlin," Hanne said. "Nothing can compare to them, my dear Tess. The fragrance is so sweet it will bring tears to your eyes."

Don't say anything, Abby pleaded silently. And mercifully, Tess for once did not come back with the kind of sharp retort that had made for some uncomfortable moments during the past week. She had her head cocked to one side, as if only now beginning to make sense out of Hanne's painfully accented English, but her real attention was focused on the cream she was licking from fingers and lips.

"I was just a girl when my parents took me there for the first time," Hanne rhapsodized. "You must translate for me, Abby, I cannot describe in English. That was before the war, of course. Everything was so different then, none of the grayness, the sadness that came afterward. All in the past now. My brother writes me such letters. I cry when I read them. To think of what has been done, what has been rebuilt in only three years. He says Germany was sleeping, waiting for this man to appear to wake her up again, to give back some pride to the German people. Every night I dream about what he tells me, and every morning I'm afraid it cannot be true. I must see for myself, I hope so much it is all as he describes. I want to show you my country as I remember her from before the war, so proud and so beautiful."

Hanne sat quietly in her chair, head high and eyes glittering with what Abby knew, as she translated, were tears of excitement and also disappointment. Then, smiling and nodding to Tess, Hanne rose, excused herself, and went to join Patrick and Miklós, walking slowly across the broad green lawn, pausing once or twice as if to subdue the emotional love of country that those others, non-Germans, could not possibly understand.

"She's either a fool or an idiot, Abby," Tess burst out. "Maybe both. Doesn't she ever read a newspaper? Doesn't she know what's going on in that beautiful Germany of hers?"

"I think your roses are beginning to wilt. You ought to take them into the house."

"Get old Tess out of the way. Shut her up before she opens her mouth again and says something embarrassing. My God, Abby, I gave you credit for having more guts than that. This coffee could use a little brandy, by the way."

The maid who answered Abby's summons took away Gustave Lebrun's glorious roses and set a crystal decanter of Courvoisier beside the silver coffee pot. Tess helped herself to the cognac with a liberal hand.

"Don't worry, kid, I'm not going to ruin things for you today. Dad and Miklós are quite capable of doing that without any help from me."

"What do you mean?"

"They're singing two different songs to each other, but it's all the same refrain. Dad's teaching him the history of Ireland, with not a single kind word for the British, and Miklós is telling him the story of the Jews in Poland and Russia. They're going to collapse out there eventually because the minute one of them pauses to take a breath, the other one starts up again. The funny thing about it is that they're really agreeing with one another, but they're both concentrating so hard on getting in the last word that I don't think they hear half of the other fellow's argument. Miklós is working up to Herr Hitler; I don't know who Dad's working up to."

"Oh, Tess."

"And you're sitting here spouting German like it was your mother tongue. Honestly, Abby, sometimes I just don't understand you." A cup of nearly unadulterated cognac in hand, Tess whistled to the dogs and stalked into the house.

And I doubt that I'll ever understand you either, Abby thought, pushing away the coffee, which suddenly tasted bitter. Pleased that Patrick and Tess had accepted her invitation to come to France this summer, she had nonetheless puzzled over the letters each had sent, trying to read between the lines because, as she explained to Joseph, where a Sullivan was concerned, you very quickly learned that that's where it was likeliest the truth lay, or something that was at least close to the truth.

Of the two, Patrick's had been the more transparent. When Bridget died the year before, she had extracted from her husband a promise to go to Ireland someday and sit for her on the stone wall where, as a girl, she had watched the tinker caravans come down the lane. He'd spent all of his years in America claiming he never wanted to go back to Ireland, but Abby suspected that all along, Patrick yearned to do just that. Grumbling, protesting, laying the return to the whim of a dying woman, Patrick could now accomplish his most secret wish without the danger of losing face. And he was taking Tess with him. "She's the most Irish of you all," he had written, "though why she wants to waste her time and mine watching some half-naked boys race around a track in Germany, I'll never know. Blackmailed me, she did." Tess's condition, it seemed, was that Patrick go with her to the Olympic Games in Berlin at the beginning of August. And not just Patrick. "We might as well all go," she had proposed. "Make a party of it. God knows, the last time I was over I nearly died of boredom listening to all the eligible old bachelors you invited to dinner every night."

Somehow, Abby thought ruefully, Tess had a way of making people fall in with whatever she planned, if she cared enough to make the effort. And for some reason, she had cared enough this time to wheedle and cajole until even Joseph threw up his hands and surrendered. The seeds of what Tess had become had always been there—the volatile temper, the crazy sense of humor that expressed itself in practical jokes that often seemed as cruel to others as they were hilariously funny to her, the laziness and lack of discipline that got her fired as often as her enormous appetite for food and liquor. Sheila Gruber, née Cohen, kept an eye on her in New York, writing voluminous letters to Abby that seesawed between hope and despair and were a catalogue of escapades that Tess claimed never to regret. And with each trip that Abby made to America or Tess made to Paris, the disintegration was more marked.

Tess was beautiful still, but in the saddest of all possible ways. She had the face of an angel, the hair of a Titian nymph, but ludicrously poised atop a body grown sloppily fat with years and years of enthusiastic dissipation. Her fondness for the bottle had grown into a love affair that began each morning with a little something to get the blood circulating and ended more nights than Abby cared to think about in frank and often obstreperous drunkenness. Yet somehow Tess still had the gift of making people care about her. No matter what she did, no matter how often she was a source of embarrassment, worry, or anger, you forgave and continued to love her. Maybe it was the naughty child smile she turned on you; maybe, as Joseph said, it was because you and she both knew that the world could be a rotten place and Tess Sullivan simply couldn't face it sober for more than a few hours at a time. She was singing now, one of Bridget's old ballads, the words slurred and the voice slightly off-key, but the melody still lovely for all that as it drifted out over the terrace and the gardens. Abby smiled to herself. There was never any point in trying to make Tess change, even in wishing that she would.

"She sounds in good spirits this morning," Joseph said, pausing to listen, waving away the coffee Abby offered.

"She ought to. She's been into the cognac already."

He shrugged his shoulders. It was a subject too often discussed over the years to offer anything new. And he had something more important on his mind than Tess's tippling. "Georges spoke to me last night. He's still planning to take Marie-Claire to Deauville in August."

For eleven years the four of them had spent that month together, walking the beaches in the morning, lunching in favorite cafés and restaurants along the Normandy coast, gambling away the long summer evenings in the hotel's casino, drinking champagne when any of them won big, commiserating over the occasional and never very serious losses. This year Georges and Marie-Claire would be alone.

"What else did he say?"

"Only that. He wouldn't ask, Abby. You know he wouldn't. Neither would she."

It was terrible to be torn between people you loved, each of them needing you, needing something different.

"It isn't only Tess now, Joseph. If it were, I'd say cancel Berlin in a minute. But we've promised Hanne too. It would have broken your heart to hear her a little while ago. Germany won't be as she remembers it from before the war. It can't possibly be the same with what's going on there."

"She'll have to learn that for herself, my love."

"I wish Miklós would change his mind. Sometimes I think that refusing to go with her is the only cruel thing he's done in his life."

"Don't be too hard on him, Abby. He's a frightened man."

"He has no more reason to be afraid than you have, Joseph."

It was a strange thing for Abby to say, and he wondered if she really understood what she *had* said. For both Miklós and Joseph, the religious beliefs and practices of Judaism had been abandoned in young adulthood, of no more significance in their lives than any of the other, more secular memories of childhood and family. Except when reminded by someone else, each had tended to forget that he was a Jew. But nine months ago, when the Nuremberg Laws stripped German Jews of their citizenship and prohibited all intimate relations with non-Jews, Miklós suddenly remembered. "Hitler has finally succeeded in making them nonpersons in their own country," he said. "Each law, each exclusion was leading inexorably to this, and every time another profession was forbidden them, the world sighed and then turned its back, telling itself that this was the worst, that Hitler would go no further. Listen to me. I say *them*, when what I should be saying is *us*. Can you imagine a Germany without its Jews? I think Hitler can and does. Even worse, I'm beginning to believe that he envisions an entire world without Jews. He's a madman, Joseph, and he will someday plunge all of Europe into another war."

It was one of the few astute things Joseph had heard his brother say in a lifetime devoted to the trivial and the obvious, but Miklós would not let the subject drop. Every dinner became a battleground, every evening spent together erupted into violent discussions that soon became angry quarrels and ended only when Hanne began to cry. It was very, very possible that Miklós was right, but in Joseph's view he was also an alarmist.

Hitler had been contained, was being contained, within his own borders, German military reoccupation of the Rhineland excepted. And that step should have been foreseen from the moment the Treaty of Versailles was signed. It was inconceivable that the nations which had brought Germany to its knees only twenty years ago would allow a repetition of the horrors no one who had lived through them could ever forget. Anti-Semitism had always been a cyclical pattern of behavior, virulent in times of economic hardship, quiescent when prosperity brought more pleasurable distractions than Jew-baiting. As bad as the situation inside Germany was for its millions of Jews, there had been signs lately that they would get no worse, that even, in time, they would begin to improve. It wasn't Hitler's treatment of the Jews that was the true barometer of his intentions, as Miklós believed, but the growing size and strength of the army and the paramilitary organizations he had caused to spring up all around him, and for that there were watchers and analysts in all the European countries counting every man in uniform and every piece of military hardware. Long before threat turned into reality, England and France would call the Allies together again. It might come to war, but on a severely limited scale, Joseph thought, and then new treaties would replace the old, and the watching would begin again. Living on the same continent with Germany was like trying to sleep in the same cave as a hibernating bear.

Yet for all Joseph's reasonable explanations and reassurances, for all Hanne's pleading, Miklós would not go with them to Berlin. "I don't care how many thousands of tourists would be there with me," he said. "I would still be alone. A lone Jew swimming in a sea of anti-Semites. Anything could happen. My passport could be found to be irregular, my French citizenship questioned. Who can tell? At least in Paris I know who I am, I know I'm not a nonperson. And Paris is where you should stay too, Joseph. Only a fool dives into a sea of sharks."

It was being called a fool by this most foolish of brothers that had finally stung Joseph into agreeing to Tess's proposal, though he had allowed Abby to think that he had simply grown tired of arguing about it. Somewhere, at the very back

of his mind, was the barest trace of a niggling fear he had not
known since North Africa, and he could not, would not, allow
it to grow unchallenged. He smiled to himself now. Repeating Georges' remark to Abby had been a sly reach for reprieve, and, all-unknowing, she had shown him exactly what
it was.

"Joseph?"

"Forgive me, darling. My mind was wandering. Of course
it's too late to change our plans. Georges understands that. I
think he was just tired, just remembering the past."

"The Games end on the fifteenth. We can catch the first
train back and still spend two weeks in Deauville."

"Are you hinting that after Budapest you'll need two
vacations?" Their semi-annual visits to Joseph's mother and
widowed sister were as much of a strain on Abby as they
were on him, but a duty about which she had never complained. The lovely house on the Tabakgasse had become a
living mausoleum to the memory of Kelemen *père*, and the
two women who tended it seldom spoke of anything but the
doctor whose dedication to his patients had robbed him of his
sons. "I want to try to persuade Magda to come back with
us."

"I'll speak to her, Joseph. Berlin won't be to her taste,
but Paris might be. She hasn't seen Miklós in years."

"How did we become so enmeshed in other people's
lives and concerns, Abby? Sometimes I think we rob ourselves
to pay what they demand of us."

"Getting married was what did it," she answered, only
half seriously. "If you'd been content to make me your mistress instead of your wife, there'd be no Tess or Miklós or
Magda for the two of us to worry about. I've never once
heard Marie-Claire agonize over Georges's wife or daughters.
As far as she is concerned, they simply belong to another
world."

"And would you have preferred that? It's not a very
American type of arrangement, but you've never been very
typically American, my love."

"Would you, Joseph?"

"I always thought of you as my wife, Abby, from the very
beginning. Anything less would never have satisfied me."

"Nor me either, Joseph. I could have wished for only
one thing more."

"It doesn't matter, Abby. It never did. Not to me, at least."

It was an old hurt, one they seldom dwelt on, deeply buried except at moments such as this when Abby remembered and could not keep silent. Four years ago, when Joseph had given her Les Roses as an anniversary gift, he had also, without a word to her, hired an architect and a decorator to transform the two empty rooms in their Paris apartment where infant furniture had been gathering dust since the first year of their marriage. When they returned at the end of that summer, Abby had found an exquisite little salon and a small library, no trace remaining of unrealized hopes to gnaw away at the otherwise smooth perfection of her days. She thought she had accepted the unanimous diagnoses of her French doctors and the specialists Sheila Gruber insisted she see in New York, but even now she could not quite believe them, even now, every month, she prayed they might be wrong. They never were. It was the only emptiness in her life, the only failure over which she had no control.

"It doesn't matter, Abby," Joseph repeated. "We were always more than enough for one another."

Loving him, secure in his love for her, she had to believe the truth of what he said, that nothing and no one could truly touch or diminish what they had created together. Nothing—not the world, not parents, brothers, sisters, in-laws, or dear friends—could reach or destroy their essential oneness. They were Abby and Joseph, an entity apart from all others, so inextricably bound one to the other that, like Marie-Claire and Georges, not even death could separate them for more than an instant.

Paris and Les Roses were oases of summer quiet after Tess and Patrick left to spend July in Ireland, but the ten days of Abby and Joseph's visit to Budapest, though quieter still, were disturbing and unsatisfying.

Mama Kelemen seldom if ever left the house where she had spent all of her married life, and the few guests she received there were widows like herself, frail, elderly women in black who clung as tightly to their pasts as they did to the teacups over which they shared lugubrious memories and tales of ungrateful children. Magda, widowed, childless, fifteen years younger than Joseph, had a thin, strained look to her, and dark circles under eyes that had once sparkled with life and vitality.

"When was the last time you went to the opera or the theater or even dined out in a restaurant, Magda?" Joseph demanded angrily.

"So long ago I don't remember when." Her smile was sad, vague, quick to die on pale lips that barely moved.

Abby's approach was gentler, more subtle. But no matter how often she begged her sister-in-law to spend an afternoon with her in one of Budapest's celebrated art museums or parks, the answer was always the same: "Mama might need me."

"She wasn't always like this."

"I know, Joseph. I remember."

"In some ways, she was a lot like Tess, always laughing, always ready to try something new, always surrounded by friends who were just as lively as she. Eight years, Abby, and she's still wearing black, still mourning a man she was married to for less than six months. If she didn't have a photograph to stare at, she wouldn't even be able to remember his face."

"It may be what she wants."

"What *he* would want," Joseph answered bitterly. Every room in the house had its portrait of Julius Kelemen, a stern, forbidding presence glaring down from walls that seemed to tighten around his oldest son with every day that passed. "Miklós hasn't been back since the day we buried him. Or thought we did."

In the end it was only the grand piano on which he had played as a child that made Budapest bearable for Joseph. Alone in the music room for hours that seemed endless to Abby, he poured out his soul through his fingertips, filling the otherwise silent house with music that thundered and raged and at last was simple, poignant, and merely sad.

"You don't come often enough," his mother scolded on the morning they left for Berlin.

"There were times when I didn't think she even knew we were there," he told Abby as the outskirts of the city flashed by their compartment windows.

"You had to try, Joseph. You always have to try."

"They could mourn him just as well in Paris as they do in

Budapest. They could bring every scrap of furniture and every one of those damned portraits with them."

"Mama would be miserable in any house but that one."

"Miserable perhaps, but safe," he muttered.

"Safe, Joseph?"

"Closer to the Channel." And then, as if he thought he had already said too much, he folded his arms across his chest and closed his eyes. They would be in Germany before nightfall.

A cold shiver ran up and down Abby's back, almost as though fingers were tapping on her spine. A goose walked over my grave, she thought, wondering why and how that stupid, waddling bird had come to represent a portent of disaster.

Berlin was a city pulsing with new life that summer of the XIth Olympiad, a city and a people aflame with a peculiarly rabid spirit of nationalism that exalted all things German and scorned whatever could not be given the ultimate accolade of being purely Aryan. Everywhere Abby and Joseph looked there were flags, the oddly menacing swastika of Hitler's National Socialist party flying side by side with Olympic banners. Streets were crowded, but tourists and Berliners alike strolled along them in high good humor, smiling at strangers as though they were old friends. It seemed, after the gloom of Budapest, as if they had emerged into sunlight, but Joseph was unnaturally quiet and Abby wondered aloud why every third or fourth man they passed should be in uniform.

"The psychology of it is masterful," Joseph explained. "It both sets them apart and binds them together, in much the same way as a religious habit proclaims to the world that the person wearing it makes no secret of his special dedication. Foreigners will be impressed by the unity, the precision, the sense of order, and they'll carry that memory home with them. What are people saying about Mussolini right now? That he's made the Italian trains run on time, not that he's gobbled up Abyssinia. Over there, Abby, that building on the corner was where the gallery used to be."

She understood then the tightness with which he was holding himself, the cold irony in his voice. Two years before, so suddenly that it seemed he had made the decision overnight, Joseph had liquidated his Berlin business, selling everything the gallery contained to the man who managed it for him. The loss had been enormous, and she might never have learned the scope of the financial disaster had not Miklós artlessly mentioned it at dinner one night. Joseph had refused to explain, but later, reading the German newspapers Hanne bought and passed on to her, Abby had guessed that the sale of Galeries Kelemen–Berlin was less a matter of choice than hard necessity and held her tongue, eventually forgetting, until today, that even wealthy foreign Jews were unwelcome investors in Hitler's Third Reich.

They were staying in a hotel near the Via Triumphalis, a ten-mile-long ceremonial boulevard linking the center of the city to the Reichssportfeld complex of enormous stadia and broad playing fields. Hanne's brother had made the reservations for them, conveying, via his sister, profuse and profound apologies for not being able to house them all comfortably in his small apartment.

"What he really means," Tess remarked when told of the arrangements, "is that he's too good a little Nazi to contaminate his place with somebody like your husband, Abby. Hell, I'd rather stay with a bunch of other foreigners anyway."

The comment shocked Abby too much to repeat it to anyone; she simply filed it away with the host of other outrageous statements Tess was making that summer, most of them, she now recalled uneasily, highly critical of the country where all of them would be guests for the next two weeks. She would speak to her sister, she decided, urge her to keep her mouth shut. Or, if that proved impossible, at least to confine her criticisms to times and places where they wouldn't be overheard.

"Ireland was beautiful," Tess confided over drinks that evening, "but honest to God, Abby, I finally understand why Mom and Dad had to leave. We spent three weeks in Mayo, visiting more relatives than I ever knew we had, and I swear by all that's holy not a one of them had two coins to rub together on a cold night. The sky and the hills and the singing would melt your heart, but that's all they've got. Boiled potatoes at every meal, turf fires that make your eyes water, statues of the Virgin Mary in every corner of every room, and one precious lace tablecloth in all the houses for when the parish priest comes to tea. It gave me the creeps."

"Why didn't Dad come with you?"

"He said he was tired from all the traveling. I think it was harder than he expected to sit on Mom's stone wall for her. He was quieter after that, and by the time we got back to Paris, I figured it wasn't worth the effort to make him come to the Games. Miklós was lonely too, even though Hanne had only left a couple of days before. Dad's staying with him; they'll argue the whole two weeks and love every minute of it."

It wasn't like Tess to give in so easily, Abby thought, especially when she'd worked so hard to get Patrick to agree to go to Germany in the first place. "She's up to something," she told Joseph. "I don't know what it is yet, but she's got the look about her of someone who's laid some very careful plans, and is smugly watching them all fall into place."

"You're letting your imagination run away with you, Abby. Whatever else she is, Tess has never been a plotter."

And for the first week of their stay, it seemed he was right. The three of them went to the Reichssportfeld early every morning, meeting Hanne, though not her brother or his family, for lunch most days; while Abby and Joseph fell into bed exhausted every night, Tess partied until dawn with a *Daily News* correspondent she knew from New York. There was a feeling of unreality about that week, a sensation of being overwhelmed with pageantry, color, and the straining bodies of the world's finest amateur athletes. It was as if they themselves were running a marathon, shuttled to and from the Reichssportfeld by taxi, caught up in the shouts and tension of the crowds, carried along in the wave of Olympic enthusiasm. Politics seemed very far away except when the crowds rose to their feet to greet or bid farewell to Adolph Hitler and his entourage. Göring, Goebbels, minor Balkan and Scandinavian princes to lend an air of spurious respectability, a blend of uniformed and top-hatted figures briefly but vociferously idolized and applauded until bare legs and bare arms flashed again in the sunlight.

It was fascinating to Abby, but she sensed that Joseph was not as caught up as she. Too often she glanced over at him to find his eyes fixed, not on the events below, but on the faces of the crowd or riveted to the spot where Germany's Führer rose to his feet when his countrymen claimed their medals, clapping desultorily and with ill-concealed bad grace when foreigners stole the prizes. Joseph was storing up sights and sounds, she thought, absorbing them, but at a distance, remaining emotionally detached while everyone around them was losing perspective. His reluctance to discuss any given day's activities told her that he was reserving judgment, that only when they were back in France, months from now perhaps, would he begin to speak about Berlin. And what he would have to say then would go far beyond the surface excitement that suddenly seemed to be so very carefully orchestrated that Abby wondered, even while she cheered and held her breath and applauded as eagerly as every other tourist, why it was so easy to fall under the spell that common sense told her was being superbly manipulated by a political entity she knew she despised.

It was Tess who finally brought her back to reality, who blew away the soft summer sunshine and awakened Abby to the cold harshness of life in Hitler's Germany.

"I've got a letter for you from Sheila. I know what she's written, and what she's asking you to do, kid. I told her you weren't as tough a mick as I am, that you couldn't do it alone, and for once she agreed with me. I go places in New York every day that neither of you would dare set foot in, and there isn't a Nazi alive I'm afraid of."

In silence Abby read the letter, and in silence, stunned by the desperation she read between the lines of Sheila's request, waited for Tess to explain.

"Sheila's working for an aid-to-refugees group. They started emigrating a few years ago, and there's more coming every day. A lot of them don't have a dime when they get to New York, and some of them don't speak English, but it doesn't seem to matter much. The stories they tell, Abby. I didn't believe half of them when Sheila first started telling me, but they've got to be true. The same things over and over again, detail for detail. The Jews who have managed to leave Germany have had to buy their way out. The Nazis take everything from them—businesses, life savings, jewelry. It's a crime and nobody seems to care. Sheila wanted to come to Berlin herself, but Arnie wouldn't let her. She's pregnant again. She's been writing to these cousins of hers for months, but she thinks the letters are never delivered, or if they are, the warning isn't getting through. She's been afraid to be too blunt; someone told her the Nazis read every piece of mail that comes to a Jew from abroad. She gave me money too, German marks. All she wants is for us to contact them, talk to them, deliver the money, and then go on acting like tourists. You'll have to do the persuading. All I can say in German is "Hello," "More noodles," and "Where's the bathroom?"

"Why did you agree to it, Tess? Why did you get involved?" Looking at her, knowing the kind of uncommitted life she had always led, Abby thought there could not be a more unlikely candidate for heroism.

"I don't like punks, Abby. I never have. And as far as I'm concerned, Hitler and his toy soldiers are the most rotten bunch of punks I've ever seen. They look good in the newsreels, and I've heard people admiring them who ought to know better, but Goebbels is a skinny little pervert and Göring is so gross it's a wonder he doesn't burst the buttons on his uniform. Besides, New York was getting to be a bore. I decided it was time to have a little fun."

"You could have given me the letter as soon as you got to Paris. Why did you wait until now?"

"There's some things I understand better about you than you do yourself, Abby, and one of them is that you make your best decisions when you're backed into a corner and don't have the luxury of thinking too long and too hard about what you've got to do. Remember the Sammy Rosen audition? Marrying Joseph because he kept asking and wouldn't take no for an answer?"

"That's not the whole of it, Tess."

"You want the truth, I'll give you the truth. Right now, right this minute, you're wondering what Joseph would say. Hell, I *know* what his reaction would be, and so do you. He'd say it's too dangerous, he'd say drop the money into the nearest mailbox on our way out of Germany and just hope it gets where it's supposed to go. But it won't, Abby. Sheila's right about that. I couldn't blame him for it because he'd only be thinking of you, wanting to keep you safe the way he's always done. Face it, he'd never have let you come to Berlin in the first place if he'd had any idea of what I was carrying, why I wanted you to be at the Games. Believe me, kid, between the two of us we can pull this off with nobody the wiser."

"Does Dad know about it?"

"Not a clue. I'm not even sure I'll tell him when it's all over with."

"Foreigners who want to contact Jews are required to register their intent with the Gestapo. It was in the information packet they gave us at the border." Tess had read her correctly, Abby thought, knowing herself already a willing partner in what was surely a harebrained scheme.

"The hell with that."

"Joseph mustn't suspect."

"I've been working on that. We'll tell him we want to spend one morning shopping, just the two of us. I'll get my friend from the *Daily News* to invite him into the press section. He won't be able to resist, Abby. The only people in this town who'll tell him what it's really like in Germany today are the correspondents who've been here all along. Bob Hill said last night that there used to be signs everywhere saying Jews couldn't use public toilets or telephones, couldn't eat in restaurants or go to theaters, weren't welcome in certain towns. He said that Goebbels convinced Hitler that Jew-baiting would make a bad impression on foreigners, so all the signs came down months ago, before the winter Games started in February. There used to be anti-Semitic newspapers so filthy it would make you sick to read them. Bob said he'd bet a million bucks the signs would go up again and the papers would be back on the stands just as soon as the Games were over. I told him a little about Joseph, and he'd like to meet him. He really would. He feels that some of the French correspondents are holding back, sending dispatches to Paris that aren't exactly lies, but certainly not the whole truth either. Bob doesn't work for the best newspaper in the world, but he's got enough of a political conscience to want to do something more than file the kind of stories he's expected to. I told him Joseph had clients in the French government."

"He does, quite a few."

"You see, Abby, it works out to everyone's advantage. I figure we ought to try for the day after tomorrow."

"I don't like the idea of you and Tess wandering around Berlin by yourselves," Joseph said worriedly, taking Abby apart from the small group of tourists waiting for taxis beneath the hotel's portico.

"We won't be *wandering*, darling. The desk clerk gave

me a list of the best shops in the city, and we'll hire a cab for the whole morning."

"Be careful, Abby."

"Careful?"

"According to Bob Hill, all the drivers report to the Gestapo at the end of their shifts. Tell Tess to keep her mouth shut and her opinions to herself."

"Darling, Bob's holding a cab. Don't worry about us. We'll be just fine, and we'll meet you for lunch at one o'clock."

Not until the taxi had sped away toward the Reichssportfeld did Abby breathe a sigh of relief and turn to link her arm in Tess's. "Let's walk," she said, loudly enough to be overheard by anyone who cared to listen. "It's too beautiful a day to be cooped up inside a car, and most of the shops we're going to are only a few blocks away."

"Are you crazy, Abby?" Tess whispered. "We've got to go halfway across the whole damned city."

"Just walk, Tess, and smile as if you're enjoying it. If I find the right stop, we'll take a bus." And she told her what Joseph had said about Berlin's cabdrivers.

Two hours later, footsore and hot, jumpy with looking over their shoulders at every intersection, they reached a quarter of Berlin where few swastikas were to be seen, where homes and shops flew only the five ringed Olympic flag, the sole decoration Jews were allowed to display. They found the shop owned by Sheila's cousin, but the door was shut and locked and all the windows barred. The strains of a Mozart quintet grew louder as they climbed the steep, dark staircase leading upward to the apartments above the shops, and at first their knock went unanswered. Only when Tess repeatedly rang the bell beneath the neat white card bearing the name of Isaac Goldman did the music abruptly cease. The door opened just a crack and a frightened dark eye peered out at them, but when Abby began to speak, and all Tess could make out was Sheila Gruber's name and the words "New York," it was flung wide, and they were made as warmly welcome as if they hadn't been strangers at all. Only afterward did Tess learn what had been said. As Sheila had warned her, none of the Goldmans spoke a word of English.

"Our grandfathers were brothers," Isaac Goldman told Abby. From a village whose name would mean nothing to you, but not far from Berlin. Mostly Jews living there. Yankele dreamed of America, even as a boy; my grandfather could think of nothing but Berlin. Nobody had much money in those days, but nobody had heard of National Socialism either. We were all good Germans, except Yankele, and that's all my grandfather wanted to be, as good a German as he was a Jew."

"Sheila has written letters to you," Abby explained. "She's afraid you haven't gotten them. She wants you to emigrate before it's too late, before they stop letting Jews out of Germany."

She thought that the shrug of Isaac Goldman's shoulders was remarkably like the gesture Joseph often made. Tea was served by a dark-haired woman only weeks away from bearing a child, while Isaac and the four other men, who had laid aside their instruments, seemed to be hanging on her every word.

"Last year, after the Nuremberg Laws, I was crazy to leave. But so were too many others. You have to pay, you know. Sell everything for a fraction of its value. And my father was ill. The doctor said he would never live to reach America. I waited. Anneke became pregnant. We waited again. Now, since February, things are easier. No new laws, no more restrictions. I make almost as good a living as a Gentile. It's happened before, this kind of madness. And always it passes."

"You're a relative of an American citizen. The United States takes that into consideration."

"Yankele came back once, in 1912, just before he died. He said it hadn't been easy to learn English, that America had been good to him, but it wasn't the Promised Land. I remember. I was a small boy, but I remember."

"For the sake of your child, Herr Goldman, for the sake of your child. Think what it will be like for him to grow up in Adolf Hitler's Germany," Abby pleaded.

"I thank you for coming. My unborn child thanks you. But it's better that we stay. We draw no attention to ourselves. I sell a piece of jewelry now and then, trade in gold and silver. We manage. I ask myself, would it be that much better in America?"

"You could become a citizen," Abby said. "They took that privilege away from you in Germany."

"Words. Papers. Can they take away the fact that Goldmans have lived in Germany for longer than any one of us can remember? I had my doubts. I admit it. But also I understand this country. When times are bad for everyone, they're worse for Jews. So. We have the Nuremberg Laws. But things are getting better now. One by one the laws will be repealed. A year from now, two at the most, it will be as if they never existed. Germany needs her Jews. From time to time she forgets how much she needs us, but eventually she always remembers."

"Not this time, Herr Goldman." She told him the stories that Sheila had recounted to Tess, the absolute conviction of the refugees who had reached America that they had escaped barely in time from some as yet unimagined ruin, from onerous restrictions on their freedom that would someday culminate in a pogrom to rival the horrors of the past. "At least let me assure Sheila that you will think about emigrating," Abby said at last. "At least take the money she's sent, put it away until you reach a decision, then use it."

Smiling, he shook his head and would have refused, but the very pregnant Anneke laid a gentle hand on his arm, and finally his fingers closed around the roll of bills. Not knowing what else to do, empty of argument in the face of such stubborn optimism, Abby scribbled her Paris address on a scrap of paper. "If you need help when the time comes, Herr Goldman, if you need more money or you want to send a message that you know will reach America, get word to me. Sheila is like a sister. For years she visited my parents when I was an ocean away and they were too proud to ask for what they needed. My people became hers, and hers are mine. You must understand that. I have a debt of honor to your cousin, and no way to repay it except through you."

There were tears in Isaac Goldman's eyes, and tears running openly down Anneke's cheeks. "It isn't wise to stay too long," he said quietly. "We are still in the not so good time. You did not register with the Gestapo. We would have had a visit, instructions on what to say. Some of our friends have told us how it is being done. For all our sakes, in case there are eyes watching, I will take you out through the shop into the alley."

He shook Abby's hand warmly, and on impulse she

reached out to embrace the fragile young woman whose belly seemed too heavy a burden for her body to bear.

With hardly a word said between them, the two sisters walked the long blocks back to where flags bearing the sharp angles of the swastika began to outnumber Olympic banners. Emotionally drained and physically exhausted, they were also strangely exhilarated by the ease with which they had accomplished the mission Sheila set for them. "Whatever they decide to do," Tess said at last, "at least we'll know we warned them. Christ, Abby, if we grab a taxi, we'll have time to go back to the hotel and change our clothes. It's not even noon yet and I stink so bad I can smell myself."

"I should have known better," Abby told Joseph later. "I should have wondered why an empty cab was so conveniently close by."

"It wouldn't have changed anything. They would have picked you up in any case."

But that was hours and hours after a nondescript man in nondescript clothes greeted them in their hotel lobby, politely presented his credentials, and asked for a few moments of their time. The clerk behind the desk stared at them with frigid dislike, and it seemed that every other German in the lobby froze in place until the Gestapo agent led them back out into the street again and into an unmarked but painfully official Mercedes whose very upholstery smelled of fear and power.

"It would have been better had you arranged your meeting through the proper channels," he told them smoothly and in near perfect English, offering coffee and schnapps in the bare office of a building they would never be able to find again, so circuitously had they come to it. "We do not encourage such visits, but neither do we forbid them. That should have been made clear to you at the border. But perhaps it was not, and thus it is we who are at fault. It is a question only of filling out the appropriate forms. I will translate, if you wish."

Abby glanced at the papers he pushed across the desk to her. Names, addresses, dates. Time, length, purpose of the visit. Relationship to the Jew in question. She shook her head, shrugged her shoulders, ignored the coffee, but sipped delicately at the schnapps. "Delicious," she said. "But I'm afraid I don't understand what this is all about."

"I think, on the contrary, that you know very well why you're here, Frau Kelemen. The Reich welcomes all its foreign visitors, but we do expect that they will conduct themselves in accordance with our laws, and with the very few precautions we must ask them to take for their own safety as well as the good of the country."

"I really don't know what you mean, or what you're implying. I wasn't aware that sightseeing was a crime. Actually, we got lost."

"Visiting Jews without the required authorization, Frau Kelemen. Not a crime precisely, but surely an imposition on the hospitality the Reich has extended to you. I'm sure you will wish to cooperate, after the fact so to speak."

"I don't know any Jews in Berlin," Abby said.

When he did not immediately contradict her, did not throw Isaac Goldman's name in her face, she realized just how well she and Tess had succeeded, and how narrowly the Goldmans had escaped detection. That they had been followed was now obvious, but equally obvious was that their very skittishness, the frequent stops to loiter in front of one shop window after another, the anxious, fearful glances over their shoulders had both marked their behavior as suspicious and, in the end, saved the Goldmans. That short, narrow street had had dozens of doorways, into any one of which they could have ducked. The Gestapo agent, whoever he was, had not wanted to spook them, had kept so safe a distance behind them that, when he turned the corner, they had already disappeared.

She thought that Tess suddenly realized this also, realized, too, that they must have been several blocks away from the Goldmans' shop before they were sighted again, that one man, at least, the one before them now, had already gone back to intercept them at their hotel. Unless they could be trapped into making an admission, there would be no proof that they had done anything more serious than accidentally wander into one of the many small Jewish neighborhoods in Berlin. The important thing was to get out of that office before either of them could be goaded into revealing Isaac Goldman's name. Beside her, Tess tapped her fingernails on the immaculate wooden desktop, a clicking that grew more and more rapid even as Abby tried frantically to decide whether indignation, a continued pretense of honest bewilderment, or a demand to call her embassy would best shake the overweening confidence of the man who seemed to believe he held the upper hand. An instant later, Tess had stolen the moment.

"I've had just about all I'm going to take from this bastard," she snarled. She was on her feet, leaning across the desk, spitting into the face of their interrogator before Abby could so much as put out a hand to stop her. "Now you listen to me, bub, and you listen good. You can harass and intimidate your own people as much as you please or as much as they'll put up with, but don't you think for one minute that an American citizen is going to take this kind of treatment lying down. We do things differently in our country, and we'd flush crud like you down the toilet except that you're so rotten you'd foul up the sewers. I don't give a tinker's damn for your required authorizations or your hospitality. I wouldn't know a German Jew if I tripped over one, except that he'd probably look and act a hell of a lot more human than you. You can have me declared persona non grata or whatever you call it, and escort me to the border right this minute, and all you'll get for the effort is a Bronx cheer and a hearty halleluiah. If you don't know what to do with these papers I'll be glad to show you. We're not answering any more questions and we're leaving. Right now. You lay one finger on me or my sister, you so much as mention the word 'arrest,' and we'll make headlines in every paper in Europe and the States. Big headlines. I have friends who will absolutely guarantee it. Nobody will know whether Germany won any medals today, but everybody who can read a newspaper will know how the Third Reich treated a couple of women who tried to spend a quiet morning in Berlin doing a little sightseeing. Let's go, Abby. I don't like the smell in this place."

Amazingly, Tess was actually halfway across the room, Abby just two steps behind her, before the command to halt rang out and a soldier suddenly barred their exit. They could hear angry raised voices in the outer office, a babble of what seemed to be German, French, and English all being spoken at once.

"Relax, kid," Tess whispered. "The cavalry's arrived."

Moments later Joseph was holding Abby in his arms while Bob Hill, furiously waving his press credentials, demanded to know why the Gestapo was detaining a celebrated stage personality like Tess Sullivan against her will. And, just incidentally, the American consul, who was also on his way over, would want to know the same thing.

"It was Joseph's idea to try a bluff," Hill explained once they were back in the Kelemens' now only relatively safe-seeming hotel suite. "Frankly, from what I've seen of those guys in action, I didn't think it would work."

"I told him what we were planning to do, Abby," Tess confessed. "I thought we needed a little insurance in case things got complicated. Which they did."

"Your husband should have been a newspaperman. He had the whole story out of me before I realized I was telling it. You know something else? I think the Gestapo has had its eye on Tess ever since she got here. I think one of their people in New York passed along the word that she was a shade too sympathetic to your friend's refugee group."

"Is it over?" Abby asked. "After what Tess did, after the names she called him, how can he just let it drop, let us go?"

"The power of the press, Mrs. Kelemen. Goebbels understands what the fourth estate can do better than any politician I've ever covered. He controls every newspaper in the Third Reich, and he'd like to control every foreign correspondent too. Right now, because Hitler is cultivating the peacemaker image, Goebbels has enough influence to keep even the Gestapo in check. At least until the Games are over and the tourists have gone home to sing Germany's praises. The worst that will happen to the three of you is that every time you turn around for the remainder of your stay in Berlin, you'll see a goon in a raincoat. My credentials will almost certainly be lifted on the last day, but I was planning to ask to be recalled to New York anyway. The only thing that gripes my ass is that I won't be able to write a single word of what happened today."

"And that," Tess laughed, pulling Bob Hill to his feet, "calls for some serious drinking. We'll be down in the bar if you two want to join us."

Alone with Joseph for the first time since he and Hill had forced their way into the Gestapo office, Abby could think of nothing to say. Guilt at having deliberately deceived him, at having drawn him into a situation that could have ended disastrously for both of them overwhelmed her. Remembering now what Tess had told her about the anti-Semitic newspapers and signs that had so opportunely and temporarily disappeared, she thought she must have momentarily taken leave of her senses to risk drawing the Gestapo's attention to Joseph. How could she have forgotten that to put herself in jeopardy could have called down on him more serious consequences than the swift expulsion from Germany that Tess had claimed would be the worst thing that could happen to them? She had sensed his unease in the Reichssportfeld, the wariness with which he entered and left the hotel; known that he often tossed and turned beside her at night, unable to sleep, counting the days until they could leave, his promise to her fulfilled. The Goldmans were strangers, yet she had put their welfare before the safety of her own husband. Her motives no longer seemed pure; they smacked of cheap heroics.

"Don't blame yourself, Abby. I would have tried to stop you had I known in time, but I'm proud of what you did, proud that you cared enough to do something I'm not sure I would have had the courage to do."

She crept into his arms, laid her head against the heart that beat so strongly, so steadily, while hers seemed to have turned into a leaden weight in her chest. Yet there was anger too, most of it directed against herself, but some, fueled by the panic she had managed to control before her interrogator, some of it focusing now on Joseph.

"You shouldn't have interfered," she said through lips that trembled. "We were never in any real danger. A few hours of detention at most. Tess and I were handling it, Joseph, we really were."

"I had to, Abby. When Hill and I went back to the hotel and found out that you'd been taken away by the Gestapo, I knew what I had to do. I had no more choice in the matter than you did."

"You didn't stop to think, Joseph."

"Did you?"

"That was different."

"Only in degree. You took a terrible risk for people you didn't even know. Could you expect me to do any less for the woman who means more to me than life itself?"

She felt tears pricking at her eyelids, but whether they were from anger, self-disgust, or the so recent fear, she didn't know.

"Cry if you want. Lose your temper if that will help, Abby. I *did* act like a fool, but so did you. Sometimes that kind of foolhardiness is the only weapon that can be used against injustice and cruelty. But remember, a brave front and a bluff aren't always enough. They weren't in this case, though they got us into the building and the office where you were being questioned. To get you out, Bob had to promise that not a word would be leaked to the press, by him or by anyone else, and that no complaint would be made to either the French or the American consuls."

"Was that all, Joseph?" she prodded. "Was it that simple?"

"These people aren't simple, my love. To think so is a mistake too many are already making. Your captor had his hand out and I filled it. You might say I bought his silence as effectively as he bought ours."

"I wish someone could know, Joseph."

"Sheila will. Tess will tell her, and she in turn will make sure that some others know also. Every small success makes the next one easier. It teaches you your enemy's weak points, makes it a fraction easier to outwit him."

"Do we have to stay until the Games are over? All I want now is to cross the border so I can breathe clean air again."

"Four more days, Abby. It's important to continue to act as if you never had anything to hide. By staying and not attempting to contact the Goldmans, not warning them, you make your story more plausible."

"Will you tell Miklós? Should we talk to Hanne about it?"

"No to both questions. You're holding Sheila's cousins in the palm of your hand. One slip, even from as far away as Paris, and their chances of getting out could be ruined."

"I'm not even sure they'll decide to go."

"They will, my love, in time. And they'll have you to thank for their escape."

"I'm so sorry, Joseph, so sorry for everything."

"I'm not, Abby. In fact, I'm glad now that I came, glad I saw it all with my own eyes."

"Why, Joseph?"

"It means that every decision I make in the next few years, every choice we decide on together, will be the right one."

*   *   *

By the time they reached Paris, by the time they were sitting once more on the balcony of the Kelemens' apartment overlooking the Seine, much of the fear and the sense of foreboding had faded. Abby had even begun to ask herself if she had imagined the interrogation that had ended so dramatically. Hanne was euphoric, still half caught up in the splendor of the closing ceremonies, describing to Miklós and Patrick, over and over again, their last night in the Reichssportfeld, the dimming and the dying of the Olympic flame, the cries that had erupted. *Sieg Heil! Unser Führer Adolf Hitler! Sieg Heil!* And how no one chanting that cry wanted to leave, but finally all had done so, filing out in silence, as if the moment were too sacred to profane by ordinary conversation.

Tess sniffed and shifted restlessly in her wicker chair, but she was too conscious of being the keeper of a secret and too far into the champagne to protest. Miklós held his wife's hand with exquisite tenderness and a look of utter desolation that Joseph pretended to ignore and Abby could not bear to watch. She was tired. She wanted Tess and Patrick's visit to end; she wanted quiet days alone with Joseph; she wanted Hanne to stop talking and Miklós to begin to smile again.

A week later Tess and Patrick packed their bags. "I told a man at the American Embassy about you, Abby," Tess said. "Told him you had two passports and might not have the sense to use the right one when the time came."

"Tess!"

"We had lunch together a few times. Dinner, too. What the hell, Abby, I take it where I can get it, and nobody's complained yet. I figure he owes me one, and I let him know what the price was. Whatever you want, it's in the diplomatic pouch, no questions asked. Anything you want me to take back to Sheila? I know about the safe-deposit box."

Tess's frankness made it easier. Eleven years before, when Abby had been Madame Kelemen for less than five days, she had given all of Sammy Rosen's jewelry into her friend's keeping. The box was registered under two names, that of Sheila Gruber and Abby Sullivan. And whenever extra money had been needed—to send Thomas to Columbia, to pay the taxes on the house on Long Island that Joseph had bought for Bridget and Patrick, to bail Tess out of months of overdue back rent or support the gamblers and the never successful writers who regularly moved in with her—Sheila had sold a ring or a bracelet or a pair of earrings, and Arnie, never charging the lawyer's fee to which he was entitled, had doled it out. Because she suddenly saw Tess in a new light, suddenly remembered how she had shaken her fist in the face of the smooth-tongued Nazi who had never before been confronted by such a woman, Abby handed her every spare franc she could, and a diamond pendant she hadn't worn in over a year.

"I'll see that Sheila gets it all," Tess promised. "Though God knows I'll probably have to touch her again sooner or later. But if you need my man at the embassy, or if you want to send anything else out, at least you've got a lifeline and security that nobody but you and she can get to."

11

Europe was relatively quiet for the remainder of that Olympic year and throughout 1937, a lonely period of time during which Abby wrote more frequently than ever before to America, long, long letters to Sheila Gruber, shorter ones to Tess, who, still drifting from show to show and man to man, seldom managed more than a quick scrawl in reply.

She worried about Isaac Goldman and his family, not knowing, and with no way to find out, if the Gestapo had moved against them. "We were so naive," she told Joseph, "even Sheila, who should have realized that anyone traveling to Germany who was even remotely connected with refugee Jews would be marked and watched. I dream we're in that office again, but you and Bob Hill never find us. We're taken to a dark cell somewhere, and the last sound I hear before I wake up is a heavy metal door slamming shut. And I know that I'll die there, that it will never be opened no matter how loud I scream. Sometimes I'm alone in that office and that cell. I don't know where Tess is or what they've done to her."

He tried to comfort her and dispel the nightmares by reducing what had been extraordinarily dangerous to the level of the mundane. "What you've got to remember is that there must have been other foreigners in Berlin trying to do exactly what you did. And the authorities knew they would. Otherwise, why make an issue of obtaining permission to talk to Jews?"

"Do you think some of them could have been picked up and interrogated as we were?"

"Very possibly, Abby."

281

"Will there be a war, Joseph?" she whispered. "War against France? Again?"

It was a long time before he answered her, and then, as she listened, she thought he must have been anticipating her question and formulating his response since long before she asked it.

"Possibly. It makes sense if you look at a map of Europe and remember what Germany has done in the past, if you consider that what Mussolini is doing in Italy makes him Hitler's dupe, but that the dupe has already swallowed Abyssinia. In a sense, Spain is a testing ground for the future. That's why the young, the idealists, and the intellectuals find themselves drawn there. Only the politicians equivocate, but that's to be expected also."

"So Miklós is right, after all?"

"Not entirely. I would respect his judgment more if he'd ever learned to tell the difference between a good and a bad painting, but even after all these years, he makes more mistakes than I would tolerate from any other employee."

"What does good taste in paintings have to do with it, Joseph?"

"It has to do with judgment, Abby, with the ability to distinguish the false from the true, what is of lasting value from what merely shocks or momentarily excites. Listen to Miklós, really listen to him some evening. He mouths the latest editorial he's read or oversimplifies the most recent book he's finished. The past is not the present. Germany can move outside her borders only if a vacuum of power exists among the other European nations, and that's simply not the case. One step into Austria, Czechoslovakia, or Poland would bring France and England and all their allies down on her like giants stepping on an ant. Hitler is webbed in by the treaties and alliances that grew out of the last war."

"He has an army. We saw it. Isn't that in defiance of the Treaty of Versailles? Yet no one has protested."

"It's not a real army, more a mad and temporary solution to unemployment. The wars of the future will be fought less with men than with planes and ships and weapons that haven't even been invented yet. That's what Hitler can never have, and what Miklós should realize. Europe was a charnel house in 1914, Abby. It simply won't be allowed to happen again, not that way."

"What about the Jews, Joseph? What about the Nuremberg Laws and people like Isaac Goldman and his family? Will the world just stand by and let them be deprived of the kind of basic human rights the rest of us take for granted?"

"What of the colored people in your own country, Abby? Would you say that what they suffer is cause for intervention by a foreign power?"

"It's not the same thing."

"Isn't it? I grant you that they're citizens, but how many of them are really free to vote in your Southern states? How many have been lynched for crimes they never committed? And America isn't free from anti-Semitism either. You would have felt it when we were together in New York if I'd been as ordinary and as poor a Jew as Isaac Goldman. Money is power. I learned that a very long time ago. I proved it again in Berlin. It may not buy you everything you want, it can't bribe death to pass over you, but it does keep the ignorant and the prejudiced from spitting in your face. I'm sorry for Isaac Goldman, for all the Jews in Germany today. I believe they'd be better off in almost any other country you could name, though none of them is perfect, none really wants them. You know how hard I've tried to get Mama and Magda to leave Budapest, to come to France. Do you know why, Abby? France tolerates her Jews a little better than the eastern European countries. There was anti-Semitism in the Legion; it still exists today in the army and the citadels of political power. But look at what I've accomplished here, tick off on your fingers the intellectuals who are the real life of this country, and then go back over the list and see how many of them are Jews."

"So Miklós isn't right?"

"Neither completely right nor completely wrong. But the important thing to remember is that I have clients in the government, clients in the upper echelons of the army, clients and old friends, Abby, in the capitals of every country in Europe, in England, in the United States. Many of them you've met; we've entertained them at Les Roses. If there is ever any real danger to us, to France, we'll know it long before Miklós can read about it in a newspaper. I'm not a fool. I fought for France in North Africa and again in the last war. I know what war is, my darling, in a way that I will never allow you to experience. Trust me. I changed my nationality once; I won't hesitate to do it again."

She wrote much of what Joseph said in that conversation to Sheila, following the logic of his argument as carefully as she could, sometimes quoting whole sentences, remembering his compassion for Isaac Goldman and his family, but making the point, as strongly as she could, that their situation was so different that there were simply no grounds for comparison. It was months before she received a reply. The Goldmans were in America, impoverished but alive and well, studying English, planning to apply for citizenship as soon as the law would allow. It was Anneke who had made the decision to quit Germany, not Isaac. Their child had been a son, Sheila wrote, and at the moment she felt him leave her body, Anneke claimed, she had heard Abby's voice asking what kind of future that infant would have in Hitler's Germany. From that minute until the day they sailed, she hadn't given Isaac an instant's peace. Their first daughter would be named after the woman who had given them a new life and a new country.

Abby wept, but when her tears were exhausted, she felt not relief, but a curious mixture of anger and frustration. The rest of Sheila's letter had been a point-by-point refutation of the argument that had sounded so logical when Joseph made it. And yet what could Sheila possibly know of Europe, living as she did in a country that hadn't known a foreign invader for more than a hundred years? Don't wait too long, Sheila counseled. Don't put your trust in government officials or army generals. Tess was drinking again, had been fired again from a show that wasn't even going to open in New York City, for God's sake, but at some second-rate hotel up in the Catskills. There was very little cash left in the safe-deposit box. The next time Tess needed money, Sheila would have to sell another piece of jewelry. Did it make any difference to Abby which one? Nothing ever changed.

Marie-Claire lived long enough to celebrate as authentic an American Thanksgiving as Abby could manage, extracting a promise, toward the end, that there would be neither a funeral Mass nor tears to clutter up the clean, swift death she administered to herself. Georges's affairs had been put in impeccable order within days of the doctor's diagnosis and his mistress's decision to die intact in her own good time. He lived until well after Christmas, for the sake of the two daughters, the wife, the grandchildren. But January was too hard, too cold, too empty without the woman he had loved for as long as he could remember. He died at the end of the first week in February, willed it, slipped away calmly, with the same measure of dignity and grace that he had lived. For Abby and Joseph his passing marked the end of an era.

The Anschluss and the takeover of Czechoslovakia were like stones thrown into a pond. Once the ripples beat themselves out and the waters were smooth again, Abby forgot the stabs of fear that had made her fingers tremble whenever she turned on the radio or opened a newspaper. For weeks Joseph was unusually quiet, tense, and preoccupied, Miklós almost hysterical, Hanne shaken and so pale that their Friday-night dinners together were exercises in self-control, the bridge game that always followed subdued, the air for once unblistered by incomprehensible Hungarian curses because Miklós was a wildly inspired bidder and Joseph demanded order and perfection in everything he did.

Then gradually, because nothing else happened, because Neville Chamberlain's phrase about peace in our time came so glibly to everyone's tongue that it took on the weight of truth, they, and everyone else in Europe, it seemed, persuaded themselves that Hitler was satisfied, satiated, that the ignominy of the Treaty of Versailles had finally been erased, that Nazi Germany, though probably never a neighbor upon whom one could turn one's back, could be lived with. Only a madman would want another war, and no one could quite bring himself to believe that Adolf Hitler was not simply another head of state, as open to veiled threats and reasonable conciliation as any other. Now, when one of Sheila's letters arrived from America, Abby read it to herself, put it away without a word to Joseph. It seemed disloyal somehow, as if she trusted Sheila more than her husband, to repeat the warnings, the arguments, the pleas that they leave Europe before it was too late. Later, she would bitterly reproach herself and never quite understand how she could have walked in a dream for so long, but by that time everyone else had awakened also, and they could only stare at one another in wonderment and fear.

Austria had ceased to exist as a separate nation in March of 1938; Czechoslovakia had disappeared in October. In early January of 1939 Hanne renounced her German citizenship, confiding her intentions in no one, not even Miklós, until it was done.

"I filed the documents years ago, all but the last one," she wept, spreading the official papers out on Abby's dining room table, her fingers as cold as the marble over which she bent. "In the end it was merely a formality, and over so quickly. I felt nothing, except shame and gratitude. I was the only German there to take the oath. The others listened to me, and moved away. They knew what I was."

"Why, *Liebchen?*" Miklós asked softly. "Why now, after all this time?"

"It was the only way to prove to them and to myself that I wasn't, that I could never be what they asked me to become. A spy, Miklós. Two men from the German embassy. Months and months ago. They came one day when I was alone in the apartment. They said that Germany needed me, that I could be her eyes and ears, that there were other good Germans in Paris who had not hesitated to offer themselves to the Reich, that later, when the undesirables of Europe were weeded out, it wouldn't be held against me that I had married a Jew. They brought a letter from my brother, from Anton, urging me to remember who and what I was."

"What did you tell them, Hanne?" It was Abby who asked the question, Abby who was remembering the booming, profane magnificence of Tess two and a half years before, remembering her own fears and nightmares that had been so real until Joseph soothed her out of them.

"That I would cooperate, that I was as loyal a German as they. I was so afraid. I would have promised anything, anything, just to be able to close the door behind them."

"And then?"

"I walked, I shopped, I went to the movies, I sat for hours in Notre Dame. Every morning, as soon as Miklós was gone, I left the apartment, and I didn't go back until I knew I wouldn't be alone there for more than a few minutes. I filed the final citizenship paper. I hid. They won't come again now. They'll know. They know everything."

Later that same month, Joseph had the outside doors to their apartment taken down and replaced with steel doors half an inch thick, the front one sheathed in carved walnut, both bored through with peepholes and further strengthened with steel bars set into supports firmly anchored in the walls.

"Is it because of Hanne?" Abby asked. "Because of what they wanted her to do, what it means? I can't live in a prison, Joseph."

"I should have done it years ago," he answered. "I'm tired of worrying about my Lautrec sketches every time we go away." There were other, much more priceless paintings in every room, yet his custom had always been to understate the value of the things that passed through the gallery and often stayed for months or years in his own home. But except for one business trip to London, the Kelemens hadn't traveled outside the borders of France for more than a year.

"You never worried before, Joseph," Abby reminded him. "It *is* because of what Hanne has done, because now she too is afraid of war."

"Times change. The new doors will cut my insurance costs by a fourth."

It was the first time in all their years together that he cut off her protestations and refused to answer her questions, refused to discuss with her a decision he had made. Abby was shocked and hurt; he had never before treated her in much the same way that he behaved toward Miklós, as if she were a child with whom he, as parent, was not to be expected to consult, to whom he owed no explanation of his actions. She roamed the apartment for days, coming back over and over again to stand in front of the steel doors hidden between the slabs of polished walnut, wondering what they could mean, what he was hiding from her. It wasn't until an almost frantically pleading letter from Sheila arrived that she finally understood.

"You won't go," she said to him that evening. "No matter what happens, you won't leave Paris. Even if Germany cannot be contained, if Hitler does the unthinkable, you'll stay. You'll stay, Joseph, won't you? But why? I don't understand why."

"It won't come to that."

"But you believe it could. You've thought so all along. And for reasons I can't begin to imagine and you don't believe in me enough to explain, you're making preparations. Do you think that some morning you can simply hand me my passport and I'll creep dutifully off to the United States and leave you behind? I won't, you know. If you believe you'll be safe behind your steel doors, then you'll have to believe that I'll be safe behind them too. What's happening, Joseph? What are your clients and your friends in the government telling you that nobody else suspects yet?"

He refused to answer. That night, and for many weeks thereafter, she slept alone in the bedroom that Marie-Claire had helped her decorate when she had come to Paris as a bride, a room whose walls were paneled in silk tapestries cut from the boudoir of a Renaissance château, whose dressing table was a relic of the Bourbon monarchy, whose bed was one in which a king and his mistress had made love. "Privacy is an indispensable part of a good marriage," Marie-Claire had insisted. "You must have a retreat of your own, and so must he." Now Abby lay awake in what seemed to her a luxurious cell of her own making, unable, because the door to Joseph's so much simpler room was so tightly, so firmly shut, to break through the only barrier he had ever erected against her.

If he had ever spoken to her of Rahel, of the lost and lovely child Emmanuel, there might have been no need for him to close himself away from her, to wrestle in lonely isolation with memories of the past and fears for the future. There had been a time when he had thought of her as Rahel reborn, when the old love had been so mixed with the new that they seemed one and the same. But that was years and years ago, and when, finally, one day, he had forgotten to search for Rahel in Abby's eyes, when he knew that he loved her for herself and not merely because she had once appeared to be the reincarnation of a dead woman, he had rested, he had dared to believe that the ghost of Rahel would be no more than that, a beloved ghost.

But no one, except O'Brien, who was surely dead also by this time, no one else had ever known that he held himself solely responsible for the loss of two lives. It wasn't the will of Allah that had killed Rahel, but the will of Joseph Kelemen, who had loved her too selfishly to leave her in the safety of her father's house, who had brought her into mountains too high and cold and cruel for her to endure, among a people so primitive that they believed illness and death could be caused by evil spirits. He had thought, once, that he could not bear to live without Rahel, yet she had been his for so brief a time. Abby, the miracle of Abby, was more flesh of his flesh, more the very heart of him than Rahel had ever had a chance to become. More, she was his atonement, the daily, visible proof that a tortured and tormented soul could find redemption and release.

If other truths be told, and finally they w~re, Joseph had grown even more deeply pessimistic than Miklós. War with Germany was inevitable, the only question being when and how it would erupt, what single deliberate act of aggression or unforeseen accident would precipitate hostilities. No rational part of him truly believed it could be averted, yet the memories of what he had seen in Fez, what he had experienced when, as O'Brien predicted, France had thrust a rifle into his hands in 1914, those memories forced him to hope that it would not happen again, even sometimes to deny that it was possible. He thought that the steel doors had been a mistake; he should have waited, should not have had them installed until he had gotten Abby safely out of the country on some pretext or another. And when would he send her away? How could he? And hadn't he known, hadn't he really known that she would understand the meaning of the half-inch-thick steel?

What he did not believe, what he later knew to have been suicidal blindness, was that Jews would, could suffer any more greatly in this new madness than they had done in 1914. He was a proud man, and he did not think of himself as a Jew. He had left that part of him behind in the desert of North Africa, shed that skin as he had shed so many others. He was wealthy; he was respected; he had carved out for himself a kingdom in which no one dared to suggest that he was any less to be respected than the Christians with whom he dealt every day. It had been an intellectual exercise, nothing more, to remind Abby that anti-Semitism existed almost as nakedly in America as did the prejudice against people of color.

And there was something else, something he would have denied as vigorously as he did the vulnerability that was his simply because he was a Jew. He had come to love France, to love the ideal of the country and the country itself almost as much as he loved Abby, as highly as he prized his art. It was an unreasonable love, one that belonged more to boyhood than to a man who had lived fifty-two years, most of them with his eyes wide open. Patriotism of the kind that might ask for the sacrifice of one's life was a young man's dream, but for the past fifteen years Joseph had aged very little in body and not at all in mind or soul. It was as if the opposite had happened, as if the process had been reversed, as if the man who had felt so very, very old in North Africa had grown younger in France, so gradually, so imperceptibly that until now he had not noticed it. It was Abby, of course, who had made the change possible, who had erased so much of the heartache and vanquished the despair, and now, paradoxically, it was because of what she had given him that he must send her away. Because he would fight for France, again, in whatever way he could, whether she truly accepted him as a son or not. He had no choice. He wanted no easier alternative. But how could he explain that to the woman he loved? How could he tell her that, unbeknownst to him, he'd been acquiring a mistress all these years, and that it was through Abby that he had come to love her?

Germany struck at Poland on September 1, 1939, the day of Abby Kelemen's thirty-sixth birthday. Ironically, it was Miklós who brought them the news, ringing their bell and pounding frantically on their front door within a half hour after the first garbled radio broadcast had shattered the city's early-morning calm. Hanne, deathly pale, clung to her husband's arm as if afraid that at any moment he would thrust her from him.

"We didn't get back from Deauville until after midnight," Abby explained. "I took the phone off the hook so we could sleep late. We came home two days early." Nothing of what she was saying was important, yet she could not stop the flow of ordinary words, ordinary concerns. "Be careful," she warned. "We were so tired last night that we told René just to leave the suitcases here in the foyer." She lifted one of them, set it down, lifted it again, stood not knowing what to do next.

"Make some coffee, Abby," Joseph said.

As she turned toward the kitchen she saw him kiss Hanne on both cheeks. It was the way he always greeted her, but this morning there was something infinitely poignant about the gesture. It was as if he were reassuring his sister-in-law that nothing had changed between them, that nothing would. He spoke to Hanne in German; she answered him in French.

The collapse of Poland was heartbreakingly swift. In the brief space of two days its air force was eliminated; the wreckage of planes that had never left their runways littered the bombed-out airfields. Within a week the bulk of its army had been defeated or surrounded; Cracow was taken, smaller towns and villages were simply engulfed by waves of German infantry. A dying Warsaw, encircled, besieged, fighting from street to street, was a barely flickering beacon of resistance. While the German army reduced the city to rubble, Hitler continued to proclaim his desire for peace, vowing that he had no quarrel with either France or England, both of whom had delivered ultimatums and then declared themselves at war with the Third Reich. Almost immediately after Warsaw surrendered on September 27, Poland was partitioned between Russia and Germany. The long nightmare of Nazi terror had begun.

When France declared war on Germany on September 3, Abby was among the many Americans living in Paris who sought reassurance and instructions from their embassy. A harassed junior officer gave her the same advice he had already given to hundreds of his compatriots that morning. Get out of Europe as soon as possible. But almost in the same breath he assured her that the United States would not become involved in a purely European conflict. Tess's friend, a surprisingly boyish-looking member of the cultural-liaison staff, said the same thing, and when Abby reminded him of the promise he had made her sister three years before, he blushed and stammered and finally agreed that if things got worse and if Madame Kelemen had something vital to send to America, he would put it in the diplomatic pouch under his own name. But he could only do it once, he insisted. Only once. It could mean his career if he was found out. And yes, he was staying. No one at the embassy had orders to leave yet, nor did anyone expect to receive any such directive unless or until the Germans got too close for comfort. He was a romantic, Abby suspected, and she thanked God and Tess for having found him.

Caught in the same paralysis of disbelief that seemed to grip most of the city's population, Abby did nothing else. The country was mobilizing; there was talk of a huge British force that would be dispatched to swell the ranks of the defenders of the Maginot Line; housewives remembered the shortages of the last war and began to stock their pantries with non-perishable staples, but there was no sense of panic anywhere.

By mid-October some elements of the French press were openly congratulating the government on not having rushed precipitously to Poland's aid. France had not been attacked after all. Since war had been declared because of the Polish question, and since that troublesome and insignificant country had now virtually ceased to exist, what point was there in continuing to antagonize a man who had somehow managed to place the blame for Poland's dilemma squarely on the shoulders of the Allied leaders who had refused to negotiate with him? Why not accept Herr Hitler's peace protestations at their face value? There were arguments in every café and around every dinner table. The country was divided between those who could not forget the devastation of the last war with Germany and those who screamed that French honor had already been unbearably compromised. Russia's invasion of Finland at the end of November released one final paroxysm of moral outrage, but even that was weakened by the memory of the Führer's narrow escape three weeks before when a bomb exploded on a Munich speaker's platform less than fifteen minutes after his unexpectedly short address. He was vulnerable; there was opposition inside Germany itself.

As winter closed in, cold, snowy, and bitter all over Europe, the French and German armies, within easy shooting distance of one another all along the frontier, sat behind their fortifications and grew bored. In Paris, life went on as usual, except for the minor annoyance of a nightly blackout and the ridiculous dictum that restaurants and public places of amusement were to close two hours before midnight. No German planes appeared over the city; there were no wounded to nurse, no casualties to bury and mourn. There were even some fools who boasted that Hitler had already been beaten, that the present stalemate was no more than a gesture to save face before the German people; that when spring came, peace would be declared and this war that was no war would be over. The French had a name for it, *la drôle de guerre.* The Americans called it the phony war.

*   *   *

Late on the night of January 10, 1940, Joseph and Abby climbed the hill from the Quai de Passy to the Place du Trocadéro. The narrow, winding streets were deserted at this hour; Paris slept behind its blackout curtains, no automobiles disturbed the peace of the Rue Franklin. In the Place itself the statue of Marshal Foch on his horse was a roost for sleeping pigeons; the sculptured white walls of the Palais de Chaillot glimmered in the dull sheen of a wintry moon. Abby would have lingered, in spite of the cold, but Joseph took her arm and led her down twisting side streets, stopping finally in front of an apartment house she could not recall ever having visited before.

They groped their way up two flights of unlighted stairs. A door opened in the hallway ahead of them, but no voice called out a welcome. Someone is watching, Abby thought as she felt hot air against her frozen cheeks; someone is watching from a window, counting our steps, waiting for us. She caught her lower lip between her teeth, biting down just long and hard enough to stop its trembling.

Princess Marie embraced her warmly and exclaimed over the state of her wet shoes, but she spoke a few quick, utterly incomprehensible Russian words to Joseph, certainly an exclamation of dismay and confusion. The Russians had always struck Abby as odd, forming, as most of them did, a formidably close-knit community of proud exiles. Abby had dined in restaurants with the princess and her husband, Prince Nikolai, gambled with them at Monte Carlo, shared their box at the races, but never, until tonight, had she been invited to their apartment. "Invited" was the wrong word, she reminded herself. Only Joseph had been expected.

"You are the last to arrive," Princess Marie said. "The others are in the dining room."

She led the way, walking briskly, a tiny woman weighted down under too much jewelry, dressed in a style that had gone out of fashion twenty years before, so heavily made up that powder and rouge were caked in the creases of her face and neck. Wisps of dyed black hair straggled out from an elaborate pompadour. She clung to her eccentricities as tightly as she did to the title that meant nothing now and the icons and fringed shawls and red-shaded lamps that cluttered the rooms in which she lived. A gypsy, Abby thought. If you did not know that she had once owned a palace in St. Petersburg and summered on an estate that was measured in miles rather than acres, you would think her a gypsy woman about to tell your fortune.

Five men sat around a long table from which a Russian Orthodox abbot had once surveyed his monastery's refectory. Their faces were as grave as had been those of the monks dead and buried three hundred years ago, and their silence as profound as though the lector still read pious admonitions to dispel the pleasures of food and drink.

Prince Nikolai was a better actor than his wife. He greeted them in the doorway of the dining room, blocking the other men from Abby's view as he bent over her hand. He had been a giant of a man in his younger days, and even now, gaunt, stooped, approaching his seventy-fifth year as he was, his nearly fleshless bones continued to give the impression of enormous size. Gracefully, as if he were partnering her in some antique dance, he kissed Abby's hand and turned her toward Princess Marie. She felt the old woman's arm slip into her own, and the almost imperceptible tug as the princess began to lead her away from this room and the men whom she could now see had averted their faces, leaned back from the pool of light that illuminated only the center of the table and the gleaming samovar steaming there. Ladies, it seemed, retired to a boudoir when gentlemen gathered to discuss serious affairs.

"I can help," Abby said, freeing herself from the little hands that were as sharp as claws. "I already know too much, don't I?" She had recognized one man by the smell of his pipe tobacco and the signet ring on his right hand. "Good evening, Monsieur Boncour."

"One of the dogs barked as I was leaving," Joseph said. He switched to Russian in midsentence, and although Abby could not understand the remainder of his explanation, she watched the effect of it register on the prince's face. Joseph had given away no secrets, merely telling her that he had matters to discuss with old friends and urging her to go back to sleep again. But she had known intuitively that he was hiding something, and in that same instant the real reason for his reluctance to leave France had become clear.

During the weeks that Warsaw had been fighting and falling, while half of France clamored for accommodation and the other half screamed for all-out war with Germany, rumors about the forming of civilian resistance groups throughout the country had been everyone's favorite topic of conversation. It was only talk, three or four friends who were beyond the age for military service concocting outrageous plots over a glass of wine, boys too young to be conscripted boasting of what they would do to the first German they saw. No one took it too seriously, and when Hitler apparently lost interest in France, as the situation at the front dragged on unchanged, the rumors died down and were quickly forgotten. Only the serious-minded, the pragmatic realists, Abby now realized, the very few who, like Joseph, were unswayed by political cant, only that handful of men and women continued to meet and to talk, convinced that someday they would be called upon to act. But what, she wondered, what could they do?

Joseph had stopped speaking. Prince Nikolai continued to block her way, but now he reached out a hand and tilted her head back so that he could look into her eyes. He seemed to be examining her face for signs of weakness, probing her mind for steadiness of purpose. She thought he looked like the pictures she had seen of Count Tolstoy, the bearded old man wearing a peasant's white blouse belted in at the waist, haughty and always angry. "Are you still an American citizen?" he asked.

"I have dual citizenship," she answered. "And two passports, both of them valid."

He smiled then. It could easily come to forged documents someday. In his own time he had known many men who had not scrupled to kill for the precious papers that could mean the difference between life and death. "So. Will you have a glass of tea, Abby, or vodka? A clear head or something to put fire in your veins?"

"Vodka, please, Prince." No one, not even his wife, called this man by his baptismal name.

There were glasses in silver holders around the samovar, a plate of sugar cubes, and boxes of long, thin Russian cigarettes. On a sideboard stood bottles of vodka, a tray of tiny glasses, a bowl of caviar ringed with half-moons of lemon and boiled egg, slices of black bread, crystal dishes of pickled beets and sour cream. Princess Marie carried them to the table, helped by the man whose name Abby had called out. There were no servants in the apartment, though the prince and princess normally lived surrounded by them, and it had been Marie herself who had opened the door. Conspirators, Abby thought; we are all conspirators here tonight.

The dining room was large; in daylight and furnished in the normal way it would have seemed spacious. But as she entered the room on the prince's arm, and the men around the table rose politely, Abby felt as though she were being conducted into a crowded tent barely large enough to hold all of them in comfort. The windows were shuttered and draped, overlapping carpets of Oriental design covered the floor, candles burned before icons in all the corners, the air was stuffy and close, and the chandelier with its tiny bulbs glowing beneath red paper shades emphasized the shadows just beyond its pool of light.

She knew them all: Roger Boncour, who had taught classes in Renaissance art at the Sorbonne until his retirement last year; Antoine Aymard, whose lectures she had attended when he was one of the curators at the Louvre; Paul Michaud, whose gallery was only two doors down from Galeries Kelemen; Martin Rouault, reputed to have one of the most discriminating small private collections in Europe; Samuel Koch, a distant Rothschild through the maternal line. Five of the finest minds in the world of European art, old friends all of them, old men also, not a one of them less than fifteen years Joseph's senior.

"*Na strovya,*" Prince Nikolai said. The response came back from every throat. *Na strovya. A la vôtre.* To your health. They served themselves from the dishes passed by Princess Marie; the prince refilled their glasses, as gravely dignified as an English butler. It was late, past midnight, but silver knives clinked against plates, drops of lemon juice sparkled over the caviar, little sighs of appreciation punctuated their eating. They were participating in a ceremony, a ritual, a sacrament.

"The rape of Poland is nearly finished," Prince Nikolai said. "A few more months, and there will be nothing left." He turned to Abby, explaining what the others already knew. "I am talking about the most precious fruits of civilization, my dear, about the art that the soul of humankind has created. We have been told that in Warsaw and Cracow Göring has had whole trains of boxcars at his disposal and as many soldiers as needed to fill the packing crates and drive the trucks to the station. They came with catalogues of what was to be found in private and public collections, names and addresses of gallery owners. And because the Jews were the first to be plundered, many Poles who should have known better believed that the action was directed only at Jews. And were secretly glad of it. They know better now, but it's too late."

"We've kept good records here too, just as they did in Poland," Paul Michaud interrupted. "Somewhere in Germany there is a clerk who has transcribed the title, the artist, and the worth of every painting hanging on my gallery walls."

"I have lived one life as a parasite," Prince Nikolai said, "and another as an exile recreating the appearance of what I lost. I don't have many years left to me."

"Herr Hitler wants France," Samuel Koch said. "He lusts after Paris the way a man hungers for a beautiful woman who has scorned and mocked him. We've never hidden our amusement at their deadly Wagner, their sweaty thighs and ridiculous pretensions, the foolish, beery young men who cut one another's faces with sabers, the palaces crudely modeled after ours. The Germans will make us pay dearly for having despised them."

"First the Scandinavian countries," Martin Rouault said. "The Reich needs their coal. Then Belgium, Holland, Luxembourg. They are just as vulnerable as they were in 1870 and 1914, and there is no more efficient way to reach France than across those plains. Our enemy worships the little god Efficiency."

"It was not difficult for us to find one another." Prince Nikolai smiled. "I spoke to some others also. A few listened but were not convinced; three or four had more pressing concerns and obligations than the ones I offered them."

"We are forgers, Abby," Antoine Aymard said. He lit one of the long Russian cigarettes and paused for a moment to watch the spiral of smoke dance above his head. "When I was at the Louvre, the very suspicion of forgery could make me sleepless for weeks. Now I am proud to have joined that confraternity of charlatans."

"We've barely begun," Samuel Koch said quietly. "But without Roger's help, we could not have done even that."

"Some of the students I taught continue to call and bring their paintings by," Boncour explained. "I always kept my little studio and continued to paint, you know." It had been one of the great sadnesses of this man's life to accept that his personal talent was a minor one. He had become a renowned academician, but Abby had once heard him remark that he would gladly have given up all the honors he had received over the years in exchange for a fraction of the genius possessed by the masters about whom he lectured. "We drink a glass of wine together and talk about theory, about technique, about what it is to live the life of an artist. I've never changed the advice I give to all of them. 'Paint the masters,' I tell them. 'Take your easels and your brushes into the museums and paint what you see before you. When you can feel the reason a stroke is made just so and understand how that special light is mixed into the paint, you will have begun to learn the secrets that will be your own foundation.' Some of them protest, of course, but you see the wisest and the most dedicated working away, oblivious to the crowds that gather to compare their copies with the originals. It's only an exercise, but I have seen a few copies that would make the most experienced expert pause for a moment and wonder. Artists are romantics at heart, and young ones often nearly impossibly so. When Prince Nikolai approached me, I realized that many of those young men would be useless holding a gun, but invaluable wielding a brush."

"I am a selfish man. I admit it," Martin Rouault said. "I don't want to fall asleep at night knowing that Hermann Göring is filling his belly with schnapps and feasting his drunken eyes on my Giotto *Madonna*. I decided that I could almost laugh my way through this war if all he took from me were forgeries."

"In a week or two the first forgeries will be completed," Roger Boncour said.

And at last Abby understood the role that Joseph was to play in the conspiracy. "Les Roses," she whispered.

"Just so," Prince Nikolai confirmed. "That was always our greatest worry, of course—where to hide the originals so they would be safe."

"At the Louvre they are talking about moving whatever they can out into the country, into holes in the ground all over France. Giving as much of the national treasure as they can into the safekeeping of ordinary Frenchmen who may never have set foot inside the Louvre. There may not be enough time, and there may not be enough Frenchmen to hide it all, but that is what they are talking about," Antoine Aymard said.

"Unfortunately, we are all too well known to hope that the Germans will not search in the obvious places," Samuel Koch said. "We cannot save everything we own. We are forced to be selective. In the coming months, if we have that much time, Martin and I will buy only the best of what is offered for sale. The copies will hang on our walls until they are repatriated to Germany. That is the word they are using in Poland to describe their thefts."

"The gardens at Les Roses," Abby said excitedly, her eyes flashing with the daring of what these sedate old men had schemed to do. "There's a shallow pond that can be drained and refilled in a single night, and even an enormously tall manure heap behind Gustave Lebrun's cottage. If we raised the seat of the Citroën only slightly, we could create a space several inches in height all along the width of the car."

"Joseph? You have said nothing." Prince Nikolai poured more vodka, filling Joseph's glass last, resting his hand lightly on his friend's shoulder before returning to his place at the head of the table.

Abby looked at her husband, then at the faces of the men studying both of them. Roger Boncour and Samuel Koch were widowers; Antoine Aymard had never married; Martin Rouault's wife had lived apart from him in California for years; Paul Michaud's only two interests in life were his Church and his gallery. "It's me, isn't it?" she asked.

Princess Marie's sunken black eyes glittered like beads of jet. "You are still young, Abby," she said gently. "And very beautiful. The Germans do not take kindly to resistance. We know that from every story that has come out of Poland. They take hostages and torture a man through his family. They are cruelest of all to women."

"That's why you've been urging me to go to London, isn't it, Joseph?" Abby asked.

He nodded. "You, Miklós, Hanne. All three of you must leave."

"No," Abby said.

"For all our sakes, Abby," Prince Nikolai interrupted. "You know as well as I do that Joseph would betray any one and any cause to save your life or spare you pain. We understand that. We wouldn't do any differently ourselves. But each of us is old, each of us is alone in the world. We have no human loves that we fear losing."

Abby glanced at Princess Marie, a mute appeal in her eyes.

"We are agreed, the prince and I," the old woman said. "They cannot break us."

"I stay," Abby said firmly.

"There is another way," Samuel Koch said reflectively, and now he spoke directly to Joseph. "Sell me Les Roses. Nothing of what we have planned changes except the ownership of the property where the paintings will be hidden. You are a young Jew, my friend; I am an old one. Believe me, to be still in one's early fifties is to be young. Take your lovely wife and get out while you can. If you were my son, I would beg you to go. We can do what we have to do without you."

"He can't sell it to you, Monsieur Koch," Abby said. "Les Roses is legally mine."

"Why do you want so badly to stay?" Prince Nikolai asked. "This is not a game we are proposing to play. You will not be able to quit once you have begun."

Abby remembered the way he had examined her face before allowing her to enter this room, the look that had seemed to strip away layers of skin, to penetrate to the most hidden corner of her soul. What had he seen there that had made him decide to trust her? What had he read in her that not even she herself understood?

"You have no children," Princess Marie prompted. Abby turned to her gratefully, silently thanking her for having supplied the words with which to begin. The princess was also childless, the cause of the extinction of her husband's proud line. From the distance of age, of revolution, exile, and a woman's special sorrow, she had understood Abby's need, the ache of years that had begun to seem so empty under the lovely ease of them.

"I have no children," Abby said. "Nor will I ever have any." Joseph's shoulder touched hers. She moved away from the comfort he was offering. She had to be alone in what she would say, prove that she could be alone in what she was asking to be allowed to do. "If I were to die tomorrow, I would leave nothing behind me, nothing of value, no contribution of lasting worth. Not to the world of art, not to literature, science, economics, music, any field you can name. Not to the United States, not to France. I'm not educated in the way that the rest of you are. I doubt that I could earn my own living now if I had to. I have no skills, no talents that are not common to thousands of other women whose husbands are as successful and as loving as Joseph is. Only twice in my life have I made a difference to people who loved or depended on me. Only twice. I want to stay, Prince, because in what lies ahead there will finally be work I can do that no one else can. I'm not a Jew; my baptismal certificate proves it. Can any of you envision a day when Joseph will have to act through me? When I can go out into the streets in perfect safety, but he cannot? It won't end when the Germans arrive. There will be other paintings to save, and the temptation to steal them from right under their noses will be one that none of you will be able to resist." She bowed her head, raised it again. "I hate the thought of war as much as anyone else, but Herr Hitler has, is, and will force it on us. There will be an offensive in the spring, not peace proposals. Nothing can stop it, we all know what's coming. And I will admit to you that I need it. I need this war."

"In Poland the ghetto has come into its own again," Samuel Koch said. "Identity papers are stamped 'Jew,' and the restrictions are worse than they are in Germany itself."

"The decision is Joseph's," Prince Nikolai said. "He is the head of his house."

Abby sat with hands folded before her on the table. There seemed to be a buzzing in her ears and a curtain of gauze interfering with her vision as she waited for her husband to speak.

"We will stay," Joseph said. "Both of us."

12

Joseph became a different man after the night at Prince Nikolai's, yet only Abby and Miklós were aware of the change in him, and only Abby understood it. The daily routine that was familiar to friends, clients, and business associates remained unaltered, but Abby's critical eye detected carefully disguised signs of impatience, a lack of real interest in everyday gallery affairs and a marked indifference toward the performances of the horses in which he owned shares. It was as if all his mental energies were concentrated on that unknown day in the future when a conquering army would appear on the streets of Paris. Despite the braggadocio of the government and the general staff, neither of them doubted that it would happen, but while Abby could do no more than wonder what it would be like to see the swastika unfurled atop the Eiffel Tower and fluttering before public buildings, Joseph knew and remembered the harsh realities of a city under siege, a city occupied by foreign troops.

His first concern was for their personal safety. "If we are to remain, Abby," he told her, "we must be as anonymous as possible." She smiled at the qualification in his statement. During the days immediately following the visit to Prince Nikolai's apartment, he had several times tried to persuade her to change her decision. She had refused, yet he continued to remind her, in small, oblique ways, that it was not too late. He had no real hope of dissuading her, but it was as if he had promised himself that he would not entirely give up.

"Samuel Koch reminded me of something I should never have forgotten," Joseph said. "Jews will be the first targets.

The pattern of what was done in Germany and what is being done in Poland will be followed here also."

"Ghettos?" Abby was horrified at the very sound of the word, yet she had only a confused notion of what it meant.

"Not here. Not in France. Our economic situation is very different, and there aren't that many of us. I don't think even the Nazis will dare go that far, but they'll use the Nuremberg Laws to strip us of our civil liberties. They'll gradually make it illegal for Jews to practice law or medicine or teach in any of the universities. The more successful a business, the more quickly it will become a target for confiscation."

"We could get you false papers, Joseph. Birth and baptismal certificates proving that you were born of Christian parents."

"I'm too well known, Abby, both here and in other countries. I've had hundreds of clients over the years; my name appears on thousands of documents. I think it would be safer to tell as few lies as possible." He stopped her half-formulated protest with a wave of his hand. "Have you forgotten your friend in Berlin? Other people also know, my dear, and they will remember. Hitler has only made anti-Semitism legal and respectable again."

"Are you afraid, Joseph?"

"I've lived with fear before; it can be conquered. And I haven't been as blind as Miklós would accuse me of being. You guessed that yourself. Your friend Sheila was perfectly right to warn us. Long before 1935 there were hints from colleagues, but even more significant were the pieces they began offering for sale and the identity of the exceptionally prudent and farsighted owners who were eager to part with them. In times of peace a man buys as many lovely objects as he can afford; he wants to surround himself with a beauty that doesn't fade with the passing years; he builds a small collection. But that same man knows that he can neither eat the magnificence hanging on his walls nor can he sew it into the lining of his coat when the mob turns on him. These people are already gone; they're starting over again in America, like the Goldmans who made it in time only thanks to you. I don't fault them for it. In fact, I applaud their instinct for survival."

Joseph was silent for a moment. A procession of the prudent men he had known was passing through his mind, each of them accomplished, talented, well established in his profession, national and family roots holding him to a soil from which he could no longer draw nourishment. He felt their pain as they wrenched themselves free, but he also saw the sons and daughters clinging to their fingertips. If he had had children, he too would have left. He did not. Abby had struck to the core of her own truth, and it was his also. Knowing that he had once sired a son as easily and as effortlessly as he had loved, he had feared that to tell her his seed bore fruit on fertile ground would be to destroy her. He had feigned indifference whenever she brought up the subject of children, but every word and every hope of hers had done no more than echo his. That had nothing and everything to do with what he wanted to tell her.

"I knew, Abby, I worried about the eventual danger to you of my being who and what I am, even while I denied it. I gambled for more time to be together, and I was winning. Every additional month, every extra year was as unexpected and as gloriously exciting as a good run of cards. I knew that I would stay no matter what. I even knew, long before Prince Nikolai approached me, that somehow I would find the means to play a game that no more than three or four people knew was being played. The odd thing about it is that I never considered myself a nationalist until now. I didn't weep when I left Hungary; I served France faithfully, but for my own interests as well as hers; I've never contributed a single franc to the Zionists. All that has changed, and I can't tell you precisely when or how or why. But as a Frenchman and a Jew, and I am both those things, Hitler is as much my personal enemy as a tough on the street or a bully in the schoolyard. I recognize my enemy, I know he's driven to try to destroy me. But he's ponderous and large; he's established a set of rules he believes will conceal the unfairness of the battle, and he must abide by them or lose face. My only rule is that I will acknowledge no code. I'm small; I'm agile; I will eventually outwit him."

There was a fallacy in what Joseph was saying, a very deep and basic flaw in his reasoning. Abby knew it was there, knew that it was terribly important that she find and identify it. It was, of course, that he was reasoning at all, that he was applying rules of logic to a situation whose first truth was that logic no longer existed. She would have said this to him, perhaps not clearly, but searching for the right or nearly right words, had he not spoken again.

"You see, my dear, in my own way, and I cannot hope that you will completely understand, because I don't myself, I too need this war."

It was the end of trying to explain, the last conversation into which the lure of what might have been, what could be, was allowed to creep. They were caught, both of them, but willingly so, each separately and both together reaching for another plateau, a high, windy place of testing.

The steel outer doors of their apartment were checked and checked again. Nothing and no one could break them down. Joseph began to buy gems, discreetly and never in large single purchases; they were sewn into the hems of everyday garments. Abby wrapped her American passport in oiled cloth and buried it in one of the flower boxes on the balcony. It would have been safer to burn it perhaps, but it was also the most valuable object either of them possessed. It was worth any risk just to fall asleep at night knowing that it still existed.

The maid Françoise left them of her own accord, weeping insincere tears because she suspected that her parents' farm in Normandy would soon become a far safer place to be than Paris. They were glad to see her go, even though it meant that for the first time in their married lives they would be servantless. Joseph had worried about Françoise, hesitating to offer any of their paintings to Roger Boncour's copyists because the maid was, as he said to Abby, a typically suspicious peasant whose keen eye noticed everything and whose narrow little brain stored up imagined slights as efficiently as the file of a bureaucrat. René, in the Reserves since September, was also a potential problem. Joseph simply filled in a form that changed his chauffeur's status from essential to nonessential to an important national industry. "It was bribery to begin with," he told Abby when René was immediately called to join his unit and went proudly, willingly, eager to erase the stigma of having allowed his employer to shelter him for as long as he had. "I will be back, monsieur," he boasted, "when we have taught the Boches a lesson." Thousands of young men were saying the same thing to wives, mistresses, parents, friends.

"The next thing is to send Miklós to London," Joseph

said, "ostensibly on gallery business. But I'll insist that he take Hanne with him, and that while they are there she look for a flat in the city that all of us can share. I'll urge him to get back as soon as the business is completed and the flat is found. When he tries to leave, there will be a question about their papers; my partner there will offer to use his contacts in the government to straighten it out; their passports will disappear in a bureaucratic muddle for as long as necessary. Miklós has never been any good at dealing with bureaucracy; he doesn't know how to cut through red tape. Without passports, they'll be safe; they won't be able to cross the Channel again."

"Will he go, Joseph?" Abby asked. "And if he does, will he ever forgive you?"

"He'll go. If I make the request urgently enough and if we can convince him that we mean to follow. It's what he's been telling us we ought to do for years. I think I understand my brother, Abby. In everything to do with business I've made all the decisions, small as well as large. That kind of long dependence gradually strips a man of his pride, even someone like Miklós. In this one thing I must allow him to believe that it is he who is right and that I now acknowledge it. With a single stroke he repays years of indebtedness and reclaims the pride I've taken from him. Whether he'll forgive me when he learns the truth, I can't say. I don't care. Miklós would be swallowed up and lost in the new world the Germans will force all of us to enter. That can't be allowed to happen to him."

"He's not a child, Joseph," Abby argued.

"He is. He'll always be a child. Someone has paid his bills and kept him from stumbling since the day he was born. He hasn't the guile to pretend, nor the discipline to keep from speaking out. And like a child, he's curious. When we start making frequent trips to Les Roses by ourselves, he'll wonder why we go alone when for years he and Hanne have always gone with us. He reads. He picks up every rumor as soon as it begins to circulate. How long do you think it will take him to figure out what we're doing? Not long, Abby, believe me. He'll want to help, he'll forget his fears temporarily, but they'll come back even stronger than before when it's too late to escape. He won't want to betray us, but he will. By a certain anxious guilt in his eyes, a sudden start when he turns a corner and sees a German uniform, a stammering if he's questioned about something as insignificant as the lunch he's carrying in his briefcase. All the qualities that make him the innocent he is will work against him. And two other things that are even more important. He's a Jew, much more of a Jew than I am, and I suspect that he's already beginning to regret that he ever forgot to remain one."

"And the other thing?"

"Hanne herself," Joseph said sadly. "Every German in the city will come under special scrutiny, especially those who changed their citizenship as she did. She's committed two monstrous offenses, and there will be terrible pressures applied to make her atone for them. The German army will tell her she betrayed the Fatherland by adopting her husband's nationality, and the Gestapo will revile and threaten her for having married a Jew. That's what will destroy Miklós. And us."

They had reckoned without Miklós' stubbornness. He listened to Joseph's explanation of why he wanted him to go to London, nodded his head as each point was made, even jotted down a few notes on a scrap of paper. But then he crossed through each item, tore the paper into tiny bits, and refused to make the trip. He didn't argue with his brother, and Hanne said not a word, but it was apparent that the two of them had been prepared for just such a proposal, that they had discussed what they would answer, and already made their decision.

"I've always tried to do everything I could to help you, Joseph," Miklós said with quiet pride. "I've made mistakes, but they haven't been serious ones. And in small ways, handling the details of paperwork, just seeing that your other employees gave you full value for a day's work, I've freed you to accomplish things I could never do. You're flattering me now by pretending to admit that in this one instance, my judgment was better than yours. You have no intention of leaving France, and somehow, I don't know how, you would make sure that Hanne and I could not get back. My heart thanks you, but it cannot accept this gift you want us to have. Hanne agrees with me. The four of us will leave together, or none of us will go."

"Don't you realize that it's Hanne who will be in the worst jeopardy?" Abby asked.

It was Hanne herself who answered, struggling with the language she still hadn't quite mastered. She had refused to speak German, even in private, since the day war was declared. "No one escapes justice, Abby. My nephews were in Poland in September. I learned that in a letter my brother wrote. I know what's coming for me; he told me very clearly. Every shopkeeper hears the voice of his enemy when I speak. They are, were, my people. I share the guilt of what they did in Warsaw and in other places; it is only just that I share the punishment they will mete out to the innocent of this country."

"Brother does not abandon brother," Miklós said.

"A wife does not leave her husband," Hanne said.

And there the argument finally ended. Neither Joseph nor Abby could deny to Hanne and Miklós the rights they themselves had claimed, the right to choose their future, the right to sacrifice themselves in the name of blood and love, the right to pursue their choice in dignity.

In early March, Abby and Joseph made the first of what became dozens of trips to Les Roses during the next few months. They seldom stayed longer than a night or two, and if Roger Boncour called in the middle of the week, Abby went by herself, often creeping back to Paris in nearly total blackness on narrow, twisting country roads. Only four or five times did they drive openly through the village that had provided Les Roses with summer help for so many years. It would have been unusual had they not come at all that spring. Every city dweller with a second home spent as much time as he could away from the capital and its constant reminders of the tense stalemate along the Maginot Line.

In past years Abby had often attended Mass in the village church. The curé had sent her a score of young girls eager to work for the good wages the Kelemens paid, and Abby had been generous in her donations to the parish. "We will not be opening Les Roses as we have in previous seasons," she now explained to him. "Monsieur and I will probably spend very little time there. But I don't want that to cause a hardship for the people who may have been counting on working for us again. Would you explain to them that monsieur's health has suffered this winter, and that because he needs rest and quiet, we have decided not to invite any guests this year?"

"But you may need someone from time to time, madame? Just one or two girls to make things ready for you when you do visit?"

"Perhaps," Abby lied. "I would let you know in advance, of course. It's a delicate thing, Monsieur le Curé, but I felt certain you would be able to persuade those who have served us so well in the past to accept a small token of our appreciation." In the envelope she handed him was enough money to pay the full salary of every villager who had expected to be employed at Les Roses again that season.

He was gratified at the weight and bulk of the envelope, but he did not open it. "They will feel themselves bound in honor to serve you whenever they are wanted," he said. Thousands of hours in the confessional had trained him to display no surprise at whatever curious things people felt themselves compelled to do. He was a keeper of secrets; he recognized instantly the bribes Madame Kelemen was asking him to pay. She and her husband wanted absolute privacy at Les Roses. He wouldn't question their motives, and he would exercise the considerable authority he possessed in the village to keep the unavoidable speculation down to a minimum. In the fullness of time, all would be revealed. Later, when he counted the bills, he discovered that madame had bribed him too. "To repair the old leak just over the side altar of the Virgin," she had written on a small white card. There was enough money clipped to the card to pay for an entire new roof. The priest smiled to himself, spent as little as possible to stop up the leak, and hid the rest of her gift in the sacristy. He too expected the Germans to come; what Madame Kelemen had provided for a new roof could be better used by the young men who would have to go into hiding.

The village priest kept his suspicions to himself, and so did Gustave Lebrun. A load of pipes was delivered and stored in one of the potting sheds that had fallen into disuse after the new greenhouse was built. Monsieur Kelemen spoke vaguely about the damage suffered by the gardens when summers were hot and dry, and Madame praised the efficiency of the greenhouses she had seen in Holland, where a system of overhead sprinklers reduced the time-consuming task of watering to a turn of the wrist. Gustave Lebrun did not wholly approve of such innovations as irrigation and imitation rain, but he kept his opinions to himself. As the weeks passed, he refrained from asking when work was to begin on the projects, satisfied to let the pipes lie where they had been placed and to watch spiders weave their webs over them.

After the Kelemens' fourth visit in less than two weeks, Gustave Lebrun's alert old eyes found a barely discernible path trodden down between the shed that contained the pipes and the ripening heap of manure that was the source of the garden's extraordinary fertility. The gardener considered the meaning of the word "gallery," remembered the secret caches of the last war, and understood what the Kelemens were doing. They had planned it well, he thought, recalling how he had puzzled over the arrival of a second, much smaller, truck whose driver he had seen Monsieur Kelemen pay in cash, and whose vehicle did not bear the name of any company. Somewhere among his papers Monsieur would have a bill of sale that specified the exact number of lengths of pipe he had purchased, and that number would eventually be reached, though now there were far too many in the shed.

They had done a very good, a very careful job of concealment, but Gustave Lebrun knew every inch of his garden as well as he knew the callouses on his hands. A man worked the soil in patterns that no one else could quite duplicate; his pressure on rake and hoe was as individual as a fingerprint; even the angle of the manure pile was due to his particular understanding of the relationship between sun and air and the material rotting there.

The one thing that might betray the Kelemens was the evidence of their own feet. A hedge separated the shed, the compost pits, and the manure heap from the rest of the garden, and because there were never enough hours in the day, Lebrun had allowed the grass to grow and weeds and wildflowers to take root there. Now he scythed them all down, plowed up the ground, and covered the bare earth with a thick matting of straw. In time, when by counting the lengths of pipe he knew that the work of hiding was over, he would scatter handfuls of grass seed in the straw, but until then it could be raked and rearranged as often as necessary and give no sign that any special activity had taken place at the shed. Madame exclaimed at the ugliness, but Monsieur Kelemen only looked thoughtful, and early one morning the gardener saw him standing on the terrace staring back at the lawn over which he had just walked, his eyes tracing the clearly visible line he had made in the dew-wet grass.

It went more quickly than anyone had dared hope, even though the copying had to be done with painstaking attention to details and every forgery was subjected to an intensely critical inspection. Although nothing was explained to the six young painters who were the only ones Roger Boncour felt he could trust, they often went without sleep or even a glass of wine to get them through the nights. Some of the paintings Joseph and Abby hid were not copied first. These had been sold in England or America, they would claim, and as proof of this they could produce genuine letters of inquiry from private collectors and now forged bills of sale and copies of the guarantees of authentication that had gone with them to their new owners. Entire ledgers were rewritten to make it appear that the majority of these transactions had taken place shortly after the fall of Poland when, as the Germans well knew, there had been a flood of valuable things leaving Europe. Martin Rouault grew younger as each forgery was hung on the walls of his home, but he would not allow everything to be saved. "They're not stupid," he said, "and they have experts of their own. Some will slip by because they'll be in too much of a hurry to examine everything, and their greed will make them underestimate our intelligence, but to attempt to keep too much from them would guarantee failure."

They met together in Prince Nikolai's apartment one last time before France fell, while bombs were raining on the beaches of Dunkerque and ships of every size carried off some two hundred thousand soldiers of the British Expeditionary Force and over one hundred thousand troops of the French First Army. The last vestiges of the impossible hope of holding back the Germans had vanished. Denmark and Norway had been invaded at the beginning of April; The Netherlands had lost a savage five-day war six weeks later; Belgium had surrendered that morning, May 28, 1940. No one knew how long the thousands of men who were fighting to cover the withdrawal could last, or how many would have to be left behind. The only certainty in their lives was that after the ships had pulled away for their dangerous final crossing of the Channel, France would lie like a helpless, beaten woman beneath the boots of her conquerors.

They drank French wine that night, the best the prince's cellars could provide, liquid rubies that eased the constriction in their throats and the pain in their hearts because this, at least, would never pass smacking German lips. They were tired, all of them. The fatigue showed in their faces and blurred the precise syllables of their beautiful language, but in the depths of their eyes shone a quiet pleasure at the work they had accomplished.

"We will say good-bye," Prince Nikolai told them. "Unless we meet accidentally in the street, we must forget that the others exist. We are too suspicious as a group to avoid attracting attention."

"They're going to be very angry when they get to the Louvre," Antoine Aymard said. "Not everything will be saved, but they'll discover that much of what is listed in their catalogues has disappeared. They did well there."

"So did we," Abby said proudly. "And it's not over yet."

"Yes, it is, my dear," Roger Boncour said quietly. "My young painters have already left Paris."

"But there is so much more," she cried. "Surely we can't let the Boches have it all."

"We're not the only ones," Paul Michaud said. "I was at a gallery yesterday where I saw half a dozen magnificent fakes on the walls, each of them elaborately protected by an electric alarm system. It was difficult, but I allowed them to believe they had fooled even me."

"I wonder how many there are," Samuel Koch mused. "Is it too much to hope that there may be hundreds?"

"I doubt we'll ever know the precise number," Martin Rouault said. "One thing does concern me." He swirled the Château Haut-Brion 1918 in his glass while the others waited for him to continue. "I hesitate to speak of it, but we cannot ignore the possibility. It would be criminal if the world were to lose forever what we have attempted to preserve." He looked around the table, at the familiar faces that tonight were dearer to him than any of the masterpieces he had ever owned. "We could all die," he said, "and if we did, our secret would die with us. There must be some precaution we can take, some way of smuggling knowledge of what we have done out of France, some repository beyond the reach of the Germans where a list would survive even if we did not."

It had never occurred to Abby that she would not see

this war through safely. Hardship, a shortage of food, rationing of ordinary necessities such as sugar and gasoline, yes, but not death. She had even thought that the period of deprivation was likely to be short, because surely the United States could not remain neutral for very much longer, not with France falling and England so close and so alone. Everyone, everyone hoped that America would be quick; everyone counted on its richness and its strength; everyone knew that the Yanks were more than a match for Hitler. She had been away for so long that she did not understand that Americans still thought of this war as a European problem, that the very few men who understood its nature, who were capable of thinking in global rather than national terms had to battle their own countrymen's prejudices before they could begin to fight the real enemy. She thought it possible that one or perhaps two of these old men might die in the next year or so, but all of them? And she herself as well? It was inconceivable.

"Martin is right to be concerned," Joseph said. "One man outside our circle may know what we have done, but he's nearly eighty years old. Healthier and tougher than any of us, and his father, so he once told me, lived to be ninety-three, but one can only tempt fate so often. Our gardener. He won't betray what he's learned; in fact, he has already proved that he will work to keep anyone else from suspecting, but he's not the answer to our problem."

"We've waited too long to be able to get a list to England," Martin Rouault said. "Amateurs, my friends. I wonder how many other mistakes we've made."

"It's not too late," Abby said. "We can send it to the States through the American Embassy. In the diplomatic pouch."

Princess Marie's head nodded approvingly. "Bravo, my dear," she murmured.

"Will they take a sealed envelope without knowing what it contains?" Antoine Aymard asked worriedly. "Will they take anything at all from a private individual?"

"I know of someone who will," Abby declared positively. "One of the younger officers." Again Princess Marie nodded, this time with a smile of wholly feminine complicity.

"I've never met your partner in New York, Joseph," Samuel Koch said. "Is he the kind of man who might be tempted to hint to one or two colleagues that not everything they will presume lost has been sent to Germany?"

"I don't know," Joseph replied honestly.

"Then the risk is too great," Prince Nikolai decided. "We have to assume that the German Embassy in Washington is also an intelligence center. And the consulate in New York as well. They may already have people watching the overseas businesses owned by Jews they are about to capture. Enormous sums of money could be extorted in return for promises of good treatment. I put nothing past them, and I remind myself that nothing escapes them. They are flies on every wall."

"Wouldn't it be safer if the individual who has the list is in no way connected with the art world?" Abby asked.

"Don't mention a name," the prince cautioned. He looked around the table, seeking a consensus. "We will leave this to the two of you to arrange. Only take no chances. It would be better to have no record at all than one that might fall into German hands."

Abby knew that Joseph would agree to what she intended to propose, that the all-important list be sent to Sheila Gruber. And Sheila, a conspirator of fifteen years' standing, would place the envelope atop Sammy Rosen's jewelry in the safe-deposit box no one but she had opened since the day it had been leased. In this one thing, at least, Abby felt certain they would be safe.

"I shall breathe more easily knowing that a manure heap will not become a grave," Martin Rouault said. "I think of all those paintings as possessing life, you know. Sentimental and foolish, but . . ." He shrugged his shoulders. None of them laughed or even smiled. They all believed as he did.

No one had expected that the enemy would come quietly; the terrible silence of the city abandoned by its government shocked all who remained behind. At the very last moment, when German troops stood poised on the outskirts of Paris, hundreds of thousands of Parisians suddenly awoke from their dreaming and attempted to escape. The boulevards that fed into the roads leading southward were jammed with vehicles rapidly running out of gasoline as their engines idled and their drivers found their way blocked by bicyclists, by families fleeing on foot, by wagons that had been used to haul fish and vegetables through Les Halles now piled with bedding and crying children. Retreating French soldiers stripped off their uniforms and threw them into the ditches with their rifles, knowing that prison camps in Germany awaited them if they were caught; old men and women urged their sons and daughters to carry grandchildren on ahead and leave them where they had sunk to the ground in exhaustion; people crowding into the fields on either side of the road sobbed as the last trains roared by and the lucky ones who had fought for places aboard them hung from the windows and thanked God they were not part of the mob that moved so slowly.

German planes flew low overhead, and when the first German trucks and tanks appeared, strafed the highways to clear them of their human obstacles. The madness did not last long, though to some it seemed a day and a night that would never end. They were cut off, turned back, the homeward journey more bitter than the flight, for now Germans on motorcycles hemmed them in, drove them off the road so their troops could pass by, did not trouble to hide their triumph at ordering them from their own streets. For the first forty-eight hours of the occupation, no one but the occupiers was allowed to be seen.

Abby watched the taking of the city from her balcony, hands gripping the iron railing, ears assaulted by the rumbling of tanks and the precision of goose-stepping units on parade, tears blurring the first sight of a huge swastika unfurled atop the Eiffel Tower. Everywhere she looked she saw the uniforms, the helmets, the reflection of the sun off their rifles and polished brass. She heard their laughter and then the sound of shutters slamming as fellow residents of the capital chose to turn their backs on the conquerors and mourn their defeat in private. In the salon Joseph sat in front of the piano and with one finger picked out the "Marseillaise." When the last note died away he closed the lid down over the keys and drew her inside, away from the sunlight and the sight of the Germans, into the dimness where from now on they must learn to live.

America was more than an ocean away. It was another time, a far country as yet untouched by Europe's woes and France's ignominious defeat. To dwell on, to remember, to dream about that place of safety, hope, and sunshine would only weaken her, Abby decided. She bade an anguished mental farewell to Tess, to Sheila, to the younger brothers she hardly knew, to every memory of the past that could betray her for as long as Germans ruled the streets of Paris. No matter what, she would not look back. She would discipline herself to forget.

The first two weeks of the occupation gave them little hint of how terrible it was to become later. It was an organizational period, and because every day there were new directives and new rumors of what the French government in Bordeaux was planning and preparing to do, the illusion of comparative freedom persisted. Surely the British could not have scuttled the French fleet lying off the coast of North Africa? Surely that was just the first taste of German propaganda. Government in exile was far preferable to government in submission. When would they finally be told that Pétain had taken the fight to Algeria?

On the evening of June 18, most Frenchmen who sat by their radios waited for news from Bordeaux. Only a few twisted the dial and heard a general whose name they did not recognize talk of destiny and a world war. Later, those who had happened accidentally on De Gaulle's first broadcast from the studios of the BBC would claim to remember every word he had said. But by that time listening to the BBC would have become a crime. The armistice was signed on the night of June 22, in the same railway car at Compiègne where the victorious French had humiliated their German foes in 1918. The symbolism of the act was lost on no one, and although few young men who heard De Gaulle's broadcast from London that night answered his call, they slept better for knowing that at least one general had not submitted. Three days later, when the armistice went into effect, when even anticlerical Frenchmen crowded into the churches and cathedrals to observe what Marshal Pétain had proclaimed as a Day of Mourning, the country was told that its defeat was due to moral slackness, to the destruction of the spirit of sacrifice by indulgence in pleasure. Liberté, Egalité, Fraternité must give way to the less-trenchant ideals of God, Country, and Family. They were privileged, Pétain told them, to be alive at the birth of a New Order. Many Frenchmen believed the old marshal. Many more would later claim to have smelled out the lie from the beginning.

By the end of the summer of 1940, Paris had begun to settle into what it believed would be an onerous but bearable period of German occupation. When the Nazi hammer was raised again in earnest, its initial blows fell chiefly on the Jews. Hardly anyone else noticed them.

The Gestapo came for Joseph in August. He went quietly, knowing it was useless to resist, wondering, as he entered the elevator and stood between his two silent captors, if there would be time to use the capsule tacked into the collar of his coat before he was reduced to screaming and babbling out the few secrets he possessed. The only thing he regretted was not being able to wring a promise from Abby that she would dig up her American passport and claim the protection of her embassy as soon as he was dead. She was walking the dogs on the narrow island in front of the apartment. He saw the two spots of white fur just before he entered the car that took him away, but he could not call to her across the distance that separated them, and she did not turn in his direction.

He was driven, not to Gestapo headquarters as he had expected, but to the Louvre, escorted to a tiny chamber tucked beneath the curve of one of the grand staircases, offered the choice of brandy or coffee to drink while he waited. Packing cases and piles of lumber lined the halls of the Louvre; the sound of constant hammering echoed from its high ceilings. Eighteen- and nineteen-year-old boys with hammer-bruised fingers and mouths full of nails were despoiling France of her treasures, working their way methodically through the galleries, oblivious to the beauty and the glory assembled there from all over the city.

Two hours later Joseph was home again, untouched, unharmed, grimly amused at the irony of the task he had had no choice but to agree to perform.

"A forgery was discovered in Berlin. Not one of ours," he reassured Abby. "They're frantic not to repeat the mistake, and they've suddenly realized that they don't have enough experts of their own in Paris to authenticate every item before it's sent to Germany. The difficulty was explained to me quite reasonably. We possess so much worth stealing that the criminals are forced to make accomplices of their victims. They're mad, utterly, totally mad."

"What do they want you to do, Joseph?" Whatever it was, she would continue to help him.

"The same unit that did so well in Poland will soon be at work here, an elite band of robbers called the Einsatzstab Rosenberg. But in order to meet Göring's timetable, they've had to set up a committee of French experts to assist them, chiefly to visit the private collections and ensure that no more forgeries slip by. They mentioned seven or eight names to prove I'd be in good company. Antoine Aymard's was one; almost all of the others are Jews. Elderly men. I suppose they think we're more easily bribed, more easily frightened than young men."

"Will you do it?"

"I wasn't given the option of refusing. I would have leapt at the chance in any case. It's an opportunity to do more than any of us dreamed would be possible, Abby, larceny on a much grander scale than we've already attempted. But I want you out of it this time. You were all I could think of when they were taking me away. You've kept the promises you made to Prince Nikolai and the others. This is something entirely different, much more dangerous. The few Americans still in Paris are managing to get out one way or another, and I want you to be among them. If I'm caught, my darling, I'll be executed. There will be no appeal, and no hope that my death alone will satisfy them."

"You're not going to be caught, Joseph, and neither of us will die. We haven't come this far and done as much as we have to fail now." The resolution in her eyes matched his own, and reluctantly, because it was the hardest truth he had ever had to acknowledge, he admitted to himself that he needed her strength in what he had to do, that even while he was begging her to leave him, he was praying she would refuse.

For as long as Joseph worked for the Germans, they would be exempted from the new regulation that made it illegal for ordinary citizens to possess a car, a condition that was turning the city into a population of cyclists. Gasoline, tires, spare parts as needed, all these would be provided them. Of even greater potential use would be Joseph's daily contact with the dozens of German clerks across whose desks the inevitable paperwork would flow. Somewhere among them he expected to find at least one who could be bribed to secure the passes without which travel outside the city was impossible. It was of vital importance not to lose the link with Les Roses and the garden where so much lay hidden.

By the end of September the work of identifying all the Jews in Paris and preparing devastatingly complete dossiers on the most important among them was nearly finished. The decrees already in effect in other areas of the Reich were then introduced into occupied France. You were a Jew, a member of a race, not a religion, if only two of your grandparents had been Jewish; suddenly there were good Catholics, even priests and cloistered nuns, who learned that long-ago conversions, their own baptisms, years of faithful attendance at Mass and reception of the sacraments meant nothing at all.

The census-taking went on throughout most of October, and never before had a population been so minutely scrutinized, so carefully indexed by every possible grouping: name, profession, street address and apartment number, nationality if you were not purely French. The Gestapo knew where to find you at every hour of the day and night; it knew the names and whereabouts of your relatives, your business contacts, the contents of your bank account, the state of your health. The letter *J* on your identity papers set you apart from other Frenchmen, and that specially marked card in the meticulously kept files of the SS meant you were already as good as dead, although only the few who chose early suicide believed it.

When shops owned by Jews were ordered to display signs that identified their proprietors as non-Christians and a date was set for their registration as non-Aryan businesses, Joseph moved quickly. Small shares he had owned in two galleries in Vienna had been swallowed up at the time of the Anschluss; afraid of losing everything to a government growing daily more cooperative with its German allies, his Rome partner had bought out his interest in that branch and immediately changed the name; the firms in London and New York, as remote as if they existed on another planet, could not be touched. For all practical purposes the Paris gallery was the only one remaining to him; it was also his special jewel, the first he had created, the model for all the others. Before the war it had been worth millions; now, with the new edict, it could cost him his life.

He turned to a man named Victor Cavaignac, the only

Christian besides Antoine Aymard whom he both knew well enough to trust and whose wide interests already included part ownership in several galleries, though none in Paris. Victor was paying huge bribes to a dozen German clerks and officers just to ensure that his businesses in both the occupied and the unoccupied zones continued to operate. One of the clerks, greedier, more daring than the others, with ice water in his veins and numbered accounts calling to him from Switzerland, requisitioned documents, shifted files, rewrote and restamped papers so efficiently, so openly, with so much calm bravado, that no one, not even the Gestapo, could prove that anyone but Victor Cavaignac had secretly owned Galeries Kelemen for years, ever since Joseph had sold it to him when his personal fortunes had brought him close to bankruptcy. Of course Monsieur Cavaignac had never taken over the day-to-day operation of the business, any more than he had personally interested himself in some others of his properties. One hired an experienced manager, and for that position who better than the individual whose name had remained on the letterhead and on the discreet brass plaque beside the door? No money changed hands; it was supposed to have done so long ago, and everything was as legal as any government could wish.

At Joseph's suggestion, both he and Miklós were dismissed. When the announcement of their departure was ceremoniously read to the assembled employees of Galeries Kelemen, henceforth to be called Galeries Cavaignac, a few of them smiled openly at the Jew's downfall. That was as much of a shock to Abby as the realization that not another franc would be paid them from the gallery until the occupation ended. If a business could be lost that swiftly, then how much easier it would be to lose a bank account, a portfolio of stocks and bonds, the contents of a safe-deposit box. Les Roses and the fortune hidden in its cellars and attics now seemed an ocean away.

So far that was all. There was no French version of Kristallnacht; no one had been relocated to the east. You knew only that you were marked, and because practically every German to whom you offered a bribe took it, you began to believe that as long as you did not run out of money or small, easily exchanged objects of value, especially jewelry, eventually even the marking could be done away with.

That was a mistake. As the files grew and became more tightly organized, the opportunities for bribery shrank; some owners of those numbered Swiss accounts lost their comfortable office jobs, were transferred to units far removed from sources of power. Many of them, desperate deserters in the last days or simply unable to avoid the bullets marked with their names, never lived to walk into the vaults in Zurich and Geneva. Nothing could be proved. Whatever you gave up, you counted as irretrievably lost. But Joseph had Victor Cavaignac's solemn oath that on the day the war ended, the gallery and all its contents would be returned to him. His two sons, had they been in Paris that fall, would have sworn also, but one was in a prison camp in Germany and the other was in either North Africa or England. No matter. It was a question of honor, and for generations the Cavaignac men had prized honor above their lives.

The weather turned cold, and by the middle of November not a single English-language book was left in the apartment. Page by page Abby tore them apart, soaking the paper in the bathtub until it disintegrated into a pulpy mess like papier-mâché, shaping sodden masses of it into balls that were dried and then burned for warmth. There was no heat in the building; only the Germans enjoyed regular deliveries of coal, and even when a Parisian's ration card entitled him to purchase fuel, it was scarce everywhere and prohibitively expensive on the black market.

The bathroom was their salon now. It was the smallest room in the apartment and it held whatever heat was thrown out by the stove Abby had installed in its center. Cushions stuffed with rags softened the lid of the toilet and filled the bidet. A wooden plank and more cushions had turned the bathtub into a sofa; narrow Oriental rugs from the hallway absorbed the chill of the tile floor. The little dogs were encouraged to leave their wicker baskets in the evenings, welcomed into laps that had once been forbidden them. They were warmer than hot-water bottles and more economical. Only tepid water flowed from the taps, and sometimes not even that.

In early December Abby spent the last of the money she had hidden in the apartment before the Germans came. For six months she had been using it to buy food on the black market, not only for herself and Joseph, but for Hanne and

Miklós also. It had seemed an enormous sum to begin with, but even pre-occupation necessities quickly became nearly unobtainable. Other Parisians were trading jewelry, silver, and treasured family heirlooms for the price of a few decent meals, but she and Joseph had agreed that for them the risk of attempting to sell such objects on the illegal black market was too great. Somewhere there were insurance and jewelers' records, lists of the pieces he had given her, descriptions of the silver. Let one item be traced to them and it would be assumed they possessed others. Blackmail was certain to follow. Everyone knew that the marketeers were allowed to operate only because many of them were informants; it was also known that the greediest among them reported or withheld information for one consideration only, money. As absurd as it seemed, they had developed a hellishly straightforward auction system. Loose gems were by far the safest commodity and brought the most return for the danger involved in disposing of them. Before the Einsatzstab Rosenberg decided that it no longer required the expertise of Joseph Kelemen, before they lost the car, Abby must get to Les Roses.

Abby drove slowly, conserving the gasoline that she estimated would be barely sufficient to allow her to make the trip to Les Roses and return to Paris. When she was stopped and her papers checked at the outskirts of the city, she silently blessed Victor Cavaignac, who had obtained the precious travel permit and coached her on how to deal with the German soldiers manning the barricades.

"Your name, your face, and your papers will tell them nothing," he had said. "The most important thing to remember is that they are accustomed to taking orders. Wear your best mink coat and enough jewelry to convince them that you're someone of consequence. Hand them your documents as though you are slightly offended by the request to see them, tap your fingers impatiently on the wheel, don't turn off the engine unless you are told to. If there is an officer present, perhaps a smile. For an ordinary soldier, as glacial and haughty a look as you can manage. The document attached to the travel permit states that you have been given permission to visit your country home and to bring personal effects back to Paris. They will probably search them, Abby. Be careful."

"I will, Victor." Implicit in her answer was the promise not to compromise him in any way.

"Speak only German," he warned.

"I'll remember."

And it had worked like magic. Fellow Parisians were rudely shoved aside to make way for the car on whose front fenders fluttered two of the hated swastika flags that marked all official vehicles; Abby's papers were returned to her with a flourish of salutes; she was safely through the barricade within moments of reaching it. But one old Frenchman spat on the sidewalk as she passed. He believes I'm either German or a collaborator, she thought; he's promising himself to remember my face on the day of reckoning. She wondered how many times Joseph had met accusatory stares that judged and condemned in the same instant. To be unable to speak, unable to explain was the most difficult part of the masquerade. The temptation to stop the car and shout out who and what she really was became so strong that it terrified her. It surfaced and disappeared as quickly as a thought, but it left her weak and trembling, bowed down under the awful weight of realizing how fragile were all her protestations of strength in the face of the contempt of one old man.

Gradually, as she drove through a countryside in which nothing seemed to have changed except the language of the road signs, she regained control of herself. Until today, in spite of seeing German soldiers thronging the streets whenever she went out, in spite of hearing the comments her fellow Frenchmen either pretended to or did not really understand, she had never actually had personal contact with any member of the occupying army. Six months and they were still as unreal and as unknown to her as actors in a play. That had been a mistake, she thought. There had been instances, many of them, when she might have stepped up to a soldier or an officer obviously on leave, standing bewildered on a street corner, map or guidebook in hand, and offered, in her perfect German, to direct him to the monument or the street he was seeking. Each harmless conversation would have given her courage for another; she could have practiced the charming smile, the small talk, the air of absolute innocence that she knew would be her best defense in an unforeseen situation. She reminded herself that she had once been an actress, and she chided herself for having forgotten the hard lessons Sammy Rosen had taught her. She would change all that as soon as she got back to Paris. No matter that her actions might be misunderstood. The more you knew of your opponent, the more frequently you bested him, the less you feared him. And Joseph had reminded her more than once that fear was the strongest weapon in the Nazi arsenal.

So hard was she thinking, planning, visualizing the encounters that she had decided were both inevitable and actually to be sought out, that she had driven more than halfway along the narrow private road leading to Les Roses before the unevenness of its surface told her that only the tires of heavily laden trucks could have produced the now frozen ruts that almost wrenched the wheel from her grip. At nearly the same instant, two armed German soldiers materialized from among the pines, their rifles lowered quickly to their sides as they spotted the swastika flags that were like red-white-black beacons in the bright winter sunshine.

She hesitated for only a fraction of a second, then stepped down hard on the accelerator. A glance in the rearview mirror told her that she was trapped. The soldiers had moved into the center of the road, dropped to one knee, trained their rifles on the vulnerable rear tires. What business had a woman in civilian clothes behind the wheel of a Citroën flying flags that could be purchased anywhere? There was no time to think, no time to do anything but react. She slammed her right hand against the horn; the sound was deafening in that quiet place, arrogant, demanding, as if she had expected to be met, escorted, and was angrily announcing her presence. The tires spun and the car slipped sideways as she roared into the circular gravel driveway in front of the house. She saw trucks, soldiers leaping out of the way, and a long, low Mercedes staff car parked insolently before the front door. She braked as viciously as she had accelerated, coming to a stop only inches from the highly polished bumper of the Mercedes.

A sergeant was beside the car within moments, flinging open the door, stiffening into the kind of outstretched arm salute she had seen so many times in newsreels and on every Paris street. She neither returned his "Heil Hitler" nor indicated by so much as a nod that she was aware of his presence. Her coat swirled like an opera cape and her heels pelted like hailstones on the broad stone front terrace of Les Roses. A glance at one of the sentries, and the door was opened for her. She had come so far, and without a second to plan what she would do next.

The foyer was dim, but a quick glance to either side told her that nothing had been removed, every piece of furniture was exactly as she had left it. From somewhere, perhaps the library, she heard the faint strains of music, and at first she thought it was one of the radio concerts the Germans now broadcast between propaganda programs. But the music broke off abruptly; she recognized the familiar sound of the piano bench scraping against parquet flooring, and she smiled. Whatever else he might be, the commanding officer of this small company that had taken over her home was also a skilled musician. Perhaps she would be lucky, and he would turn out to be one of those plump, slightly myopic misfits she had seen in Paris lingering outside the Opéra, buying postcards to send home to equally plump, myopic wives in Germany. That type of man she could handle as easily as if he were not wearing a too tight, wrinkled enemy uniform.

The same sergeant whose "Heil Hitler" she had ignored now appeared beside her. "Inform your commandant that I am here," she snapped, turning away before he could ask her name and business, stripping off her gloves so that the sapphire ring she wore on one hand and the diamond ring she wore on the other flashed sparks of light. The click of his heels reassured her; the murmured acquiescence to her demand further raised her confidence. This is my home, she told herself. I may not be able to force them to leave, but I can certainly remind them that their own regulations require a document of requisition. She couldn't remember where she had read that, but she was certain it was true. "Tell him I must be back in Paris before dark. I will not wait long."

The large salon with its Louis Quinze furniture, Aubusson carpet, and very minor Impressionist paintings was only four or five steps away. She opened and slammed the door behind her. Again, nothing had been touched, but it was a ghostly room she entered, the furniture still draped in the sheets she herself had placed on each chair and sofa, the carpet overlaid with a protective canvas cover, the paintings hidden behind shrouds of pale linen. Where was Gustave Lebrun? In his cottage, she supposed, or perhaps busily repairing the daily damage these soldiers must surely be inflicting on his rolled lawns and dormant gardens. He would not have left Les Roses; nothing short of death could have removed him. She shuddered, wondering how long these Germans had been there, wondering if they had questioned the old man. Joseph said he knew about what had been done in the gardens. Could he also know about the trunks in the attics and the jars of preserves in the cellar?

"Madame?"

He had come into the room so quietly that she had heard neither the click of a latch nor the sound of a footstep. She whirled to face him, startled, her expression unguarded for a second or two, the fear as easy to read as the surprise. It was only a moment, but the balance of control she had tried to establish shifted. The German officer waiting for her to respond to his greeting was the undoubted master of Les Roses, she the uninvited, unwelcome intruder. His insignia gleamed on a spotless, perfectly fitting tunic; he held himself erect, but not tensely so, and even before she was able to make out the features of his face she was aware of the waxed-leather smell of his boots and holster.

"I received no notice of requisition," she said. "That is surely a breach of the protocols of occupation."

"You speak German well, madame. I congratulate you." He turned aside her accusation as deftly as a tennis ball.

"And you, monsieur, do you speak French?"

"As you wish, madame. I am comfortable in either language." His French was unaccented, as fluent as her own. "I must ask to see your papers. The times require it. I am sure you understand."

He stepped toward her, out of the shadows into a pool of sunlight streaming through the glass doors that led to the terrace. He was neither young nor old, thirty perhaps, his skin tanned very dark, gold hair only a few shades paler than her own burning with a reddish hue in the special winter brightness. A breathtakingly handsome man, with deeply set dark eyes where one expected to find blue or gray, tiny wrinkles around his mouth and along the bridge of his nose, wrinkles such as one saw on the faces of sailors whose lives were spent staring at sea and sun. He held out one hand, confident she would obey.

"I've come from Paris," Abby said. "My travel permit. A

letter authorizing me to remove personal effects from the house."

He took the papers she offered him, read them over carefully, handed them back to her. "Your identity card, Madame Kelemen. Without it, these others are worthless."

Furious that she could have made so stupid a mistake, she searched through the jumble of ration books, makeup case, loose change, shopping lists, address book, and handkerchiefs that cluttered her purse. Two red spots began to burn on her cheeks.

"In one of the pockets of your coat perhaps?" he suggested smoothly.

A glove fell to the floor. He made no move to retrieve it.

"There. You will see, Herr Hauptmann, that I am who I claim to be," Abby said. She would match him now, give back as good as she got, her cold politeness a trifle chillier than his, her tone of voice a shade more arrogant.

"You read our military insignia as perfectly as you speak our language," he said.

"It is a skill every Frenchman has had to learn. With so many of you in our country, the lesson is quickly assimilated."

"My apologies for having doubted you, madame." Her identity card disappeared into the breast pocket of his tunic. "I shall keep this for you until you leave, I think. So important a document should not suffer the same fate as a glove." He moved so swiftly that it was not until she saw the glove in the palm of his hand that she realized it no longer lay on the floor like a gauntlet thrown down between them. Her scent came faintly from the crushed leather. "I am glad to learn that the rumors of shortages in the capital are grossly exaggerated. One would not like to contemplate the distress of so lovely a lady deprived of her favorite perfume."

"You are deceived, Herr Hauptmann. There are shortages of all the necessities of life. That's one of the reasons I'm here."

"I should like to hear the others as well, madame. There are so few opportunities for amusement in the country. Perhaps you will enlighten me over a glass of wine? The cellars provide an excellent selection."

"My cellars, Herr Hauptmann. The list was meticulously kept. I expect to be reimbursed for every bottle."

He laughed then, a full, ringing burst of honest appreciation of so ridiculous a demand. Abby stood before him watching, listening to the proof that what she had once owned was no longer hers. "I offer you wine that belongs to the Third Reich," he said at last. "Remember that as you drink it, madame."

"I am not thirsty."

"You mean that you're afraid you would choke on it. But I insist, Madame Kelemen. You intrigue me. How did you come by the car you drove here, for instance? There are many questions I could require you to answer."

"Are you detaining me for interrogation, Herr Hauptmann? Do you have that authority?"

"Every German officer has as much authority as he may need to exercise over every French man or woman who crosses his path." There was no trace of laughter in his voice now. "We will go to the library, madame. It makes a very comfortable office."

She had no choice but to pass through the door he held open. For a moment, when she was sure he could not see her face, she relaxed the muscles that ached with the strain of controlling them. Desolation at the loss of Les Roses, anger, fear, an insane desire to reach for some sharp object and slash it across the strong, even features of the man walking closely behind her, all these emotions showed nakedly in the few seconds it took to reach the library, but there were no mirrors along the walls of the hallway to betray her. When she had settled herself in the chair that had been Marie-Claire's favorite after-dinner spot, the face she turned to her inquisitor was unreadable, absolutely blank, as though she had been newly born that instant. But behind the emptiness her mind was racing and an erratic pulse throbbed in the hollow of her throat.

He was tall, broad-shouldered, slim-hipped, with the long legs and straight back of an expert horseman. She studied him as he stood in profile in the doorway, ordering a white Bordeaux to be brought up from the cellars. Something about him was tantalizingly familiar. The hair perhaps, so like her own after a month of bleaching in the August sun of Deauville, so like that of the brothers who had squirmed under the Saturday-morning barberings years and years ago. More than that. The nose was slightly aquiline, the cheekbones high and distinct, the skin stretched taut over muscles

unmarred by any suggestion of fat beneath. She had seen a
face like that somewhere, alike but different also, as dark as
his, hawklike, but lacking the bleak severity that was only
noticed when the eyes were turned elsewhere. It would
come to her, where she had seen his near twin, but now was
not the time to search her memory. She read his name on the
desk where Joseph had written letters on summer evenings.
Stefan Helldorf. Hauptmann Stefan Helldorf. Captain, her
mind said in English. Don't think in English, she told herself. German. Think in German; speak only German.

"The wine will be here in a moment," Hauptmann
Helldorf said. "Will you remove your coat, madame?"

She wanted to tell him that she did not intend to remain
long enough to make that necessary, but she bit back the
words and allowed him to slide the supple, silken mink from
her shoulders. There was a man beneath the uniform, and it
was on the man, not the German, that she had decided to
concentrate all her energies. Victor Cavaignac had not said it
openly, but the hints had been there, implicit in all his
instructions. You are a beautiful woman, Abby. Don't forget
that. Use it. The most forbidding German is just as susceptible to your charms as the French policeman who tries to be
severe with you for letting the dogs off their leashes in a
public park and who ends by hoping that you will break that
unimportant regulation in the same spot the very next day.

She smiled at Stefan Helldorf, anticipating his first question. "As to the car, Herr Hauptmann, my husband has the
honor of serving the Reich. The position he holds is an
important one; we receive certain privileges."

"They tell me that Parisian women will soon have the
most beautiful legs in the world now that so many of them are
forced to get around the city only on bicycles. Is that true?"

"I wouldn't know, Herr Hauptmann, not being interested in observing other women's legs." She smiled again.
"You have not been to Paris yet? I thought the Führer had
promised every German soldier a leave there."

"We go where we are sent. We serve there as long as we
are needed."

"Of course. No criticism was intended. When your time
comes, when you are no longer needed here, you will undoubtedly find Paris as magical a city as have so many of your
brother soldiers." That was a mistake. She had not been able

to keep the acid from her voice, had not even been aware of the bitterness with which she spoke until the words were said.

"Your husband, madame. I am curious to know what important work he does for us." The wine had been brought in, and two dusty crystal glasses. Abby would have instantly dismissed any servant who failed to present them on a silver tray. But these were barbarians, she reminded herself, wincing slightly as a thin film of dust rose to coat the exquisite Bordeaux she forced herself to taste.

"He is a member of a special committee," she said with deliberate vagueness. "French and German working together."

"And what is this extraordinarily cooperative group called?"

"They assist the Einsatzstab Rosenberg," she answered, praying that the name would be unfamiliar.

"Strange," Stefan Helldorf said. He took Abby's identity card from his pocket and laid it on the desk between them. "Are you a secret Jewess, madame? If so, you possess false papers. Forged papers. We hang people like you."

She had read about it in novels, that half-scream rising in the throat, but always she had thought the writer exaggerated. Now she thought it was a poor description for the sensation and the sound of panic. The room seemed to swim and whirl. She could smell wine and perfume and leather and even newly turned earth, and the sinking afternoon sun appeared to shine as hot and bright as July on the Côte d'Azur. The moment pulsed away, the room became her library again, it was winter; she shivered and wanted to hide herself in the warm darkness of her mink coat. "There is no *J* on my identity papers," she said finally. "Look for yourself, Herr Hauptmann."

"I have, madame. And I ask myself if a woman like you would knowingly marry filth. Perhaps your husband lied to you, deceived you. There were instances of that in Germany. Not many, but we established procedures to deal with them in any case. Attempts at outright deception were far more common. Jews lied to us. They claimed to be something else. We trained our doctors to become specialists at detecting the physical proofs of racial inferiority. Were you deceived, madame, or are you one of the deceivers?"

She had to gamble. It was everything or nothing—Joseph, Miklós, Hanne, all their lives on the turn of a phrase and a bald challenge. "There is a branch of your military service that deals with such things as false papers, I think. The Gestapo, the SS. You have a telephone on your desk, Herr Hauptmann. Place a call to one of the black uniforms. Tell him you suspect a Jewess has outwitted him. Bring him down here to the country. Show him my papers. Demand that he verify them with my prefecture. When I am vindicated, I will file a complaint against you in Paris. We are a defeated people, but we are not slaves. Your own courts protect us."

"Perhaps you are not a Jew, madame, secret or otherwise. But your husband almost certainly is. The methods of the Einsatzstab Rosenberg are as well known as its remarkable record of efficiency."

"Do you want me to tell you my husband is a Jew, Herr Hauptmann? That I married him knowing he was a Jew, that it made no difference to me then and makes none now?"

The crystal glass shattered in her hand. White Bordeaux streamed over Joseph's desk, spatters of blood. She reached for the identity card lying there, but just as her fingers touched the gray cardboard, it was snatched away from her. Hauptmann Stefan Helldorf's black eyes bored into hers; she caught the look, deflected it without flinching.

"You are a very brave woman, Madame Kelemen," he said. He held the wounded hand in his, wrapped an immaculate white handkerchief tightly over the tiny cuts, handed her the unstained document that was life and safety. "Whatever else you may be, I salute your courage."

"I'm not brave and I'm certainly not courageous," she said. "I'm hungry, Herr Hauptmann, and I'm cold. I've come to my own house to find what food remains in the cellars and take back to Paris the trunks containing clothes I would have donated to the poor of this parish had your Führer left us in peace. They are small requests, but I'm growing tired. Either allow me to claim what is rightfully mine or call the Gestapo. My pass expires at sunset."

For a very long moment he continued to hold her hand. She was dizzy. She hadn't lied when she said she was growing tired. A terrible fatigue was creeping along her limbs. She wanted nothing in the world but to lie down and sleep, whether it be here or on a prison floor. Almost convulsively, as if he could read her thoughts, he released her. Two soldiers answered his summons. "Madame is to take with her anything she wishes," he ordered. "See that whatever she selects is carried to her car."

"Exactly what I told you, Herr Hauptmann," Abby said quietly. "Some preserves from the cellars, whatever root vegetables my gardener stored there. Trunks from the attic. I should like you to accompany me. I wouldn't want to be accused of stealing what belongs to the Reich."

There was one bad moment. Only the shrewd eye of a housewife could have detected any difference between the jars of jam and candied peaches Abby selected and those she left on the shelves of the cold cellar, but one of those jars whose contents were only marginally darker than those of any of the others slipped from the fingers of the soldier who was packing it into a straw-lined basket. The whole fruit shimmered and shook with an odd clicking noise. "Pits," Abby said disgustedly. "One pit per jar to keep the fruit from spoiling. That's all that's needed. I'm afraid the girls in the village are very lazy. I turn my back for a second and grate my teeth on pits all winter long. Do you have servant problems in Germany, Herr Hauptmann?"

He didn't answer. His eyes swept the shelves. "Open it," he said, pointing to a glass jar of perfectly preserved strawberries. "Now pour it on the ground." The soldier obeyed. The floor of that cellar was made of tightly fitted, unmortared blocks of stone. Stefan Helldorf's boot crushed the strawberries to pulp and flowing juice. When he raised his foot there was a red stain, nothing else. He took a jar of peaches from the middle layer of the basket, shattered it against the wall. Peach pulp and brown pits clung briefly to the stone. Nothing else.

Two of Joseph's old jackets were shredded, one of Abby's favorite dresses. He found nothing. "Ruin everything," Abby challenged defiantly. "Leave me nothing but rags." He ordered the trunks closed, watched as they were loaded into the car. "They'll do the same thing at the barricade at Saint-Cloud," she mourned. He wrote her a special pass exempting the contents of the car from inspection.

"I will remember you, madame," Stefan Helldorf said. "I'll see that headquarters sends you a formal requisition for the house and its contents."

"Enjoy Les Roses, Herr Hauptmann, if you can. I was happy here once. When all of you have been pushed back to Germany, I'll be happy here again."

"I could have you arrested for that remark, Madame Kelemen. I could telephone Paris and tell them I suspect you of smuggling. As you drive, you will have to wonder if the call has been made, if your obvious charms are perhaps less powerful than you believed them to be. And I think you should also remember that the Gestapo doesn't deal any differently with women than it does with men."

"Worse, so I've been told."

It was the last salvo in what had begun as a simple confrontation between predator and prey, a contest of wills charged by a different kind of tension the instant Hauptmann Stefan Helldorf touched Abby's bleeding hand. She had tried to deny the change because it frightened her, but even in the damp cold of the cellars and the chill of the attics she had been aware of the heat of his body, the sexual warmth and smell of him, the lazy, too-knowing way his eyes watched her. She had won, she had retrieved much of what she had come for, but now she began to fear the price of her success. She had lost that precious anonymity Joseph insisted was so important. She would not be able to forget, in the days and weeks and months ahead, that very close to Paris was a German officer who had promised to remember her, who had scrutinized her papers with more than routine attention, who had guessed immediately that the husband recruited by the Einsatzstab Rosenberg was a Jew, who had amused himself at her expense and then released her, but who could find her again anytime he wished.

The sky had turned gray, promising snow before morning. In the peculiar light that heralded the approaching storm, bright and dim at the same time, she watched the figure of Stefan Helldorf captured in her rearview mirror until a bend in the road finally obliterated him. There had been no formal words of leave-taking, no heel-clicking salute, not even the purely ceremonial kissing of her hand that she had half expected. A warning. That casual reference to the Gestapo had been either a warning or a threat, she was not sure which. And then, just before she lost sight of him, he raised his arm in her direction, as if he knew she was looking back. He was the gracious host of Les Roses waving good-bye to a departing weekend guest; she had seen Joseph stand on the steps of their home in just that same attitude hundreds of times. A sense of foreboding nearly overwhelmed her. Before she turned onto the Paris road she pulled the handkerchief from her hand and threw it from the car window. The tiny cuts smarted and stung. Good. She needed that small pain to remind her of the real peril in which Joseph walked every single day, the danger of forgetting for even an instant that both of them had committed and would continue to commit acts for which death by hanging was the routine punishment.

It had all been too easy these past six months. If not Joseph, then she at least had been lulled into a false and deadly feeling of security. One minuscule slip could destroy them. She had fenced with the Hauptmann, perversely enjoying the thrust and parry. Now she feared that he had enjoyed it too, that he would seek another match. On every street in Paris you saw German soldiers staring insolently at French women, and occasionally you saw them strolling arm in arm, little islands of collaboration in a chartless sea. She would die before she became one of those women, Abby thought. But a truer voice spoke just as quickly, telling her with insidious softness that she would do anything, anything, to keep Joseph safe. It was the deeply hidden heart of the promise she had made in Prince Nikolai's apartment when she had claimed to know that what she begged to be allowed to do was not a game. Princess Marie would understand, would, with one glare of her glittering black eyes, confirm what both women had always known: that to be a woman in wartime was to learn to be a very special type of victim.

She trembled all the way back to Paris, and she was shaking uncontrollably long before she managed to park the car beneath the apartment house on the Quai de Passy. She and Joseph washed sugared fruit from diamonds until sunrise. "After I've had some sleep," she told him, "after I've had some sleep I'll slit the hems." Her brain had forgotten, but her fingers remembered all the small stones and the tiny stitches. "There was no trouble, no questions asked," she lied. "They are all obsessed with the authority of documents and seals and affidavits. Everything else is safe. The Hauptmann won't soil his hands digging in a manure heap." She was desperate for sleep, but she tossed and turned on her bed until well after noon, battling waking nightmares in which Stefan Helldorf stood outside her door and whispered "Jewess" through the peephole.

13

Abby waited more than a week after the trip to Les Roses before disposing of the smallest least perfect stone on the black market. She jumped every time the telephone or the doorbell rang, and spent as little time alone in the apartment as she could. But there was really no place else to go. The few friends left in Paris from pre-occupation days shunned the Kelemens now; the dogs shivered and whined if she tried to prolong their walks; even the hours she spent standing in the lines outside every shop that had food to sell were never long enough. She told herself that her fear of Stefan Helldorf was irrational, that nothing could be proved against her, but she continued to see his face in her dreams nearly every night—his face, the broken body of Gustave Lebrun, the gardens blasted open as if by a bomb, fragments of canvas and broken pipes scattered everywhere. Joseph had mixed handfuls of precious gems with mud, sealed them inside pipes he shoved into the very bottom layer of the pile that lay inside the potting shed. In her dream those stones were spread over the wreckage like shards from a thousand broken bottles.

There were other worries also. Miklós and Hanne were changing, both of them slipping into the states of mind that Joseph had feared and foreseen. More often than not, the books Miklós carried with him everywhere he went were volumes of Jewish history, commentaries on the Talmud he had hated to study as a boy, even a child's Hebrew grammar. Abby was afraid to ask where he had obtained them, afraid he would tell her he was visiting the quarter of the city where Jewish refugees from the east lived in closely packed misery.

335

Hanne's physical metamorphosis was shocking, its spiritual cause complex. The Gestapo had never summoned her to explain, if she could, why she, a German, had married a naturalized French Jew. The expectation and the fear aged her; she shrank, becoming as wrinkled as a piece of dried fruit. Night after night she sat at her kitchen table with Miklós' identity card in front of her, concealing the *J* with her thumb, uncovering it, hiding it again, as though by some miracle it would have disappeared the next time she looked. It never did.

Blaming herself for that card, that damning, dangerous letter, her mood swings grew erratic. She alternated between a torturing guilt and a self-righteous anger that he should be a Jew at all; worse, that he had only begun to remember what it was to be a Jew when no sane man could wish for anything but to be able to deny it. Somehow it became apparent to her that the fault lay entirely with him. And then she would come to her senses and remember that she had been the one to scoff at prejudice. The penance she set herself was semistarvation, but the anger and the mental confusion persisted. Miklós feared for his wife's sanity, loved her and watched over her in silence, but could not, would not change what he was.

On the night of Tuesday, December 24, Abby made a soup of dried peas flavored with onions and thyme, and a tart of sorts with the last bits of flour and butter and a jar of preserved apricots. There was a bottle of wine from the cellar, a loaf of slightly stale bread that would be improved by a last-minute toasting, and a very small round of cheese. The black marketeer who had bought her diamond had cheated her; she would have to go back again far sooner than she had planned, but not until that imperfect stone had been stretched into as many meals as possible. She laid the best of her linen tea cloths over the enamel-topped kitchen table that had once been used only for the rolling-out of pastry, set four places with fine china and sterling silver, created a centerpiece of dried flowers and a single white candle. Miklós and Hanne were expected; they would eat here, warmed by the heat from the stove, ignoring the stark walls, the sink, the icebox, the cabinets for pots and pans, the garde-manger, the rugless floor, and the steel door with its heavy bar and ugly locks. A brave front was as important as the fact of courage itself. You needed both of them just to be able to get through each day.

She poured two glasses of wine and carried them through chilly hallways and her frigid bedroom to the bathroom, where Joseph was feeding more of the paper balls into the stove. The little dogs whined and yapped halfheartedly when she opened the door. Their coats were dull and lusterless, they hadn't adjusted to this war as well as their human masters. You saw few pets in Paris now; there was a place you could take them if you hadn't the heart to watch them starve to death, and every morning Abby awoke hoping they had willed themselves to die, as animals and old people sometimes did in such times. But these last two of the several Westies she had owned were either very stupid or very stubborn. They still hoped for steak in their dishes when the only decent beef in the city was being consumed by its conquerors.

Before the occupation they had passed the hour before dinner over their newspapers, Abby drinking her champagne and reading the Paris edition of the *Herald-Tribune*, Joseph wrestling with a crossword puzzle. Now they talked, and although at first she had shuddered at the stories he told her, she had gradually come to welcome them. There were so few visible signs that anyone else was doing anything at all that often she felt they were entirely alone. It could not be true; among the millions of Frenchmen there had to be thousands who resisted in whatever ways they could, who had helped the British survivors of Dunkerque make their way back to England, who escorted their own countrymen into Vichy territory and then to North Africa or Portugal and finally to De Gaulle's ragtag headquarters, who hid or sent on refugees who had already fled from Hitler once and thought they had found safety years ago. The whole country could not have cravenly accepted domination and forgotten the meaning or the price of freedom. Joseph told her every day of people he had seen in the apartments he was forced to visit, of men and women giving up who only a few months ago had been vigorously hopeful and full of life. She was determined it would not happen to them. If she did nothing more while this war lasted, she would badger, cajole, and command the people she loved to make it through.

He thought she looked exceptionally lovely with her face

flushed and her hair curling from the steam of the soup over which she had been laboring. Its fragrance had come with her down the hallways and into this make-believe salon. He missed the other smells of her, the perfume she applied sparingly now and the American cigarettes that had been used up months ago. He had intended to slip his New Year's gift to her beneath her pillows while she slept, but her right hand suddenly looked so achingly empty without a cigarette wafting its smoke between the fingers that he could not wait another week to surprise and delight her. It was an insignificant present, the sort of thing one formerly tossed to a chauffeur or bought with the evening newspaper, but he doubted that anyone else in Paris could boast of possessing anything as reminiscent of pre-war days.

"Close your eyes," he said, "and hold out both your hands."

"Joseph, what in the world?" She felt slick paper, two square, light packages over which her fingers curled. She saw camels standing before palms and pyramids, the yellow-and-cream-and-brown label that had once been so familiar. "American cigarettes! Where did you get them?"

"Smoke," he said, "and I'll tell you."

The smell of the smoke she exhaled was like nectar, she thought, dizzy with the pleasure of it. One of the dogs sneezed and shook its head. She laughed and then she choked, laughing even harder at the absurdity of the surge of enjoyment this fragile cylinder produced, the illusion of normality that drifted over them as they sat in their bathroom with blankets wrapped around their knees and more blankets draped over their shoulders like oddly cut cloaks.

"I was in an apartment in the seventh arrondissement a few days ago," Joseph said. He never told her the street or the family name of the people he saw, only the general area of the city in which they lived. "Obersturmführer Dornberger was with us. He has a good eye, better than the average, and that makes him a little easier to fool than some of the others. He can occasionally be convinced he detects things which do not exist. They were a rich couple, Abby, an old man and his wife who must have been investing in art for most of their lives. Beautiful things everywhere, and no place to hide them. From the look on the husband's face when he opened the door, he had been expecting this for months. Dornberger is polite, you know, as long as there are no arguments, and so far there have been only one or two halfhearted protests. He smiles without showing his teeth, like a snake concealing its fangs. It has a mesmerizing effect, but this old Jew recovered quickly. He was anxious to cooperate, but behind Dornberger's back he gave me a look like none I've ever seen before. Not pleading, like some, but full of deep sorrow, almost a question, as if to ask me why I was betraying my own people. I don't know how Jews recognize one another. I had forgotten that kind of intuition ever existed until the Germans reminded me of it. They're making good Jews out of bad ones, like the Romans did with Christians."

He paused, as if trying to decide whether to include himself in that category, then shrugged his shoulders. Not yet. There was no faith, no belief in God, only a reverence for old and beautiful objects, and this was now deepening to include traditions that had endured for thousands of years and were therefore humanly, if not divinely, sacred.

"We took everything, of course. It's never any different and it never takes very long. They're like ants, the soldiers who do the lifting and the carrying. In and out, up and down the stairs, never pausing until the job is done. One painting bothered Antoine. When it's a Jew who's being robbed, he's the one to shake his head first; when it's a Christian, I become the doubter, if it seems we can get away with it. No discussion, no plans laid before we arrive. We go on instinct, and sometimes we disagree. It reassures the Gestapo." With his hands Joseph measured off a space perhaps two feet by three. "Nineteenth-century English," he said. "Exquisite." If he was caught, she would know nothing, not even the name of the artist. "Antoine took out his magnifying glass, which he has never needed, and the little knife and brush that make the operation appear so serious. He examined and he scraped and muttered to himself; he took the painting over to a window; he stepped back from it, went over every inch of canvas with the glass again. I think it wasn't until the performance was nearly over that the old man caught on and had the sense to pretend to be outraged. 'I bought it from a reputable dealer,' he said. He was a good actor. I've never heard the truth sound so much like a lie. In the end, it was two votes to one, Herr Expert Dornberger and Antoine calling the old man a fool for having spent good money for a fake,

I half convinced, but not absolutely certain. So we saved him one of his possessions. Sometimes we can't manage even that. I found the cigarettes in my coat pocket. I don't know when or how he put them there."

"Oh, Joseph." She lit another of the cigarettes and thought about the lovely pastoral scene that would not go to Germany. "Will you miss it terribly when you have to stop?"

"No. When we first began I could think only about the paintings we saved, but they have been so few compared to the hundreds I've had to let go. We don't try to keep back the best. Minor artists have a better chance of slipping by. There's very little left now anyway."

"What about the black market?"

"We've been fortunate so far. Nothing traceable to us has turned up there. Antoine thinks it inevitable that someday something will. I'm not sure he's right. I have a feeling that the owners we've helped will find some other way of surviving. I think they'll find ways to hide their paintings, to hold on to them no matter what."

"How much longer before it will be our turn?"

"I don't know. There must be a master list of victims somewhere, but they're careful to keep it from us. It could be tomorrow; it could be months from now. When it does happen, they'll take everything. Antoine will authenticate the fakes, and he won't even have to pretend that he's enjoying it. Expect him to be rude, Abby. It's for his own protection. Stealing from Jews is one of the surest proofs of your own racial purity.

"Racial purity!" She spat the foul-tasting words. "What nonsense, what utter nonsense. How can they even pretend to believe in such a thing?"

"Empires have been built on flimsier lies before. But the weakness inherent in a lie is that eventually someone questions it. Once doubt sets in, the whole structure begins to collapse. You have to stay alive and move quickly to avoid the debris when it falls."

The doorbell pealed and she got up to answer it, slipping the cigarettes into the pocket of her skirt. Hanne used to smoke, but even when there were plenty of cigarettes available and they were cheap, she never fitted more than half of one at a time into her ebony holder. Too many of them ruined your complexion, she had always said when they teased her about her idiosyncrasy and the precise way she rationed herself. Maybe, Abby thought, maybe what she needed now was a reminder of that habit, something about which she could laugh, some common, ordinary remembrance of the years when they had shared so much. Old guilts and new guilts were driving Hanne apart from them, and Abby knew that in that self-imposed spiritual isolation her sister-in-law would destroy herself. They had always believed her to be so strong; surely some remnant of that strength remained.

Miklós sniffed appreciatively at the soup, exclaimed over the apricot tart, admired the perfection of the table setting, and drank half a glass of wine, all while fussing with Hanne's coat and unwrapping a little package of newspaper that contained a few scraps of fat for the dogs, fat he should have eaten himself. The small kitchen seemed no larger than a closet with all of them crowded into it.

"Do you know what today is?" he asked, rushing on so quickly that no one had a chance to answer him. "Dreidels and latkes and coins hidden under our plates. What does that tell you, Joseph?"

There was such childlike delight in his voice that Abby turned from the soup she was stirring to look at him. His eyes were aglow with some secret joy. He reminded her, in the dim light of the single bulb that hung from the ceiling, of the drawing she had once seen of a mischievous leprechaun caught in the act of dancing in the moonlight, gleeful, wrinkled face and long nose quivering with excitement. She saw that Joseph was staring at him too, and that the wine he had been about to drink had been forgotten.

"It's Christmas Eve," she said.

"For some, maybe. For you and Hanne. But for others, for me and for Joseph, it's the first night of Hanukkah." He reached into his pocket and took out two small round caps of black felt, one edged with silver piping, the other plain. He handed one of them to Joseph, who hesitated and almost drew back his hand before accepting it. "Do you remember what it was like at home when we were children, Joseph?" he asked. "Hanukkah, Passover, and Yom Kippur, three times a year Mama and Papa remembered to be Jews. The rest of the time, who cared? It was too much trouble."

"Where did you get the yarmulkes?" Joseph laid the little round cap on the table as if it had burned his fingers, picked it up again, raised his hand to shoulder height, then stopped and lowered it.

"Put it on, Joseph," Miklós whispered. "For Mama. For yourself."

Tears were running down Hanne's cheeks, oozing through the fingers she had pressed over her mouth, dropping onto the china plate in front of her. This was the worst, the beginning of the end, the final proof that Miklós had embraced the terrible thing the Nazis said he was. Terrible. Glorious. Terrible. A Jew. She wept and wept, and none of the other three made a single move to comfort or to stop her. They stood and watched and listened, looking at one another occasionally, sipping their wine, thinking their own thoughts, knowing that when she raised her head at last, it would either be to leave them forever or to face and banish the shadows that had been driving her closer and closer to mental darkness. No one could help her. It was too late to pretend any differently.

She left the table finally, without a word, leaving the kitchen door open so that the air in the hallway rushed in and chilled them. They heard her heels on the bare floor of the foyer, then silence.

"Put it on, Joseph," Miklós said softly, and Abby nodded. Put it on.

It changed his face somehow, crowned him, gave him a look of completeness, as if for a long time there had been something missing, and his scrap of cloth was it. He smiled, embarrassed, patting the yarmulke into place, smoothing out the hair around it. "All we need now is for Abby to be holding a rosary in her hand," he said, and laughed. The tension eased.

"You look very handsome, both of you. Like prophets without beards," Hanne said. She stood in the doorway, a handkerchief clutched tightly in one hand, the other fingering the pearls around her throat. Her face was streaked with the tears she had shed, and her eyes had a ravaged look, but her voice was firm.

A moment later she was in Miklós' arms, weeping again, but softly now, as if the pain were less and the tears were ones of thankfulness that it was nearly gone. He stroked her hair and murmured to her in German, the last time he would speak that language until the Allies came.

"Do we pray?" Abby asked, trying to remember what Joseph had told her about Hanukkah so many years ago on their first trip to Budapest.

"We light candles," Miklós said, pulling out Hanne's chair, bending over to kiss the top of her head when she was seated. "One more each night until there are eight." He took a narow book with worn leather covers from his pocket. "I don't remember the prayers by heart, just the way it always began, with the candles and Mama's potato pancakes, all the children taking turns to spin the dreidel, and Papa telling the story of the Maccabees. Joseph ought to be the one to read them; he's the eldest and his Hebrew was always far better than mine." He held out the book.

"No. It was too long ago. I've forgotten whatever Hebrew I was taught. The only prayer I learned by heart was that of a dying Jew." Rahel. Emmanuel.

Abby lit the white candle, remembering the flame of the votive light that Bridget had kept burning before the plaster statue of the Blessed Mother. Whatever we believe, she thought, we do the same things. We light candles, recall and repent our sins, make a holy feast out of bread and wine, place our trust in a faith that there is something, someone, somewhere that is eternal, caring, just, and loving. We are more alike than we are different. Racial purity. Had they rewritten history? Was Jesus no longer a Jew? But then she remembered that Hitler and his swastika had replaced Christ on His cross, and the meal of soup and apricot tart became for her the Midnight Mass of her childhood.

When they had finished, when they sat savoring the last of the wine and the lingering taste of sugar and fruit, she brought out the two packs of American cigarettes and gave the unopened one to Hanne. Joseph repeated the story of how they had been given to him, an act of trust that made Hanne weep again and Miklós' eyes shine. He had suspected what his brother was doing, but never dreamed that he had dared so much. Joseph was careful to make it sound as though he had acted entirely alone. His own life he would put in their hands, but he hadn't the right to offer any others.

Hanne and Miklós left well before curfew, standing very close to one another in the elevator, walking arm in arm the length of the two dark blocks to their own apartment. Abby watched them from the balcony; they made her think of young lovers and springtime. It took her hours to pick out the threads from the seams of the yarmulke, but eventually all the triangular pieces were safely hid, like bits of dusting cloth nestling in the drawers of the furniture whose surfaces they polished. If it became a crime to be more than a racial Jew, if it became a crime to practice the religion as well as bear the name, it would be better to leave no sign that Joseph had ever done so.

In early March Joseph suffered a mild heart attack. Two soldiers of the Einsatzstab Rosenberg squad half-carried, half-dragged him into the apartment. Antoine Aymard, ashenfaced, explained what had happened.

"I thought he was pretending, Abby, I swear to you that at first I didn't know it was real. We've done that before, gotten a few extra minutes in which to think and decide what to do by feigning an old man's weakness. They humor us because they find it amusing, and today there was one painting in particular that we both knew ought to be saved. I caught him as he fell. He whispered Émile Vautrin's name. Thank God those people had a telephone. There wasn't any pain, just pressure, he said. He was dizzy, he was sweating like a man who's just run a race. I told Émile all the symptoms. He promised to meet us here."

"It's all right, Monsieur Aymard," Abby said soothingly. Joseph lay on the couch where the soldiers had left him, struggling to sit up, falling back again. Abby knelt beside him, loosening his clothing, watching the color slowly return to his cheeks, murmuring reassurances, trying to prevent him from speaking. "The front door, monsieur," she pleaded. "Let the doctor in."

"I'm fine, Abby," Joseph whispered. "Aymard exaggerates. He needs a brandy. No hospital. No matter what, I won't go to a hospital." They both knew that only Germans received good medical treatment now. A Christian Frenchman could expect minimum care, but a Jew would be left in his bed to die or recover as best he could manage on his own.

"Any heart attack is serious," Dr. Vautrin cautioned when Joseph had been examined and made comfortable. "This time we were lucky. It was a warning."

"Will there be another, Émile?" Abby asked. She had known and admired and trusted him for years. He was the finest heart specialist in Paris and an avid collector. When Bridget had been dying, it had been Émile Vautrin who had told her what to expect, Émile Vautrin who had urged her to go to the States as soon as possible.

"Almost certainly. But if he is careful, if you are a stern nurse, Abby, we can hope that the next one will not come for years. The damage is minimal; I've known men with far worse hearts live to dance at the weddings of their grandchildren. The most important thing is that he cannot continue to do the kind of work he's been doing. He's not the only one of my patients who's risked his health and his life since the Germans came, my dear. The younger ones can survive it, if they escape hanging or a firing squad, but older men like me, like Joseph, we fool ourselves. We deny the evidence of our own bodies until we've pushed them beyond endurance. It's up to you to convince him that he's done enough."

"How did you know, Émile?"

"I know nothing, Abby." He smiled. "Except my patients. A doctor is a little like a priest, remember. After a certain number of years words are no longer necessary. I can arrange things to satisfy the Gestapo. They're not very interested in sick old Jews yet. We shall tell them that Joseph nearly died, may die at any moment."

"What of the danger to you, Émile?"

"Nonsense," he scoffed. "The nature of medicine is to make mistakes. Can I be blamed if my patient lives? It will only enhance my reputation as a worker of miracles."

"He's a brave man," Joseph said when they were alone.

"No braver than you, my darling. Sleep now."

"I'm fifty-four years old, Abby. I've outlived my father."

"That doesn't mean anything. Rest, please rest. We'll talk later, I promise." Émile had said that the speed with which Joseph recovered would depend to a great extent on her nursing and the control she could exercise over him. She wanted desperately to stay by his bed and talk, but her needs were no longer important. She must be mother to his child, and she remembered all the things she had done for Bridget, the poignancy of the moment when she had first realized that mother and daughter had reversed roles, that the one who had given life was entirely dependent on her child for a dignified passage into death. Where Joseph was concerned, Abby refused even to think the word.

"I don't want to be a burden to you," he said.

"I have strong shoulders," she laughed. "That's the only criticism Madame Thérèse has ever made of my figure, that my shoulders are too broad. It comes of generations of peasant ancestors." He smiled then, weakly, but a smile nonetheless. His eyes closed. He slept.

If it had to happen at all, Abby thought distractedly as she paced the length of the dining room, barefoot so as not to awaken or disturb him, if it had to happen at all, then thank God it happened at the beginning of spring. There were still cold days, damp days, but the worst of the bad weather was over, she no longer had to wear several sweaters or a coat just to be able to survive in the apartment. She could open the door between Joseph's bedroom and the bathroom and hope that the small amount of heat from the stove would warm him, ward off the pneumonia that had killed so many in Paris that winter. As he got stronger he could sit on the balcony in the sunshine; he would have the best of everything the black market could provide, no matter how many stones she had to sell. She was an experienced trader now; she bargained as shrewdly and as tenaciously as the men and women who tried to cheat her. What difference did it make if the stones went quickly? There were more of them at Les Roses, sealed up in the mud-stoppered pipes in the potting shed.

There was an edge of hysteria to her pacing and her thoughts; she recognized it, knew it was born of fear, relief, and the realization of how narrow and slippery was the step between life and death. And she knew also that she must let it take its way with her now, that she must permit it to exhaust her, that once it passed it would never come again. Later that night, waking suddenly from the nightmare she had not dreamed in months, she remembered something else. The car, the only means she had of getting to Les Roses, the Citröen with its swastika flags and concealed space beneath the floorboards, would be confiscated within hours after Émile Vautrin informed the Einsatzstab Rosenberg of Joseph's heart attack. They had lost the link with Les Roses and everything hidden there. In her dream it had been Hauptmann Stefan Helldorf who reminded her of that, the handsome, puzzlingly familiar face only inches from her own, sharp white teeth elongating, becoming pointed fangs as he smiled and sneered at her distress. Mozart played by a master musician and the crack of a pistol or of shattering crystal.

The frightening days of mid-March were no more than a memory by the end of April, but the consequences of the decision they had made then remained. Joseph was nearly well again, restless at being confined to the apartment, arguing with Émile Vautrin on every visit that he could and would go back to work for the Einsatzstab Rosenberg, that to continue to feign a serious heart condition when there was so much still to do was cowardice. "What else can you call it?" he demanded.

"Medical prudence and ordinary common sense," the doctor replied. "This euphoria of well-being you're experiencing is temporary, my friend, and dangerous. You flirted with death and won. You think you're invincible. That's not true, Joseph."

"I watch your face when you listen to my heart, Émile. I've seen that same look a hundred times when a painting pleased you."

"I'm pleased because I'm trained to expect the worst, because in your case I detect none of the signals every physician dreads. I'm delighted that you will live to quarrel with me for many years yet."

"Then why, Émile?"

"What I did for you cannot be undone. We agreed, the three of us. I acted quickly, but not precipitously. I was thorough; the case I presented was so well documented that no one questioned it. My reputation helped, of course, but so did the records of the dead man that are on file now under your name. Recovery from that kind of damage is impossible; the patient may linger for a year or two, but he cannot climb stairs, he cannot walk quickly or too far, he struggles for breath at the slightest exertion. I made you a dying man to save your life; if you insist on refusing to act like one, it could cost me mine."

"How long, Émile?"

"Until the Germans leave."

"Impossible."

"You learn patience in your business, do you not, my friend? You watch a young artist for years, half a lifetime. You buy his early works and store them away against the day of greatness. You must do the same thing with yourself; Abby knows I'm right. You're in a vault, safe, protected, and there you remain until the world changes, until the time comes for you to show yourself again."

"A prison," Joseph said bitterly.

"A cocoon of love," Abby whispered.

The arguments with Émile Vautrin were mild outbursts of the passion with which Joseph struggled every night. She heard him pacing his room hour after hour. She read his thoughts. She watched him during the day when in his mind he was with Antoine Aymard, playing another round of the game he had said he would not miss when it was over. Nearly eight months of calculated deceptions had infected his blood; he had gloried in the secret, sustained the danger of it, become entranced by his own success. She remembered what he had told her of the canny, agile street boy pricking at his ponderous, slow-moving enemy. He believes that he's run away, she thought; he thinks he's turned his back out of fear; he's trapped himself in his own logic; he's forgotten that he once admitted the game could not go on forever.

"They will move against the Jews soon," Émile Vautrin cautioned. "I am called in on difficult cases from time to time, I hear things. It would have been over for you in a few months even without the heart attack. God watches out for the fools who do great things in His Name, and you're one of them, Joseph. A little pinprick of pain, and *voilà*, He removes you from the arena just before the lions rush in. Accept it."

"Antoine can do nothing working alone," Joseph muttered.

"He's made his plans," Émile said cryptically. "The Gestapo won't bother you, and neither will your clever Einsatzstab masters. Trains get derailed, trucks blow up, the Resistance does what it can; the paperwork is not as difficult to manage as the Germans would have us believe. Antoine's life is also in your hands for a while yet."

"I don't want that, Émile, I don't want that kind of power, I don't want the responsibility."

"You have no choice. It's done or being done."

"I didn't ask for it."

"You did. You stayed in France when you could have left. You worked in concert with others, you had as much care for their safety as they did for yours. If Antoine were the

Jew and you the Christian, wouldn't you reason with him as I
am reasoning with you? Wouldn't you?"

"Yes."

"Then stop arguing; don't waste any more of my time.
Read the papers, listen to the radio. Every new decree is
another warning, part of something greater, some mad master design that only exists so far in the deranged fantasies of
their Führer."

"What more could he want?" Abby asked. "The continent is already his. Must he have England also? America as
well? The world?"

"Possibly." Émile Vautrin would not, could not bear to
put into words the stark truth that his analytical mind had
pieced together from the dozens of clues he had at first tried
not to believe. Resettlement of an entire people to some
eastern wasteland was a horror in itself, but also illogical.
Millions of human beings could not be moved like so many
head of cattle. And even if they could, where was there a
stretch of empty land vast enough to contain and support
them? Resettlement was a myth, a blind. The only alternative
solution to a hate-crazed mind would be annihilation, but that
too was illogical. How was it possible to kill millions without
unleashing a wave of desperate resistance that must succeed
because of its very size and fury? He hoped he would never
know, hoped that before a devil out of hell answered that
question, Hitler would make the mistake the Reich could not
survive. Émile had bought Joseph time. For the moment he
could do no more.

The roundups began in mid-May; hardly anyone raised
his voice against them. At first they were limited to those
whom the Germans defined as non-French Jews, but the
Jews who had been French for centuries knew that after their
foreign-born coreligionists had been dealt with, the sweeping
arms of the SS would reach out to embrace them also. There
was never any warning and no way to escape. You could not
run from a street that was cordoned off at both ends; could
not slip through a line of men standing elbow-to-elbow, ready
to beat you back with the butt of a rifle; could not hide in
attic or cellar because there was no corner of a building they
did not search, no mattress or drapery that was not pierced
by a bayonet. Thousands of refugee Polish Jews were the first

to go, but as the summer wore on, more and more French Jews, waving papers that were ignored or torn from their hands, were forced into the trucks and buses that transported them to Drancy, and after Drancy to relocation camps somewhere to the east, no one knew where.

In June came the startling news of the German invasion of Russia. Parisians nudged one another and prayed for an early winter, for mountains of snow that would do to the Nazis what every schoolboy knew they had done to Napoleon. And June was also the month in which Hanne and Miklós gave up their apartment, made a gift of it and all their possessions to a fellow Frenchman who would swear that he neither knew nor cared what had become of the people who had lived there. Frightened by propaganda pictures taken in Poland of German-born women who defiled themselves with Jews—heads shaved, stripped half-naked, tied to wooden stakes on scaffolds erected in public squares—they decided that their only hope of remaining together was to disappear. They moved into Abby's room and did not reregister with the police, climbing the stairs barefoot late one night, each carrying one small suitcase, already fugitives. They were part of an exodus of French-born and naturalized Jews fleeing into hiding places throughout the city, trusting others to conceal and protect them, edging their way toward the imagined greater safety of the farms in the surrounding countryside. Once you went into hiding, you did not dare come out again. Without valid papers you were as good as dead if you were picked up.

Summer ended finally. Now Abby stood on line for coal as well as bread and vegetables. She bought everything her ration card and Joseph's entitled them to, stretched what was barely enough for two into not nearly enough for four, and began to feel as much at ease dealing on the black market as she had once felt in the familiar shops of the quarter. By now there was a system. Certain Germans took half of what a man with a truck brought into the city, made it possible for him to continue his commerce by providing him with gasoline and tires and spare parts for his vehicle, and he, in turn, sold his goods for ten or twenty times their real value. Paris ate; her citizens grew poorer, but they survived.

They also began to resist more openly. Posters and placards were defaced almost as soon as they were plastered to the walls of métro stations or public buildings; nearly every-

one with a working radio tried to dial in the jammed broadcasts of the BBC; and, in a few of the prefectures, the forging
of documents took up almost as much of a working day as the
legal activities with which the Germans had made the French
police their agents of collaboration. It was costly to go too far,
however. Hostages were taken and shot or hanged—ten,
twenty, fifty or a hundred for a single German life; almost as
many for charges of insulting behavior toward the Reich or its
flag.

By November, when the worst of the cold began, the
curious existence the Kelemens were leading had become so
routine that it was difficult to remember the flavor of freedom. Of the four of them, Abby was the only one who could
leave the apartment, the only one who could chat with the
concierge, pick up rumors on the streets, attempt to take the
pulse of the city, breathe fresh air. Much as she dreaded
going out, she hated even more the days on which the shops
were closed, the stretch of silent, empty hours, the strain of
whispered conversations pitched well below the level of the
radio.

Yet it was only when she was at home that the others
could move about, and then only one person at a time. The
creak of a floorboard might betray them to the apartment
below; everyone in the building knew that Monsieur Kelemen
was bedridden and dying by inches. The tiled floor of the
bathroom was safe, and so was the reinforced floor of the
dining room; sometimes, very late at night, they wrapped
their feet in rags and glided from the rear of the apartment to
the balcony that was their eye to the outside world. But
mostly they sat or slept. Joseph and Miklós huddled beside
the bathroom stove, playing rubber after rubber of honey-
moon bridge, the game a soundless parody of past matches.
Cards were laid on the table as lightly as feathers; neither
man said a word; only their eyes snapped the old Magyar
curses as their wins and losses climbed into the millions of
pre-occupation francs. Hanne, curled up in the bathtub,
watched them, dozed, awoke to watch and fall asleep again.
She was frequently as exhausted now as she had once been
energetic, no longer quite so thin thanks to the food Abby
provided, but listless and preoccupied. It had been Hanne
who had urged and pleaded with Miklós to go into hiding. It
had been the right choice because it was their only choice,

she told herself, but she had not reckoned with the effects of the tedium, the press of minutes that ticked by as slowly as years, the lethargy and loss of interest in anything at all. Only when Abby came in was she able to rouse herself, and then, for an hour or two, she cooked and cleaned and came alive again while Abby sat and rested. It was like a macabre ballet in which only one member of the corps moved while all the other dancers remained frozen.

Five days after the United States entered the war, a thousand Jewish lawyers and doctors were picked up in retaliation for the attempted murder of a German officer. That same day Abby began to sew an American flag. She cut up scraps of sheets for the stars and the white stripes, a crimson silk shawl for the red, an old navy skirt for the field of blue. She gave one of the stars six points. It was foolish, no more than a symbolic gesture of defiance, but the hope of hanging that patchwork flag over the balcony some day enabled her to continue the exhausting struggle to keep all of them fed. There were days when she thought that if she were asked to do more than that, she would simply collapse under the strain.

By mid-January she had begun to long for spring again, forgetting that armies come out of hibernation in the spring, men shake themselves in the sunshine and laugh, look about them for moving targets to shoot for sport and objects on which to work out the lustful dreams of their long sleep. Once, a long, long time ago, it seemed, she had asked to be tested, even prayed for the opportunity to prove herself. She had been soft then, safe, wanting to grow hard and purposeful. Fate and God and Allah and the djinn had all smiled and together decided that the time had come to grant her wish.

They thought they were mistaken at first, that the doorbell had rung in their imagination. It was after ten o'clock, past curfew. Only the Gestapo moved about at night; only the Gestapo came unannounced. For thirty seconds, perhaps a minute, they stared at one another. The drill, so often practiced, so often discussed, but never before used in earnest, suddenly seemed hopelessly inadequate. But then they moved, swiftly, silently, automatically: Joseph to his bed, Miklós to the narrow ledge beside the bathroom balcony on whose railing towels were hung to air on sunny days, Hanne to the pantry and the coffinlike false-fronted space at the back of the deep closet where brooms and mops were stored. It was Abby's task quickly to remove anything the others had left behind, her charge also to unbolt the front door and confront whatever monster waited there.

There was no time for more than a whispered, wordless prayer, more sigh than petition. The door could not be broken down, but those outside must not discover its invulnerability. Not yet. Not until all you hoped it would buy you was enough time to end your own life in dignity and self-respect. Nothing, she thought as she sped down the hallway, we've done nothing to bring them down on us. Only once had the Germans entered the building, but they had demanded no more than that the concierge verify the list of tenants. None of the apartments had been searched. "Someone is bribing them to stay away," Madame Dupont had said. Now Abby wondered if that unknown resident had stolen quietly out of Paris, if the German in his pocket had decided to flush out another source of income. It wouldn't be difficult. This was an expensive quarter in which to live, apartments in the elegant buildings along the river highly prized and occupied only by the wealthy.

She had never unbolted the front door without first looking through the peephole. Years of habit overcame the need for haste, and even as her hands began to lift the steel bar she paused, released it, stood on tiptoe to peer through the lens that magnified and distorted the landing, but left no corner of it hidden. Nothing. She saw nothing. Blackness. The lights in the stairwell were activated by push buttons on every floor, timed to provide two minutes of illumination but not a second more. Yet there was someone there, some mass that moved, a voice cursing in German. The bell rang again, so close to her head that the sound vibrated like bells in a high church tower, and then the dim, economical light flashed on. He wasn't whispering "Jewess," wasn't leering like the gargoyle of her nightmares, but it was Hauptmann Stefan Helldorf's face she saw, and it was Hauptmann Stefan Helldorf's gloved fist that began to pound on the walnut-enclosed steel against which she slumped.

"You were not in bed, madame?" he asked perfunctorily, dark eyes flicking over and past her as if probing for secrets. "I do not intrude too late or disturb your sleep?"

"No, Herr Hauptmann," she said, taking a step forward,

one hand remaining on the door, inching it closed behind her. "I'm surprised, that's all. The curfew."

"Does not apply to us, of course. Or is it that my presence here surprises you?"

"You are on leave in Paris then, Herr Hauptmann?" He was alone on the landing. She heard no sound of boots echoing up the stairwell, no fists pounding on the doors below.

He waited, not answering, until the light ticked off. She felt his gloved hand brush hers, and the uniformed menace of him move closer, force her back into the apartment. A thin shaft of light from her bedroom streamed into the foyer. "My husband is very ill," she protested.

"Dying, I am told. You will make a very young and a very attractive widow, Madame Kelemen. But you will have to learn to speak in whispers, I'm afraid. Or is it that monsieur your husband only pretends to be ill and you are warning him of something? I have seen the medical report. Your performance contradicts it. I have always thought it unseemly to shout where a man is struggling to hold on to his soul."

Had she spoken louder than necessary? Neither Miklós nor Hanne could possibly have heard her, and neither would come out of hiding until she tapped the all-clear signal on window and cupboard door. But Joseph—had she unconsciously raised her voice to pin him to his bed? No. The Hauptmann was trying to intimidate her, attacking while she wondered and worried and might be trapped into showing fear. She remembered the library at Les Roses, the duel between them that she had won. "What do you want, Herr Hauptmann?" she asked. I am your enemy and you are mine. Let's get it over with, whatever game is in your mind to play.

"Two things, madame, and the first is time and a place to talk as civilized creatures one to the other."

She led him to the grand salon, flicking on lights as they passed down hallways and through the small salon that was seldom used, glancing apprehensively at the tall windows with their tightly drawn blackout curtains. One sliver of brightness shining onto the street would bring a German patrol and a stiff fine. In the back of her mind was the certainty that it was vitally important to attract no attention tonight, to conceal from the entire world Hauptmann Helldorf's presence in her apartment. A tiny voice was whispering that murder might have to be done, but it was so hysterical, so absurd a suggestion that hiccups of nervous laughter stuck in her throat.

"You live luxuriously, madame. One would say in pre-war style," Stefan Helldorf said. He stood in the center of the grand salon, slowly peeling the gloves from his hands, unbuttoning and removing the heavy gray overcoat he flung over the back of a chair when she made no move to help him with it. "It's a beautiful room, one of the loveliest I've ever seen."

She had lived so long surrounded by perfection that at first she thought he was merely being polite. But through his eyes she saw everything anew, saw that the objects she took for granted were both priceless and damning. The homes of other wealthy Jews had been stripped and pillaged; hers had not. How to explain? How to satisfy the dangerous curiosity that must inevitably ask why they had been spared?

"I am not interested in the lies you contemplate telling," Helldorf said, reading her mind. He too was glancing toward the windows that overlooked the quai, also checking for fissures of light. "I have come alone. You may inspect the street if you like. No trucks, no soldiers, no Gestapo."

His reassurances calmed her, restored her nerve. And there was something else about him. The fine lines of fatigue that were like strands of a spider's web across his face, the puffy discolored skin beneath his eyes, the momentary tic at the corner of his mouth, the swift turning away as she continued to stare at him, examining that face and finding both truth and a suspicion of hidden pleading there. But his method was to attack, she reminded herself. She waited, in silence, her mind tossing her answers to questions yet unasked, trying to anticipate the weak point at which his thrust would be aimed. He lit a cigarette; the plume of exhaled smoke was acrid and thick; it hung like a winter snow cloud in the cold purity of the salon's night air.

"Your brother-in-law has disappeared from Paris, Madame Kelemen. Where has he gone?"

"I don't know." She almost smiled. This was nearly the question she had anticipated, the one for which her answers were the most practiced. But why Miklós, who must be unimportant to them in every way except that he was a Jew? Why had he not asked first about Hanne?

"Is it common practice among the French to lose a family member and care no more about his whereabouts than if he were a stray dog?"

"We presume he is in Vichy territory. I can't tell you any more than that. Letters are not permitted from one zone to the other."

"When did he leave the city?"

"We weren't close. There was a great deal of confusion, so many people attempting to get to the south. I don't recall precisely when we realized he had gone."

"That's a lie, madame. He was registered with the police as late as May. If he crossed into the area administered by the Vichy government after that date, he committed a very serious crime. The punishment is death."

"Miklós was always headstrong and stubborn."

"Tell me about the woman called Hanne Kelemen. Where is she?"

"They may both be dead, Herr Hauptmann. Sometimes one receives word. Someone with a pass makes a telephone call. It's not a crime to comfort a family, to let them know a relative has been seen. No one has ever contacted us."

"She wasn't French. I have seen copies of her papers."

"She was a naturalized citizen, Herr Hauptmann. A good wife."

"A German woman who lives with a Jew is not a wife, madame."

"This is France, Herr Hauptmann, not Poland."

"It's all the same Reich. The sooner that lesson is learned, the better."

"All I can tell you is that they're no longer in Paris. There are suicides every day, many of them unidentified. They may be in Vichy or they may not be. They were very much in love."

"I don't think you know your own mind, madame. You claim to know nothing, then you pretend to believe your husband's brother has crossed into the unoccupied zone, and finally you suggest a suicide pact. Which is it to be?"

She shrugged her shoulders as if it didn't matter, as if the problem were too insignificant to cause concern. "Miklós and my husband never got along very well, Herr Hauptmann. There was an old quarrel between them. I was fond of Hanne. As I said, I thought she was a good wife and they were in love. Anyone who knew them could tell you that. But as for their personal lives and the decisions they may have made out of fear for what might happen to them, who can say?"

It puzzled her, this interrogation that was almost desultory. Even the anti-Semitic epithets were pronounced without scorn or anger. He wasn't really interested in her replies, she thought. His eyes lacked the coldly satisfied gleam of the pursuer whose prey lies within easy reach of his claws. It was as though he were making the polite, meaningless remarks with which one led up to more serious talk, passing the time, shuffling mental feet before the real dance began. It struck her then that he cared just as much as she that this visit go unremarked and unreported. Why else come alone and so late?

Wearily, as if tired of the game, he smiled, so slight a movement of his lips that it came and went like a shadow. "No one knows I am here, Madame Kelemen, not even your concierge."

Abby nodded her head, waited for him to speak again. He lit another cigarette, then, like a schoolboy who suddenly remembers his manners, offered one to her. "They're very strong," she said.

"Wartime tobacco."

"Nothing is quite as it was before. Everyone misses really decent coffee."

"Do you want coffee, Madame Kelemen?"

"I think not, Herr Hauptmann. We French are a thrifty people. I am sure I would find the price too high. May I offer you a glass of cognac before you go? Something against the cold?"

She left the room without waiting for a reply, moving gracefully but swiftly, hiding, fighting back the urgent need to scream or laugh or simply give in to the nausea that was rising from the pit of her stomach. All of her imagined confrontations with this man had been a series of rapier thrusts; in none of them had she seen him exhausted and afraid. And he *was* afraid. An animal could have smelled it on him; she recognized it as the same emotion that weighed on Hanne and looked at her out of Miklós' eyes. He wants something from me, she thought. Needs something, she corrected herself, needs it desperately. Were there men, even in the

German army, whose fear of death was so great that their souls were in despair and the only comfort they craved was a woman's body? The little death of sex and sleep? Paris was glutted with German officers who had made "arrangements": found mistresses, furnished apartments, were living night-time lives that were a travesty of their daylight hours. Was that what Stefan Helldorf had come to ask her to do? One meeting between them, thirteen months of silence, long enough to begin to forget what she had whispered to herself she was willing to do, long enough to hope that it would not be asked of her. Princess Marie would never have been so fooled.

She thought Helldorf had left the salon, and she nearly dropped the tray on which stood the bottle of cognac and two tiny Italian glasses. Even directly in front of it, you couldn't hear Hanne breathe in her cubbyhole; Miklós would by now have crept along the ledge to the back of the building; but Joseph, Joseph had to play the role of invalid, motionless and supremely vulnerable in his bed. No, the Hauptmann was still there, standing at the far end of the room, hands clasped behind his back, smoke wreathing his head, studying the portrait of her that Joseph had had painted in the first year of their marriage. Not until she had poured the cognac did he turn away from it.

"A beautiful portrait, madame," he said. "Has it ever been exhibited?" His eyes squinted against the cigarette smoke, hiding whatever expression she had thought to read there, but the way he clipped his words off hard and sharp told her that he was sure of obtaining whatever it was he had come for. She sensed impatience, saw it when he drank the cognac at one swallow and reached for the bottle to refill the glass himself. He had unfastened the top button of his tunic and taken off belt and holster. Her eyes flicked over the tabletops until she found the gun. Far away from her, across the room. And he would always be between her and it. No matter what happened, she must not cry out, must make no sound that might drive Joseph from his bed. He could arm himself with the pistol hidden in his mattress, but what good would it do? She could see the bloody German corpse crumpled at her feet, and no way to dispose of it.

"The painting has only a sentimental value, Herr Haupt-mann," she said. "I don't even remember the name of the artist, it was so long ago."

He paced slowly about the room, looking at every one of the paintings, at each of the silver-framed photographs standing atop the grand piano, at the miniature treasures in crystal, enamel, and marble displayed on every table, at the graceful curves of the Louis Quinze furniture. He paused before the empty shelves that had once contained her English-language books, the toe of one boot rubbing meditatively at the magical colors of the Oriental carpet beneath his feet, eyes returning to the portrait even after he had seated himself in one of the chairs that suddenly seemed fragile enough to break under the weight of his body. And Abby, so used to seeing that reminder of her younger self, stared at it also. It was as if a third person had come to join them in the salon, someone with an undeniable right to be there, but distant, floating just beyond the range of conscious thought.

The artist had painted her against a background of pale sworls of green and gray, her hair like the ocean sky at sunset, eyes looking directly out at you as if asking a question, the mouth slightly parted, the beginning or the ending of a smile. It had always been the first thing a visitor exclaimed at when he entered that room, and for as long as anyone remained there it held him, a presence over the shoulder that seemed about to step out of its frame and offer its hand to be kissed. She had felt the allure herself at times, as though a scalpel had excised some part of her, and an ancient Egyptian priest preserved it undeteriorated for centuries. Strange thoughts that came in the night.

"Do you hate all of us, madame?" Helldorf asked suddenly. "Do you despise every German?"

"I am French," she answered.

"Did you love the sister-in-law who may or may not be hiding in the unoccupied zone, who may or may not be dead?"

"Very much."

"Can a Frenchwoman care for a German woman?"

"When has any woman ever begun a war?"

He was sparring with her again, tossing questions at her whose purpose she could not fathom. She knew that the answers she gave were important, that he was weighing each one, probing for kernels of truth, anticipating deceptions.

"I want to bring my wife to Paris, Madame Kelemen. I

want her to be happy here." Once more he was staring at Abby's portrait. "It reminds me of someone," he muttered.

"Herr Hauptmann?"

"Please don't interrupt. My wife has been ill for a long time. She begs me to take her out of the hospital. She's afraid of dying there."

"I'm sorry, Herr Hauptmann."

"Don't lie, madame. You're not sorry. She means nothing to you."

"I understand personal sorrow. Sometimes I think it's the only thing that really touches us, even in the midst of a war."

"I can get the drugs she needs, but I cannot remove her from one hospital only to put her in another. She can't be left alone." Again the portrait stole his attention. He got up and with a viciously sharp twist snapped off the powerful gallery light illuminating it. That corner of the room was dark now, the presence gone. "The reason you cannot lie to me, madame, is that your face reveals everything, every thought, every hope, every fear. Surely someone else has told you that. The artist who painted you perhaps? I'm not asking that you care for Marta in these rooms. I think we both sense how very dangerous that could be." Another warning? "The apartment across the hall will be vacated in a few days. Monsieur and Madame Millot have a daughter living in Paris. A son-in-law, two grandchildren. They will be allowed to take their personal effects with them. They'll be no worse off and no more crowded than thousands of others."

The suddenness and the strangeness of it all had momentarily stunned her. "When will she arrive, your wife?" His wife. Why had she never thought of him as married? "What will you do if I refuse?"

"Arrest your husband, Madame Kelemen."

"On what charge? A dying man?" Fight back. Scrabble for a foothold. Give nothing away, and especially not an admission of guilt.

"Dying? Perhaps. That will be part of the bargain you and I are making tonight. I have his file, madame. I can keep it indefinitely or return it tomorrow to the cabinet from which no one knows it's missing. I can also temporarily erase your Jew brother-in-law and his whore."

"Wife."

"Wife. A man named Antoine Aymard died recently. The Gestapo would eventually have become interested in him, I think. The corpse was badly decomposed when they pulled it from the river; the fingers had been nibbled at by fish. But his name was neatly stitched in the lining of his coat and his papers were very carefully wrapped in oilcloth. Intriguing, is it not?"

"Are you Gestapo?" Abby breathed. They were everywhere, or so the horror stories went, even infiltrating the ranks of their own army, spying on one another.

He shook his head.

"How can I be sure you'll keep your word?"

"I haven't promised anything yet."

"My husband, Herr Hauptmann."

"May continue to die in peace, if you like. The unfortunate couple will not be the objects of a serious search. You will care for my wife as tenderly as if she were the sister-in-law you claim to love. You will not leave her side unless I am there to take your place. Your concierge will know nothing of our arrangement. I will provide the physical necessities of life. Your coffee, Madame Kelemen. Within reason, whatever else you ask for." In one breath he had ticked off a list of demands, of concessions. No need to think them through. That had been done long before he had rung her bell.

"Who are you?" she whispered, not realizing she had spoken aloud. He was of relatively minor rank, yet he had access to Gestapo files; he could promise protection; he could arrange to have a sick wife transported from Germany; he knew about or suspected the connection between Antoine Aymard and Joseph. He spoke French with the ease that came only from a superior education. A native tutor? Childhood holidays spent in France? "Who are you?" she repeated.

"A man whose colleagues will scarcely be able to believe that his French mistress has volunteered to care for his ill wife. The envy of half the officers stationed in Paris, I imagine."

"Mistress, Herr Hauptmann?"

"In name only, Madame Kelemen." Her question seemed to amuse him. "Unless you prefer it otherwise?" He smiled at her, the cognac, the cigarette smoke, and the ease with which he had won making him languid, lazy, Mediterranean in mood if not in appearance.

"Your gun, Herr Hauptmann," Abby said. Had he noticed her moving toward it, picking it up, holding it awkwardly in both hands? Was he testing her again, one final, dangerous challenge to end the strange evening, to seal the compact with an illusion of trust?

"I wonder which of us has won the victory tonight," Stefan Helldorf mused. The light on the landing clicked off. It was cold out there, colder than in the apartment, but Abby's face burned and droplets of sweat coursed like fire down her back. *"Au revoir, chère madame."* Somehow he found her hand in the darkness. His fingers held hers lightly; his lips brushed the suggestion of a kiss across them.

Not until the door closed behind her was Abby able to answer his question, and then it was too late for him to hear.

"I have, Herr Hauptmann," she said aloud. "I had the most to lose."

"He wants me to be a nurse to his wife," she said. Joseph stared at her, Miklós' teeth were chattering, and Hanne seemed on the verge of breaking out in hysterical laughter. "That's all, that's all he wants."

"It can't be. You misunderstood, Abby," Miklós said.

She vomited into the kitchen sink, clutching the sides of the basin as wave after wave of spasms brought up nothing but bile, leaving her weak, aching, and nearly blinded by pinpoints of light dancing before her eyes. When it was over she rinsed her mouth with water and then with wine. "It's nothing. The taste of him," she whispered incoherently. "I had to get rid of the taste of him. We'll have heat in the building again. It's always that way when a German officer moves in. Heat and hot water we don't have to boil on the stove."

"We'll have much more than that," Joseph said, reaching out to support her. "We'll have information. The husband will talk to the wife and the wife will confide in her loving nurse. We'll know their plans in time to act if we have to. We have a margin of safety now. We had nothing until tonight."

"Can you do it, Abby? Can you care for his wife without openly hating her?" Hanne asked.

"I'll think of you and Miklós and Joseph whenever I look at her. It won't be difficult to pretend I care."

"We can't continue to hide here with him so close," Miklós decided. "It's too dangerous for all of us."

"I agree," Joseph said. "Before the wife arrives, Abby, you must persuade the Hauptmann to take you to Les Roses. Talk to Lebrun. He has sons, grandsons, nephews. One of them will surely have contacts in the Resistance. Explain the situation to him. Tell him that Miklós and Hanne *must* be gotten out of Paris."

"Why should he risk himself for us?" Miklós asked. "Better we simply leave and take our chances in the crowds."

"You'd never get out of the city," Abby declared. "You'd be caught at the first barricade."

"To bluff a German officer," Hanne said wonderingly. "To use him to find the Resistance."

Abby's smile was slightly crooked, but it held. "Promise you won't do anything rash," she pleaded. "Give me a few days, a week. It will take time for him to arrange transportation for his wife."

"Suppose he goes back to Germany tomorrow? What if he plans to bring her here himself?" Miklós said softly. "And what if he will not do as you ask?"

"He will. He doesn't dare refuse," Abby replied, ignoring the first of Miklós' questions. "He's hiding something just as we are, Joseph. I know it. I can feel it."

He held her close and Hanne crept into Miklós' arms. The two brothers stared at one another. Bleakly. Their lives were cupped in the slim hands of Joseph's American wife. To Miklós they appeared fragile vessels. Joseph, almost twenty years the husband, twenty years the lover, did not doubt that they were strong enough to keep them safe, strong and supple enough to bend and curve and fight off any threat, destroy any predator.

14

*I*n every way, Abby decided, she would treat the arrangement she had reached with Stefan Helldorf as a purely business contract between two equals. For every demand he made of her, she would exact a price. Formality and the illusion of legitimacy were to be the keystones of their fragile, separate truce. A life for a life, she thought. She would remind him in a thousand small ways that his wife's care and comfort depended solely on his protection of Joseph, that a heartbeat was all that stood between the keeping and the breaking of her promises. No threats, no restrictions on her other than those to which she willingly agreed, no invasions of the privacy of her apartment would be tolerated.

"It may not be that simple," Joseph cautioned. "And it may not be the most desirable thing to do either."

"What other choice do we have? I can't pretend a friendliness I don't feel. That would only make him suspicious, make him determined to ferret out whatever secret he believed I was hiding. If you could have seen him, if you could have heard what he said to me and how he said it, you would know that I am right. He attacked, he tried to catch me in a lie, he hinted that he had the power to expose you. He told me about Antoine. It was obvious that he suspected the body to be that of someone else."

"It was. A derelict fished out of the Seine and thrown back in again."

"Why didn't you tell me?"

"Neither of us was supposed to know. Émile was not supposed to know. They're very skillful in tracing the ways in which information passes from one person to another."

"Have you asked him yet, Abby?" Hanne begged.

"No. But I will. And he will take me to Les Roses." Her chin went up in a stubborn gesture that reminded Joseph of Tess, and he smiled.

"And why do you want to go there?" Joseph asked quietly playing the inquisitor, thinking that she armed herself too flimsily with only determination and not enough guile. "There is no logical reason for such a request."

"I'll find one," she promised. "And if logic fails, then I'll fall back on womanly whims and tears and whatever else will move him."

A shadow passed over Joseph's face; his eyes slipped into a distant look, as if he had heard but yet not heard what she had said. In all their conversations about Helldorf and his odd request they had shied away, both of them, from the single question that was of any real importance. The burden of saving the three people she loved was entirely on Abby. How far would she go, what was she willing to sacrifice in order to keep them safe? If they could have spoken openly of it, each would have assured the other that it was nothing, an act of the body performed without passion or the heart's involvement, a price exacted by the fact of war, as a soldier kills and violates his soul because he must. They did not speak of it because neither of them truly believed that it was or could be so, and because Hanne and Miklós could not have borne it that she would offer her body for their sakes. Abby was alone in whatever she consented to do, and she knew instinctively that the luxury of confession would never be hers.

"Once the wife arrives, I'm trapped," Abby said briskly, wanting more than anything else to wipe away the puzzled look on Miklós' face and the hint of vaguely dawning realization on Hanne's. "But he'll want to make certain of me long before then. I've had time to think, time to change my mind. He'll come again, and when he does, I'll ask him to take me to Les Roses."

Stefan Helldorf slammed viciously through the gears of the Mercedes staff car. He had snarled at the soldiers manning the barricade at Saint-Cloud, and spoken not a word to Abby since the moment they pulled away from the Quai de Passy. Her special pass lay on the seat between them, a hard-won concession to which he had agreed only because she had insisted that she would not, could not care for his wife unless he took her first to Les Roses.

"Your story of pits in the fruit didn't fool me, Madame Kelemen," he had said angrily. "What else have you hidden there?"

"Nothing," she had replied. "But in the attic, in the trunks I did not take with me that day, there are letters, pictures, personal momentos of the past."

"And they have suddenly become important to you, these things you probably haven't looked at or thought of for years."

"I am losing my husband, Herr Hauptmann. Is it so unusual to want to hold on to whatever I can of him?"

Every conversation with him, every meeting was a test of wills. She had won again, for the third time, but only because necessity made her inflexible. She thought he had responded to that strength of purpose in her, and that as long as she showed no weakness, no fear, she would continue to win in all the little ways that were so important. She knew he would be watching her every movement, would be instantly suspicious if she tried to speak privately with Gustave Lebrun, and she had no plan, no idea of how she would manage it. She only knew she must, and that she would not leave Les Roses until she had the gardener's assurance of help for Miklós and Hanne. Joseph had warned her that the contact must be verbal and quick. "You cannot carry a note and hope to slip it to him," he had cautioned. "Anything in writing is incriminating; even a shopping list can be a code." So she had left the apartment with nothing but her wits upon which to depend, and, as on her first visit to Les Roses, she had dressed richly. There had been a spark of something, admiration perhaps, in Helldorf's eyes when they had met on the landing, but only for an instant. He hadn't troubled to conceal his anger, nor had his mood softened in the slightest since leaving Paris. Every mile, every minute of silence brought them closer to Les Roses, closer to Lebrun. If he would not speak, then she must.

"Are you really angry with me, Herr Hauptmann?" she asked quietly. "Or simply annoyed?"

"Both, Madame Kelemen. We had reached an agreement, the two of us. I could say that you broke it."

"You didn't give me time to think," she said softly, using

the conciliatory, persuasive tone of voice that had made her the peacemaker at the bridge table during all the years that Joseph and Miklós had fought over the playing of a hand. "You told me I could ask for anything within reason. I was too surprised that night to know what I wanted."

"I was speaking of food, Madame Kelemen, the things a woman like you might miss from before the war—perfume, cosmetics, silk stockings."

"Those things mean nothing to me. I've learned to do without. Many of us consider it a point of honor not to complain about what we cannot have. Some even refuse when gifts are offered to them. Was the pass very difficult to get?"

He didn't answer, but the car slowed as he leaned back in his seat, fumbling in his pocket for cigarettes and lighter. He tossed the pack into her lap, glancing briefly at her as she shook out two cigarettes and lit them. Her hands were steady; they betrayed nothing. She saw him taste the faint smudge of lipstick on the thin paper, watched the muscles of his face begin to relax as he smoked. The countryside was no longer a dizzying blur of bare tree branches and wintry fields, she was no longer flung against the car door with every turn in the road.

"I apologize if it was," she said. "No, I don't. What you've asked me to do is a very hard thing. This is nothing, a few hours away from your desk. I won't make any other demands. I promise you that."

"We are not engaged in blackmail, Madame Kelemen. The price each of us is willing to pay cannot fluctuate on a whim."

"It is blackmail, Herr Hauptmann. To call it anything else is to deceive ourselves."

"I'd rather call it a truce."

"As you will. The word is unimportant." She could see the steeple of a church far off in the distance, rising arrow-straight and strong above the flat plain. "I would prefer not to go through the village, Herr Hauptmann," she said. "There is another road to Les Roses; it will take no more than an extra ten minutes."

"Are you so afraid of what the villagers might think?"

"Yes," she said simply. "Women who collaborated in the

last war had their heads shaved. They were paraded through the streets."

"The circumstances are different now. Are you forgetting that we have already won, that we will continue to win?"

"It's not over yet, Herr Hauptmann. Please, the other road."

"The English are trapped on their island, and the Americans are a soft, flabby people with most of their navy lying at the bottom of the ocean. Who else is there to threaten us?"

"Please, Herr Hauptmann, the other road. The turnoff is just ahead."

She thought he was going to ignore her plea, but at the last possible moment he downshifted and made the turn. The car slowed to a crawl. She had taken him onto a narrow dirt road used only by farmers moving stock and hay carts from one pasture to another. And she had gained time—fifteen, perhaps twenty more minutes—in which to work on him.

"You must tell me the nature of your wife's illness, Herr Hauptmann. How am I to care for her if I don't know what to expect, what she needs?" Abby lit two more cigarettes. "If a doctor ought to be in attendance, I can recommend my husband's physician. His specialty is the heart, but he also runs a clinic for the poor; he's treated every disease imaginable. He's a very gentle man, and he speaks German."

"No doctors," Helldorf said harshly, "and no more hospitals. I've promised her that. Keep your Dr. Vautrin away from her, Madame Kelemen."

Somehow it didn't surprise her that he knew Émile's name. He must know things about them that both she and Joseph had long ago forgotten.

"The drugs you spoke of," she pressed. "Isn't it dangerous to administer them without medical supervision?"

"I will tell you what you need to know when the time comes, Madame Kelemen," he snapped. He was angry again, angry at her questions and angry at the rutted condition of the road that was torturing the tires and axle of the car.

"I am only anxious to avoid mistakes, Herr Hauptmann. I didn't mean to pry."

He said nothing, ignoring her, swearing fiercely under his breath as they crept around the village. There wasn't a soul in the fields, not even an animal to hint that this was something other than a landscape inhabited by ghosts.

"We're almost there," Abby said, leaning forward, rubbing at the fogged-up windshield. "The gate to Les Roses will be on the left, just a few hundred meters after we come out on the main road again. I assume the house is empty, that no more of your people came later on?"

"I don't know, Madame Kelemen. I thought it better not to make inquiries. But it's not an important location from the military point of view, and the German army doesn't loot. Cooperative civilians have nothing to fear from us."

"I was cooperative. I didn't file a complaint, I didn't demand payment for the use of my home. I could have done so."

"You bluff badly, madame. It's a temptation you ought to resist. There was never any possibility that you would do anything to draw attention to yourself or your husband. We both know that. Why pretend any differently?"

"It was a foolish thing to say," she agreed. At least they were talking to one another, and much of the tension between them had eased. This was a game she was adept at playing. Ask a question, shy quickly away from subjects he obviously did not want to discuss, ask again, a little later, in a slightly different way. It was slow work, but she had already gleaned two very important facts: An extremely ill woman was to be kept away from the best doctor in Paris, and Hauptmann Helldorf was as anxious as she that there be no official record of the connection between them. She would have to depend on Joseph to interpret the contradictions.

Moments later she saw the gate that barred entrance to the estate's private road. It had been smashed and crudely repaired; strands of wire held it to the post from which a chain and padlock had once hung. For the first time since Joseph had told her she must make this trip, she was afraid of what she would find. And yet what was there to fear? There were no Germans there now, of that she was certain. They did not mend broken gates with strips of warped, unpainted wood, did not secure them with baling wire, did not leave any road leading to a headquarters unguarded. Her fellow countrymen then? People who had fled a city, frightened souls without good papers, perhaps a band of young men from the Resistance seeking a few days or weeks of concealment? If that was the case, surely they would be warned by the sound of the car's motor; surely they knew how and where to hide.

Yet her hands shook so badly that she hid them in the deep pockets of her mink coat, willing the fingers to stop twitching and the palms to remain dry.

The road was like a track cut through wilderness. Heavy vehicles had churned it into mud, and then freezing cold had made the ruts left by the tires as hard as brick. Tree branches had broken under the weight of ice and fallen, dead limbs that snapped and cracked under the wheels. She remembered that the December rains had turned to snow just before Christmas. Germans had been here sometime during those weeks, a patrol at least, perhaps a squad of them, camping in her rooms, stamping from attic to cellars, using the furniture for firewood, rifling through her trunks, smashing the few remaining jars of food and the bottles of wine in their wooden racks. She knew instinctively that the house had been used and abused in some horribly cruel and impersonal way, that she would find the kind of wreckage left by mindless, rampaging drunks. None of it mattered, she told herself, the only thing that counted was contact with Lebrun. And he was too wily, too clever an old man to have allowed himself to be caught.

"We'll have to walk," Helldorf said. One of the enormously tall, enormously straight pines lay across the road, impossible to lift aside, the trunk too recently dead to have begun to rot.

They struggled around it, into the woods; the heels of Abby's shoes sank into the matted pine needles. Helldorf took her arm, and she stumbled against him more than once, several times, each contact a little less awkward than the previous one, until at last, when they came out onto the road again, she forgot to move away from him, let him remain so close that her breast pressed against his arm. He unsnapped the flap of his holster. A squirrel scrabbled up a tree toward its nest high above their heads. The gun in his hand followed the sound, tracked it.

"The gardener is an old man, harmless," she whispered. "Don't frighten him. Let me go on alone."

"No."

By now she should have been able to make out the line of the roof, the chimney tops. Nothing. Gray sky through the pines. She had left her gloves crumpled on the seat of the car. Her hands were cold and she slipped them into the sleeves of her coat.

They smelled it before they saw it, smelled the soggy dead ashes and charred wood. The road ended suddenly, and the lawn on which peacocks had once strutted lay spread out before them, a battleground of churned-up soil and mounds of straw-colored grass. Beyond it were the ruins of the house, walls that had tumbled in on empty space when the timbers that supported the roof collapsed. No effort had been made to put out the fire; the house had been abandoned to burn for as long as anything flammable remained. A month or more ago; the wreckage didn't have the settled look of old ruins.

She shook herself loose from Helldorf and walked toward what was left of Les Roses. *Les Cendres*, she thought confusedly, I should rename it The Cinders. The terraces that had fronted it and stretched toward the garden at the rear of the house were intact, but buckled, as though the flagstones had risen up out of a volcanic earth. They were littered with glass from windows that had shattered explosively, and, here and there, bits of the velvet draperies that had been hurled through them. On one of the steps stood a stone urn, miraculously undamaged. She had planted red geraniums in it every spring, sturdy, hardy flowers whose stems gave off a pungent scent when they were broken.

"Parts of Berlin look like this," he said.

"You are in France, Herr Hauptmann," Abby hissed. "Men set this fire, not bombs."

"You don't know that, madame."

"Tell me it was lightning then," she said, "and I'll believe you. SS lightning."

He recoiled as if she had struck him. The gun went back into its holster and he drew himself up ramrod-straight, clicking his heels, reaching out to take her by the arm again. "There's no reason to remain here. What you came for doesn't exist any longer. I have work to do in Paris."

She felt the sting of tears in her eyes even while she willed herself not to cry, not to break down in front of him, not to acknowledge the end of all hope of finding Lebrun. Hot tears. Why were tears always warm when the heart from which they came was cold? They stung like acid on her cheeks. They would eat away her fingers if she reached up to brush them away.

"Don't look," he said. "Don't think about it." The hand beneath her elbow slid upward, caressing the soft flesh of her arm. She could barely make out the face bending toward her. The expressionless dark eyes changed color, became lighter, almost gray; shutters clicked open; a warmth she had never expected to feel from him poured over her. "Houses can be rebuilt."

"Not this one," she said. "Not the lives that were lived here."

"Why would you want to recreate the past? Why would any of us want to go back?"

"I was happy here. I was young here. Memories are the only things you and your army haven't stolen from me."

"Bury the past. Let the memories die a natural death. Holding on to them will kill you."

"What do you know about memories, Herr Hauptmann? All you've created are nightmares."

"Say my name."

"No."

"Say it." The pressure on her arm became pain.

"Stefan." The pain increased. Through the fur, through her clothing, he was bruising her. "Stefan," she repeated. "Stefan, Stefan." To wrench herself away from him was impossible. Her head fell forward; the buttons on his overcoat pressed into her forehead.

"I've waited for more than a year to hear you say my name, say it just the way you did. Did you guess that, Abby Kelemen, the night you opened your door and tried so hard to keep me out of your apartment?"

She was too empty to answer, too tired to think any more. She leaned against him, let him support her weight, let the smell of him fill her nostrils, the heat of his body thaw out her fingers. She hardly heard what he was saying. The vapor of his breath pushing out the words warmed her cheek, but her mind refused to listen, refused to accept the declaration he was making.

His arms tightened around her, forcing her to take one tiny, stumbling step that pressed the length of her body against him. He was whispering in her ear now, his lips sending shudders along her spine. She forced herself to concentrate. She had to remember every word so that later she could wade through the emotions that seemed to be driving him, could separate what might be true from what surely had to be false.

"I'm a man who has always lived by duty. All my life. Until the day I allowed you to take, what was it, Abby? What did you have in those jars of fruit and sewn into the linings of the clothing my men carried to your car? Diamonds to sell on the black market? Of course that's what it was. I knew it then, and I tried to do my duty. Do you remember the jars I smashed? You couldn't realize how desperately I was hoping to find nothing. And your luck held. I could let you go with only a slightly abused conscience. You intrigued me. So beautiful, so courageous, to walk into a nest of your enemy and emerge unscathed, the victor actually. It's been a long war for some of us, beginning years before Poland. I had just come back from North Africa, where the women smell like camel dung and have the dispositions of sheep. You were the first European woman I'd really looked at, really spoken to. You almost frightened me, married to a Jew and proud of it. Later, I saw you many times in Paris. I watched you walk your dogs; I was so close to you at Mass one Sunday that I could hear your prayers; I kept the Gestapo from your building. And then North Africa again, for more than eight months. I dreamed of you every night, I forbade you to leave Paris, I willed you to stay strong and safe. And when I was given a leave to Germany, there was Marta, needing me, growing worse, hysterical whenever they reduced the dosage of the drugs that keep her calm, begging to live with me again. Duty, Abby, and for once it's brought me more than I dared ask of it. Sometimes the gods relent for a while and smile on us. A dream of the past comes so close that all we have to do is reach out for it. Had I come with wine and flowers you would have spat in my face. I knew that; your integrity is part of your charm. But coming as an enemy, as what my uniform proclaims me to be, offering a mutually beneficial truce—or blackmail, if you prefer to call it that—you had no choice but to smile and agree to my terms."

He released her, turned away after one swift, searching look. The burned-out, wasted smell of hard-packed ashes was all around them. There was no one else at Les Roses; it was as empty and silent as a tomb from which the body has been taken.

"You needn't fear me," Stefan Helldorf said bitterly, two

paces away from her, gloved hands gripping one another in the vulnerable small of his back. "I won't ask anything of you other than what you've agreed to, I won't force myself on you, I won't even blacken your good name unless you need the protection of being thought to be my mistress."

It was as though he hoped she would stop him, hoped she would either touch him or run away, back down the rutted, icy road. She waited, shivering in the cold, a kernel of pity struggling with the need to know more, thinking that this weakness, this folly, this delusion of his, for surely it could be no more than that, this unlooked-for, unwanted attraction was too vital to conceal from Joseph, and yet too painful for her to tell and him to hear.

"Marta, my wife, is a fragile child, both physically and mentally. She miscarried twice and then gave birth to a dead infant three years ago. Most of the time she lives in a world of pleasant dreams; but occasionally they become nightmares and she has to be confined. The German state does not easily tolerate her kind. For a long time she lived in the country, with a woman who was both compassionate and glad of the money I paid her. There was a private clinic nearby for the bad times. The woman is dead now and the clinic will not remain open much longer. Accidents have been known to happen in clinics and hospitals where the staff is more political than medical. So you see, Abby, I have no more choice in the matter than you do. She will be safe in Paris, and once more I will have done my duty. I don't love her; I wronged her by marrying her, but that also was a duty."

"I love my husband," Abby said. She was enclosed in a block of ice, part of her making feeble mewing sounds of protest, the voice and the brain forcing out the only words she thought he would hear and believe.

"A man sixteen years older than you, half dead already?"

"I will always love Joseph."

"Loving a Jew could cost you your life. If you say it's duty, that I can accept. But love? Not possible. Not with what he is and the way he is. When was the last time he made love to you?"

"Stop, Herr Hauptmann!"

"Can you bear it? Can you stand the feel of an old man's flesh on yours?"

"Stop, Herr Hauptmann!"

"Or what?" He turned to face her again, and she, looking for physical signs of the truth of what he had told her, found nothing. The eyes that had seemed gray for an instant were nearly black again, flat, without depth, as hard as ebony. For a moment she feared that he would reach for her, and she knew that even to attempt to fight him off would be useless. She didn't understand any of it, and especially did she not understand the man himself. Surely he must know what he had done, surely he must realize the advantage he had given her. Was it a ploy, was it just another aspect of the game, one she hadn't dreamed existed? She had been prepared for a coldly calculating lust, but not for a confession of caring, not for this sudden withdrawal that denied every word he had said.

She clenched her hands into fists, digging her nails into the palms, deliberately hurting herself. Hauptmann Helldorf wasn't human, was no more than a symbol of what she had remained in France to fight, but Stefan, the man who had forced her to call him Stefan, the man whose wife was no wife at all, this man was living, breathing, vulnerable flesh and heart. She needed desperately the armor of being able to hate him unreservedly, but she felt already the looseness of the plates with which she had covered herself, felt compassion for him stealing in around their edges.

She wanted something, someone, the branch of a tree or a merciless hand to slap her across the face and remind her that to cease to hate, even for a moment, was to invite discovery. More than anything else, standing there in the icebound forest, the ashes of Les Roses beneath her feet, she feared that fear itself would eventually impel her to give herself to him, and worse, that she might find some pleasure in the act. The physical pleasure, not the act itself, was what would torment her until the day she died. A long black tunnel stretched before her, and she could see no escape from it, no redeeming source of light anywhere. She prayed for release from this new nightmare, a babbling plea addressed as much to the mother who must surely be a saint as to the God who had given her Joseph. She believed forever after that her cry had been heard.

The forest was enchanted. A tree moved, broke apart from its fellows, developed eyes and a mouth, limbs from which stretched human fingers. Gustave Lebrun and his ax stood within killing range, a blade of sharp steel and a pair of sharper, more deadly eyes raking over them.

The gardener was quick for an old man, quicker than a boy, with a shrewdness bred into him by generations of men who have learned to outwit their masters. He read the warning and the relief on madame's face, and knew what she was doing. There were women who collaborated for pleasure or because they were weak, and there were others who fraternized only until they had saved those who depended on them. His cap was in his hand, his ax lowered to the ground within seconds after she spoke to him. He was used to hiding his feelings; he smiled internally, not a twitch of the lips betraying him or her. Monsieur remembered him. That was all he had to hear.

Shuffling noisily through the rubble, vacant-eyed when the German looked at him, dragging the ax as if having lifted it once had exhausted him, he led them toward the hidden entrance to the cellars, those medieval stone vaults untouched by the fire that had raged above them. "I thought madame would want me to remain to look after things as I have always done," he said, exaggerating the Norman accent, swallowing half of every word. Kings had had their fools; madame would have her faithful idiot.

It was fragrant and dim below ground. He had strewn the smallest storeroom with pine boughs, chiseled out ventilation holes in the foundation and the roof, built a fire pit for warmth. Their footsteps echoed hollowly as they went from chamber to chamber, not a single cobweb to absorb the sound, nothing but surfaces of stone swept obsessively clean. Order had been Gustave Lebrun's passion in the old days. The sheds where his tools were kept had often been cleaner than the rooms of the house.

"What happened, Gustave?" Her voice sounded absurdly loud in that small place, as if she had shouted the question. But it was here, in these spotless stone cells, that she wanted to hear the story. She did not think she could bear it if she had to stare at the ruins and smell the fire while he talked.

"There is not much to tell, madame." He shrugged his shoulders in perfect imitation of helplessness. "They came just before Christmas. I don't know the ranks of the officers, but there were more than half a dozen of them. And women. I spoke to one of them. She was French. All the women were

French. They came in long black cars, but there were trucks also, soldiers with guns and dogs on leashes. Someone in the village had told them that the house was vacant. They were afraid for their daughters, you see." Hauptmann Helldorf turned away, one fist striking against the cellar wall. The gardener's eyes flashed brightly and Abby nodded at him. By the time the German looked at him again, the old man's head had drooped onto his chest once more, and his voice droned tonelessly on. "Every night for a week there was a party, music and dancing and shouting, singing you could hear as far away as the gate. They kept fires roaring in all the fireplaces; I could see them through the windows. The women wore the clothing you had left in your closets, madame, when they wore anything at all. It snowed almost every day and the woods were very quiet, but at night the singing would begin again."

"Why was the house burned?"

"They had finished with it, madame, and they were angry because there wasn't as much wine in the cellars as they had expected to find. The women were coarse creatures, worse than the men. One of them, she had dyed her hair yellow, said that the New Year should be celebrated with a bonfire. The soldiers siphoned gasoline from the trucks and splashed it over the walls and the furniture. They watched it burn for a while and then they left. Monsieur le Curé told me they saw the flames from the village, but everyone knew it was hopeless."

"Was nothing saved, Gustave? Nothing at all?"

"Not a thing, madame."

All the loose gems she and Joseph had laboriously hidden in tiny holes nicked out of the timbered walls of the attic, a fortune she had had to leave behind when she had retrieved the clothing from the trunks. Gone. She remembered the day he had brought those strange stones home and spilled them out on the cover of her bed, a rainbow of glittering color, the facets of the cut stones nearly blinding her, the larger, uncut gems lying among them like pretty pebbles picked up from a stream. All he would tell her was that they were old, very old and very valuable. They had lain for years in a bank vault somewhere in Paris, a king's ransom winking away in darkness. She knew then that they belonged somehow to his past, to Morocco. Stolen? Found in the bowels of the earth in some secret, long-forgotten robber's lair? She hadn't asked where they had come from; it was during the time when they made trips to Les Roses every few days. It had seemed such a game, such an exhilarating, frightening, mysterious game. Not to know, only to guess, heightened the sense of excitement. Now she could not even recall how many paintings they had hidden, and she wondered if they had sealed them tightly enough inside the pipes. Water and rot could have eaten them up by now. Göring or nature? In the end she supposed that what one had not managed to steal, the other would destroy. She shivered and blew on her fingers.

"Madame is cold?" The old man knelt down and began layering sticks and pine cones inside the ring of stones.

"Don't bother, Gustave," Abby said. "Is there anything you need, anything I could leave or send to you?"

"No, madame. I live off my garden and what I can trap in the forest. I trade my herbs for bread when I go into the village for Sunday Mass. Everyone is brewing tisanes again. I used to tell them they were better than what came in the doctor's bag, and now they believe me." He cackled, an absurd, old-womanish sound she had never heard from him before. A signal? A message?

"Are you still growing dill and lavender?" she asked as they climbed the steps out of the cellars. "I wanted the leaves for preserving cucumbers," she explained, "but Gustave taught me to let the plants dry and gather the seeds for tea. We infused them with mint and sweetened the liquid with honey. You have to drink the tisane boiling hot, but it makes you sleep like a baby."

"I have them all, madame, protected from the cold in what is left of the greenhouse. Sage and thyme, a cutting from the rosemary monsieur brought back from Greece, sorrel growing like the weed it is, garlic for the digestion, fennel for sausage and stewed apples. Many more. Would madame like to take some of them back to Paris?"

As if she hadn't heard him, she gazed into the rubble that had once been gracious rooms, stirring up sodden ash with the tip of her shoe. She turned a full circle, imagining walls about her and a ceiling where there was openness, her head tilted to one side, listening for echoes from the past. Hauptmann Helldorf never took his eyes from her; she let the loss she was feeling show on her face, let him read a sadness that was near to despair. "I would like to take something back," she said slowly. "I'd like to walk for a few minutes, I think. I'd like to see something growing, something that's still alive." Stefan Helldorf's arm was at her elbow. "I could make tisanes for Marta," she said, smiling at him.

They followed the gardener across the rear lawn, toward the caved-in structure that had been the greenhouse. Once Abby stopped beside a tangle of dead twigs, reaching out to snap off a sharp thorn almost as long as her fingernail. "There used to be beds and beds of roses here," she said. "On a warm day the perfume was overpowering. I wish we hadn't come. I'll never be able to think of Les Roses again as anything but the way it is now."

They had to stoop to enter the greenhouse. It was a tiny place, barely large enough for the three of them, and in the spaces where panes of glass were missing, Gustave Lebrun had woven pine boughs and straw. Charcoal glowed in an iron cooking pot; the air was moist and warm and smelled like a hundred steamy kitchens. "It used to stretch for twenty yards or more," she said reminiscently, "and there were pipes running along the frame so that the plants were always bathed in mist. One year we experimented with orchids. Do you remember that, Gustave?"

"Yes, madame."

The dill was feathery and softer than down against her hand. She crushed a leaf between her fingers and held it to her nose, breathing deeply. "The old remedies are best. There was an elderly man from the country who came to Paris every spring, hauling a cart that carried nothing but herbs in little clay pots. The Parisians used to cluster around it and stand talking to him even after they'd bought what they needed, just to smell the fragrances. He had a medicinal use for every plant. I haven't seen him in the quarter for years."

"There is a wheelbarrow in one of the sheds, madame."

"Thank you, Gustave. I don't want to take everything. Just a few plants, the ones you have most of."

She watched him hobble off, shaking her head at the bent back, the way he dragged one foot. "I suppose he'll stay here until he dies," she said. "I think old servants who spend their entire lives serving one family are as much a part of the past as the ruins of this house. Do you mind dirtying up your car with my plants?"

"Do you think I care about old servants or how you turned cucumbers into pickles or the tisanes you can brew? Do you think I'm interested in any of that? Something other than the cold is making you shake like an old woman with the palsy. What is it, Abby? Can't you believe yet that I won't allow anything or anyone to harm you?"

"You won't be in France forever." She was going to lie to him. She had to say his name. "The tisanes are for Joseph. He sleeps badly at night, and even worse during the day. His only comfort is to have me beside him. I won't be able to be there when your wife comes. My letters are gone, all the bits and pieces of my past that I could touch. My husband needs sleep, Stefan, but he's not an easy patient. He chokes on the pills Émile Vautrin leaves for him. He'll drink the tisanes."

"If madame returns," Lebrun said, "I will have more for her." He named each plant as he nestled it into a bed of straw in the wheelbarrow. He had brought two lengths of pipe and a dozen clay pots back from the shed with him. They lay on the latticework floor of the greenhouse. "I can run the pipes from the pond as we did before." He pointed with one shaking finger toward the broken lines above them, as if to restore the sprinkling system were really possible.

"I want to give him some money," Abby said in German. "He won't take it in front of you."

"Quickly, madame." Gustave Lebrun's work-worn fingers dug at the mud stopping up the ends of the pipes. She held open the pockets of her coat, watching Stefan Helldorf pick his way over the uneven terrace, feeling the weight of the stones cascading against her hands.

"How did you know?" she asked.

"Madame was very clever, but I never allowed wood wasps to burrow into the walls of the attic. They are all here, dug out before the last group of Germans came. They ran their trucks over the garden, but they did not dig in it."

"We need a man who can provide papers, Gustave. Monsieur's brother and his wife must be gotten out of Paris."

"They are Jews?"

"One Jew. She's German. Neither would survive a roundup."

"Where are they now?"

"With us, hiding. Can you help?"

"I know someone who knows someone else. It wil be expensive, madame."

"That doesn't matter now."

"What about the Hauptmann? I pretended not to recognize him, but I remember him well. Is he English?"

"English?"

"At night, madame. They come by parachute, wearing German uniforms, God protect them. There are others too, not many, but planted in the German army years ago. Even the Resistance doesn't know who they are."

"We heard rumors, but we didn't dare hope they were really true. It's terrible in Paris, Gustave. They've turned the city into a German playground, and Frenchmen are denouncing one another every day. You can taste the hatred. All the old lies have resurfaced. The Hauptmann has a wife who's ill. I am to care for her, but he can't be trusted."

"Be careful, madame. I'll send someone to you as soon as possible."

"God bless you."

No more than five minutes had elapsed since they had been left alone in the greenhouse. Gustave Lebrun took the money Abby handed him, putting it in the breast pocket of his jacket so that a corner of one bill showed. She walked ahead of him, hurrying to rejoin Stefan Helldorf, catching up to him as he stepped across the front terrace. She kept her hands clenched around the stones in her pockets, her head lowered, never turning around to see what lay behind her. Her gloves were on the front seat of the car where she had left them, and while the gardener lovingly arranged the pots of herbs on the rear floorboard, she climbed into her seat and crushed the leather gloves into soft pads, jamming them into the pockets of the coat, wedging them against what was left of Joseph's Moroccan treasure.

15

Stefan Helldorf left Paris for Germany three days after their trip to Les Roses. Not once during those three days did he come to the Kelemen's apartment. One morning Abby found a piece of paper slipped under her door, two dates scrawled on it, and only by that did she know he had left and when he expected to return.

"We have ten days of freedom," she told Joseph. The relief in her voice was so obvious that he drew her down onto the bed beside him, cradling her head in the hollow of his shoulder. She rested there, quiet and at peace.

"Tell me what happened at Les Roses," he said.

At first she was confused. She had already told him, told Hanne and Miklós too, what Gustave had promised; how he had spotted the slight depressions where the wood had settled over the holes they had gouged out of the attic walls, his fear that other Germans would come, his decision to remove the stones.

"What else?" Joseph prompted. "I can bear it, Abby, but I must know."

The words came slowly, hesitantly, more than half muffled as she pressed her face deeper into the muscles of his shoulder. She felt them tighten, then relax again, as though Joseph expected the worst and was determined to accept it.

"I didn't want to speak of it," she began. "I'm not sure myself what it means." She repeated what Helldorf had told her about his wife, his surprise at the destruction of the house, his decision not to make inquiries about the property before the trip. And then, even more haltingly, she told him what he had said about seeing her in Paris, about keeping the

Gestapo from the building, about the months in North Africa when dreams of her had come to him every night. "He claims to be a man of duty, Joseph. Duty to country and to his wife."

"He's fallen in love with you, my darling. Just as I did. One glimpse at Longchamps and you had captured my heart; the moment when he first saw you at Les Roses must have been very similar."

"He didn't talk about love; he never mentioned the word."

"It doesn't matter. That's what he meant."

"It's a soldier's love, not real, just a dream to make the life he leads more bearable." She was desperate to convince both him and herself that it could be nothing more. "They imagine themselves in love with movie stars and the girls who sell flowers on street corners. They're lonely, all of them. He'll forget once he's seen his wife again. Coming back in the car, he didn't say a word. It was as if he'd never spoken at all."

"I think your naïveté is only exceeded by your generosity, Abby. You don't want to hurt me; you'd rather fight him alone."

"Nothing will happen, Joseph."

"I know that. And if something does, it will still be nothing."

She fell asleep, finally, waking only when she sensed his muscles begin to cramp under her weight. Drowsy, not quite certain what she had said that had brought such release from worry, she stumbled to the pallet at the foot of his bed where she had slept ever since his heart attack. She didn't hear Hanne tiptoe in with food, reacted only subconsciously to the blanket her sister-in-law threw over her, drifted away to another world in which Bridget and Patrick laughed and sang and drank tea together, Tess was young and beautiful, and Marie-Claire had not yet discovered the lump that killed her. For twelve hours she was free; reality returned with the wintry-cold light of the morning sun.

The man Gustave Lebrun had promised to send came sooner than anyone had dared hope. He stayed less than thirty minutes, and when he left he carried away with him several of the stones that Abby had reclaimed from the lengths of pipe. He told them that someone else would deliver two sets of false identity papers, and that a third person would escort Miklós and Hanne out of the city. There were few safe houses, but to attempt to cross the border into Vichy territory was next to impossible now. Madame had seen the cellars at Les Roses. Did she not think they were as safe and comfortable as any fugitive could wish for? The old man was prepared to run the risk of keeping them there and had declared the place far less likely to be searched than any farmhouse.

"I don't mind living in a cellar," Hanne said. "Anywhere but Paris."

Two days before Helldorf was expected back from Germany, Miklós and Hanne were taken away by a guide wearing the baggy pants and blue blouse of a workingman. He was young, confident; he had smuggled hundreds of people out of Paris, he told them, and never lost a single one. Before the war he had worked in a factory; now his business was the transport of human cargo. There was nothing personal in what he did; he was paid in full before revealing any part of the route they would follow. Professionals were seldom caught, he boasted. It was amateurs and anxious relatives who gave way to panic and acted suspiciously when they were asked to present their identity cards. They didn't like him, his coldness, his brusque impatience, his obvious desire to get it over with as quickly as possible, the way he counted the money Abby handed him before demanding privacy so that none of them knew where he hid it on his person, but they had to trust him. He had come from Gustave, through some circuitous network of faceless, nameless men, and all of them knew that this was the only chance of escape that would ever be offered.

They could take nothing with them, only the clothes on their backs. He searched them thoroughly, an indignity to which they were forced to submit. He took Hanne's pearls from her purse, weighed them in his hand for a moment, then flung them onto the kitchen table.

"I'll keep them for you," Abby promised. "They'll never be sold." Hanne seemed very tiny as she embraced her, as Joseph kissed her on both cheeks.

The guide found Miklós' old identity card in the pocket of his jacket. "I wasn't told it was a question of Jews," he said.

"Are we more valuable cargo, monsieur?" Miklós asked. "Does it cost more to smuggle a French Jew to safety than a French Christian?"

"Stupidity is expensive. Don't you read the newspapers?" The young man handed the card to Abby. "Burn this, madame. It's my life as well as theirs."

"How will we know when they've arrived at their destination?" Joseph demanded.

"You won't. I hand them off to someone else. If I'm not picked up, if the Germans don't knock at your door in the next thirty-six hours, you can assume that all went well. Don't try to find out. Too much knowledge is your worst enemy in this business. Be at the métro station in fifteen minutes. Don't come together. You won't see me and I won't speak to you again until you reach the Gare Saint-Lazare. Understood?"

What could they say? They kissed and held one another, let each other go reluctantly. The guide whistled as he clattered down the rear stairway. Hanne crept after him a few minutes later, and Miklós, snatching back the card that marked him as a Jew, concealing it in a tight fist, followed. He held himself as erect as a patriot en route to his own public execution.

Abby watched them from the balcony, willing them not to turn around for a last glimpse of what they might never see again. Hanne melted into the straggling crowd of people heading toward the station, but Miklós, had there been a German passing by to see him, would surely have been stopped. Everything about him screamed defiance.

Their absence meant that Abby had time to think again, time and more privacy than she had enjoyed since June of the previous year. She moved back into her own bedroom, meticulously destroying the few pieces of clothing they had left behind, searching through the apartment for scraps of paper bearing their handwriting, anything that might seem unusual for her to possess. She found little; they had all been very careful. When she finished, all that remained of Hanne and Miklós was the strand of old pearls she placed at the bottom of her jewel case.

She began to realize that the bargain she had made was not really with Stefan Helldorf, not even with Joseph, Hanne, Miklós, or God. It was with herself and some band of winged fates with hidden faces. If they were caught, if Hanne and Miklós and their guide never reached Les Roses, the forfeit would be great, inevitable, and final. Helldorf could do nothing to save them. She wasn't even curious about the type of death that would unite them all. Quick or slow, merciful or brutal, it would come in its own time, at the pleasure of the men administering it daily to so many others. If they escaped, if they went to ground like phantom foxes before the hounds, the task of keeping them safe could stretch on for years and years. It might involve many moves, other cellars, new identities, and all of it would cost money. She made another, harder bargain with herself, with the nameless, unchristian fates. She said nothing to Joseph, but she spent hours examining the contents of her armoire, willing herself to remember a time when the choice of a dress had been as important as anything else she did in the course of a day. She was preparing herself to be Stefan Helldorf's mistress if necessary, and she was doing it with the same brisk efficiency and lack of emotional involvement she would bring to the task of caring for his wife. When it was over, when the day of liberation finally came, she would wipe these years from her mind as though they had never existed, and her only true prayer was that Joseph would be able to do the same.

Marta Helldorf, thin, frail, arrived in the first week of February, carried up the five flights of stairs on a stretcher. Early every morning Abby rang the bell of what she could not stop thinking of as the Millot apartment. Stefan Helldorf was always waiting for her. They were like two nurses meeting at the change of shifts. Marta had passed a quiet night, was still asleep or just waking up. There were written instructions she was to follow, and often throughout the day the phone would ring and he would ask whether a particular medication had been given. She asked for a key to the apartment so that she could go back and forth across the landing, reminding him that she had two patients to tend. He never failed to take it from her in the evening, and although they often shared a glass of cognac before she left, and sometimes she looked up from her glass to find him staring at her with that unshuttered dark-gray gaze she remembered from Les Roses, he never spoke of that day. He called her Madame Kelemen; she caught herself wondering if she had only imagined that for a few minutes he had once called her Abby, had forced her to repeat his name, had said things she was finding it more and more difficult to recall.

Marta Helldorf was so fragile that the daily sight of her tugged at Abby's heart. She had the smooth, unlined face of a twelve-or thirteen-year-old child, skin as translucent as fine porcelain, features that could have been sculpted by the gentlest of skilled fingers, a cloud of loose, floating, light-brown hair. More than once Abby thought she would have offered to care for her even if there had been no threat, no compromise, no precarious compact between enemies.

During the first week she followed Helldorf's instructions to the letter, and twice, cradling Marta in her arms, spooning soup into the babylike mouth, she had looked up, startled to find the husband standing in the doorway watching what she did. Checking up on her. Counting the pills he had left on a silver plate that morning, pills that kept his wife perpetually half-conscious, so drowsy and disoriented that Abby found it impossible to question her. She wasn't even certain that Marta Helldorf knew where she was or realized that the woman tending her was a stranger. Gradually the telephone rang less frequently. On the tenth day he did not call, and that evening she told Joseph that she thought he had come to trust her as much as he ever would.

"Be careful," he warned. "Take only the chances you have to. Don't go too far."

The first time she withheld a medication she hid the pill in the pocket of her skirt. After that, because it had nearly fallen out when she surrendered the key, she wrapped them in a piece of tissue stuffed into the toe of her shoe. Until she had stolen a sample of each.

"Painkillers and sedatives. Medications to improve the circulation and reduce fever," Émile Vautrin said. "Without examining her I can't tell very much from these."

"It's too dangerous," Joseph said. "We can't risk you, Émile. Unless we know for certain exactly where he is, you must stay out of that apartment. If he came back, if he found you there, everything we're working toward would be lost."

Abby, coming into the bedroom just in time to hear the end of the conversation, asked what it was they *were* working toward.

"The less you know, the better," Émile said. "You have

to face him every day, my dear. Let's just say that something about the story he told you strikes me as being incomplete. He cannot be the only German officer whose wife suffers from a prolonged depression due to the loss of a child, but he is certainly the only one to go to such extraordinary lengths because of it. I've already said too much. Nothing may come of it anyway."

Outside it was still winter and the wind howled over the river and through the alleyways. Used to living with cold by now, Abby found the apartment uncomfortably warm, as if an indoor spring had suddenly oppressed them with a taste of summer. The radiators were almost too hot to touch, yet, as Abby dutifully reported to Joseph and Émile Vautrin, Marta Helldorf's fingers and toes were always tinged with blue. Even in her sleep the young woman rubbed fretfully at them.

Now Abby rarely left the building at all. There were no little dogs to walk in the evening; they had stiffened in their baskets in early December. She was freed from the ration lines and the black market; the best of what Paris had to offer was delivered to her door every few days. They ate well, better than they had in years, yet February was a terrible month. The directives came so quickly that one had scarcely been absorbed before another was added to it. There was a widespread rumor that Jews were going to be required to wear the Star of David on their clothing; then came a restrictive curfew that made it virtually impossible for a Jew to fulfill the daily business of living before he must scurry home to the darkness of his house.

Émile told them of a beating he had seen only a few hundred yards from their front door, an old man's body crumpled to the pavement and methodically abused while Parisians looked on in fascinated horror. No one had asked what the old man's crime was; no one had dared, and perhaps no one had cared. Another Jew. The sooner the Germans got them out of the city, the sooner the population would be spared such sights. How could it be the Jew's fault that he was beaten? But somehow it was so. Somehow the victim became the guilty party, and instead of compassion, his persecution engendered only resentment and a wish to be rid of him.

"There will be others," Émile predicted. "They've learned

that Parisians are as callous about their Jews as the Poles were."

The first trains left on March 28. Trains going east. Filled with Jews. Later, much later, Abby learned about Auschwitz. The world learned, and voices began to ask how it was possible that anyone could have believed in the lie of resettlement. Since mid-February, Jews had had to remain indoors from eight o'clock in the evening until six the following morning. There were signs everywhere forbidding them access to public telephones and toilets. Synagogues had been blown up; Jewish lawyers had simply disappeared. "Death to the Jews" was scrawled or painted onto walls beside posters advertising the latest films churned out by Goebbels' propaganda machine.

For Abby the departure of the trains and the sights Émile Vautrin witnessed were less real than the daily fact of Marta Helldorf. She was doing what Joseph had urged her to do, gradually reducing the dosage of the sedatives she gave her patient, working, under Émile Vautrin's instructions, toward a point at which the young woman would remain free from pain, but also able to answer questions.

"It's a very delicate thing to accomplish," the doctor warned. "She must believe she's dreamed her conversations with you. Helldorf medicates her heavily; you must always be certain she is deeply asleep when he returns."

Now it was Abby who was impatient for him to examine her, Vautrin himself who hung back, filing away in his finely tuned physician's brain every scrap of information she brought him. "She asks me for cigarettes sometimes, like a guilty child. I have the feeling they're forbidden her, but it's such a little thing, Émile. And they seem to make her want to talk."

"Not too many, Abby," Vautrin cautioned. He wanted to leave it at that, knowing the strain Abby was under, reading it in the circles beneath her eyes and the looseness of her wedding ring, but Joseph disagreed.

"She has to know," he said. "Émile suspects that they've assigned a man to watch him."

"I'm not certain," the doctor put in quickly. "But lately I seem to see a familiar face behind me everywhere I go. It could be just an overactive imagination."

"Is the building being watched, Émile?" Abby asked. "Can you tell?"

"I don't think so, but it's wiser all the same not to come here too often. If they're interested in me, they'll also be curious about the patients I visit." He hesitated. "Your concierge has gotten in the habit of walking with me to the elevator, and I often find her sweeping or polishing something in the hallway when I leave. Every sound carries down that shaft; I've noticed it myself."

"The opening and closing of a door?"

He nodded.

"You should have told me." She was almost always in the Helldorf apartment when he came, sometimes didn't even know he'd been there until Joseph mentioned it afterward.

"Any break in a routine makes them suspicious," Émile said, "but we have to make one small change. In a few days I'll call and ask if Joseph's condition is any different. You'll tell me that he seems slightly better and I'll tell you that I've gotten busier at the clinic and that unless he has a bad night, we can keep in touch by phone. If you really need me, or if I learn anything I think you should know, I'll come immediately. That should draw them away from you."

"Whose phone is tapped?" Abby asked.

"Mine," Émile said. "The one at the clinic and probably the one at my home also."

"And ours?"

"I doubt it."

"It may be Helldorf," Abby said. "He warned me to keep you away from his wife."

"If that's the case, we'll know soon enough," Émile said. "Mention to him, as casually as you can, that I won't be seeing Joseph regularly any more. That and the report from whoever is tapping my phone ought to make him call off his man."

Without Émile's frequent visits they felt more alone than ever before, completely cut off from contact with the rest of Paris. For hours at a time Joseph lay in his bed staring at the ceiling, waiting for the sound of Abby's key in the lock. They read the newspapers avidly, even knowing that hardly anything of what was printed could be believed. Much was viciously anti-Semitic, penned by Frenchmen whose virulent hatred for the Jews had finally found an appreciative forum.

Both of them were waiting, but for what? Because Émile feared a repetition of what had happened to the Jews in

Poland, Joseph waited for clues of what might be being planned to appear in print or on the daily radio broadcasts; but Abby, living with another type of fear, waited for Stefan Helldorf to break the excruciating silence between them. Every evening, when she came into Joseph's room disturbed and agitated by the incoherent ramblings she'd listened to during Marta Helldorf's brief periods of semiconsciousness, he heard her out without comment, but more and more frequently with an appraising look that seemed to ask her why she had stopped speaking of the husband. She found herself adding a whispered "Nothing else," knowing he would understand what she meant. She dreaded the day, if it ever came, when those words would be a loving lie.

She was given an unexpected period of grace toward the end of March when Stefan Helldorf told her he would be out of Paris for several weeks. "I leave Marta entirely to your care," he told Abby.

"What do I do if something happens, if I can't manage, if she needs a doctor?" It was unnerving to know that he would be beyond the reach of a telephone. And yet not to have to see and talk to him every day was something she had almost given up hoping for.

"There won't be any emergency. Her condition never changes."

"But if there is?" she persisted.

"Do nothing," he said. "Don't call a doctor, any doctor. Let her go."

From the second week in April, when he returned, until it was all over, Abby hardly slept at all.

Stefan Helldorf was different somehow, though Abby found it difficult to identify precisely the ways in which he had changed. She thought he must have been sent back to North Africa for at least part of the three weeks he had been away; his skin was darker, his hair lighter. But she found a scrap of paper with the name of a town written on it, a dated, half-burned page she recognized as being from the little book he carried in his breast pocket, and when she asked Joseph if he had ever heard of the place, he told her it was a village near the Swiss border. So he had also been to Germany.

Sometimes she caught him staring so intently at his wife that it frightened her. It was as if he were trying to will the shallow breathing to stop, as if he had set a date for her dying, a limit to the time he would allow her to live. In January he had told Abby that he wanted Marta to be happy in Paris, that she was afraid of dying in the hospital where she had been for God only knew how long. He had lied then, and every time he had accused Abby of lying to him he must have been trying to thrust her away from his own great deception. She knew now that there had never been any hope of recovery, knew that by being happy, he had meant drifting into a death that could hardly be a much deeper sleep than the one in which his wife had already been held for years.

She knew much more than that, but she could make no sense out of it, could not understand why Joseph made her repeat some things many times, virtually ignored others. The real reason behind Marta Helldorf's slow dying in Paris remained as much a mystery as ever. But what she had most feared, what Joseph too had seemed to anticipate, didn't happen, and as April warmed into May, she finally began to allow herself to hope that it would not. Yet whenever she felt herself grow too confident, too relaxed, almost happy, she forced herself to stand before a mirror and did not turn away until she saw her eyes harden again, until her back stiffened, and with it the will to go through with whatever demands Stefan Helldorf eventually made of her.

Within days of Helldorf's return to Paris, Émile Vautrin lost his shadow. He developed a bad crick in his neck from constantly peering over his shoulder, but even after he was certain that he was no longer being followed, he stayed away from the Kelemens' apartment. Whenever he telephoned, Abby assured him that Joseph's condition remained the same, was perhaps even a little bit improved. In the middle of May she was startled to hear him say that he would come by the apartment anyway that evening, on his way home from the clinic.

"Something has happened or is about to happen," Joseph said.

In spite of what Miklós and Hanne's guide had told them, they had had one last contact with Les Roses. A man had appeared at the kitchen door late one night, told them the packages had arrived safely, and then asked them one question. Were there any other packages they wished to send? If the answer was yes, it could be arranged; if no, steps would be taken to break the links of the chain. There would be no way to pick it up again. They had been given no time to discuss the proposal, but they hadn't needed any. Helldorf knew there were cellars at Les Roses; if they disappeared it would be the first place he would send the Gestapo. Abby's quick thought that he might not denounce them, might let them go because of what he had said there in January, evaporated almost as soon as it was born. She had had no sign from him that he remembered it, nothing but an abstracted look in his eyes that became almost anger, almost desolation whenever he bent over his wife.

"We couldn't have gone," Abby said. "Émile is late. What does it mean, Joseph?"

"He's being cautious, or some last-minute emergency detained him." He was much less afraid than she. He thought he knew why Émile was coming. It meant that there was still a little time, but that the waiting could not continue much longer, that the plan they had once discussed, almost dismissed as too ridiculous to be successful, was perhaps their sole remaining choice. It all depended on how accurate Abby's observations of Marta Helldorf had been.

Émile Vautrin almost hurried by Madame Dupont without pausing to greet her. He caught himself at the last moment; she couldn't fail to notice the discourtesy and would wonder what had caused it.

"It's been a long time since I've seen you, Doctor," she said. "I hope Monsieur Kelemen is not . . ."

"No, no. He's doing much better than I expected, to tell the truth."

"I'm glad to hear that. He's the only one in the building who never complained about my cats, you know." She lowered her voice to a confidential whisper. "She's pregnant, my little female. It would have been a tragedy a few months ago, but with Herr Helldorf here now, there's nearly as much garbage as in the old days. Scraps to feed the kittens."

He peered at her in the dim light. "And you yourself, madame?" he asked. "You're not giving food to the cat that you should be eating yourself?" She was certainly thinner than he remembered her being. His glance dropped to the swollen legs and the pair of men's shoes she was wearing.

"It comes and it goes, Doctor," she said. " Some days

are worse than others. What can one expect? I thought I might ask your advice, but . . ."

"Would you like me to examine you on my way out?" he asked. Was this why she had seemed to be lying in wait for him in the hallway? The relieved smile on her face told him it was. She probably had no doctor of her own, couldn't afford one, was the type of woman who suffered along quietly for as long as she could. "After all, if you're going to have kittens to care for again, you'll have to be quick on your feet."

"Won't that be lovely, Doctor?"

He forgot Madame Dupont, her cat, and the cat's possible kittens as soon as he rang for the elevator. Later, after he had told Abby and Joseph what they had to know, he would examine the concierge as conscientiously as he did all his patients, but for the moment he had more important things on his mind. All day long he had been trying unsuccessfully to convince himself that he had misunderstood, that Frenchmen would not lend themselves to so monstrous a project as the one that had been accidentally revealed to him. Tried and failed. He was too good a Catholic to keep silent, too good a Frenchman, proud to be fighting his country's occupiers through the exercise of his profession. The Nazi campaign against the Jews sickened him, and the obsequious acquiescence of many Frenchmen to what were preposterous lies shamed him.

Ever since the Germans had first marched into Paris, there had been rumors that the deportation Jews had suffered in other occupied countries would become customary in France also. Now, almost two years later, it was still a rare occurrence. They had been forced to register, had been issued the discriminatory papers that set them apart from other Frenchmen; naturalized Jews had had their citizenship revoked; many foreign-born Jews had been interned in special camps; laws had been passed limiting the professions and businesses in which they could engage, even the hours when they could be on the streets; and they were always the first to be rounded up for reprisals; but so far they had been spared the yellow star which the Germans called their badge of shame.

Early that morning the doctor had been summoned to the home of one of the men on the staff of the Commissioner for Jewish Affairs. The man had been awake all night with pains in his chest and shortness of breath, and although Dr.

Vautrin diagnosed severe indigestion and panic as the cause of his discomfort, his patient was scarcely comforted by the reprieve. The Jews were to blame if he died of overwork and exhaustion. There were so many of them needing to be ferreted out. The Germans were pressing the Commission hard. It was already the middle of May. Great plans for this summer were being drawn up. The task ahead of them was going to be enormous, and if even one Jew was left unmarked in the occupied zone they, the commissioners, would be blamed and probably suspected of secret leniency. Nothing more specific than that. The dose that cured the indigestion also closed the man's mouth. But Dr. Vautrin was convinced that when he spoke of marking the Jews, he meant that the Star of David would soon be seen throughout the capital, and not just on the coats of refugees and the foreign-born.

Joseph Kelemen's status was one that did not fall easily into any category the Germans had yet devised. A man who had won citizenship through service in the Legion was not the same as one who was naturalized in the ordinary way. But it was impossible to predict whether the Germans would honor that fine point. So far it would appear that they had. Now Émile Vautrin had to warn both husband and wife that the situation seemed on the point of changing, that at least one individual on the Commission for Jewish Affairs had hinted at some grand scheme to be begun this summer. Surely French Jews would remain in France. But only Joseph himself could decide whether or not to trust that a former legionnaire was French enough in German eyes.

They listened to him without interrupting until he had told them all he could. "I'm positive it means they'll make it a crime for a Jew to be caught not wearing the Star of David," he said. "And I'm also certain that within weeks, surely no more than a month or two after that, there will be more arrests, more foreign-born Jews sent to the internment camps."

"And deportations," Joseph said quietly. "Mass deportations. Hitler won't be satisfied until he's gotten rid of every Jew in western Europe."

"Where will they go?" Abby asked. "There must be millions of Jews. It would take years and years to build enough labor camps and resettlement villages. Russia is swallowing up his armies as fast as he can get them to the front."

Émile Vautrin hesitated, uncertain how much she had

been told of what he and Joseph had lately discussed, the chilling rumors and stories that were beginning to filter into France from faraway Russia, the even grimmer suspicions that no sane mind wanted to believe. Patients and families of patients talked openly to Émile Vautrin, and his practice was not limited to the wealthy or the socially prominent. Long, long ago he had opened his examining rooms to any poor soul who needed his special expertise. Physicians from all over Paris sent him their most impossible cases, and sometimes he managed to work miracles. The staffs of the charity hospitals knew him well; the nursing nuns considered him a fit candidate for sainthood. When his wife had insisted that he was too old to continue working sixteen hours a day, he had begun to limit the number of paying patients he treated, but refused to abandon a single one of his indigent cases. Almost more than anyone else in Paris that spring, he had his fingers on the varied pulses of the city. The agitated, frightened rhythms he picked up from his Jewish patients were, he felt, more than justified. Untouchable himself, he was better able than they to believe in the fact of incomprehensible horror.

"Tell her, Émile," Joseph said. "I cannot."

"We have no evidence other than what passes from one man's mouth to another's, but it is nearly certain nevertheless that in Russia there exist units called death squads. Thousands and thousands of Jews are being systematically worked to death building roads for the German army, but other thousands, no one knows how many, have been sent in front of firing squads and buried in mass graves. Liquidated for no other reason than that Hitler has ordered it. Wait. That is not the worst. Some of what are called labor camps are being turned into centers of extermination. Treblinka, in Poland, for one. The Warsaw Jews sent there are never heard from again. The trains that left Paris six weeks ago also went to Poland, to a place called Auschwitz. Apparently the prisoners are given postcards to address to their relatives, telling them that they are working and are being well treated. After the cards are written and signed, the prisoners are killed. Gassed to death, by some reports."

With her left hand Abby stifled the scream emerging from her mouth as a series of short, high-pitched whimperings, and with the right she made a fist that beat and pounded against the fragile cage within which her heart leaped and twisted under the blow Émile Vautrin had dealt her. The horror of it was that she believed him, believed without a moment's doubt in the hidden mass graves and the lungs bursting under the gas. Believed it so totally that he mistook her terror for denial.

"The Germans think they leave no witnesses, but a crime of that magnitude can never go entirely undetected. There are partisans in every country. They're scattered, disorganized, and largely ineffectual so far, but eyes in the forest nonetheless. They have reported trucks that drive slowly along the roads, screams from within them, and tangled masses of bodies pulled out when they finally stop. By itself that would not be enough, because often the partisans themselves are Jew-haters, but here and there, in some communities, there are Jewish partisans, remnants of Zionist organizations, a few young men and women who read the postcards and were not fooled by them. They followed the trains to some of these camps and saw and smelled what was being done there. At Auschwitz the camp commander is building shower rooms without water, and ovens in which to burn the corpses. Hardly anyone to whom they describe the scenes they witnessed is willing to accept what they say. I do. I've seen too much carnage on too many bodies to deny that man is capable of any monstrosity toward his own kind."

Her hands fell into her lap, bruised and numb, too weak to hold a glass or reach out to touch either of the men watching her. She thought they could see into her mind, could read what was written there, know what it was she had contemplated doing, was still, even now, prepared to do, and despised her. She was wrong, of course. They were simply waiting for the color to return to her face, waiting for her to tell them that she was all right, that she too could live with the horror as they had schooled themselves to do, waiting for her to pick up and begin to put together again the pieces of the world they had shattered. She managed at last to ask the only question she could. "Is Joseph in danger of being deported?"

"That's the one thing I don't know," Dr. Vautrin said. "I think he is."

"When?"

"You have time, Abby, but don't waste it. As soon as they decree the wearing of the star you'll know that deportation of all the foreign-born is imminent. The worst place to be when that happens will be a city. If the Gestapo forgets you, your neighbors will remind them."

"Please, Émile, how long?"

"A month, two at the most. My informant, before he realized that he had said too much, was bemoaning the fact that he would have to stay in Paris all summer."

"August, then?"

"I wouldn't count on that much time, Abby. If you have someplace to go, I think you should apply for travel permits immediately. I'll provide any medical certificates you may need. Doctors often prescribe country air when they don't know what else to do for a patient."

"Will you have another brandy before you go, Émile?" Joseph asked.

"Just a swallow. And for good measure I'll listen to your heart and take your blood pressure."

Abby heard them begin to talk again after she had left the bedroom. She found the bottle of cognac in the dining room and stood for a moment holding it, collecting herself, promising herself the night in which to think through and face what she did not dare consider now. Some piercing, persistent noise was knifing across her forehead, but not until she crossed the hallway and glanced toward the door did she recognize it as the ringing of the bell. And immediately knew that Stefan Helldorf was standing on the other side of the locks and the bar, demanding to be let in.

She was stone or steel, a pillar of salt or a frozen corpse. If the world kept on spinning and years went by, she would not move to open that door.

"Let him in, Abby." It was Dr. Vautrin whispering beside her, prying her fingers from the neck of the brandy bottle. "Don't be afraid of him."

"He's a murderer, Émile, a murderer of Jews."

"They're all murderers. Don't make him wait any longer. Open the door."

She ran her hands over her face, arranging the features as if they were clay she could mold into a mask. The heavy steel bar seemed weightless as she lifted it from its supports; one lock stuck and she tugged angrily at it, the other opened smoothly, noiselessly.

"Madame Kelemen." Click. The heels. He had glimpsed

the doctor standing behind her. "Forgive me for intruding, madame. I've had a telephone call." He held a key in his right hand, was putting it into her outstretched palm. Cold leather and colder metal chilling her. "I'm not sure that I'll be back before morning."

She nodded, unable to speak to him. The elevator door was propped open. Whoever or whatever had summoned him into the night was important. The flap of his holster was unbuttoned. She had never seen it loose like that except when he took it off. She was noting details, not the man, sharp pieces of what he was, all the things she had gradually come to ignore until now. The power of him, the sheen of the uniform, the light on his boots, the tailored gloves hiding his hands, the gun, the beak of his cap shading his eyes, the set of his jaw, the tight, high collar guarding his throat, most of all the gleaming insignia and the predatory eagle with wings outstretched.

He bowed to them once more, and then walked the few steps to the elevator. Abby felt her face begin to break apart; she wanted to leap at that vulnerable back and rip and claw until the uniform was in shreds and his blood and skin were under her fingernails. He looked up a fraction of a second before the automatic light on the landing went out. He hadn't seen the expression on her face, had been looking, in fact, not at her, but at the door of his own apartment. A blank stare, disbelief, some strong emotion just beginning to register.

"You did well, Abby," Dr. Vautrin said.

"I couldn't say anything. I wanted to kill him. If I'd had a weapon I would have done it."

"Come back inside. Pour yourself some brandy."

"I don't want anything to dull what I'm feeling."

She followed behind him, stumbling against the edge of a table because he had turned out the lights in the entrance-way, the dining room, the salon. She saw him outlined against the glass doors leading to the balcony, poised there, black against the deeper blackness outside, the curtain pulled aside an inch or two.

"Quickly, Abby. Is that his car pulling away from the curb?"

The same gray Mercedes in which he had driven her to Les Roses. A match flared in the back seat, the tip of a cigarette glowed red.

"Yes, that's him." The orderly drove very fast. Within seconds they could hear only the sound of the engine dying away in the direction of the Place de la Concorde.

"Good. I had to make sure he wasn't lying to us. You can turn the lights on again."

"What's happening, Émile?"

"Sit down. Drink the brandy. Slowly. I don't want you choking on it."

The marble top of the dining room table was cold beneath her hand. The glass left circles of amber liquid every time she set it down. She made a pattern of interlocking eights, not even aware of what she was doing.

"Are you all right now, Abby?" Joseph's hand rested lightly on the top of her head. His hair was newly tousled, stringy and unkempt-looking, the hair of a sick man who lies on pillows all day long. He wore a heavy sweater and had pinned a small blanket around his shoulders. All of him except his eyes looked ancient, halfway tumbled into the grave already. "In case the Hauptmann had come to pay a social call on the invalid," he explained.

The absurdity of it struck her, and she began to laugh, rocking back and forth in the chair, gasping, choking, spraying droplets of brandy across the marble, unable to stop, the place where she had locked away the screams breaking open, emptying itself in this exhausting laughter that was more painful than retching. He held her until the spasms grew weaker and finally stopped, until she wiped away the tears and the spittle with the corner of the blanket he wore, pulled away from him and sat up straight again, no longer blinded, terribly, acutely aware that she was burning alive in hell and could not, could never redeem herself.

"I must examine the Hauptmann's wife tonight," Dr. Vautrin said. "Now. She can't be allowed to know I've seen her."

"Why, Émile?"

"Trust us, Abby. Don't ask why. Can it be done?"

"Joseph?"

"Your face was never meant for keeping secrets, my darling. The less you know, the better."

"I can't take care of that woman anymore. I can't. I'll never be able to look at either of them and pretend anything but disgust."

"Abby, listen to me. Nothing must change. Everything must go on exactly as it has for the past three months. We need him. We need the travel permits. There may not be time, there may not even be a way to arrange for false documents."

"You're Joseph's lifeline, Abby."

She sat very still between them. The corners of the room were in shadow, even the edges of the table were indistinct in the dimmed light of the chandelier hanging above their heads. In Prince Nikolai's apartment above the Trocadéro she had sat like this, old men watching her, judging her, waiting for her to convince them that she was as capable, as strong as they. She remembered telling them that she needed this war, confessing, baring the insignificance and the waste of her life until then to a jury of Jews, Catholics, Russian exiles, men whose blood had been French for centuries. Lately she had experienced moments when it all seemed about to collapse, when she had begun to drift away from the hardness of her purpose, begun to tire of the game, forget that there were no respites, no little pleasures that could be snatched up along the way. Somewhere in France there must be patriots who went on and on until they dropped or died, single-minded, obsessed with justice, never losing sight of the goal toward which they strove and the vows they had pronounced. Did they ever want simply to give up and accept the excuse of being human? Were there Jewish saints? Were the squads in Russia, the SS killers lining the pits of the death camps, creating an army of holy men and women? And children.

"I'll give her more of the sedative she takes at night. She won't feel a thing, Émile. She'll never know you're there."

She had to wake up Marta Helldorf to make her swallow the sedative. Unless the dose was a massive one, her sleep was light, restless, a series of sudden awakenings, shallow dozes. She bathed the thin face with cool water, brushed the soft, flyaway hair, helped her put on a clean nightgown, even changed the wrinkled sheets and gave her one of the forbidden cigarettes. None of it was as difficult as she had thought it would be. She had done all these same things so often that her hands performed automatically.

"Sleep, Marta, and dream of cool dark forests in Germany," Abby said, smoothing a damp cloth over the hot forehead. Occasionally, on the edge of sleep like this, only that word registered. And through mumblings and broken bits of sentences Abby had stepped into Marta's childhood, into the intimacies of her marriage, into the few good years with Stefan before she had gotten so ill. Tonight, however, she tripled the strength of the sedative and deep sleep came quickly. She let fifteen minutes pass, counting off the seconds, watching the hand that moved so slowly across the dial of her watch. Marta's head lolled drunkenly when Abby shook her; there was no response when Abby called her name, no reaction at all to the sound of the heavy book she dropped.

Dr. Vautrin's examination was over so quickly that Abby could not even begin to guess what it was he was expecting to find. He listened to the heart and lungs first, but only briefly, paying more attention to the fingers and toes whose coldness he traced and retraced with his fingertips, following the blood, seeming to measure the point at which it began to warm the skin. His hands were gentle and swift, white angel's wings tapping, pressing, lifting the translucent, blue-veined eyelids.

"Cover her warmly," he said, standing back for one final look. "How long ago did she smoke this cigarette?" He held the partially consumed cylinder between thumb and forefinger, rolling it back and forth until the thin paper covering broke. It slipped from his fingers, fell to the floor, lay there amid scattered shreds of tobacco and ash.

"Twenty minutes before I let you in," Abby said.

"Poor creature. It only makes the condition worse, but they won't believe you when you tell them that." Like a priest administering extreme unction, he sketched the sign of the cross on Marta Helldorf's forehead.

"Émile?"

He shook his head and picked up his bag. "Stay with her for a few more minutes. Just in case the husband comes back."

That wasn't the reason he left her alone with the unconscious woman. He was no better at lying than Joseph had said she was. It was Joseph who had told him about Marta Helldorf, who had mentioned something so important and so surprising that the doctor had had to confirm it by examination. There was no point in trying to guess what it was; eventually they would have to tell her. She let it go, her mind too tired to wonder why cold, cramping hands and feet could interest them when time was running out and in some busy office an addition to the ration books was being printed. That would be the way they would do it, of course; a ticket to be exchanged for a scrap of yellow cloth; another way to check that every registered Jew had his star.

She smelled the coffee as soon as she opened the apartment door. Rich, heady, warm, it nauseated her because it had been bought so dearly, because it was the gift of a German officer, because she hadn't traded a piece of silver for it on the black market.

"I want you to tell me everything you know about Marta Helldorf," Dr. Vautrin commanded. "Not what the husband has said, but exactly what she remembers and talks about herself, especially what may seem disconnected and vague when the sedatives are wearing off."

"She's obsessed with death," Abby began. "One of the first things she said to me was that funerals dotted her life like signposts along a road. She thinks she has tuberculosis. She claims she can feel her lungs rotting, that large pieces of them are pulling loose and floating free inside her. She remembers the private clinic he told me about; she was afraid because they kept her apart from the other patients, in a little cottage somewhere on the grounds. Every time she woke up she heard a woman weeping."

"Go back further. To her childhood."

"A lake. Swans. Is that important? Someone died when she was very, very small, and then almost immediately some-one else. A black dress was cut down for her by a servant, and she cried and cried because there were still pins in it and they stuck into her during the funeral. Then she was happy again, but in another house. There was a train ride, and when she woke up, a roomful of toys and no more black dresses. People called her by a different name at first, but later she couldn't remember any other, just the idea that there had been one."

"Foster parents who adopted the child when her real mother and father died. And perhaps not related to her in any way," Émile Vautrin said. "I've arranged similar adoptions myself. If it's a baby or a very young child, they often grow up without ever being told about it."

"Do you think Helldorf knows?" Joseph asked.

"I'm sure of it. A document left undestroyed, an old servant with a very long memory. But he'll have done his best to make sure the records no longer exist in Germany. The only clue is the girl's own heredity. If she could, I'm certain she'd tell us that her hands and feet have always been cold, but that she assumed everyone else's were also, that it became worse as she grew into adulthood. What do you know about the husband's family, Abby?"

"Nothing at all. He speaks French without an accent. He's seen duty in North Africa."

"His parents may have been colonists there," Joseph said. "I remember meeting German settlers when I was in the Legion. We know he's been sent back several times. It's very likely that he speaks Arabic. The only other clue we have is the name of a village written on a piece of paper that Abby found in his apartment. The place is about three miles from the Swiss border, on the German side."

"An escape route?"

"Probably. Something must have prevented him from being able to use it."

"His wife's condition," Émile Vautrin said. "He waited too long."

"Is she really as ill as he claims?" Abby asked. "Is she dying?"

"In the ordinary way of things, I'd say she can't last more than three or four months."

"You're talking in riddles, Émile."

"Yes, I am. Deliberately so, Abby. Marta Helldorf has three separate death sentences hanging over her. One of them I don't think she even knows about herself. Some saint of a German doctor discovered it and never recorded it on any of her charts. Obviously, if he was to save her for a more natural death, he had to tell the only person who could protect her. And he did. She does have tuberculosis, but it's not a particularly hard disease to die from, at least not until the end. The woman she heard weeping in her cottage was Marta herself. As her body weakened, so did her mind. She undoubtedly walked a mental tightrope all her young life; she was bound to lose her balance eventually. If Hitler hadn't introduced the needle as an ultimate and final solution for mental instability, she might have been cured in time. Who can say? A sanatorium high in the Alps; cold, thin air for the lungs; a year or two for the soul to heal itself under the guidance of a psychiatrist. I think the husband has done the best he could under the circumstances. Sedatives." Émile Vautrin shook his head sadly. "I'd administer them myself if I were asked to. I hope and pray she escapes the other death."

Abby's head was whirling. Her eyes burned when she tried to focus them. "You're not going to tell me any more, are you?" she said. "I'm not to know as much as you do, am I? Why not? I've come this far, Joseph."

"And I can't let you go any further. At least not yet. Not tonight. One slip of the tongue, Abby, when you're tired or angry, and we'd lose the only advantage we have. You won't be able to reveal what you don't know."

"Go to bed, Abby," Émile Vautrin said. "I'll give you something to help you sleep. You need the rest."

She could hear them talking, the clink of spoons against cups, the sound of brandy being poured. In her nightgown, barefoot, unable to stretch her tired body out on the bed, she stood in the doorway of her bedroom listening, but only as Dr. Vautrin was leaving was she able to make out what they said.

"I think it's too great a risk, Joseph. It's blackmail, pure and simple, and there's always the possibility that he'll turn on you and do the Gestapo's work himself."

"I won't use it unless I have no other alternative. If it comes to that, he'll have to be told that I've entrusted documents containing the information to someone who will inform the Gestapo if anything happens to me."

"Will you?"

"No. I couldn't do that to any human being, especially not to one of my own kind. His wife's as much a victim of Germany's madness as I am, but at least I know it. I don't think he'll call the bluff."

"How can you be sure? You've never met him."

"Abby. I can read him through her."

"It would make things easier for her if she knew the truth about him."

"You'll have to trust my judgment, Émile. She goes out to fight for me every single day. I don't know where or how she finds the strength to keep on fighting, but I tell you frankly that I don't dare to weaken her in any way. Once you begin to pity your enemy, you might as well hand over your weapon and have done with it. You know I'm right."

"Make sure she applies for the travel permits soon. You're going to have to start dying again in earnest, Joseph. I'll have a new report ready tomorrow, and I'll tell Madame Dupont tonight that my optimism was premature. Nothing less than a clinic in the country will do you any good. It'll be all over the building by morning."

She was sitting on the edge of her bed waiting for him when Joseph came to the door of the room. He refused to answer any of her questions.

The gallery light that illuminated Abby's portrait burned all night long. She waited patiently for some trace of age or experience of life to appear on the painted face, but it never changed. She watched the sun come up over Paris, and discovered that the city too was exactly as it had been the day before. Perhaps the secret of Notre Dame's gargoyles was precisely that they had no secrets to tell. Their blind eyes saw nothing, recorded nothing, revealed nothing. She didn't know any more about the secret that Joseph and Émile Vautrin shared than she had the night before, and now she decided to guard her ignorance as jealously as some people sought enlightenment. Pity your enemy and you might as well hand over your weapons and be done with it.

She would go alone to request the travel permits, armed with the new papers Émile Vautrin would provide, knowing that the chances of their being granted were slimmer than any gambler would have been willing to bet on. Parisians returned to stand in the same long lines at German headquarters day after day for months and got no more than a laconic response to their questions. The requests they presented were in an eternal maw of being processed. A dying mother or father was usually long buried before the plea to be allowed to visit the patient was even denied.

In spite of what was happening in those places she had never heard of before, the camps at Treblinka and Auschwitz and God knew how many others, in spite of the gunfire echoing over the Russian steppes she had never seen, Abby must continue to care for Marta Helldorf, must tend her body and wandering mind as devotedly as if she did not bear the stigma of being German. Nothing, Joseph had emphasized, nothing could change. For months she had spent no more than a few hours a day in her own apartment; if she could bear it, they must be even fewer. A debt was being built up, Joseph had said, and before they were forced to call it in, they must be sure payment would be prompt.

This new, colder Abby told herself that she could, would lie with Stefan Helldorf in every hotel room on both banks of the river. She would promise anything, swear to anything, even to loving him. Joseph would not choke to death inside a truck driving slowly through a dark forest, would not walk into the waterless showers of a camp in Poland. Listening to herself, she waited for heart, conscience, honor to cry out against it, but there was only silence. So be it. If any of them ever awoke again, she would still be listening.

She went to the first Mass at Notre Dame, dropping a coin into the basket of the beggar nun half-asleep in the vestibule, murmuring "Pray for me" because it was what the sister was accustomed to hearing. She needed to lose herself in the greatest cathedral in Christendom, not to be too close to the altar in a tiny parish church. You could empty your mind while the priest droned out the Latin prayers on your behalf, made the sacrifice, served as a conduit for the blessing that flowed from his hands making the sign of the cross above your head. She had no right to take Communion, but confession was impossible. Someday a priest would bend across her bed, ask her to think of her sins and signal to him with the flick of an eyelid that she repented of them. That would have to be confession enough. The Host dissolved on her tongue, a dry, paper-thin wafer that had to be swallowed whole. It slid down her throat, the bread becoming physically a part of her, the greater mystery escaping. Her anger and her purpose were too cold and too hard to find the old comfort in it now.

She was early at the *boulangerie;* there was still bread warm to the touch. Stefan Helldorf's gray Mercedes swung over to the curb as she came out; she rode the last three blocks home beside him.

16

Debts. In times like these you called them in by inches, and prayed they would be honored. "I want someone to take my place caring for Marta Helldorf," Abby told Émile Vautrin. "Not every day, not all day long, but someone who can come whenever I call."

"Will he allow that, Abby? And why? What are you planning?"

"You and Joseph have secrets, Émile. So must I."

Because he had known her since the earliest days of her marriage, because he did not doubt the sincerity of her love for her husband, Émile Vautrin crossed himself and agreed to help her, agreed also to say nothing to Joseph. He confided only in his own wife, and she too crossed herself. "It means nothing, my love. I would do the same for you if I thought it would protect you, if there were any German who coveted wrinkles and ancient flesh."

"The order of nuns who staff your hospital, Émile," Abby said. "You told me they have orphanages, old age homes, schools. Beg the Mother Superior for a nursing sister. Tell her whatever you must, whatever you think safe. Bribe her with these." He glimpsed a handful of glittering stones before Abby slipped them into the pocket of his jacket. "She has parentless children to feed, hungry nuns, the ill and the dying whose ration coupons can't possibly stretch far enough to purchase the special foods they need. I know these women who have spent their lives serving God. They rob Peter to pay Paul and pray that Peter's chest will be filled again by faith. Try, Émile."

The old nun did not hesitate, but she drove a surprisingly shrewd bargain. "We cannot spare any of the nursing sisters who are currently working in our hospitals," she told the doctor. "We are able to maintain a certain degree of autonomy only because they need us; there are not enough lay nurses. I have one sister here with me now who might suit your purpose. She is young, she doesn't possess a nursing degree, but she is very capable. She came to us from the Motherhouse, on a temporary leave from other duties because of illness. Nothing serious; we fully expect that she will make her final vows."

Sister Paul-Marie was in her mid-twenties, Émile Vautrin guessed, a slender young woman on whom religious decorum seemed oddly strained. He had spent all of his medical career working with nuns, and this one bothered him. Her hands were hidden in her sleeves as they should be, her eyes were cast down, she walked with small, self-effacing steps, but she was alive to the room she entered, intensely aware of the elderly man whose hand she briefly and passionlessly shook. She could describe every line of my face, Émile Vautrin thought, she's memorized me with one quick glance. But her voice, when she spoke, was so low that he had to strain to hear, and her fingers wrapped themselves around the rosary hanging from her waist, as though to slip in a Hail Mary while she waited to be told what to do.

It was the middle finger of her right hand that told him what she really was. A barely noticeable stain, but one he had never expected to find, one he had never before seen on the finger of a nun. She smoked heavily, this nun who was not a nun, and any good Catholic with a sharp eye for what nuns did and did not do would spot the discrepancy. He was being offered a member of the Resistance in hiding, a girl with a Gestapo dossier probably, a Sister Paul-Marie whose real name he would never know. He shivered for a moment in the cold faith of the Mother Superior's duplicity, and then he agreed. He wouldn't tell Abby; he too could keep secrets.

She expected Stefan Helldorf to fight her about the nun, but he did not. "I'm exhausted," she told him. "I have to have some relief." She was thinner now than she had ever been in her life, pale the way women grow who never leave the artificial light of their homes, pared down to unpadded flesh over delicate, birdlike bone. She had the ethereal, otherworldly look of a fey young girl on the brink of adolescence, and the red-gold hair was turning a deeper shade of auburn with every month passed without sunlight. She would be thirty-nine years old in September, but she had never looked her age; sometimes, catching a glimpse of herself in a mirror, she felt deceived by time. Surely that was the very, very young woman who had danced for Sammy Rosen looking back at her.

"I'm hungry for Paris in the spring," she said, "for the smell of flowers and the sight of lovers strolling by the river."

"You can't go out alone," he told her.

"Why not? The streets are safer than they've ever been. Your army has made them that way."

He nodded. "Safe for ordinary women, but not for you."

She knew what he meant, had counted on it. Paris was flooded with German soldiers and officers on leave, Hitler's promise made fact. From the windows of her apartment she had seen them staring after even ugly girls, had seen the self-assured way they followed them, spoke to them, sometimes demanded identity papers in order to find out a name, an address. It was the officers who were the most dangerous; they weren't accustomed to being refused, and even the lowest-ranking of them were aware of the fear they inspired.

"I could show you a Paris you would never see by yourself," she said.

"Why?" he asked. "Why now, madame? Abby."

She shrugged her shoulders. "It's spring, Herr Hauptmann. Stefan. No one who has spent a spring in Paris is ever quite the same again, and no one ever forgets it. Even Parisians themselves never grow immune to it."

"Let the nun come tomorrow," he said. "I'll speak to her, but I promise nothing. Not yet."

She had him, and she knew it. Her allies had been the city itself and the sick woman with whom he closed himself up every night. Once he entered the apartment where she lay, he did not leave it until morning. Closed up with a dying wife he did not love while all around him other men in uniforms exactly like his crowded into restaurants and cabarets and spent the lonely hours after midnight in the arms of women and girls who might not love, but who were expert at pretending they did. They traded their bodies for protection and food and money to survive, especially the very young, because when the uniform was taken off, there was a man like

any other beneath it. Stefan Helldorf had seemed to age in
Paris, while Abby, except in mind and heart, had grown
younger.

Scentless, sexless in her black habit, almost faceless within
the depths of her starched white coif, Sister Paul-Marie answered Helldorf's questions in whispered monosyllables, eyes
on the scuffed toes of her worn shoes, head bowed, hands
tucked into her sleeves. She spoke no German, she said, and
no, she was not a real nurse, but she had sat beside the beds
of many sick old nuns in the infirmary of the Motherhouse.

"Madame sleeps in the afternoon," Abby told her. "There
is nothing for you to do but be here in case she awakens."

"She won't," Helldorf said, and Abby knew that he had
increased the strength of the sedative she took at noon.

The nun settled herself in a straight-backed chair beside
Marta's bed, rosary trailing across her lap, leather-covered
Holy Office already in one hand, the other hand moving from
forehead to breast to left and then right shoulder, beginning
to pray even before the apartment door closed behind them.

They went to the Quai de la Mégisserie that afternoon,
to the stalls of the booksellers where Abby had found strength
so many years before when her world had lain in ruins
around her feet. Nothing had changed. That part of Paris was
as eternal as its cathedrals. The same stout, red-cheeked
women, the same pipe-smoking men with dark-blue berets
worn slightly off-center, identical barges on the river, trees
leafed out with the descendants of the leaves that had shaded
Abby then. If you could will yourself not to see the German
uniforms, not to hear the guttural, mangled French with
which they bargained, you might be able to believe that the
city was still free. As they walked, seldom speaking at first,
Abby caught the stares—polite, envious, hastily broken off
because beside her was a man no brother German officer
would challenge. And finally, Helldorf took her arm in his, as
he had done in the forest at Les Roses.

They went out together frequently after that, several
afternoons a week. Sister Paul-Marie was always available,
always the same, a black-and-white presence still murmuring
prayers when they returned, assuring them that no, madame
had not awakened. Once, in the second week, they were
sitting on the terrace of a café. Ten feet away, at another of
the spindly metal tables, sat a German major and a French

girl much younger than he. When they got up to leave, the major smiled at Helldorf. One eye closed, a sly, knowing wink. They watched the couple cross the boulevard and disappear into a doorway. Above the entrance was the name of the hotel, and moments later another German, French-woman on his arm, also approached and entered. Abby felt her cheeks flame, and then the touch of Stefan Helldorf's hand on hers. But he did not ask, and when she looked at him, she thought she read pain in the eyes where she had expected to see heat and a question.

Joseph knew nothing, but still Abby worried. She hid the faint blush of sunlight on her skin with white powder, and she filled the evening hours with the sound of the radio and the rattle of newspapers. He would have to be told eventually, of course, but not yet, perhaps not until Abby had the travel permits she would ask Helldorf to get for them. Three or four months, Émile had said; Marta Helldorf would be dead in three or four months. In a little over two months it would be August, the farthest limit of the safe time Émile had predicted remained to them. It was probably a sin to pray for someone else's death, but she had whispered, "Pray for my intentions," to the nun one day, and Sister Paul-Marie had nodded, innocent, unwitting accomplice.

Often, looking up from her newspaper or leaning over to place a tray of food before him, she thought she saw in Joseph an older Stefan Helldorf. The first time it happened she spilled his wine over her fingers. Fatigue, she thought. She was seeing Helldorf everywhere she looked and even in the well-beloved face of her husband. He had even come to invade her dreams, and sometimes the two faces hung side by side in blackness, Joseph as he was now, but growing younger until he was the hawk-faced Arab she had thought him to be at Longchamps. And then the young German and the young Hungarian Jew floated toward one another, merged so perfectly that they became one face, one man the reddish-blond hair of the one eaten up and overpowered by the black hair of his double. Maybe it was true that somewhere in the world was a double of every person who lived, that there were only so many differences of bone structure, and twins of different parents, different countries must be inevitable. Some-times the impression of similarity persisted into daylight. She had to force herself not to study Stefan Helldorf's face the way she studied her own. If the dream continued, if it robbed her of the few hours of restless sleep she managed every night, she would ask Émile Vautrin for relief, some of the magic pills that allowed Marta Helldorf to escape the world.

On May 31 she left the apartment early in the morning, instructing the nun to tell Hauptmann Helldorf, if he called, that she had gone to Dr. Vautrin's office for some urgently needed medicine. She wrote out the telephone number in case there should be an emergency. Émile had been warned and would know what to say.

In the lavatory of the métro station she wrapped her shoes in newspaper and put on a pair of shapeless brogues she had worn in the garden at Les Roses. She washed the makeup from her face, covered her bright hair with a faded scarf, and slipped her arms into the sweater Joseph had worn the night Émile Vautrin had told them about Auschwitz. She wore no jewelry, and with her teeth she chewed at her fingernails until they were short and ragged, rubbing the grime of the walls into the skin on the backs of her hands. No one, seeing her as she was now, would have taken her for anything but another shabby Jewess among the crowds standing in line to be handed their bits of yellow cloth.

Women fainted as the morning grew hotter, bearded old men wearing black hats and long curls swayed back and forth as if at prayer, children cried out to be taken to the bathroom, and hungry babies wailed. Tomorrow the wearing of the Star of David, sewn over the heart, prominently displayed, the directive specified, would become obligatory all over the occupied zone. Today the Jews of Paris stared at one another, the knowledge of what had been done in Poland leaping from their eyes. Tonight, after curfew, each family would sit watching needles flash as thousands of women marked their loved ones' clothing.

Numbly, late in the afternoon, hours since she had taken her place in line, Abby pushed Joseph's ration book and Dr. Vautrin's sworn affidavit that this Jew was bedridden across the counter behind which a clerk was too tired to do more than glance at another middle-aged woman. The smell of ink was strong enough to make her giddy; she hadn't thought to fill the pockets of her sweater with food as these other Jews, accustomed to unending lines, had done. The man behind her had offered her a piece of bread sometime around noon, but she hadn't been able to take it from him. He was too thin, almost emaciated, and in his arms he held a little boy with huge, hungry eyes. Stamp, and it was over. She shoved the ration book deep into her purse and stepped aside. The man with the child said something to her in Yiddish that sounded like a blessing. He had glimpsed the photo pasted into the ration book, seen that only one transaction took place, and recognized her for a Christian woman sparing her Jewish husband.

"I want to sew it on myself," Joseph insisted. He smiled. "Every legionnaire learns to be as good a seamstress as his mother."

"Over the heart," Abby said quietly.

"I know."

His stitches were neat and tiny, almost invisible. Point by point, the yellow star grew onto the jacket he had selected from the many hanging unworn in his armoire. He had insisted that it be done, in spite of Abby's protestations that it wasn't necessary, that he would never be exposed on a public street. "It's better to be prepared," he said, "to take their new edict seriously. And Miklós would be proud to know I've accepted it."

During the first three weeks of June, Abby took Stefan Helldorf to the hidden corners of the Paris she knew and loved so well. They rode the métro or hired one of the vélocabs that had replaced privately owned automobiles. Sometimes they walked along the river or brought a picnic lunch to the Bois. Since the night that Abby had watched Joseph sew the Star of David to his coat, she had avoided cafés, museums, and especially the Champs-Èlysées. Too many Germans in one place gave her claustrophobia. For a few days there seemed to be no Jews anywhere in the city, but gradually they began to appear again. You could see the star on their clothing from a long way off, bright, bright yellow, like a sunburst or a flower until you discerned the shape of it. They were not yet officially forbidden to mingle with the Aryan population in public places, but that, too, was coming; everyone knew it would be the subject of the next edict. In anticipation, and to avoid the jeers that inevitably greeted them, many Jews left their homes only for work or the most necessary of errands.

In at least one way Stefan Helldorf was unlike most other soldiers and officers of the occupation. It came to Abby slowly, but she began to watch him closely whenever there was a Jew nearby or walking toward them along the street. He seemed not to see them, not to be aware of them at all, never to become suddenly, critically alert as she had noticed was commonplace among even the lowest-ranking soldiers. Nor did he place himself deliberately in a Jew's path, claiming the entire width of the sidewalk, forcing the man or woman to step into the gutter in order to pass by. Not once did he turn around to mock a fleeing Jew; he even seemed not to hear the epithets that made her ears flame and her heart thud erratically. It baffled her. She remembered what he had once called Hanne. Yet now that the hated species was more visible than ever before, he paid no attention to them.

The Bois was the best place to be, and also the most disturbing. Fathers in undershirts and sons in short pants kicked soccer balls back and forth on open, grassy flat places, laughing and calling out instructions, ending the games with arms around each other's waists and shoulders; but there were lovers there also, sprawled on blankets beneath the trees or asleep in the sun, heads touching, fingers entwined. Except for taking her arm when they walked together, Stefan Helldorf had not touched Abby since the day they had seen the men and their whores going into the hotel. It was as if an invisible but stern and watchful chaperone accompanied them everywhere they went. She had come to trust his control even while she did not understand it.

She let him into her life with safe confidences, laundering her past, lingering over good memories, manufacturing a childhood he never questioned, beginning and ending every conversation with Joseph's name, as if it were a talisman, the essential word in a spell of enchantment. And very, very gradually, he had begun to speak about his past also, about the days before the war began, hints of the person he had ceased to be when he put on his country's uniform for the first time.

He sought the sun, drank it up while she sat in the feathery edges of shade, close enough to be able to hear each other's breathing, but with a tiny stretch of neutral space separating them. His hair had begun to bleach; his skin was golden brown. Soon, she thought, it would be as dark as it had been the first time she saw him. "I've always envied people who could sit in the sun without burning," she said. "I've never been able to do that."

"You have to be born in a country where the sun kills or cures you like a piece of leather." He laughed, then sobered quickly. "It ages women."

"Were you born in a place like that, Stefan?" He had mentioned a boarding school in Bavaria once, where he had learned to ski and to drink stolen milk hot from a cow's udder, where most of the other boys looked forward eagerly to holidays with their families, and only two or three, like him, stayed on, unwanted, the pocket money doled out to them once a month and an occasional letter the only proof that they were not entirely alone in the world. But farther back than that he had never gone.

She thought he was sleepy from the bottle of wine they had drunk. His eyes were closed, his speech a little slurred, like that of a child protesting that it will not nap even while nestling down into the soft haven of loving arms. "It could be bitterly cold in the winter, and in the summer so hot and bright and the air so thin that you could burn your finger on a stone. My father sent me to Europe when I was ten. I never went back, not to that place."

"It's a hard thing when a parent dies," Abby said, not knowing, but guessing, hoping that Stefan's father was dead and that the remembrance of loss would prod him to speak.

"Not that one," Helldorf said bitterly, as if the man were standing there behind his closed eyelids. "I hated him. And his friend. My father's people used to stare at me as I grew older, and make the sign against the evil eye when I passed."

She thought she had misunderstood him; the perfect French had become oddly accented, as though his mind were thinking in another language and his lips were awkward translators. "My father had a terrible temper," she said. "It frightened me when I was small. My mother always made the peace between us."

What he said next was completely incomprehensible. She had never before heard that particular combination of sounds. It wasn't German; it was another language entirely.

And then, in English, with a trace of a lilt that shocked her because it was so like Bridget's, "They said she died when I was born. Her grave was on the hillside. I used to dream sometimes that he had killed her."

She was afraid to go on, afraid to ask another question. And wondering too how she would tell Joseph what she had learned, because tell him she must. The words Helldorf had spoken in that unknown tongue she had seized on with her good ear for languages and stored away as carefully as the phrases from the first lessons in French that Marie-Claire had given her so long ago. Joseph could pinpoint the province, sometimes even the town a man came from, simply by his accent or the way he turned a phrase. She sighed, lulled herself by the wine. All these weeks she had deceived him, spared him the knowledge of what she had been doing and with whom. Confession would be hard, but she could end it with the phrase "Nothing else," and with her eyes assure him that it was true.

"Abby?" Helldorf had pushed himself onto one elbow, was leaning toward her, half in sunlight, half in shadow.

"Yes?"

"I think it's almost over, this spring we've had together."

"Are you leaving Paris?"

"Eventually. Soon, perhaps."

"And Marta?"

"When I know that I must leave, I'll make other arrangements for her. Another safe place in which to die."

"I'm sorry."

"You said that once before. I didn't believe you then."

"And now?"

"Perhaps a little. I want to see your husband before I go. I want the sight of that sick old man to be as much a part of this spring as the sight of you."

"I can't let you, Stefan. It might kill him."

"Why do I doubt that, Abby? Why do I think he's as healthy as the Jews we know are paying dearly for clinic beds in which to lie and wait for our defeat? It will never happen; we'll have them all finally."

"Why do you want them? What harm have they ever done to you or your country?"

"It doesn't matter. The Führer has marked them, and

the rest of the world doesn't care. They're expendable; we're all expendable."

"No, Stefan. Every human life is sacred. The day you force your way into Joseph's bedroom is the day our truce ends. You won't kill him, or if you do, you'll kill me also."

His fingers touched the empty wine bottle lying on its side between them. He rolled it back and forth, and Abby watched, fascinated, as the grass flattened and died under the swift, hard strokes. "I told myself I didn't care that you were only playing a game with me, that every smile was forced and every hour we spent together was torture for you. I thought, you see, that the springtime magic you spoke of might begin to work on you in spite of yourself. It hasn't. It never will. I think I've accepted that now."

"I promised you nothing."

"Agreed. I only hoped that you would change, that you would soften." So low that it was almost not spoken speech at all, he added, "Begin to love me."

She said nothing, all the courage and the coldness she had been nurturing in herself suddenly gone. She could do it, she could still do it if he were to take her hand and lead her away from the Bois to one of those cheap hotels where rooms were rented by the hour, but she sensed that it would be a more bitter, an even more empty act for him than for her. And then, suddenly attuned to him as she always was to Joseph, she knew that it would never happen, knew that she was safe.

"I *will* see him, Abby, before I go. Tell him that, prepare him. He won't die of the shock, and neither will you. I have to know, that's all, I have to know."

They didn't speak again until they reached the apartment building. His hand touched her elbow lightly, momentarily, guiding her into métro cars, through jostling crowds in the stations, past other Germans who might have been attracted to the beautiful woman in the white, summery dress. Once, when two young men holding hands like lovers brushed past them, she felt him shudder violently, felt him draw back from the accidental contact. His jaw worked spasmodically, a deep, growling noise came from his throat. No one else in the car seemed to notice the young men. Centuries ago, Paris had learned to accept all kinds of lovers.

Madame Dupont beckoned to Abby, stepping back inside the hot little room that was no more than a cubicle of glass hung with transparent, gauzy curtains. It smelled of cat and old-woman odor.

"That nun, madame," the concierge whispered, holding up one of the new kittens, angling her head so the German could not read her lips, "she had a visitor today. A man I've never seen before came. I listened to the elevator. He seemed to know where he was going. He was here for only a few minutes, then left in a great hurry."

"What are you warning me of, Madame Dupont?"

"Just a feeling I have. One of my nieces is a Daughter of Charity. They breed certain things out of you in the religious life. That one still has them."

"What did she want?" Helldorf asked. The elevator creaked and groaned.

"More scraps for the kittens. The mother cat is weaning them. They're hungry, and madame doesn't have the heart to drown them."

He lit a cigarette, pulling on it deeply, filling the elevator with a cloud of smoke. "So now we have to feed the cats of Paris too," he said. "At least they're more useful than dogs."

"There aren't any rats, not even many mice left in the city." She had seen the skinned bodies that black marketeers claimed were squirrels or tender young rabbits. Her eyes still ached from the brightness of the Bois; the smoke irritated them and she waved it away from her face.

"Sorry."

A door opened and shut two floors above them, and a moment later they heard the sharp buzz of someone ringing for the elevator. Only the door to the Kelemen apartment made that distinctively heavy, final sound, the steel inside the wood absorbing, deadening normal echoes.

"We haven't been formally introduced, Herr Hauptmann," Dr. Vautrin said, "but you should know that your generosity has probably saved my patient's life. Madame has told me of your kindness to her." He was giving no indication that he was aware of how that generosity had been repaid. "You're fortunate not to have been cooped up inside a building all day. I've never seen Paris more beautiful. Of course we Parisians say that every spring, but every spring we mean it. Were you at the races?"

"The Bois," Abby answered, watching Stefan crush out his cigarette in the metal ashtray attached to the wall. It was full already and the butt teetered on the edge, a tiny wisp of smoke curling from a thread of tobacco that continued to burn.

"A wise choice. I used to ride there every morning before my bones got so brittle that my wife made me give it up. I'll give you a piece of advice, Herr Hauptmann. Don't ever grow old. The women take your pleasures from you one by one until all you have left is a glass of watered wine in the evenings." Émile Vautrin laughed at the nagging of devoted old wives, seemingly content to remain there on the landing with them, giving himself a respite before hurrying away to other patients. "I found monsieur better today," he said, "a little stronger, sleeping longer at night, he tells me." The curl of smoke from the ashtray caught his eye, and with his fine, thin physician's fingers he extinguished it, catching what was left of the cigarette as it started to roll off the heap of ash and other butts. "I suggested to madame a few weeks ago that she take him into the country for a month or so this summer. Paris can become an oven in July and August. I tell all my heart patients that. Have you done anything about it, Abby?"

How clever he was. "I've made a request for travel permits," she said, "but I was told it would probably be weeks before anyone with authority even considered it."

"Where do you want to go, madame?" Stefan Helldorf asked.

"Nowhere near Les Roses. It would be too painful."

"I recommend Brittany," Dr. Vautrin said. "Some little village or town not too far from the sea. Fresh, clean air, warm days, nights so cool that you have to sleep under a down quilt. I can check on clinics in the area, if you like. What do you think, Herr Hauptmann? Perhaps you can persuade her."

Stefan Helldorf said nothing. He was staring at the cigarette Dr. Vautrin had forgotten to put back into the ashtray, watching the cylinder roll between forefinger and thumb, an absentminded series of movements of which the doctor seemed unaware. The paper was coming apart, shreds of tobacco were drifting onto the marble floor, a little flurry of them falling like brown snow, followed by a flutter of disintegrated paper.

"Herr Hauptmann?"

"I think Brittany sounds ideal, Herr Doktor," Stefan Helldorf said. His voice was devoid of enthusiasm or interest. "If madame will permit, I will do what I can to expedite the granting of her request. And now, if you will excuse me?" He bowed to each of them, Abby last. Her hand lifted for the kiss with which he always greeted or left her, but for the first time since he had come into her life, he did not take it. He stood for a moment in the open doorway of his apartment, looking back at them as if waiting for something else to be said. They heard his footsteps in the hall behind the closed door, and then silence.

"You can't wait much longer, Abby," Émile Vautrin said. "He'll get the permits for you. Very soon. They're the most efficient people in the world when they want to be."

"She's gone, Joseph. Her bed is empty."

"What are you talking about, Abby? Here. You're shaking." He held her, stroking her hair until the tremors died away into weak shudders. "Now tell me what happened."

"There's no one in the apartment. The door was unlocked. I looked in all the rooms, but she's not there. His bed hasn't been slept in, there are clothes spilling out from the armoire, and all the medicines are missing. She's gone. He's taken her away. What does it mean?"

"It means that somehow he's found out about the night you helped Émile to examine her."

"That doesn't make sense."

"Yes, it does, Abby. It's the only explanation that makes perfect sense."

"But only yesterday afternoon Émile was telling him about Brittany. He offered to help us get our permits."

"Something one of you said must have given us away."

"No, Joseph, that's not possible. We never even mentioned her name."

"It doesn't matter how he found out. Go back to the apartment. Be quick, but search it thoroughly. Look for anything, scraps of paper, notes beside the telephone. Then go down to Madame Dupont. She must have seen or heard something."

*   *   *

"Early this morning, Madame Kelemen. I wasn't even dressed yet," the concierge said. "He pounded on the glass and demanded the key to the front door. I always lock it every night at curfew."

"Was he alone?"

"No, no, madame. He had his wife with him. Poor thing, she could hardly walk. She sat on that bench there while he went outside. The soldier who drives his car came back in with him to carry the suitcases."

"Did he say anything to you? Did you hear him tell the orderly where they were going?"

"Not a word, madame, except to ask for the key. But I talked to the wife for a moment. She seemed very confused and she was crying. I couldn't understand half of what she said. Her French is very bad."

"Please try to remember, madame. It's important or I wouldn't be asking you. Please."

"Is it the Gestapo?"

"It could be."

"Well, then." Madame Dupont's hands riffled through her gray hair, pulling out the pins of her neat bun, kneading at her scalp as if to force her brain to remember what, half-asleep, she had barely taken notice of. "She was very confused, as I said. I think she was begging me not to let him send her back to a hospital. What hospital, madame?"

"I don't know. Somewhere in Germany. Didn't she say anything else? Anything?"

"Not that I could understand. It was very sad, madame. Her mind. We saw many women like that after the last war. Vague, helpless, in and out of clinics all the time, wasting away because there was no cure for that kind of illness." Madame Dupont's shoulders slumped. "He wasn't as bad as some of the others, her husband. He carried her in his arms to the car. Very tenderly, I thought."

Abby stood in line at German headquarters every day. No matter how early she went, there was always a crowd already waiting, men and women shuffling forward without saying a word to one another, amazingly patient Parisians wholly unlike the volatile, impetuous people they had once been. Every day it was the same. Nothing. No permits, no promise that they would ever be issued, no information at all about how far the request had traveled through the bureaucracy. She used up all the food stored in her pantry, stole without a qualm every grain of rice and scrap of hardened cheese from the apartment across the hall. When nothing else remained, she set the lock and pulled the door closed behind her for the last time.

Madame Dupont left. "I don't want to, madame," she wept, "not after twenty years, but they've given me no choice. They say I was never properly registered as a resident of this quarter. Twenty years, and suddenly not a resident!" She was indignant, trying to pack all the belongings of her tiny apartment into one trunk and two suitcases, the cat and her kittens mewling in a wicker basket. "My sister's grandchildren are hellions. I've gotten used to my privacy."

Each tenant was given his own key to the front door. After a few days, fingerprints smudged the heavy glass, and bits of mud and dirt from the street accumulated on the unswept marble floors that had once been kept polished to a high gloss. Three or four times Abby thought she heard footsteps on the staircase long after curfew, but the landing was always dark when she looked through the peephole and she did not dare open the door. Even during a war, she thought, Frenchmen must visit their mistresses.

On July 8, another edict further restricted the lives of the city's Jews. The text was printed in all the newspapers, plastered onto the walls of the métro stations, tacked up on every kiosk. A people who had contributed so much to the country's artistic vitality was forbidden attendance at theatrical presentations and concerts. Their children could no longer escape the heat in public swimming pools; the parks were closed to them; all sporting events; even the vast stretches of the Bois de Boulogne and the Bois de Vincennes. The shops in some quarters were virtually empty except for the one hour every afternoon when Jews were permitted to shop.

Almost hysterical, Abby had to choose each morning whether to join the lines at German headquarters or spend hours trying to buy a soup bone and a handful of vegetables. She didn't dare risk the black market. What if she were picked up, detained overnight or for several days? Joseph could not leave the apartment without putting on the coat to which he had sewn the Star of David. She had seen what abuse elderly Jewish men suffered. The thought of Joseph falling beneath German boots tormented her.

She had told Joseph about her wooing of Stefan Helldorf, and instead of the anger she had expected, there was only laughter. "I knew about it almost from the beginning," he said. "You had such an air of purpose about you. I wore Émile down until he finally confessed his part in the conspiracy."

"I didn't want you to worry, I didn't want you to lie here wondering."

"I never did, Abby. You were as safe with him as you would have been with Émile. He loved you, still does, wherever he is."

"How could you know that, Joseph?"

"I knew. It was inevitable. I knew the first night he came here. How old did you say he was? Thirty, perhaps a bit more? I was only a little older than that when we met, but I remember what the sight of you did to me. I've aged, my love, but you haven't. You're still the girl in the portrait. He loved you; he couldn't help himself."

"Madame Dupont said that he wasn't as bad as some of them."

"I know a side of him that you do not, Abby. He was a divided man, raised on the concept of duty to country, eaten up by the duty he owed his wife. Poor bastard."

She hid nothing from him, not even the lengths to which she had prepared herself to go, not a single word of the conversation in the Bois on the last afternoon she had spent with Stefan Helldorf. He made her repeat over and over again the words she had memorized, even though she knew he had understood them as soon as she had spoken.

"Morocco," he said. "Our German was born or lived as a child in Morocco. Somewhere in or near the Atlas Mountains. He had dark skin, you said?"

"Yes. But his hair was light."

"A Berber mother and a French or German father. The Legion was never able to find all of its malcontents. It tried, but it had trained us too well."

"He spoke English too, Joseph. A few words, at least."

"There were Englishmen in the Legion. It was an army of stateless men. We became polyglots, all of us. Forget him, Abby. He's of no use to us anymore."

She was glad to do it, relieved to know that Stefan Helldorf was gone from her life forever. She slept now without dreaming, in Joseph's bed as often as in her own, huddling close to him like a child who has thought of doing something naughty but been spared the moment of rebellion. Both of them knew that they were without protection, worse, that the nun had been a member of the Resistance and that if she were ever picked up, the Gestapo would have their names before she died. But alone as they were, with Émile Vautrin's fears hanging over their heads like the death sentence it was, they were strangely content. The struggle seemed to have come to an end. They were waiting again, but together. Nothing else seemed to matter.

They went to bed early on the night of July 16, turning off all the lights in the apartment shortly after dusk, opening the windows to catch a breeze off the river, lying atop their separate beds on sheets sticky with the damp heat. Neither had eaten more than a few mouthfuls of yesterday's soup, but Abby had again waited too long at German headquarters to be able to bring home anything from the stores.

Émile Vautrin had visited them three days before, proposing to have Joseph admitted under a false name to a ward in one of his charity hospitals. "The nuns will cooperate," he had said. "There are a dozen clinics hiding Jews under forged papers." But Joseph had refused to consider it, refused, he said, unless he had reliable papers to present. And he did not. Hospital rolls were minutely inspected. He wouldn't allow the nuns to be placed in jeopardy. What they had managed to achieve so far, all the lives they had preserved, could not be endangered. He would continue to wait.

Paris was so quiet at night now. No cars speeding through the streets, no lovers' laughter spiraling up to open windows, no church bells marking the hours, only the river water slapping against the quays. Whether they slept or not, Parisians had learned to be still. Only in the nightclubs frequented by German officers was there any gaiety, any sound of music or the pop of champagne corks. You could hear the leaves rustling on the trees, even the rise of the moon across the black sky.

Shortly before midnight the peal of the doorbell brought Abby upright in her bed. It stabbed into her over and over again, urgent, quick, insistent. Gestapo, she thought, running into Joseph's room, seeing the gun that was already in his hand.

"Quickly, Joseph. I love you," she whispered, turning her head, pushing back the hair above her ear, exposing the soft target where a pulse beat beneath her fingers. Would she hear the explosion, or did death come before sound?

"Let them in, Abby," he said. Two capsules lay in his hand, sparkling in his palm. "I won't destroy beauty. Let it rest in your cheek. Don't swallow it. Crush it between your teeth if it's Gestapo, if they reach for you."

There was no point in looking through the peephole. She knew, both of them knew who waited outside. This is the last time I'll have to take the bar down, she thought as she lifted it, leaned on it like a cane, stood it in the corner. Turned the keys in the locks.

"Abby," Stefan Helldorf said. "I have come to take you and your husband for a drive into the country. It's a beautiful night. Get dressed."

I'm dreaming this, she thought, I'm dreaming this man. The capsule bulged against her cheek.

Suddenly he was inside the apartment, grabbing at her face, prying her mouth open, his fingers bruising her tongue, nails scratching at her gums. He crushed the capsule under his foot, shaking her until she could hear the bones in her neck crack.

"Abby, Abby. Listen to me," he said. "I've come to take you and your husband into the country. Look." He was holding papers in his hand, doubling them in his fist until the parchment crackled. "Get him ready."

"It's the middle of the night," she said. Dazed, she was too dazed to know what she was saying. "No one is allowed on the streets after curfew."

"Damn the curfew! I can get you out. But only if you hurry."

His arm was around her waist, holding her up. She stumbled over the hem of her nightgown, feeling her way along the walls, leading him toward where Joseph lay with the gun he had refused to fire, ready to escape with a capsule poised between his teeth.

"Get up, monsieur," Stefan Helldorf ordered. "Tell your

wife what a perfect night it is to go for a ride in the country, the only night beautiful enough to leave Paris."

For an eternally long minute Joseph stared at the young man who had invaded his bedroom. His mouth opened, and he spat the capsule of cyanide onto the floor. His face was very dark, very shadowed in the moonlight. Looking from one to the other, Abby thought she was seeing only one man where there should have been two, a profile and its exact duplicate.

"Get dressed," Stefan Helldorf repeated. "Make sure you have your papers." He wheeled toward the armoire. "This coat, I think, monsieur," he said, pulling it out, flinging it onto the bed. The Star of David shone dimly, a beacon fire newly lit. "In case we're stopped, you have the honor of being my prisoner."

They didn't speak again. Abby and Joseph sat together in the back seat of the Mercedes, her hand slipped into his pocket. Stefan Helldorf drove, slowing down only once, leaning his head out the car window to curse the soldiers who were slow to shove aside the barricade at the Porte de Saint-Cloud. He smoked as he drove; Abby thought she would always remember the acrid smell of his cigarettes that night. He took them as far as the last turnoff to Les Roses, never once asking for directions, never once hesitating or braking to peer at the countryside.

"I can't do any more," he said, not looking into the seat behind him. "These papers will allow you to travel wherever you wish in the occupied zone. There wasn't time to get passes into Vichy territory."

At the last possible moment, when Joseph was already pushing aside the rose-covered, bramble-choked gate, Abby leaned back into the car. A leather-gloved hand held hers for an instant. "Thank you," she said.

"I'll always love you, Abby, but I couldn't allow them to destroy my wife. Ask your husband what he and the doctor planned to do. No one who survives this war will ever be innocent again."

He drove away, as he had come, with shaded headlights, shadows and reflections of shadows dancing through the trees.

More than twelve thousand Jews living in Paris were taken that night, rounded up, hauled off in buses and trucks to the trains waiting to transport them to the camps and the hissing gas in the shower rooms where no plumbing had ever been installed. A woman leapt into the street cradling her baby in her arms. Both were crushed. It was a quicker death. Children, separated from their parents, cried. Later, many of them suffocated in the cars that were designed to carry live-stock, and never as many bodies as the Gestapo packed into them. The French policemen who came to the Kelemen apartment found only a German officer there. Furious at having been awakened, he threatened them with his gun and took their badge numbers. Their records were inaccurate, he informed them. The Jew they were looking for had long since been interned. He personally struck Joseph Kelemen's name off their list.

By the end of October, the cellars at Les Roses were cold. They were healthy, all of them, from a diet of forest creatures and vegetables; the monotony of living together, mostly underground, had not yet begun to take its toll. They walked in the woods, hoed the hidden garden faithfully, brewed tisanes from Gustave Lebrun's herbs. They missed wine in the evenings; water, no matter how clear and pure, did not lull you to sleep. Of them all, Miklós was the most content and contributed most to conversations that often faltered and lagged. He remembered whole chapters of the books he had read, and set out to educate Abby and Hanne in literature and history. The old gardener nodded off as soon as monsieur opened his mouth.

They had no news of what was going on in the world except the gossip that Lebrun brought back from the village on Sundays. Everyone hoped Russia was freezing the Boches to death, but nobody thought the English and the Americans would land on the faraway coasts of France that winter. Spring, they claimed, next spring or summer. Every now and then there were stirrings from the Resistance, but Paris, the magnet of all their hopes, Paris remained a German playground.

It snowed on All Souls' Day, a mist of tiny flakes melting as they fell. Abby remembered that you could free dozens of souls from purgatory on that one day every year simply by reciting a few prayers every time you went into a church. Only Lebrun could afford to be seen in the village, but he had nuts to gather and did not bother. It did not matter after all, because purgatory and its cleansing fires had now been established on earth. Heaven was again an easy reward to earn.

November 9 was the most dismal day they had endured since coming to Les Roses. The pines dripped moisture from early morning until well after sunset, a doleful sound unbroken by birdsong or the busy scrabblings of forest creatures laying up stores for the winter that was almost upon them. The deer hid in their sheltered resting places deep in the forest, wild hares and foxes never left their burrows, and even the insects folded their wings and refused to fly. Gustave Lebrun was sparing of, almost miserly, with the wood that all of them helped to gather; the fires he built were too small to throw off much heat, usually nothing more than a bed of glowing coals fed just often enough to keep the embers from dying out completely. The food they ate took an eternity to cook, but there were never any grand plumes of smoke to give them away. "They know my ways in the village," he said. "Only city people are wasteful of what the land provides."

Their clothing stuck to their skins, never quite dry, steaming when they sat close to the fire, turning clammy and heavy with the dampness when they moved away. Cleanliness was an irritating problem, and both Abby and Hanne had cut their hair as short as possible, each one assuring the other that the new coiffures were becoming. There were no mirrors to contradict them. On Hanne the effect was as disheartening as the rain, straight, lank strands that fell into her eyes and stuck out over her ears until she tied a scarf gypsy-fashion around her head. Now she had the look of a Russian peasant, broad face and calm eyes set off by a wildly colorful frame. On Abby the transformation was utterly different. The curls that had always been subdued by artful hairdressers became ringlets, a mass of reddish-gold circlets too tight to comb. Everything that was Irish in her face was emphasized, the paleness of the fine skin, the straight, narrow nose, the delicate shape of her mouth, the vulnerable chin, the changing colors of her eyes. She looked ten or fifteen years younger, the sweet-voiced colleen of all the ballads, with new touches of silver here and there to attest to her sorrows.

They had gotten accustomed to the silence of Les Roses at night, the complete stillness of the forest, the more brooding quiet of the ruined house above them. The only city noise they yearned for was the sound of a radio, not so much for the music they never heard anymore, but for the crackling transmissions of the BBC. Only once a week, on Sunday, did they discuss the war, and then it was more important to know about the movements of the Germans in their area than to speculate vainly, frustratingly, on the massing Allied armies or the battles being fought hundreds of miles to the east. Sometimes they could hear planes in the night sky, but there was no way of knowing whose they were. All the engines sounded alike.

They took turns standing watch, exhausting, lonely vigils that Joseph had insisted were merely elementary precautions. He had been furiously angry and horrified at Miklós and Hanne's carelessness, so soundly asleep the night he and Abby arrived that they hadn't awakened until he kicked at their feet. "What if we were a German patrol?" he had hissed. "They don't always roar around in trucks, you know. One grenade tossed into these cellars and you'd all be butcher's meat." They resented and fought his sarcasm, but eventually, unable to make him yield, they gave in, and a certain satisfaction at their new craftiness was born. There was no question of being able to resist if their hiding place was discovered; time to reach the trees was what he wanted to buy for them. He rigged up a silent alarm system, a length of rope looped around the ankle of one of the sleepers, never to be out of reach of the one who remained awake. "In the desert," he told them, "we used to chain ourselves to our rifles to keep them from being stolen by the Bedouins. It's the same principle."

The routine never varied. They'd cleared a space in front of one of the chimneys and piled up bricks and rubble around it, creating a sort of roofless cave just large enough for one person, a vantage point from which the road could be watched, at least as far as the bend. Their rear was blind, but not vulnerable. The forest was thicker beyond the old gardens than anywhere else; not even the deer could walk there without snapping twigs beneath their hooves. When it was your night to play soldier, you wrapped yourself in your blankets and propped your back against the chimney, fighting off sleep, learning the shadows, stiff and aching by dawn, but alive and feeling that you'd accomplished something more important than just learning to live with your fear.

When the monotonous dripping stopped and the moon broke through the clouds that had ridden the sky all day, Abby let the blanket slide from her head. It would be a beautiful day tomorrow, still cold, but sunny for a change; she could feel the air beginning to dry out. Predicting the weather was a game the watcher always played to keep himself alert. Sentry was too ridiculous a word to apply to any of them, so ludicrous that it could make the job seem far too silly to take seriously. It was hard enough not to drift into wanting to pretend that this was a way of life no different from the hiking trips they had made into the mountains when they were younger, stays of two or three nights with hired guides and a string of donkeys to carry their equipment. The harshness of it would not settle down on them until winter, she thought, and then illness could become a greater danger than the Germans.

She thought she heard the sound of an engine, listened, and decided that it was a vagrant echo borne by the wind from a plane many miles away. It was difficult at night to pinpoint sound, track it with only your ears the way animals did. Watching the blackness lighten into gray before the sun rose was like coming out of blindness. She finally understood primitive man's fear that the sun which appeared to die every night might someday not return. Perpetual darkness was too awesome to conceive, its nothingness impossible to contemplate. Belief in a place of eternal light was the only way to combat the void.

When the moon shone this purely and steadily, keeping watch was almost a delight. Every fifth night she could count on being entirely alone, on experiencing the heightened awareness that comes with physical fatigue and a mind not invaded by dreams. Looking backward, living in the past was a sickness of which she had cured herself. By day she occupied herself with the present; every fifth night she planned the future. Simple, ordinary plans, details she could catch hold of, examine, let lie, and bring out again during the next watch. Start at the beginning, she told herself; start with the day the occupation finally ends.

She would go to the Étoile at noon, stand on the spot beneath the Arc de Triomphe where the unknown soldier of the last war slept. Since June 14, 1940, almost two and a half years ago now, it had been the most heartbreaking place in Paris, because every day the swastika hung over the grave that symbolized all the brave young men blown into unidentifiable bits during the last war, and every day, on the stroke of noon, a German military band defiled the spot, marching the length of the Champs-Élysées past ranks and ranks of Parisians too bitter to weep at the sight anymore. Only when the tricolor flew there again would she really know that the long night of the occupation was over. Food would be delicious again, wine would be heady, and over her balcony she would drape her American flag, leaving it there until, tattered and frayed to ribbons like the flags that hang from the high ceilings of military museums, it became a precious relic to be folded away, brought into the light only once every year on the anniversary of the liberation. These two things she would do before any others.

There would be a life to rebuild with Joseph, and she imagined that in all its externals it would not be very different from what it had always been. That thought was strangely soothing, as it was to millions of others who wanted nothing so much as to be able to return to a time when Nazis were a joke and Adolf Hitler a Chaplinesque caricature. Deauville in August, Monte Carlo at Christmas. Another pair of Westies to replace the two whose baskets she had not given away. The difference now was that she could envision growing old, could even welcome years that passed slowly, uneventfully. Once in a while, she told herself, we'll look up from our newspapers in the evening, our eyes will meet, and we'll know that neither of us has forgotten. By then the memories will be as fragile as the frequently turned pages of an antique book, and we won't speak of them. Survivors rarely do; it's only spectators who want to relive the game.

She thought it must be close to dawn, and that one of the deer had stepped out onto the road. Too big a shadow to be a dog, too still to be human. After a long, long time, padded steps beneath the overhanging pines, a hesitant approach, as if the doe stopped every yard or two to scent the air. They came up onto the lawns sometimes, raising their legs high over the ugly mounds where the grass had reseeded itself and begun to grow again. She looked away for a moment, as Joseph had taught her, knowing she was half-hypnotized from peering at that one spot. When she turned back, Stefan Helldorf was standing in the middle of the road, his hands upraised as though someone had called out to him to surrender or be shot.

She untied the rope from her wrist and left it lying beside the chimney. She'd picked her way across the rubble so many times in the dark that her feet automatically found a silent pathway. The blanket fell to the ground, a rocklike heap in the tall wet grass.

"I came alone, Abby," he whispered.

"Why? What's happened?"

"British and American troops landed on the beaches of Algeria and Morocco yesterday. I'm leaving Paris in the morning, transferred to the Afrika Korps. They need officers who can speak Arabic. I've never been able to get the sand completely out of my boots. I'm going home, in a way. Will you walk back to the gate with me?"

She looked toward the cellars where the others lay sleeping, where there was no one now to watch over them.

"He'll be safe, Abby. I can't stay more than a few minutes."

"I didn't think I'd ever see you again," she said. The bend in the road hid them, left them alone between the trees.

"You won't, after tonight."

"We owe you the debt of our lives. When the war is over, Stefan . . ."

"Do you believe it would ever be possible for me to see Paris again, see you again? That's beyond me, Abby. North Africa is a gift. I'm not coming back."

"You won't die."

"Thousands of men will die. Others will simply disappear. Either way, the desert will hide them. Don't pretend to feel sorry for me, Abby. Don't pretend to feel anything. I've understood everything for months. We all pay with whatever coin we have. Tell your husband that he and Dr. Vautrin guessed right. Marta had Buerger's Disease."

"That's nothing but an answer to a riddle whose question I don't even know."

He stopped then, and turned her toward him so that the moonlight pooled in her eyes. "My wife was a Jew, Abby. Buerger's Disease is a circulatory ailment that's fairly common among Jews, a hereditary problem any doctor would recognize during an examination. The shredded cigarettes, Abby. On the floor beside Marta's bed, and on the landing, falling from Dr. Vautrin's fingers. It had to be you who let him into the apartment. I had the locks changed; there were only two keys."

"I didn't know."

"No, I don't think now that you did. I admire your husband's will to survive. He would have blackmailed me had it come to that." He touched the curls above her forehead. "She's safe now. She died very peacefully in Switzerland."

She had to know. The unanswered question had burned her soul for too long. "Stefan, have you ever heard of a place in Poland called Auschwitz, or a camp named Treblinka?"

He nodded, an unfathomably deep, immeasurably profound admission of a whole people's guilt. "There are rumors," he said, "loose tongues in the Gestapo after the schnapps bottle has been emptied once too often. Complaints from the Poles about clouds of greasy ash ruining their crops."

"Go away, Herr Hauptmann," Abby said. "Go away to your desert and leave us in peace."

His hands fell from her arms, hung lifeless at his sides. "I didn't expect you to understand," he said finally. He took a leather wallet from the pocket of his overcoat. "I've brought you a gift."

"No."

"It's the key to your apartment. And some papers. Open the wallet, Abby."

The leather was warm from his body, as supple as skin. A match flared above her head, the flickering flame lighting up the documents she recognized immediately. Identity cards, ration books. Joseph's face, frozen in the stark, staring expression of a passport photo, stared back at her.

"Please," she whispered.

Another match flared, and this time she searched frantically for the one mark that was missing, the terrible curl of the *J* she had grown to hate. It wasn't there. Joseph Kelemen, Jew, had become Joseph Kelemen, Aryan.

"Where did you get the picture?" she asked. Ridiculous, stupid, unimportant question.

"From the drawer of his desk. There were several of them. I only needed two. You never told me he was in the Legion, Abby." Was she listening to him, hearing what he said? "You can go back to Paris whenever you want. Everything has been taken care of, at the prefecture, at our headquarters, even in the Gestapo files. The war against the Jews is waged on paper, and on paper your husband is a baptized Catholic. I thought it appropriate for a Frenchman."

He dropped the burned-out match into the carpet of pine needles beneath his feet. "Adieu, Abby," he said.

Her kiss against Stefan Helldorf's cheek was featherlight, lingering like the passage of a tear. The fingers that traced the outline of his lips barely touched them, falling away helplessly, acknowledging that they could not bestow redemption. She watched the shadow of him disappear into the blacker shadows at the end of the road, waited until the purr of the Mercedes had died away into the quiet night. Then she walked back to the ruins of Les Roses, first steps on the journey home to Paris.

Epilogue

Abby Sullivan Kelemen did go back to Paris, did survive the war. And because of her, Joseph, Miklós, and Hanne also survived. On August 25, 1944, her homemade American flag with its single six-pointed star welcomed the first wave of American and French troops flooding into the city. That night, while the church bells that had been silent for four years pealed and pealed, while Parisians danced and sang in the streets and prayed in all the churches, Joseph opened wide the balcony doors, sat down at the piano, and played two songs. The "Marseillaise" and "The Star-Spangled Banner." Played them with tears steaming down his face and full, booming crashing chord accompaniment. When General de Gaulle made his historic march down the Champs-Élysées, Abby was in the crowd that gathered at the Arc de Triomphe and cheered and wept and surged along beside him as he passed.

Victor Cavaignac was dead, but his sons returned, decorated, wounded, claiming never to have heard of the secret agreement made in the early days of the war. There were men of honor, but men of business too, and so they kept the inheritance left by their father but made room in the gallery for the Jew who had owned it for so many years. They praised his expertise, made him a senior consultant, agreed to employ Miklós also. But foreign names were unpopular and unprofitable baggage, especially one that sounded vaguely German. Galeries Cavaignac was never again Galeries Kelemen. Abby raged; Joseph told her that the prospect of battling Victor's sons in the courts disgusted him. He accepted cash settlements from the partners in New York and

London; he was too tired to begin again, too old now. A little work in the Paris gallery in the mornings, the races in the afternoons, evenings spent with Abby. That was all he wanted, and he promised her that it would be enough, assured her confidently that they could live as they had before the war, that their remaining stones would last as long as they did.

In 1962, Joseph developed an annoying cough that was eventually diagnosed as cancer of the larynx. Abby flew to New York, bringing back to Paris the contents of her safe-deposit box. For a while he continued going to the gallery, never missed a race when one of his horses was running. Later, nurses were hired to sit beside his bed day and night. One by one, Abby sold the remaining pieces of jewelry given her almost forty years before by Sammy Rosen. Joseph died slowly, inch by inch, pound by pound, accepting it, neither desperate to stay alive nor wishing to hurry the end of it. He was buried in a grave deep enough to hold two bodies. The cross of the Legion of Honor he had been awarded for his role in frustrating Hermann Göring's attempts to rob France of her art treasures lay between his folded hands. None of the paintings they had hidden had been lost. All had been returned to their rightful owners or their heirs.

A month later Abby went to her room to rest before dinner, drank a last glass of chilled champagne, laid down on the bed and never woke up. Never knew her heart had failed, never suffered. She had not a single piece of valuable jewelry left.

Miklós died in the Rothschild home outside Paris, a lonely and bereft widower after Hanne's final stroke, crying out during the last few years that all these old Jews he was being forced to live with thought of nothing but the next meal they would eat and the doctors they claimed were neglecting them. Joseph, Abby, Miklós, and Hanne. Tess, an old woman, came from New York and paid for a stone to be erected between the two graves that held all four. She asked at the Paris gallery for the portrait of Abby. Had it been stored there? No one knew. One of Abby's French lawyers thought it had disappeared during the war, seemed to remember hearing that it had been the only thing stolen from their apartment during the months they had been in hiding. It was never found.

Stefan Helldorf fought with distinction in North Africa.

He was never captured. His name appears on none of the casualty lists, nor on the rosters of prisoners interned by the Allies. No passport has ever been issued in his name by the Federal Republic. The desert, as he had predicted, promised, swallowed him up.

ABOUT THE AUTHOR

ROSEMARY SIMPSON, who lives in Chapel Hill, North Carolina, is the author of The Seven Hills of Paradise, which Mary Renault praised as "an outstanding historical novel: steeped in its era, powerful, honest, and vividly real," and which Ruth Beebe Hill called "a fascinating view of the fourth crusade, not only for history buffs but for every reader who yearns for a superbly written story."